THE BIG CUT

Sarah,
all the best in
the art world and now for
THE BIG CUT
the legal World,

Aaron Richard Golub

St. Martin's Press
New York

ACKNOWLEDGMENTS

Without Tony Gardner, there would not be *The Big Cut.*

Johnny Ocean could fill this page expressing his gratitude to Elizabeth Beier for her wisdom, advice and editor-in-glove involvement in presenting his dogged quest for justice in the city, but Mr. K says that's not Johnny's style.

John Murphy is one of a kind. Any writer would be lucky to have him behind his book. And what about Jamie Brickhouse?

Well beyond the aggressive lawyer's demanding expectations, Ed Stackler deftly guided Johnny's journey through a forest of twisted backroads (will this story ever make sense?) to The End.

Thanks to Peter Arnell, Karen Levitas, John Rodman, M.D., Philippe Quilici, M.D., Phoebe Eaton, and Diana Kan. The works of Sterling Seagrave, Harrison Salisbury, and Emily Hahn are unforgettably appreciated.

Mr. K, dhanwade Jie, one million (das lakh bar) times.

THE BIG CUT. Copyright © 2000 by Aaron Richard Golub. All rights reserved. Printed in the United States of America. No part of this book may be used or reproduced in any manner whatsoever without written permission except in the case of brief quotations embodied in critical articles or reviews. For information, address St. Martin's Press, 175 Fifth Avenue, New York, N.Y. 10010.

Library of Congress Cataloging-in-Publication Data
Golub, Aaron Richard.
The big cut : a novel / Aaron Richard Golub.—1st ed.
p. cm.
ISBN 0-312-24538-6
1. Organized crime—New York (State)—New York—Fiction.   2. Counselor and client—Fiction.   3. New York (N.Y.)—Fiction.   I. Title.
PS3557.O452 B5 2000
813'.54—dc21   99-056777

First Edition: March 2000
10   9   8   7   6   5   4   3   2   1

Therefore the Lord God sent him forth from the garden of Eden, to till the ground from whence he was taken. So he drove out the man; and he placed at the east of the garden of Eden cherubim, and a flaming sword to keep the way of the tree of life.

—*Genesis III, 23–24*

CHAPTER ONE

A four-mile-long garden grows in New York City. Only twenty feet wide, it divides the flow of two-way traffic on Park Avenue, knotting the numbered cross streets to the main thoroughfare like the warp of an Oriental carpet until it ends where Spanish Harlem begins. It is prohibited to walk on "the mall." There are no shops, just miles of rusted rectangular steel grates concealed by dwarfed yews, pear trees, and perfectly landscaped beds of pink begonias—a thatched roof high above the deafening hell of Metro-North trains roaring out of Grand Central and off to the suburbs.

Early that morning, I was walking down Park Avenue with Barkis, my 130-pound Rottweiler, passing one grand limestone apartment house after another. Every day I see these gray fortresses and think of the people I've sued and defended who live inside, hiding in their high-rise mansions above white-gloved, uniformed doormen and buzzing intercoms, avoiding wily process servers.

This neighborhood belongs in the book *New York City on $10,000 a Day*. Felonies are committed just above Park Avenue's horticulture by affluent citizens manipulating digits and legal principles over breakfast and the *Wall Street Journal*. At this time of the morning, the hissing of watering hoses and scraping of street cleaners anticipate the filthy world converging on the big city. The maxims of Manhattan—aggression surmounts extreme resistance, manners over morality, revenge finds its time and place—are played out one more time, one more day.

Nearly all the events of my next case would occur in four blocks of this grid, as if the city were a country village or a sports field. People from good families commit crimes, but an old family name reduces scandal to biographical cachet. In this respectable East Side neighborhood every transgression, including murder, can make you a star. The once-convicted and once-acquitted Claus Von Bülow ate at the best table in Manhattan's top restaurants while being tried for the attempted murder of his wife.

At cocktail parties and restaurants, slurping and burping judges, writers, matrons, and maître d's love to speculate: "My opinion is he poisoned her." "Everyone knows he was just after her money, but he's very handsome." "She deserved it. But I always liked her."

As I approached the curb, the sun buffed the black-lacquered side of a Cadillac hearse with SING SI WANG FUNERAL HOME embossed in bronze on the windows. Putting a match to a Lucky, I read each word slowly. The hearse looked out of place parked in front of the Sixty-fifth Street service entrance to the Caprice, one of Park's most expensive residences. Not to mention the four large Chinese thugs, silently sidewalking, expressionless as frozen food. If you had the nerve to ask, they'd say they were in the "death-services business."

"An excellent day in the city," a radio squawked from a passing yellow taxi as two more Chinese strongarmers in tapered black suits rolled a gurney to the curb. A body sheathed in a blood-stained sheet and fastened under three red vinyl restraints lay on the stretcher. It could have been a Jackson Pollock interpretation of the Swiss flag, but that stiff was no work of art.

No one else on the street noticed, but another dead body is how a lawyer like me makes his pay.

There wasn't a cop in sight. At that moment, I had no vested interest in making a critical inquiry—no paying client. The body slid into the hearse behind black velvet curtains on polished chrome window rods. The rear door swung closed, and the hearse squirmed through the traffic on East Sixty-fifth Street toward Lexington. Had murder been folded away? A streak of blood now soiled the avenue. Somewhere, some lawyer would soon be opening a file on this matter.

When I take my usual morning walk with Barkis I'm not exactly looking for action or clients. But nearby, behind the paneled ebony door to my townhouse on East Sixty-seventh Street, I keep my law office. You won't find a name or a bell on the building. The first two floors are offices, and I live on the top three, but I haven't been to the fifth in four years except to dig out a dusty bottle of 1962 Château Haut-Brion.

Inside the office, my Indian butler, Mr. K, was sitting behind the receptionist's desk on the ground floor, acting busy while slyly reading poetry. Clients treat him like the rare ornament he is—a wafer-thin Sikh with a long, white Van Dyck beard tied in a double knot. His skin is tan and parched, worn as an old wallet. His business card reads: "Mr. K, Managing Director, Eyeballs, Inc.," but I own that private investigation agency.

Mr. K thinks of himself as my bodyguard. He practices *gatka,* the Punjabi art of self-defense, and carries a *kirpan,* or sword, concealed under his shirt. It is one of the five "Ks" of dress and appearance required by the Sikh religion, known also as the *Panth,* the path. The other four are: *kada,* the steel bracelet that reminds the Sikh not to steal or commit bad deeds; *kesh,* the vow taken by Sikhs not to cut any of their hair, as it permits them to be recognized as the selfless servants of all mankind; *kangha,* the comb, to keep hair neat and secured under the turban; and *kachha,* undergarments worn to ensure self-control and sexual discipline.

The *kirpan* cannot be displayed for mere amusement. Once the weapon is unsheathed, violence is inevitable. But in moments of crisis, K is the first to say, "Be cool, sir, be cool." Violence is always the last resort. I try to achieve a state of coolness in this unforgiving city, although it is difficult.

K straightened his pink turban. Although K abhors change, he "tucks up" a different colored turban every morning. Instructing him to change an unpressed suit or a wrinkled, threadbare shirt is part of my daily ritual. The same tie has hung from his neck for months.

"That's a great outfit, K."

"Pink on Tuesday. Fine dress is very important. It makes the man, Sahib. We must look our best for the clients. Gird up your loins and get ready for your legal battles. Sahib, don't give up, don't give in. We will be victorious."

K is a loyal, God-fearing family man absorbed by religion and the belief that he is on this planet to serve me and mankind.

"Sagai." K clasped his hands and bowed. That meant he was turning right. He disappeared upstairs to prepare breakfast and I went to my office on the second floor.

During the next hour, the telephone seemed to ring incessantly. I answered the last call ahead of Mercedes, who handles my secretarial work even though it is beneath her Mount Holyoke B.A. in art history and M.A. in political science. But she tells me she needs the money for another degree.

A dignified female secretary who sounded more like a Palm Beach socialite than a law-office drone asked me to hold for Mr. I-didn't-catch-the-name before I was swallowed in a disconnect. Then it rang again.

"Call for you, Mr. Ocean," Mercedes said on the intercom, and I picked up.

"Johnny. Sorry I was cut off. Got a minute? Something interesting for you."

It was Jack Dyson, a good friend who worked for one of those fifty-partner, two-hundred-associate law firms on Wall Street. Hidden well by his Ivy League education and three-piece suits was a rough background.

"We've got a hot one here. The computer calls it an 00868— means 'not for us.' The case is fixed. The judge is wrapped around the other side's finger."

"That puts another small crack in your Yale Law School mug, Jack." Dyson sent over cases every few months that were too small or politically loaded for Davis & Shiring.

"Right, the firm doesn't want it. It's an estate matter, ripe for the Ocean Liner. You've been around the Surrogate's Court before, haven't you?"

The second I heard Surrogate's Court, I knew it was messy but probably very lucrative.

"Yeah, sure, but only to use the men's room."

"This is a good case for you." He paused. "The client only wants you for a limited purpose."

"What's that? Some sort of—"

"Power play. The case needs new blood. Just come on like a grizzly, intimidate the shit out of the opposition. Take a deposition for about 100K, including all your expenses. It'll take some complex legal research and some investigation. But it'll be like a summer job. Like when I was a tennis pro in Southampton."

That was the summer he tore the ligaments in his right knee racing for a bitchy drop shot that ended his amateur-circuit tennis career. But now wasn't the time to remind him.

"My kind of case, no long-term commitments."

"Don't kid yourself, there's time involved." Dyson continued, "It's a cat fight between two sisters-in-law. Your client is being sued for 170 mil by her sister-in-law, Babette Longwood. Seems Babette loaned her dear brother Marcel the dough. He croaks, leaves everything to his wife, the sister-in-law, your client. Makes Babette little angry, *comprendo?* You've heard of the husband—" a long Dyson cigar draw—"Edgar Longwood?"

I had, but he didn't give me chance to get a word in. Edgar Longwood, Babette's late husband, was a powerful man. The Longwoods were one of the richest families in the country, playing an almost historic role in national and local politics and international finance. Edgar had run the family fortune while he was alive.

"You'll be taking Babette's deposition. If it gets complicated, I'll see to it that you get no less than 200K. Whack her around, scare the fucking shit out of her from the other side of a table. Shouldn't take more than that, and you're out. If it goes well and stays relatively uncomplicated, you could get another hundred grand. The client's that way. You don't even have to appear as the attorney of record. She's already represented by some senile geezer named Rupert Hargrove. She probably found his name in an old *Social Register.* And from my point of view, you don't have to know the whole case inside and out. It'll take too long to learn the details of the entire file, lots of junk facts in a billion-dollar estate—too many cardboard boxes, thousands of documents, manila up the ass. Just kill. Rip Babette's heart out and drink her blood! Got to call you right back."

Such are the carefully chosen words of top trial lawyers. I already knew it wouldn't be easy.

Long before I'd ever thought about a deposition, some twenty years ago, Jack and I met in Criminal Court at 100 Centre Street. Dyson was an assistant district attorney. I was well out of law school but not practicing. In fact, I'd never even taken the bar exam. Two junkies—one black, one white—had broken into my small apartment in the West Village. They'd beaten my brains out, wrecked the place, and stolen my driver's license, some gas credit cards, and an engraved wristwatch my father gave me when I was sixteen. Some young plainclothes cops collared them when the black one produced my New York State driver's license with a photo of my white face after he was asked for identification somewhere in the East Village.

The cops called me as a witness. I had to appear at the arraignment, conveniently set for midnight at 100 Centre Street. When I stepped up to the counsel table in front of the bench, Jack and I seemed to know each other from someplace. Dyson insisted that he knew me from summers on the Jersey shore during his Budweiser-blurred college years. I had never driven an inch off the New Jersey Turnpike. We never figured it out.

Jack is a red-haired, freckle-faced Irishman. His looks don't fit this truly tough guy. He grew up in Hell's Kitchen, while I was raised in a bad neighborhood in a factory town in Massachusetts. Jack's parents owned a bar. Mine owned a small grocery store over which I grew up. His father never made a mixed drink or served a highball, just beer and shots. My father rang a cash register; butchered meat, poultry, and pork; and bagged fruits and vegetables. My mother worked as a secretary who never touched a drop, but Dyson's mother was no slouch when it came to boozing. Jack's folks gave this world a lawyer with granite nuts and a lethal mouth who could make anyone cringe on the stand. As an assistant district attorney, Dyson didn't just cross-examine witnesses—he nailed them to the cross.

That's what the two guys who broke into my apartment soon discovered. They were swiftly prosecuted and convicted. In the courtroom, I watched Jack perform. Like all good trial lawyers, he was a great actor, and I got angry at myself for not taking the bar exam. It'd been five years since law school and three since I was discharged from the military. I had been doing investigative work and liking it because it was bringing in the bucks. But after I left the courthouse that morning, I was determined to change my life.

Jack and I became fast friends. Every few months over the years we'd get together for a fast lunch at Grand Central's Oyster Bar, talking as if one of us were going to be late for a train. In a way, in exchange for inspiring me to pass the bar exam over red snapper and stone crab claws, I encouraged Jack to make some real money, leave the DA's office, and take a job in a large, civil, private practice with the white-shoe firm Davis & Shiring. The most senior partner, Bud Davis, took a real interest in Jack and introduced him to the city's heavy hitters on Wall Street—and to real-estate moguls, media tycoons, the team owners, and the movie stars.

Dyson plugged himself into the circuit of big-time judges and politicos, quickly made partner, and landed in a hallowed corner office. When it finally happened, it depressed him. Older partners who'd been retired to mid-floor offices when their client list shortened loved rainmakers like Jack, who graciously turned over all his business—three million plus dollars per year—to the firm. He drew an annual salary of five hundred thousand dollars while Davis and his best buddy, Shiring, pulled five million each. The firm sold Jack on the prestige, but there was no big money in sight. Jack was disappointed that Davis & Shiring was a one-way street, but he didn't make a change. For all that it was worth, he could say, "I'm a partner in Davis & Shiring." That alone got him into every important midtown club. He could read the *Wall Street Journal,* smoke Cuban cigars, drink cognac, play backgammon, and fall asleep in a green leather wingback chair alongside ten WASPy geezers who attended Ivy League schools in the twenties. Fortunately, any time a party invitation allowed him to drag a friend along he called me, which was my introduction to the swells.

Dyson rang back.

"So Jack, who's the client?" I asked.

"Pandora Markham. You probably know the name, or Pandora's face. On her way to her late thirties. A thoroughbred. In great shape the last time I saw her, two months ago. Long brown hair. Lives in a seven- or eight-million-dollar co-op on Park Avenue. Your type, very good body, very tall, very fucking desirable. Loves to challenge men. Her sister-in-law, Babette, will be scared shitless of you. Evidently, Pandora met you at a party some years ago, and everyone was buzzing about the way you destroy witnesses."

He paused, and I inhaled the compliment.

Then the looks profile continued. There wasn't any need to take notes. I recalled Pandora fine because we had met at a chic event, which always makes beautiful women larger than life. If I'd met her in my kitchen over a beer I'm sure she'd come down to size. Context is always misleading.

Pandora and her brother, Webb, had been with Edgar and Babette Longwood when we met at that party. A crowd had collected around me, the token maverick, while I reenacted a dramatic cross-examination I'd done that afternoon in the federal court. I'd been practicing law for about ten years by then, and my white-collar-crime clients lived elegantly on the Avenue.

While I performed I didn't fail to take in her two thin strands of pearls, lavender dress that revealed a delicate collarbone, and beautiful shoulders. Pandora's long brown hair full of curls and ringlets was swept back over diamond ear clips. The nose was sharp, provocative, to the point; her aristocratic face chiseled, angular. What could Dyson tell me that I didn't already know?

I wanted the case, and I wasn't about to give Dyson an excuse to call the next lawyer on his list.

"She's about five-nine. An excellent body."

"C'mon Jack, you're repeating yourself," I said.

But he went steamrolling along at the pace of a sportscaster. "When she was eighteen, she did a famous cult film—great scene in which she stripped in the ballroom of some white-columned mansion in Southampton and displayed the small Persian carpet. Parents and society went nuts—the whole nine yards of rebellion on Park Avenue."

I knew the profile—quietly ferocious.

Dyson went on, "The movie, *Violet Avenue,* was released in the early eighties. She was Violet. Banged around with the Valentino

and Hollywood crowd for a while. I went out with her years ago,
before she was married. She wouldn't fuck me then, and now the
firm, old D&S, can't take this case on. So why don't you do both?"

"How do I get paid?"

"A no-brainer. She inherited a lot of cash from her old man,
who owned a big racetrack, a Long Island steel mill, and some
other high-number assets. He checked out with about a hundred
million dollars, and she's too smart to lose it. She has plenty of it,
and it's growing, but she'll never admit it. Always claiming she's
broke or doesn't have access to the money. I don't know, you may
not get to see her. These days, it's all E-mail, fax and phone—the
safest way to go."

"That's fine, I can handle a voice-mail relationship."

"Look, Ocean, nothing to complain about. There's nothing in
this case but a good time. It's not just another sleepy litigation,
especially if she sleeps with you."

I'd already made an unsuccessful pass at her at that party. But
so many men hit on her, I doubted she'd remember.

"Anyway, I'll start with the case," I said.

"Are you one of the few lawyers who say they won't have sex
with a client? Is there something in the code of ethics about it?"
Dyson was more than half serious.

"Maybe. I'll research it if it gets that far."

"Good. You're a man with a steel heart and I'll be shocked if
you nail her. No, I'll be angry."

"At me or her?" Now he had me thinking about it.

Dyson laughed. "I'm outta here. I'll call her and she'll call you
in ten minutes. By the way, how's your boy Slade?"

"Don't really talk to him that much. See you later."

That was none of Dyson's concern. My ex-wife committed suicide and my son was raised by his stepfather, an ex-criminal client
of mine who I disliked.

I hung up the phone and drank some cold coffee from the

breakfast tray while I called up some Nexis articles and cruised the Web for something interesting on Pandora.

An hour passed and the new client hadn't called when Mercedes brought in a small white package with my name scribbled in black ink along with a "Personal/Confidential" legend. No return address. I opened it and found a video. Mercedes said the mailman found the package leaning against the front door.

I put the tape in the office VCR.

Over a gray background a male voice said, "Welcome." No picture. "This program was developed for friends of Pandora Markham. As her attorney, you may be interested in this product, your future client."

Pandora slowly materialized wearing a short blue dress, facing the camera. She brushed the shoulder straps to the side and pulled the dress down over her hips. It fell to the floor, and she was nearly naked. Her long fingers unhooked a black bra. A nude Pandora sauntered across the room to a black lacquered 1920s vanity.

The camera zoomed to a lit cigarette in an ivory holder. Smoke rose from a mother-of-pearl ashtray. The camera panned up her legs, crossed on an ottoman covered in leopard skin. She picked up the cigarette, took a long drag, and studied the reflection of her breasts in the vanity's mirror.

An attractive man in his mid-forties, possibly the "Man in the Hathaway Shirt," walked into the frame wearing a black silk dressing gown. He guided her to a large four-poster bed with fringed pillows that were carefully arranged on paisley sheets. The camera followed them as he untied his belt and removed the robe. She picked up the belt and tied his hands behind his back. An oil painting of two Egyptian lovers hung on the wall over the bed.

Pandora spread her hands across his back, vampirishly biting his shoulders. Her body was far more curvaceous than I had imagined. She pushed him onto the bed and slapped him. A small, evil smirk walked across her face. The picture faded to black. But the sound of sex continued, no images.

Several minutes passed. Pandora slid open a pair of thick red-velvet curtains to a view of the Metropolitan Museum's Temple of Dendur wing. A breeze blew through an open window as she ran a hairbrush through her curls. Sitting at the vanity, she clipped her stockings to a lavender garter belt and took a pull on the cigarette. For a moment she hesitated before tapping out a number on a white telephone. The camera zoomed to a piece of paper next to the ashtray. My telephone number was written on it.

The voice-over: "Mr. Ocean, she's got your number. You just bought a one-way ticket to the Dead Sea."

The tape ended. I was sold on this case.

Then the phone rang and I grabbed for it.

I watched Mercedes answer it from my office. She held the receiver and listened a few seconds. "Please hold," she said, her tongue stopping just before "bitch."

It was Pandora.

I told Mercedes to get the number and say that I'd phone back in about an hour.

Mr. K nodded to me from Mercedes's desk and said, "Cool, sir. They are crazy creatures. Clients."

Then I played the tape for K.

"Give me your opinion of this."

"I enjoy films, especially when they are connected to our cases," he answered and watched the screen with great interest. When it finished, K thoughtfully pulled at his beard, leaned forward in his chair, and jabbed two index fingers at the screen. "Sir, it is merely a film, entertainment for my boss, but it is intended for enticement. In India, movie stars are revered as gods."

"But K, what do you think of the woman?" I was toying with him, which he liked.

"Sir, I am only opining at your behest. The lady wants you to admire her and to be intrigued. You are the judge of what is going on and can extract the truth from her."

"But what do *you* think? She may be a new client," I pressed him.

"Sir, that would be fine, very fine. A very good thing for your adrenaline." He fixed his turban, gripping the folds at the top with his fingertips, and left.

For about twenty minutes I sat behind my desk, my willpower playing havoc with my mind as my fingers traced the desk's Victorian scrollwork like a crisp stack of hundred-dollar bills I was deciding how to spend. Who was the voice? Had someone somehow listened in on Dyson's call? Or was Dyson behind all of this? The picture was clear—she wasn't that single gardenia I was looking for growing out of the city's concrete.

For once, money was irrelevant. The woman was unbelievable, but I knew it was too soon to return the call. I didn't want to appear *too* eager.

About three o'clock I accompanied K outside while he was telling me that the TV was now out of order. "Sir, the rays, they are not coming to the roof . . . or if they are coming, the TV is not catching them. The screen is all confused, crazy and coughing." He pointed to the roof and laughed. "It is because the video was 'hot as coals of a glowing fire.' William Shakespeare."

Although he said he was going to the TV repair shop, K headed in the direction of Third Avenue and Fifty-ninth Street, where there's a newsstand owned by a Sikh. Hours from now Pandora Markham's name would be on the lips of the Sikh community. I'd return her call sometime tomorrow. A little sweat would do her good.

CHAPTER TWO

That night I wrote some legal letters, returned calls, and gazed at the clock. Nine. It was hard to concentrate. Even though I wasn't hungry I wanted to get my scrambled brain off the video and was doing my best to keep my fingers from dialing Pandora's number. Around 9:30 I went over to the Black Curtain on East Sixty-third Street, just four blocks from my house. A cuff-link box of a French restaurant run by André, a downbeat, ultracool, whisper-voiced Frenchman, this square room was a source for information and a place to pass it.

The Black Curtain is my dining room. I eat there almost every day, sometimes for lunch and I turn up for dinner at least three times a week. If I don't go, Mr. K chases me around the house with a brown paper bag full of cherries or a plate of sliced cantaloupe, screaming, "Sahib, you must take. Take something."

But I prefer restaurants to fruit. Potential clients believe they're getting free advice over a bowl of cucumber soup, but sooner or later they wind up at my office, paying a healthy retainer for those back-table visits. André recommends about half of these clients, provided they not mention to anyone else where they heard about me; he doesn't want the customers I'm suing to know about these referrals.

As usual, André was performing his "resto-bar-owner" stage act before a table of Euro diners, running his skinny fingers through his wavy, unwashed raven hair, which hung like fresh fettuccine over the back of his chair. His clothes never changed: a silk shirt and taut, nearly pegged, zipper-pocketed black ski pants tucked into his dark Wellington boots.

I told him I wanted to have a pasta plus a word with him. The table's custom-tailored foursome seemed offended, raising their heads as if an odd smell had wafted in their direction or something unchic had been perpetrated.

André and I squeezed our way around packed tables, finally sliding into a corner banquette in the back. As André signaled for a draft Beck's and my order, I asked about Pandora. He danced me through a few facts. She hadn't been around in some time, possibly years, but she used to come often.

"You know, Jahnnie"—he lifted his half-full beer glass with two hands to his long, narrowing face, magnifying his chin and nose—"I am certain, *bien sûr*, she like this place, although I have not seen her for a while. *Le menu ne change jamais.* Same conversation, same food each day of the year. *Tu vois les femmes, tu aimes les femmes, tu connais les femmes,* Jahnnie." (You see women. You love women. You know women.)

I wasn't getting much from him except broken French mumbo jumbo when the mercurial André spotted a strange-looking customer at the door who needed greeting. He left the table and I figured he wouldn't be back.

The penne was good but a bit salty. Everyone in the know says the same thing about the Black Curtain: "The pasta is terrific but there's a weird vibe in there." Tonight was no different.

Some of the customers were scribbling with crayons on the sheets of white paper used in place of tablecloths. It's a perfect setup for taking notes and illustrating legal scenarios for clients, plus calculating their fees. I knew just about everything there was to know about too many of the patrons, whether or not they were my clients. I had heard most of their squalid stories—the infidelities, the drugs, the sex or lack thereof, the white-collar and other crimes. Rumors and stories that were full of facts were launched there like airborne viruses. Many of the patrons had entered into deals with one another that soured. Some of them fucked women but most of them would rather screw a bank. But they ate and cordially conversed because bad business was de rigueur in café society.

I checked the black velvet curtain concealing a small stage behind the bar and thought about what was written at the bottom of the menu. *"Toutes les maisons ont un rideau noir."* (All houses have a black curtain.) The customers never knew when André was going to sweep back the curtain. Sometimes weeks or days went by and André pretended to be uninterested in the curtain. Nothing happened, and the crayon-doodling intensified. Then, one night, he'd suddenly pull it to one side, or it would rise tentatively on its own and André always made the same announcement, *"Mesdames et messieurs,* Le Rideau Noir—oh, *excusez-moi,* we are not in Paree, the Black Curtain presents . . ."

Some of the great performances have been: Sean Penn sitting in a high chair in diapers, eating baby food and bawling his way through the meal; Al Pacino reading Dylan Thomas backwards wrapped in a tomato-sauce-stained red-and-white-checked tablecloth from Pete's Tavern; an ersatz Francis Bacon painting displayed on an easel with a nude model next to it, who was eating the painting of himself; a black and white couple eating chocolate and vanilla ice cream from each other's genitalia. The most memorable was a Bengal tiger in a steel cage, devouring a live goat. André's ideas were endless and often portrayed literal conspicuous consumption.

I sat back at my table, listening to everyone and no one in particular speaking fractured French and English about everyone else's money, who's sexy, who isn't, rock 'n' roll, and simple-minded bestsellers purchased at the airport that they want to produce with a friend in LA.

André is obsessed with the atmosphere, mood, but most of all placement. The best customers get the right table where they believe everything happens. But nothing satisfies them.

The second-rate artists, artistes, bums, investment bankers, models, unworried has-beens, sun-baked socialites, and onlookers spill over to the sidewalk to small-talk.

"If it's happening, it's at the Black Curtain," people say, because the Curtain had defied the city's rule of thumb that says when a place is hot it's over.

André returned to the table. "Maître, I heard people claim that you come to the Curtain to hustle business, and that you use the table in the back like a consigliere, eating the salade niçoise."

André had his weird moments, and I didn't exactly take it as a joke. There were good reasons to be careful of what I said to him. I didn't know who his backers or buddies were—for all I knew they were my archenemies or legal adversaries. But I'd decided to take a chance and have André check out Pandora. All lawyers use intermediaries, but no one does a favor without debiting your account. André was about to get a credit on my books.

"Some information I can have about this woman," he said. "I know her family but it will take some days. One of my customers, the guy lived with her, I can't think of his name right now."

Suddenly the black curtain swept halfway back, its folds gathered nearly to one side. André smoothly turned toward the stage as if it were the most natural thing in the world and suspended our conversation.

He announced, "Le Rideau Noir," and the crowd's noisy reaction drowned out the word *presents*.

I could see a hiked-up black skirt and a pair of perfectly shaped legs in black mesh stockings leaning on a black chaise longue. But not the ankles. The curtain pulled to the side another few inches and everyone gasped at the heavy, iron shackles clamped around the ankles. A samba number oozed over the speakers: "Just one gaze and, into the haze, one or another, come be my brother, you gave yourself to me . . ."

Silence. An almond-shaped face with purple lips and black-rimmed eyes peered around the curtain. As a pair of slender arms reached out to the crowd, beckoning them, I found it impossible to tell if it was a man or a woman, and whether the androgynous face was connected to the lovely legs. The act was outrageously erotic and sexually confused. When the curtain abruptly closed, the show was over, the crowd stunned. Standard at the Black Curtain.

André left, nothing having happened as far as he was concerned.

Finishing the last of the pasta, I ordered a shot of cold vodka to clear my head of the performance. Then I used the house phone at the bar to call the office for messages. I often did this because the pay phone was bugged. In New York, drug dealers deliver to their customers wherever they're dining. The cops would not overlook the Black Curtain, although the thought of the police recording K and me was hysterical.

I got K's usual confusion about "Mr. Ocean's residence" and "Mr. Ocean's office." Finally he said there were no new calls. I downed another vodka, settled the check, and went outside to a phone halfway down the block for some quiet.

Betty picked up for the answering service. Big, black, with golden vocals, Betty had been working for Verbatim Telephone Answering Service for the past twenty years.

"Johnny O, just one for you." Her voice was a haze of cigarette smoke and clinking highball glasses.

"The usual?"

The usual is a crank call I've been getting for three years from a lawyer who flipped. He claimed that I'd killed his parents in San Francisco and that I was tied to the CIA. He normally calls around three in the afternoon, seven in the evening, and about five times a week in the early hours of the morning, crying like a baby, always leaving long, complicated messages. But this time I sensed trouble by the tone of her voice.

"No, it's from a man named Bill Rogers. Says he knows a prospective client of yours, and she's no Mary Poppins. Then he said something so foul I don't want to repeat it."

"Come on," I insisted impatiently.

"No, I can't. It tore me up! I just can't." She laughed nervously.

"Come on, Betty. What did he say that you haven't heard before—or from me, for that matter?"

"He said *plenty*. You know we can't repeat curse words on the service, Mr. Ocean. But since it's you, I'll tell you. He said, 'You fucking cunt. Tell your boss that if he takes this case, I'll cut his balls off and put them in a Mason jar in the basement of my uncle's house in Yonkers. Tell him that Pandora Markham is a fucked-up bitch who gives the best head on Park Avenue because she knows how to use her lips and tongue, and he hasn't heard the last from my mouth.'

"Then I politely asked him for his phone number; I said Mr. Ocean requires that I ask all callers to leave their number even if he has it. He said, 'O.K., it's 752-shut-the-fuck-up.' Then the phone went dead. I punched in Caller ID and dialed the number, 756-4575. No one answered."

"Did you ask him for the address of his uncle's house in case my heirs want to retrieve my family jewels?"

"You got to be careful, this one sounds seriously scary. And he violated 240.30 section 2 of the penal code. You taught me."

"What's that Betty? Remind me."

"I got the law posted right in front of my board. 'A person is guilty of aggravated harassment in the second degree, when, with intent to harass, annoy, threaten, or alarm another person, he or she makes a telephone call, whether or not a conversation ensues, with no purpose of legitimate communication.'"

"Betty, almost every conversation would land someone in the slammer if that law was enforced. Keep your voice in shape and thanks."

I hung up and, in fact, was concerned. No one likes those calls or the kind where nothing is said—just weird silences. It wasn't my case yet. But my good name was already rooting around in some warped brain.

Walking up Madison Avenue, I thought about Pandora. On top of everything else, I sensed I wouldn't be paid enough if the case was dangerous and I stayed with it. Beautiful female clients eventually stop paying their lawyers. Some tourist passed by and muttered to himself, "Big city, no action." I thought about going back to the Black Curtain for another drink, but decided to try the telephone number Betty got from Caller ID. At another pay phone I dialed it and a woman answered.

"This is Johnny Ocean. Mr. Rogers there?"

"He comes around." Her voice had a sexy resonance. "Want me to tell him something?"

"Can you be trusted?"

"Believe me. I give good message. What do you want to say?"

"Tell him I got his message. I'll have *his* balls in my martini glass—shaken, not stirred."

"Will there be anything else, Mr. Ocean, because he's never around when it's high tide."

She didn't sound a bit sarcastic, which really got me. I dropped the phone and left her hanging.

I fired up a cigarette and walked home. K wasn't around, so I turned on the computer and reviewed the notes I'd made on Pandora. After a while I got bored and wondered where that videotape had gotten to. Typically, I was alone on a weeknight, working under a chrome lamp on papers that were somehow going to affect the rest of a client's life. And my life. At 11:30 I pulled down a new quart of vodka from the liquor cabinet, poured half a glass, looked at it like a dissatisfied chemist, and dumped it out.

A loud knock came at the door to my office. The night man's craggy, oversized face craned into the room. Axel used to work security at a hotel around the corner. He was a little off-putting, but then, that was his purpose.

"Mr. Ocean, this was just left for you." Axel lifted a package and shoved it into my chest. "Some messenger. Tall guy with long black hair and a long black coat."

I fixed myself a stiff one and ripped at the package—a reckless habit for a lawyer, because you never know if evidence is being mutilated or if your face is going to wind up on the ceiling. The profession is a natural for letter bombs.

I pulled out the contents like turkey stuffing, but it was just the usual documents-by-the-pound.

On the top of the pile was a note written on light lilac paper with a Park Avenue address in milky ink.

Everyone in the neighborhood used that stationery shop. I knew it was from Pandora. The engraved telephone number read Trafalgar 9-5698, but it was lined out. The note said:

Johnny,

You didn't call me back. Couldn't sleep, was lounging in my red silk pajamas (I bought them in Hong Kong—you'd love it there), watching late-night television, and I was so anxious for us to be working together. Your reputation tells me so much about you. You're a man of intensity. And you're quick. You don't have to accept the check, it is just the first insurance you have that I am sincere about retaining you and that I need you, not just as an attorney but as a friend. I took the liberty of sending over these files because I'm so eager for us to get started.

I have more. The papers start off with the will of my husband, Marcel. The story my sister-in-law, Babette, tells is something to be believed only by her. The money is mine. After all the brain damage she's suffered, no one trusts a word she says. She would never have asked for the money back in a million years if my husband was alive but since Marcel is dead, sure, let's get it back from me as his sole heir. She wanted to give it to Marcel, and now I've rightfully inherited it. And I will not get the raw end of the deal.

Babette should have come to me when Marcel died. She could have politely asked for all of it back, but instead she sued me. We could have worked things out, but it's just too late.

Pandora

There was no check enclosed. An old client's trick. When it comes to payments, the gimmicks are endless.

The letter was scented a deep, rich lilac. The cliché worked, and I was amused because I'd been down these lilac-strewn roads before. But every time I got to know the client, the love affair was over. And these femmes fatales don't come along often in my business.

She had sent a lot of files. Pawing at a stack of documents, I found an original grainy black and yellow death certificate. Pandora had piqued my curiosity. I mentally punched in and went to work, for free.

Rummaging through the stuff, I discovered the usual unusual: First, the death certificate of Marcel S. Markham, dated January 17, 1995. Cause of death: (suicide) cerebral hemorrhage. Age: 40. Occupation: Businessman/investor. Residence: New York City. Born in Santa Fe, New Mexico, 1955.

Markham's personal lawyer was one James Kerrigan from a WASPy law firm with a small stinger down on Broad Street that had a former president of the United States on the letterhead. Big firms, like the old Nixon Mudge Rose Guthrie Alexander & Mitchell, use politicians' surnames in the firm's name. It's very much like a sinker pitch—it starts out high but drops low at the plate.

I read about twenty different letters and memos relating to a deal that Marcel set up with his sister, Babette. One hundred seventy million dollars was to be transferred to Marcel and he could do whatever he wanted with the money. No strings attached.

I found out through the bumps and humps of the files that Babette had the bucks, which she had gotten from her husband. All of the papers I read so far were dated around 1985.

I put the stack down for a second, lit up a cigarette, and blew smoke out of the side of my mouth as my concern deepened. I was not discovering the kind of thing every lawyer hopes to find— something in a case that'll make money, or in this case, save it. So far it just wasn't there.

About an hour later, I decided that I'd seen enough for the night. I started to put the files in order so that I could deal with them in the morning. One particular piece of paper didn't quite fit into a file. It was stuffed in at the bottom—a partially torn, legal-sized sheet of yellowing, brittle onionskin. I stamped out my smoldering cigarette and slowly removed the document. Like crab legs, my fingers carefully smoothed it out. It read:

Greenwich, June 1982

Dear Marcel,

This letter, when signed by us, shall constitute our understanding with regard to certain sums of money you owe me. Over the years 1980 and 1981, I advanced you the sum of five hundred thousand dollars. For this amount you have given me promissory notes due this month. You have expressed to me that these sums cannot be paid, and there is no prospect of payment because you are not gainfully employed.

Accordingly, I forgive the indebtedness, wish you well as if you had succeeded, but have put from my mind the thought of repayment. You will always be my friend, my brother-in-law, but not my debtor.

Edgar

This was the first potentially important thing I'd seen in this mess. Marcel's and Edgar's signatures appeared on the letter. The forgiving of a large loan could be important evidence. I took out some tape to repair the document. But then I remembered the file was trial evidence and I changed my mind. I wasn't going to tamper with the condition of the letter.

I thought for another moment or two and began to go through the stuff again, coming across mostly standard letters—lawyers to lawyers, lawyers to accountants, the most unrevealing sort of correspondence—until I found a bad copy of a promissory note. This one was for $170 million, signed by Marcel S. Markham, "Payable to Babette Longwood, any time fifteen years after date, June 12, 1985, with interest at 7%." Seems Markham went from bilking the peanut gallery to raiding Fort Knox, and the trip reinforced the old saying "Blood is much richer than water."

There was a note attached to it from Kerrigan to Markham. Marcel's lawyer sounded sleazier and more condescending by the sentence:

Dear Marcie,

If the note's okay, sign it. You'll be able to get all the money immediately. It's a great deal, and in ten years you can renegotiate when the note is due. After all, you're dealing with Sis. Enclosed is a copy of my paid bill for 250 grand. Sis took care of it but I have to say I was shocked when she asked me how to spell thousand. I got mine, call me when you get yours.

J. Kerrigan

The scam was obvious to me—avoid the federal gift tax by making the arrangement appear to be a loan, a very friendly loan. At this point, I was thinking about phoning up Pandora and getting a few things straight—namely, I had to work out a better fee. The money was too big and the case too complicated to work for a pittance if

I rendered services past the deposition. Besides, if I was being threatened as Betty said, I should be compensated immediately.

I was tired and didn't want to think about the case, Bill Rogers, or Pandora Markham for the rest of the night, so I closed it out until I could speak to Pandora the following day. I wanted my head to clear. Barkis was fast asleep under my desk. I turned the lights out, shut the door to the office, and went to my bedroom upstairs on the third floor.

At four-thirty, I woke from a dead sleep. There was a ruckus in the lobby, and the noise was propelled right into my bedroom. My brain was moving like a weary old draft horse. It was completely dark in the hall stairway. Those lights should have been on. Was Axel drunk and falling all over the furniture? Did he shut the lights off? He was supposed to be in the house taking care of things, not destroying them. I listened for him, any sound. Nothing, just deadly silence. I pulled my nine-millimeter out from under the pillow and soundlessly made for the door.

Slipping out into the hall, I flipped the light at the top of the stairs. Still nothing. Had the power been cut or just a fuse blown? Where was that goddamn Axel? But something told me not to holler "Axel."

I could hear Barkis growling downstairs in my office. I imagined he was baring his huge teeth, but the damned door was shut tight.

Approaching the stairwell, I slowly descended the steps. A rustle seemed to be coming from the lobby. Or was it closer? I was hearing too many things and trying to focus on what was or wasn't in the stairwell.

I had to get down to the office and let Barkis figure it out. That fucking coat, was it that coat? Was it coming after me? "This is brilliant. Shit!" went through my head as I inched down several steps while my heart punched against my chest.

Throwing all of his 130 pounds of angry dog at the door, Barkis knew I was only a few yards away from liberating him.

Material brushed against the stairway's steel spindles. I could hear someone coming toward me. Then it seemed like he was moving away. Was it one person or two? I froze for a moment, not wanting to reveal my location. I slid my foot onto the next step and cautiously edged my way downward. My hand reached out, searching for the knob in the blackness. I had to get to the office and let Barkis out.

Then a heart-stopping sound—unmistakable—a revolver being cocked. The sound echoed in the marble hall, bouncing off every turn in the building. My back went flush against the wall. Cold marble and me.

Slowly I backtracked up to the third-floor landing. Footsteps, and not Axel's lumbering Timberlands.

The circumstances dictated my moves. I rolled and lay face down, flat as a sheet, waiting for a shadow on the steps, on the walls—any noise louder than my breathing or the pounding of my heart. There wasn't any delay. Three shots came, each clipping on the heel of the other, drowning out all other real or imagined noise, and all of them carrying my logo.

My face was pressed to the floor, tasting some of the finest Johnson's Wax I'd been buying for the past twenty years. I told myself that this kind of trouble is always the fault of the client because we are their stand-ins. I had to get up and shoot back, but I couldn't see a thing. Raising myself off the floor, I returned the fire into the void, tearing apart nothing but my house.

Another crack. A bullet ripped through my left shoulder and I went down as the wall behind me washed in a flashlight beam. The only thing I could think of was my father in the Second World War. He'd been wounded by mortar shrapnel outside a French farmhouse near the German border, and he woke up in a ditch next to a dirt road. Two SS officers were talking excitedly, just beyond sight of him. My father's instinct was to shout for help, but when he heard those thick German voices, he forced himself to be silent.

Now it was my turn.

CHAPTER THREE

One uniformed cop and two detectives stared down at me. They were talking about the "swami" telling fortunes and predicting the weather for the nurses. From my hospital bed I had the comforting thought that Mr. K was watching over me. I recalled him saying, "*Swami* is a respectable Sanskrit word, Sahib, it can mean a spiritually awakened person." That's where I lost consciousness.

The next day a doctor informed me that I was in New York Hospital. The detectives came back, but I was too delirious to be of much help. They informed me I'd been found by Mercedes, who usually came in at about eight A.M. and who had indiscreetly told the cops about Pandora's case when they asked if there was anything unusual going on at the office. Axel, the night man, had been shot dead, right through the heart. A note pinned behind his ear with an acupuncture needle read, "Mr. Ocean, No fee is adequate when the price is death."

For the next week, I was in the hospital and in serious pain. The bullet had entered through my biceps and then torn through my shoulder blade, where there were now smashed bits of bone. I had been winged from below by someone on the staircase, unlike the time I'd been "shot at" with a .22 pistol by a guy I sued for fraud. He went to jail and the day he was released, he called and made an appointment for a consultation using a phony name. He entered my office and nervously pointed the gun in my face. Just then K appeared, his *kirpan* drawn, and stabbed him in the neck. The gun went off, grazing me.

K later said, "My boss always gets bang out of the first consultation," and laughed like a hyena. But that was a superficial wound, not this purple-heart business.

Every couple of hours Pandora shuttled into my day-and-night delirious dozings—Pandora on horseback buck naked except for muddy riding boots, her long chestnut hair knotted together with the horse's tail, at a full gallop out of Central Park and through a police precinct past detectives and cops; Pandora parachuting nude into the middle of Park Avenue onto the hallowed mall at midday; Pandora waiting for me in my office, lying across my desk, laughing hysterically, undressed, firing bullet after bullet into the promissory note for 170 million while Axel tried to wrestle the gun out of her hand.

The detectives reappeared before the weekend. This time there was no getting out of it. Lieutenant Victor Slice formally introduced himself with a bone-crushing handshake as if he'd graduated from a Bronx charm school. "Finally we get to meet a celebrity, Mr. Johnny Ocean, shyster to the guilty and a real Shylock Holmes."

I freed my hand and replied, "Thanks for the greeting, Lieutenant. Now I have two injuries—a wounded shoulder and some busted knuckles."

"So what, Counselor? Sue the fucking city like you sue everybody else," said bulldog-faced Chief Detective Oliver Windows as he exhaled a nasty cigar breath in my face.

"That's right, I haven't got any friends, so I sue people to meet them. We'll be pals soon," I answered.

Same old story with the cops, jealous as hell about the fact that I own a profitable P.I. agency. They despise lawyers like me who embarrass cops on the witness stand. We've solved crimes that they had buried in their dead files, pissing them off to no end. I don't need them and the last thing my Park Avenue clients want is to be interviewed by a cop—or the IRS.

They questioned me about every case I was on, investigating my life in general and anyone I'd seen in the past month or so. They were stymied by K, who kept telling them—or rather, interrupting them with—stories of his boss's great courtroom triumphs: "Oh, see, my boss, when he enters the courtroom, the judges show their respect for his perspicacious arguments. They are mesmerized by his power and quickness of mind."

Slice and Windows indulged him. In a sense, they were getting directions in a strange neighborhood. K called them "police cops," sarcastically praising them for "protecting and servicing the public of this great city."

The detectives had already found out from the "mud runs," the local phone records, that Pandora was one of the last people to call my office. But she had no criminal record and her social status protected her, initially.

I told them about Bill Rogers, but they already heard about him from Betty at Verbatim.

Windows looked at Slice, wrinkled his nose at me, and said, "Ocean, this cruise ain't over 'til the boat's in the harbor." But they left and I pictured the two of them on a tugboat chugging up the Hudson searching for the shooter.

Mercedes brought the Markham files and a pile of last week's newspapers to the hospital. I tried to work. The story of my shooting was all over the place. The *New York Times* had it as the lead in the Metro section: "PROMINENT EAST SIDE ATTORNEY SHOT AT HOME, EMPLOYEE KILLED." The *Post* ran it as a second headline, "UNSUCCESSFUL HIT ON BOSS, BULL'S-EYE ON EMPLOYEE." Mercedes told me it was aired on every television and radio news show. Pandora would have to be in a coma to miss the word on my famous whereabouts. Why hadn't she called?

Flipping through the files I found some old society-column

news clippings about Pandora. The client was described all right, by herself, in a foolish interview she'd given to the *Sun Valley Expression,* a resort newspaper that was long out of business.

"I go to social events, enduring my inbred peers quietly, bored by the repetition," said Pandora. "I hear people say I have a hard time loving anyone or anything. That I'm insincere. That's not true. No one knows about my real life. I almost joined the Peace Corps."

Meanwhile, K was on the case because the New York "police cops" were not satisfactory. He had already drafted his Sikh friends to assist him. K's Third Avenue newsstand buddies knew everything about anybody who was ever written about. Multicolored turbans were bobbing and bouncing around town day and night, checking out every lead and every possible suspect, including Pandora and Rogers since I showed K the video.

Dyson came by the hospital to see me. As he removed his double-breasted navy suit jacket, the overhead light annoyingly flashed off the carved gold griffins mounted on his double-sided, enameled cuff links.

"Love the white shirt Jack, no blood on you."

Sitting at the end of the bed staring at a nurse taking my neighbor's temperature across the hall, Dyson grinned and rubbed his manicured fingers together. "Hope you don't think I sent you to Vietnam. I don't see how this is connected to Pandora Markham, but I guess it's possible. Maybe they'll get some clues from the note."

"Or the needle. Man, you got me into something; no wonder D and S passed on this case."

"I didn't know, and the last place I thought I'd see you was here," he replied, turning back to check out the nurse's legs.

"Hey, remember the patient."

"Okay, for you, J.O. There's some dirt I didn't tell you which is another reason I came by."

"I'm listening."

"Heard about Vito Bellicoso, Babette's lawyer, a fine member of the bar?"

"Know the name. It's always around during election time. He rides around in open cars, seated next to a politician, whenever there's a parade on Fifth Avenue. And he's one of the bigwigs at the San Gennaro Festival. I saw him stuff a cannoli into his wife's mouth." I realized that we were on the subject of the judge's connection to my new adversary.

"Yeah, Vito Bellicoso. Where do you begin with that grease trap? He was the mayor of White Plains, no big deal, Westchester County, but the office has tentacles. I never had a case with him. Johnny, you can handle anyone in the courtroom. That's real good as far as it goes, but I'm concerned about what happens in the rest of the courthouse. Watch out."

I'd first heard of Bellicoso a few years back when he ran for Senate and nearly won. But right before the election there was a scandal about Bellicoso's family-owned construction company, something about a scheme to defraud the State of New York in a highway-repair contract, overcharging for equipment rental fees. After the election, Bellicoso was cleared of all RICO charges by a judge he'd shoehorned into office. He'd lost the election but managed to hang on to his political power.

The courts could be bought and Bellicoso knew how to work it—by running into the right clerks by accident and handing them envelopes, or by playing cards or golf with the judge and just letting His Honor win as much as the case was worth. And if the judge was someone Bellicoso couldn't control, he'd reach for his personal legal argot and got his "fuggin" point across in chambers.

"Vito's got his own style—friends in high places that can make your life rocky."

"I'll take care of him in my way."

Jack told me as he was putting on his jacket that he'd tried to reach Pandora a few times, but to no avail. "She just disappears for weeks at a time with no explanation," Dyson said, twisting his French cuffs through the sleeves.

His visit got me thinking again. I had all sorts of suspects in my shooting. Babette Longwood could have wanted me off her back, but that seemed too unlikely and not the style of a rich socialite. Still, she was known for being shaky and her late husband had had some underworld connections. I kept her on the A list. The other prime candidate was Bill Rogers, who'd already impressed my answering service and me with his telephone voice. I had no idea and every idea in the world about who'd shot me. Almost every other case I was working on had at least one maniac who could have tried to do me in for coming on too strong. But this was a professional job: the lawyer was wounded as a warning, and Axel killed.

There wasn't anything going on in the hospital that kept me from working on the case except contacting Axel's ninety-year-old father and arranging for the funeral. He had no other family, and the little money he had went to his church in Queens.

Making calls and reading over every piece of correspondence in the Pandora case as if one sentence, one word, would give me a clue, I plowed on. But nothing came until I got to a letter from Babette to Marcel:

June 4, 1985

Dearest:

Because you are my favorite person in the world, I want you to have one hundred seventy million from Edgar's estate. Marcel, I am never going to press you for these funds. The court ordered it to be paid to me this week along with enough for me to be comfortable.

More litigation is going to come out of Edgar's business deals, which makes it a very complicated estate. I want to see you succeed in something. You're my brother and should share in my good fortune. God knows there is nothing wrong with luck or inheritance.

I have arranged with the lawyer to have the money wired to your account and for you to sign a promissory note Kerrigan has prepared—the terms are that you'll pay me back in ten or fifteen years or so at a respectable rate of interest. Seven percent?

Love you,

Babs

Although this seemed like a great piece of evidence against Babette, the fact that a promissory note was signed would override Babette's disingenuously charitable nature.

As I tucked the note back into the file, the phone rang. Pandora. Finally.

"I know we haven't spoken before, Johnny. There's been a lot going on, and I had to reach you. I've received several calls from Babette; she's frantic. She wants me to come by for lunch or tea to discuss the case. Fine thing for that bitch. Now that she's sued me for the one hundred seventy million bucks, she wants to chat. I don't trust her, and if she wants to settle, her attorney can call you. Right?"

The breathy, ego-driven voice was careening down the road at me as if I'd crossed against the light. My health was obviously a nonissue. But 170 million sloshed around my mind like champagne bubbles—a heady consolation prize. I had represented beautiful defendants before, but never one *this* beautiful and *this* rich.

"You know I'm in the hospital?" My first sentence, a pitiable bore.

"Yes, *I* called you, remember? So what happened to you?" she asked as if I were in for an annual checkup.

"I was shot in my house." I abruptly changed the subject. "Do you know Bill Rogers?" I was testing her.

"You changed the subject, Johnny."

"To me, life's one long case and *everything*'s relevant." Heartfelt concern wasn't on her agenda, so why ask her to fake it?

"Shot?" she exclaimed and then switched to her caring mood. "Forget about Bill. He's crazy but he wouldn't shoot a cap gun. He's been calling me a lot lately. Says he sent you a tape. Standard for him, I'm afraid."

I said nothing more about the tape. The material was too hot. She must have known the contents. I wanted her to explain it but couldn't bring myself to ask.

"Who would want to attack a lawyer? Especially such a charming, bright, and dedicated one like you, working nights and weekends? Jack told me everything about you! What about Babette? Maybe she shot you. She's motivated to see that I get nothing, not even a decent lawyer to represent me. You should tell that to the police."

"It happened right after I read the file you sent over."

"That night I had the file delivered. And then I didn't hear from you." She sounded indignant. "I thought you didn't want the case, so I immediately called Jack, and he told me you were in the hospital. He didn't say why. And as for Babette, you should get it straight—her money can buy anything."

She had never spoken to Dyson. That was the first lie, but it wasn't major. Cases and people are full of them. The facts were always different, depending on which witness I wanted to believe. Was I going to believe Dyson or Pandora, my future client? Probably Jack, because today's client is tomorrow's enemy.

"I'll be here for about two more weeks, and then I can become a moving target again. But maybe I don't want to be."

"I want *you*—no one else—to represent me. It's your case now. You *have* to take it."

Something in that beautiful, musical voice made me want to believe that she chose me to the exclusion of all other lawyers. It certainly felt like my case, especially now that I'd been shot in the line of duty. And here she was, begging. I liked that.

"Well, I've read the file—the beginning of it, anyway," I said cautiously. "And I've got a lot of questions. But before I go any further, I want to make sure we have a clear and firm financial agreement—a written retainer."

"Don't think that I'm wealthy!" she said. "Whatever you've heard isn't true. My trust barely pays me the maintenance on the apartment. The one hundred seventy million hasn't been freed up by the court yet, and the court has turned down all our motions to release the money. Only the income is distributed to me on the estate. So with that in mind, tell me what you require. And remember, I just want you for the deposition." Then she switched modes and sweetly added, "And maybe more later."

The income on the 170 had to be close to ten million a year, a sum that didn't inspire pity.

Without hesitation, I upped the fee that I'd had in mind because it was already apparent that she might stiff me down the road. "The case will go farther and you'll need me. I want two hundred thousand. You won't have to pay me anything else for the trial."

"That's outrageous," she said. "Jack told me fifty thousand now, and possibly fifty thousand more in four weeks, depending on the work. That's one hundred max for your role in the case."

"I set the fees, Jack doesn't. And just to get up to speed on the file, it's nearly fifty thousand."

"One hundred thousand, that's all. Don't take advantage of me under these circumstances."

"I'll take two hundred thousand; the deal is that if I'm out after the deposition, I'll refund the other one hundred thousand."

She said nothing. Maybe I would have taken it on for free, but now I set the retainer and there was no going back. Anyway she was getting a great deal—Johnny Ocean in for a surgical strike.

The truth was I was crazy to handle a two-hundred-thousand-dollar case with no other fee and with the trial thrown in for practically nothing. I'd wanted her to be above haggling. But now I had the feeling there wasn't much she was above. The conversation ended.

In the afternoon a messengered draft drawn on the Morgan Guaranty Trust Company arrived at my hospital room. The gray cashier's check for the sum of two hundred thousand dollars came along with a note: "You're in my world now. I know we'll have great success together. Yours ever, Pandora."

I sent it to the office with a memo to Mercedes to deposit it tomorrow morning.

A couple of days later, I was released from the hospital and greeted by a jubiliant K at the door. Barkis sat in the background, staring at me, confirming his unpredictable nature. K said the dog was in a strange mood. Last night Barkis had played with a cat in Central Park; a week before he killed one. We never clown around with Barkis.

Things hadn't changed, except I wanted to go right upstairs and check the spot where I'd been hit. The police were finished with the crime scene and the place was just as it always had been, except for the bullet holes in the wall on the second floor—one from my nine-millimeter and three from the other gun.

K said that Axel was watching "Magnavox TV" in the basement when he was iced. He should have been upstairs watching the house, but that wouldn't have saved his life. He'd left the service entrance open as he was taking the trash out. That's when the killer must have slipped into the house. Security was tight but there was "a screw loose in this gentleman's head," K remarked.

K has seen so much murder in India that his reaction to homicide is initially dramatic, but seconds later death becomes just another fact of life.

I wanted everything out of my path so I could concentrate on Pandora's case, find out who shot me, and figure out how the two were related, if at all.

It was becoming a complicated case. The facts were breathing, growing, the players threatening. Now I couldn't—and wouldn't—simply do what Dyson suggested: "Come in for the prep and the deposition."

The deeper you get into a case the more you discover that no one is telling the truth or even knows what the real truth is. So the lawyer is forced to invent what really happened and hope that it flies.

This case was about $170 million that Pandora inherited because Marcel died intestate, without a will. In New York, his estate would go entirely to his wife. Further, it could easily be interpreted from the letter between Marcel and Babette that the money was purely a gift to Marcel. In that case, 60 percent of the $170 million would have to go to the IRS who'd call the "loan" a sham transaction, a disguised gift, and go after Babette for the tax. Did Babette know that pushing and losing the case might cost her $102 million in taxes, interest, and penalties?

On the other hand, there was some hard evidence that was bad for my case, like Babette's letter that told her brother to sign a promissory note. But I was going to make the letter cut the opposite way—Babette said on the same page she was never going to press Marcel for repayment.

My defense, which was more like a threat (as are all legal defenses and most claims), was that the loan was really a gift and the plaintiff would have to pay a hefty federal gift tax if she persisted in this lawsuit and failed to prove it was a real loan. My threats, seemingly extortionary, had to be tempered and delivered with the right timing.

When I got fully into my work, which took a day, I reviewed the file as intently as possible. Next to the folders on the desk was a note from K: "Sir, you may not find these documents in the papers you received from the client." There was a brown manila envelope stapled closed. Pulling it apart at the top, I withdrew the document, a report filed at the police department regarding Marcel Markham's death. It was a cold piece of paper.

NAME: Markham, Marcel

VITAL STATISTICS/DESCRIPTION

SEX: MALE

WT: 200

HT: 6' 3"

COLOR: CAUCASIAN

EYES: BLUE

DRESS AT DEATH:
Gray flannel pants, black socks, shoes (size 11) brown, oxford shirt (green and white stripes).

OTHER: Subject was last seen at 4:30 P.M. on the corner of East Sixtieth and Madison.

For a few minutes I reread the rest of it. Markham was found with eighty-two cents in his pants pocket, described as three quarters, one nickel, and two pennies. All coins U.S.

From the report I knew he'd been discovered at the bottom of an air shaft and probably wouldn't have been found at all if his suitcoat, vest, and wristwatch hadn't been left in his new offices on the fourteenth floor of a Madison Avenue address.

The medical examiner's report was more revealing; the circumstances of the case were as follows:

Subject may have jumped or fallen or been pushed. Posterior portion of the head severely depressed. Back of subject's head admits of several gashes that may not have resulted from fall. Eyes not opened, one split. Teeth intact, good condition. Chest well formed and developed. Other extremities extremely developed. Thin, long lacerations on shoulder and back.

I wondered about Marcel Markham's death. Would he commit suicide when $170 million was supposedly in his bank account in 1995? Was Pandora pressing him not to pay Babette back and driving Marcel right up the wall? Had he been torn between his wife and his sister and left this world to let them fight over the bucks? Or did he blow all the dough—it wasn't in the bank—and couldn't face Sis to tell her he couldn't pay it back?

At the time of his death, Marcel was starting a new company that imported art and antiques from Europe. He was excited about the prospect. It was hard to believe there was anything that could bother him except running out of tonic water in the summer or scotch in the winter. Suicide was not a credible choice. I suspected that he might have been murdered.

I jumped into a cab and went to the building where Marcel Markham died, figuring I'd find out for myself how it felt to be him for ten minutes. His old office on the fourteenth floor was now an Israeli travel agency called Up Up and Oy Vey.

Passing down the hall, I went to a gray steel door that was marked with a small red sign AIR SHAFT, KEEP LOCKED AT ALL TIMES. After I stuffed a portrait of Ben Franklin in his shirt pocket, I asked the building superintendent if the shaft doors on each of the building's twenty-six floors were locked and how long had that practice been in force. He said he'd been in this piece of real estate since emigrating from Dublin in '48 and had never been near any air shaft except to dig out the guy named Markham back in 1995. Although several building employees had heard a thud, they made no investigation. No one knew the victim because they all minded their own business.

The sense I got from the place was Markham didn't do himself in. But that was a job for the cops and the DA, not me. The on-site exercise was interesting, but why hadn't Pandora briefed me about her husband's death? Some clients leave all the squalid details to the lawyers and the city's sanitation department. Evidently, she was one of them.

As I returned home I thought the next thing I wanted to do was find out as much as I could about Bill Rogers. But that was too big a job for today.

On the way upstairs, K asked, "Boss, have the police discovered any evidence of the crime committed against you and this respectable house?"

"No, K, and it appears we have not been very diligent in finding any clues."

"Sir, they have the facilities, fingerprints if any, and any other information they gathered while you were in the hospital. We have a handicap. If they give us their findings, things will move faster." He was quietly angry and exasperated.

"They won't do that. I've had enough for one day. I'm beat."

"We will take the law into our own hands," K muttered and walked away.

The next morning I received a call from Pandora's regular lawyer, Rupert Hargrove.

"Mr. Ocean, we must meet immediately. This case has seriously escalated. I am having a time of it. Mr. Bellicoso is demanding documents and threatening to have me sanctioned every time he calls. Since you're handling the deposition of Babette, I think you should step in right now."

"No problem. I'll come by and we can talk."

Although argumentative phone calls with an adversary are the profession's staple, they are stressful for most attorneys. The elderly Hargrove realized long ago his sparring days were over. So he didn't mind deferring to me, didn't mind the lawyer getting shot, as long as it wasn't him.

"I don't mind yielding to you," he said nervously. "Heard you're a killer in court, even got shot at in the case."

"No, shot. Guess you couldn't notice over the phone I'm wearing my jacket over one shoulder."

"Ooh, sorry. That's too bad, but you're fresh blood in the case. What would anyone want with me?"

"Heard that before. Let's just say 'I'm new to the matter.' Sounds better to me."

His office was at Forty-ninth and Fifth in Rockefeller Center, *not* overlooking the ice-skating rink or the plaza. It had a depressing view of some dilapidated West Side buildings. I rang a raspy buzzer to get in. The tarnished brass plate on the door was simple enough: LAW OFFICES. After a few minutes, an octogenarian secretary pulled the door open and let me in. She slowly led me to a bunk bed–size office. It was as if someone had pressed a button and time had stopped. The year was 1934.

Hargrove introduced me to the secretary—his wife—who sat right next to me. It felt like she and I were traveling companions on a Greyhound bus. Hargrove silently went about tidying a few things on the desk. His head was the size of a small grapefruit. Sparse pinches of gray hairs had collected in and around his ears. He had remarkably tiny hands and a shaky voice. Nervous was written in one eyeball and wreck in the other.

"Let me relate some of the Markham facts and the approach I'd taken. The two children, Marcel and Babette, were very close since they were kids. That's probably why there was no real contract between Marcel and Babette. This is just another case of overreaching in family matters. Marcel and his sister being represented by the same lawyer, Kerrigan. Now that's a conflict of interest." Hargrove jerked his chin down, making his last point in the other side's favor.

I disagreed. "Not necessarily. It depends whether they both agreed to it. Babette might have signed a waiver. All this has to be looked into."

"Speaking of family ties, Pandora's brother, Webb Hartford, now takes care of Babette's health, if you want to call it that. That Babette, now she might have been on drugs which Marcel might have supplied her or maybe he forged her name or pushed her into the loan. I don't trust what Pandora says about how sweet her dead, do-nothing husband was. All of these things I have tried to investigate, but I'm getting no help from the client," he said disgustedly.

So Babette was a patient of Webb's. I deduced that Webb met the Longwoods through Pandora, but I wasn't assuming anything with this cast of characters. But why was Hargrove trying to attack his own case? It made no sense and all of those theories seemed way out of whack. Gripping the peaked lapels of his baggy woolen suit jacket, shuffling around piles of yellowing Law Review articles, Hargrove tried to justify his shoddy legal work, but the intellectual connections in his legal arguments were weak and remote. I'd be soloing on this mission.

His wife didn't say a word, just kept nursing ageless black coffee from a lipstick-stained Starbucks paper cup. Disturbed by her noisy sipping, Hargrove kept telling her to keep quiet.

"Does it bother you?" she asked meekly.

I tried to smile. It took a while, but what I finally got from Hargrove was somewhat informative.

"Babette was diagnosed by some expensive uptown doctors to have suffered brain damage from mixing pills and booze. That was long before the loan, when she was in the middle of marriage to Longwood. Too often she came home from some fancy party loaded, or she showed up in after-hours joints downtown and spent the wee hours on amphetamines and whiskey. She was miserable and bored in her marriage. Maybe that's just an act because that woman's pretty coherent." Maybes: I hate them.

"The case had actually been going on for only about two years—not long for the Surrogate's Court. That's a good laugh—a court and a judge are your surrogates the second you die, making certain your estate taxes are paid and the net goes to your hungry heirs."

I agreed with his cynicism.

"Edgar died in late 1983, leaving the heirs with a net estate, after taxes, of over a billion. Babette's share was eight hundred million in works of art, about one hundred million in trust, and a cash legacy of about three hundred million—a good chunk of which Marcel had managed to get from her. But he was dead months before he was supposed to deliver a check to Babette for one hundred seventy million."

"Why the hell would anyone want to kill himself holding a wad of cash loaned to him from his loving sister?" I asked Rupert, who just rubbed the cheap, silver-plated pen set on the desk and didn't respond.

Hargrove's wife looked at me queerly, as if I'd taken her on a midnight toboggan ride. But I now understand that she knew what was about to happen because she'd seen it many times.

Rupert grasped his nose, inhaled deeply, and said in a thick German accent, "Vell on that point, Counselor, I schmell . . . zometing creaminal." Then his right hand slid down his nose and he pressed his fingers and thumb together as if the smell was contained therein. He looked at me, his lips together, and nodded knowingly. He delivered a small laugh and said, "I studied German in college and worked in Switzerland. The Swiss start criminal cases to compel settlements in civil cases. I'd like to do that if we could prove the other side was involved in Markham's death."

It was clear to me that Hargrove "schmelled" criminal behavior from the other side in all his cases, and he used that pitch to extract larger fees from his client. The client most likely believed that instituting a criminal case was going to help resolve the civil dispute. In New York, it is considered unethical for a lawyer to threaten someone with criminal action in order to settle a civil case. Hargrove was coming off as a nut.

"But, Rupert, there's got to be more to it," I said, stopping myself from laughing in his face.

"Marcel Markham was a high-class bum, Mr. Ocean. He was a failure in just about every respect, except his good looks and his charm with the ladies, especially where his sister and his wife were concerned. Pandora, she's a tough one, but this Marcel—he had a hold on her. Finally, she married him, gave up the film business, and left California. But he had nothing except a sister married to Edgar Longwood, one of the world's richest men."

That made me remember one of Mr. K's sayings: "Rich people have the opportunity and the facilities, not like ordinary people. They can use telephones to fulfill their missions in life."

"And Pandora stayed with him through that. Sounds like a boring life to me," I said.

"What did she care? You see, Mr. Ocean, every designer dress and weekend in the tropics—summers in Cannes, Portofino, Sardinia—were paid for by the Longwoods."

Hargrove lurched to his feet and opened a small coat closet next to his desk for no apparent reason. On the inside of the door were two vertical rows of small, cheap, dust-covered picture frames with membership certificates to various organizations, only a few of which were related to the law. Not one of them connected Hargrove to any professional achievement—all of the legal memberships were indiscriminately awarded upon receipt of the application. I counted ten of them: American Bar Association, New York State Bar Association, American Society of Matrimonial Lawyers, AAA, Knights of Columbus, Grand Lodge of the

Independent Order of Odd Fellows of the State of New York, Home Nest of the Order of the Owls, New York City Subordinate Grotto of the Supreme Council of the Mystic Order of Veiled Prophets. And he was a member of the Great Council of the Improved Order of Red Men of the State of New York. The door looked like the chest of an overdecorated boy scout. But this is all he had.

Hargrove mistook my shocked expression for interest. "My wife is a charter member of the Dames of Malta and she's on the council of the Degree of Pocahontas. When you've got some time, I'd like to talk to you about joining a club."

His wife tightly smiled through her coffee-stained, deeply grooved teeth and kept staring ahead, seemingly at nothing. I thought about Pandora, represented by this fool. There were great lawyers in New York City who would die to be her attorney.

As I was about to leave, I asked Hargrove for the court papers—pleadings and motions.

"I'll send them over along with my regards to Pandora. Hardly ever saw her," he said, walking me to the door. "You know Mr. Ocean, when Mr. Bellicoso called last week, I told him you were coming into the case. I told him that I heard about your reputation and that you were a great trial lawyer."

"Were you trying to frighten him?"

"In a way, but . . ."

"But what?" I asked and backed away.

"He said he never heard about you. That was all. I thought you might want to know." Hargrove's eyes traced an imaginary line along the floor.

"I keep to myself," I answered. "Good-bye, Mr. Hargrove." But his last remark bothered me.

CHAPTER FOUR

A week passed with Pandora and me missing each other's calls—mostly she missed mine. Clients usually don't wait for the lawyer to call a second time before ringing back. But then, she wasn't a typical client. I was behind in the work that usually pays the bills, but I could concentrate on nothing but this case and recuperating. My shoulder was healing very slowly, and I was supposed to stay in one place and rest. The soreness was excruciating at times and I refused to take any painkillers.

I found out a few more things about Marcel, Pandora, and the Longwood family. An ex-security guard for the Longwoods, who was disgruntled and intelligent in equal measure, was discovered and interviewed by K, while Mercedes tape-recorded the conversation. I read the transcript, which showed their special world was one unto its own, from their Fifth Avenue apartment to the country estate in Greenwich, Connecticut.

Each night, the Markhams went upstairs in the building's wood-paneled elevator to the Longwoods. They were the professional companions of the Longwoods, visiting their "Mausoleum on the Park"—thirty rooms on Fifth Avenue overlooking Central Park at Seventy-third Street. Marcel and Pandora had a smaller, ten-room apartment six floors below, purchased for them by

Edgar, who exerted his considerable influence on a very strict co-operative board to get his in-laws accepted by the building. They'd eat in Edgar's half-block-long dining room, each of them solo on different sides of a forty-foot mahogany table, surrounded by the Vermeers, Rembrandts, and Cézannes. Edgar told his attorney when his will was being drawn that his real friends were his paintings, including the frames he chose. After all, the Old Masters couldn't borrow money from him.

The property in Greenwich, which the Longwoods used on weekends with Marcel and Pandora in tow, consisted of two identical Tudor-style manses next door to one another and connected by a 350-foot underground tunnel, done up with Turkish mosaic tile. One house was for guests, the other for the Longwoods. There were never any visitors other than Marcel and Pandora.

I couldn't help thinking how odd it was—receiving no word from Pandora since I received the retainer check. Although there were some interesting questions developing and I was itching to review the case with her, I stopped calling her.

Then the phone rang one night as I was parked comfortably on the red mohair sofa in the living room. I thought maybe the police were calling to say they had a prime suspect. Wrong. It was her.

The voice was unmistakable, overstaged and overpowering. Was I about to get the phone version of the video? Thousands of white angora cats purred in my head.

"Feeling all right, Johnny?"

"I'm fine."

"I . . . I just have to sleep with you, I mean speak with you."

"If you're locked out of your apartment, I have a king-size water bed," I joked.

The client-fucktress laughed uncontrollably. "I'm sorry. I just, I just mispronounce things occasionally."

"So did Freud. Anyway, I'm much better, except the pain is so sharp, I've been working on the couch. It's the only place in the house where I can be comfortable."

"Have they found out who did this thing to you?" she asked with more concern than I expected.

"No. As a matter of fact, when you called, I thought it was the police with news."

"Babette's been calling again and again." So much for concern. "She's really confusing me, telling me that I should come for lunch and bring some friends, that she's so lonely in that giant apartment. I think her lawyer is putting her up to it. Is that ethical? They know I have a new lawyer."

"That's strange. She's suing you for a hundred seventy million dollars and she wants you to come visit? How does she treat her friends?"

"Is it proper for me to see her?"

"Her lawyer can't talk to you, but it's all right for you to speak to Babette alone. Maybe the two of you can settle it."

"No, I don't think I should do that. She's very crafty. Being friendly to anyone is a throwaway for her. That's the gimmick, kill people with kind expressions but give them nothing. She uses that pathetic face, that's been lifted more times than a drawbridge, to fool people. She talks like a crazy person. Nothing's logical. Nobody's had a sensible or decent conversation with her since the second time she overdosed. She lost her speech but now she's got it back. The therapy helped, unfortunately."

"Who's the doctor?" I asked rhetorically.

"Actually it's Webb Hartford, my *darling* twin brother to whom I don't speak. During her crazy episodes he treats her, which is all the time. You probably heard that from Hargrove."

That twin connection was a shocking page in an off-beat case, without clipping it together with the fact Webb obviously worked against his own sister. That took the cake and the candles.

"And with all that brain damage? You believe she's capable of being shrewd?"

"Wait and see, she's no one's fool. Webb had rich patients, but he's no Einstein. He wants to retire from his medical practice.

Not long before Edgar died, Webb was suddenly around all the time. Left his wife, got divorced after being married for eighteen years or so. Nice timing, just as Babette comes into the fortune. Essentially, he's keeping her company, watching her health and her wealth. I suppose he's very devoted. I never really spent much time with my brother when my husband was alive. Webb was intimidated by Marcel."

"How's that?"

"Marcel was very handsome, athletic, a brilliant raconteur. He had the best-looking ladies of the world on his arm before I wrestled him down. Webb was the direct opposite—a bookworm, not bad-looking, but I think he was never confident with women. How he became a doctor I'll never know—with that kind of manner—but he's family and I . . . love him."

She worked her way through the entire baggage-claim area, dredging up one emotion after another. I imagined how well her style would play to a jury.

"Interesting." It wasn't at all what I meant to say. It's one of the worst things a lawyer can tell a client because the fee usually plummets to something nominal in their mind.

Ignoring my remark, she mysteriously flashed back to her childhood. Mother was dressing her for a birthday party.

". . . Mom was pinning a flower on my white cotton dress just below the collar. We were standing side-by-side on the front lawn of our house . . ."

I went with the digression, got the picture—a four-story white Victorian house with a long driveway snaking through a huge estate property up to a porte cochere. Not exactly how I was raised.

"Tears were streaming down my cheeks. Two hours before I'd screamed at Webb for ripping the eyes out of my Madame Alexander doll. He was so cruel. Once on a Sunday, when our parents went to a wedding, Webb tied me to a tombstone in the town cemetery during winter. A grave digger found me hours later, practically frozen to death. Webb was never punished."

I listened, imagining the rest of her childhood from the sound of her voice. I saw a woman's beauty glaring from a child's face. I wondered if she was sage enough to sort out what every man was after. I soon got the answer.

"I grew to detest all the attention heaped upon me. But at the same time, I thought it suited me. It wasn't my fault that I was pulled into the social world—cocktail parties in the city or weekends in Palm Beach or Newport. From the time I was sixteen, men made passes at me in cars, cabanas, under bridges, everywhere. Many proposed. People screamed things at me on the street that I won't repeat. I'd answer with a laugh, or 'maybe,' or 'I think I'm getting married next week to . . . whomever.' But it got to the point that I hated men, even the men I knew because they were dull and all so alike. Stiff, glossy socialites— same schools, same clubs, same brokerage firms. Anyone different would do, so long as he didn't have the same background."

She was getting morose, desultory, ridiculous. It was turning me on; she was *human.* Her hard side was a transparent defense. Maybe she was 100 percent hard sides, but I didn't see it. In a way, she was still a child. She needed help and was reaching out for someone to guide her through the maze. For a few seconds, I forgot the reality—that she had backed into 170 million plus because of Marcel's death and wasn't about to give up a penny without a bloodbath in the courthouse.

The subject abruptly about-faced, back to the lawsuit. "Anyway, Johnny," she whispered, "wait until you have the pleasure of meeting Babette. She's very sexy; she's got plenty of charisma. There's also a stupid rumor going around that the lawsuit is Babette's revenge for a love affair between her and me that went bad."

"Now that might settle the case."

"Very funny. Nothing happened. Don't get excited."

"You think she might try me?"

"That won't settle things either. And if you don't behave, it'll get you fired."

"This is a plain-vanilla will contest. I promise I won't get distracted." I was being sarcastic. There was no vanilla in this one.

"I'm confident that you'll behave ethically." She paused a couple of beats before pronouncing the word *ethically* in an almost lascivious manner.

Then there was a long pause in the conversation during which time I listened intently to nothing. "What?" I finally said to cut the silence.

"What? What if you were touching my tight little ass with your nervous fingers?" she shot back.

"Uh, nervous?" I coughed, jittery as a guy juggling three chain saws.

"Have you ever fucked one of your clients?"

She'd caught me off guard, which was her objective. It was as if she'd said, "Fuck me." I pretended I didn't hear, although someone else, a far more clever lawyer, would have said, "I want to fuck you in that tight little ass." She had me and I wavered between whether she had been referring to fees or sex. I could feel a hang-up coming. I didn't want that. My furnace was roaring. I couldn't face the rest of an empty night after this.

"Johnny, I have to go. There's someone waiting for me downstairs to take me to a party at the Armory on Park. Can we meet sometime later tonight or, better yet, during the week?"

"Absolutely. I'll get my calendar. Can you hold on?" I asked quickly and reached for the diary like a weight-watcher at mealtime.

"There's no time right now," she said. "I'll phone you later or tomorrow. Sleep well."

She was gone.

CHAPTER FIVE

"My boss wins trials in front of juries. Sometimes his methods are not popular with trial judges, but he likes judges anyway because they seek out the justice."

One of K's Sikh friends was listening to K pontificate in front of the house. As I reached for the door, K asked me to lend his doctor friend "a helping hand with his daughter's Green Card," to which I replied I'd be glad to, but thought K should be telling him the truth: If the judge were a politico, and my adversary a member of the club, I was a dead-bang loser. I'd get screwed by the favor factory.

K just shrugged and told his blue-turbaned, full-bearded friend, "My boss will find a solution."

A day had passed that wasn't wasted. I was adding to my knowledge of Babette's lawyer. He'd left a message that Hargrove told him I'd be doing Babette's deposition. Late in the afternoon I called back.

"Mr. Bellicoso, this is Johnny Ocean."

"Thank you for calling back. Pleased to meet you, Counselor. I've heard good things about you."

Odd, in view of Hargrove's comment.

"Who's been talking?"

His manner was polite, paternal, and patronizing. "Lot of people, can't remember their names, but you've got a fine reputation for a young lawyer, and I'm certain we'll get along well if you play by the rules." The admonition and voice change came together. He was threatening me already.

"You'd like me to behave a certain way? I don't exactly get the drift," I answered.

"My client is an elegant, fragile person and I want you to respect her position. She's the plaintiff and just wants her money returned." This was a technique to take the case out of the zone of litigation and put it on some subjective moral plane.

"That's all? Wouldn't it be nice if we lived in a perfect world without courts, and plaintiffs could simply make a call and get everything straightened out for a quarter?"

"How's that?"

"That's a point of view."

"You'll have a short deposition with her, I'm sure. She only knows the essentials and I don't want her to be upset."

"When is she available?"

"Next Monday at the courthouse ten A.M. I will tell her that you are a gentleman. You should think seriously of settlement. There is no defense."

"There's nothing on the table that I know of at this stage of the case," I said and shut off the dialogue, leaving him with no hope of an early resolution.

That conversation had me on my feet walking to the window. I looked out to Sixty-seventh Street. Babette had hired a specialist, a member of a club that had closed its eyes and ears to what most folks call justice. I'd be up against a power broker, stuck in a court where I had no influence: Surrogate's New York, New York County. Maybe Pandora was no better off with me than Rupert Hargrove.

The judge who had finally announced a trial date ninety days from now was Humphrey "Ringside" Macefield, a Democrat like

Bellicoso. There are only two judges in the Surrogate's Court. Both are elected. These judges and the lawyers who practice estates and trusts all deal in nicknames. John Lee Hooker once remarked, "You ain't nobody unless you gotta nickname." His was "the Original Bogie Man." Vito Bellicoso was called the "White Knuckle." Dyson warned me and I found out what everyone else apparently knew—that Vito and Humphrey were old pals, both in their indeterminate sixties.

Whether belonging to the same clubs in and out of the city, attending the same conventions and conferences for the past forty years, hiring each other's family members as court clerks or associates at the firm, or placing a son or daughter securely at a client's business, these Surrogate Court lawyers and judges were joined at the hip. They discuss the cases in gross detail in terms of what's in it for them. But what was unusual in this case was that Bellicoso was from outside New York County. Lawyers from New York County usually rule in the city but are regarded as virtual foreigners outside the county. Similarly, the prejudice against outsiders in New York can be overwhelming. Every case in any state is local, and winning goes to the locals—the home-court advantage. It takes twenty years just to know the players, and another twenty to know the game.

But Vito Bellicoso was a notable exception. He had clout in New York County because he was involved in politics statewide. And Judge Macefield helped any way he could. There were a million and one tricks to play havoc with attorneys like me who opposed lawyers like Macefield's pal Vito. Typewritten court rules were handed out every Thursday at nine-thirty when the court heard motions.

Macefield's Rule No. 1: If Macefield's name was not pronounced or spelled correctly by an attorney, then the case was automatically dismissed because "Macefield has been a family name in New York State for over 100 years and if a lawyer can't say or spell it, he doesn't deserve to appear in court. Rule No. 2: No papers in the courtroom other than legal documents. Newspapers are disrespectful to the court.

Another fifteen rules were equally arbitrary.

There is no right to a jury in the Surrogate's Court. The judge solely controls the result. The trial might be a bitter battle in the public's mind, but on the inside it could just as easily be a straight fix. Men in custom-made navy blue pinstriped suits called it "putting in a contract." Should I persuade Pandora to let me bail from the case since I was up against the impossible? An interesting career question.

I checked with Mercedes and Verbatim for my messages, but there was no word from Pandora. I had called and left word that I wanted to discuss the case. We needed to prepare for Babette's deposition. The dedicated clients always call to go over the facts before the trial or the deposition. They know the story or how to make it up before the lawyer weaves his own fiction. Although most lawyers never want to talk to the client, it is necessary. If I telephoned Pandora, there'd assuredly be no answer, and I didn't want to give in to the weakness anyway.

I began to get angry for letting myself get sucked into the madness. During the deposition I would concentrate only on the questions and the pressure they would create. A deposition is testimony taken before trial, under oath. If the story changes at trial, the witness will look like a liar when the opposing lawyer reads contradictory statements from the deposition transcript during cross-examination. Bellicoso had not yet scheduled Pandora for her deposition. I wondered why. Maybe he thought he didn't have to bother with it in this court.

I had other matters to focus on. The first thing was to get Bellicoso intimidated, and from our brief conversation I got some insight. He could be riled. That'd make Babette more nervous. It was going to be difficult, but it can be done with any adversary.

Still, a direct threat could make me come off like a loose cannon who didn't care about the law or the club. I'd put him to the test by throwing Babette up against the wall. Maybe she'd settle for 10 million in her pocket and walk away from the other 160. Could I make the deposition last two to four days, six full hours a day? I would need that much time to break her.

About 9:30 that night, it suddenly hit me that the deposition was now a week away and I felt queasy. I barely looked at the salad and curried chicken on a Chinese mother-of-pearl tray K had left on my desk. I stared at the black telephone, wanting it to jump in the air and scream my name in Pandora's voice. It rang. Manna had dropped through the ceiling of my house. I felt a surge in the veins in my arms. I was addicted to the calls.

"Johnny? Hello, Johnny, is that you?" she asked in her sea-breeze voice.

"Yes" was all I gathered together.

"Johnny, what are you wearing? A three-piece suit?" She knew how to throw me further off-balance.

"No. Levis and a black T-shirt."

"Button-fly or zipper? I hope you're not going to dress that way when you appear at Babette's deposition."

"I wouldn't do anything to jeopardize the case," I said, suddenly getting angry at myself for letting her get a reaction from me. When in doubt, repeat the question. "What are *you* wearing?"

Silence.

Then: "Johnny, I would really like to see you tonight."

"Let's make it happen."

She finally bit into one. "We can meet later. It's important that I see you personally, to show you something that I'd like you to keep in a safe place. You . . ." She hesitated, as if someone were eavesdropping, then continued, "You have something like that, don't you?"

I couldn't help but smile until she added, "A safe-deposit box or an offshore bank account?"

"Of course I have, I mean—what *do* you mean?" I shook my head and laughed. "I don't have a foreign account."

"You sure you don't have one in Liechtenstein or Luxembourg?"

"Yes."

"I'd love to meet you tonight when this party is over. Where would be a good place?"

"The Black Curtain. Ever been there?" A test. André said he knew her.

"Don't know it." She dropped it like it didn't exist. "There is a club, a private club I am a member of . . . the Veranda. It's on the East Side. I doubt that you know it, because it isn't open very often and they won't admit you unless you're with a member. You know, it's one of those places, chic, snobby, but we can talk alone and you could see how the other half lives."

"Which half?"

"I'll have to phone you back. I need to break a few commitments," she said.

I had a feeling that she was sitting right next to one of those commitments. He was probably in his forties and looked like the Marlboro man, a mansion dweller from Long Island in black tie about to spin her around for the night.

"A little stealth is necessary in almost every situation," she said.

"It's hard for me to do anything except in a straightforward way," I said. "You know, lawyers are like that. Even in their personal lives."

"That's good to know. I feel like I can rely on you. Call you back."

In twenty minutes, the telephone rang.

"Pandora."

"How did you know it was me?"

"When and where?"

"The club. Half hour?"

"Okay."

"It's near the Seaport at Pier 13. You'll see an old service station. Park anywhere around there. The lot can be used at night; they don't tow. Then walk around the back, and the club is at the end of the wharf. Haven't you ever seen it from the FDR Drive? It looks like a Roman building, like a small courthouse. You won't have a problem. It has columns and a statue—Zeus—is out in front."

"I think I know the place. I always thought it was a mortuary. See you there."

"If you arrive first, just sit tight. I'll be in a black limousine . . . alone."

I dressed hurriedly: dark blue serge suit, navy tie, white shirt. I looked like an Italian playboy or a charter member of the Veranda Club. Barkis was ready too; he shook off a day's worth of dust from the house. I clipped a short, tan leather leash to him and took him to the car.

The parking garage was next door to my house.

My 1963 triple black Chinese Eye Bentley coupe was always parked in front. It was the only car originally made by Rolls-Royce as a Bentley. Later, Rolls-Royce called it the Silver Cloud 3 Continental. It was the last in a series of coach cars made by H.J. Mulliner in England. Every time I stop at a city traffic light, someone ambles up to the driver's side, gives the car a fresh set of fingerprints, and asks me, "How much does it cost?"

Jimmy, the attendant, wasn't in sight. About fifty cars were parked there, ranging from limousines to Shelby Cobras. I called out; Jimmy emerged from the garage office.

"Hey, Mr. Ocean, you look slick," he said with a toothy grin. His right hand went out to Barkis, who sat down like a pile of muscles and turned his head away. A few minutes later, I was racing down FDR Drive. There was hardly any traffic, and an August half-moon cast an uneven shadow across Roosevelt Island's serrated skyline. It was warm, but a cool breeze was coming off the water. A yacht cruised down the East River lit for an elaborate bash, with black-tie Pandora people on deck. Passing the United

Nations, I reached over, shut the air-conditioning off, and slipped my right hand around Barkis's collar. He was sitting up in the passenger seat staring straight ahead, as if he sensed trouble.

"What's up, boy? Looking forward to seeing Pandora as much as I am?"

Barkis looked at me quickly, then climbed into the backseat. He hardly ever makes a sound and only barks when I'm in a jam. Other than that, I can't recall a whine, howl, or even a squeal from him. The strong, silent type.

The Seaport exit came up. I circled under the FDR Drive and began to cruise the waterfront looking for the Veranda Club. The only thing I could see was the Gulf gas station. It was nearly pitch black. Then I noticed a small passageway to the left, almost blocked off by several oil drums stuffed full of garbage. I wheeled the car over and drove past the station. The left tires of the Bentley chafed the wood curb, making blunt, rubbery screams.

The Veranda Club was there, just as Pandora had described it. It looked exactly like a miniature Roman temple with Doric columns in front, probably faux-finished wood, and Zeus. Three granite steps led up to a set of high narrow doors painted blood red and outlined in black lacquer. A bouncer the size of a Hummer paced near the door. There was a row of stretches and my Bentley. I was early, so I let the engine run without making a move to get out. Barkis lay down on the backseat with his head between his paws, pretending not to be a dog.

The bouncer swaggered toward my car as I hit the electric window. I was in the mood for love with a client, not trouble.

"Who you here to see?" he asked in a schooled tough-guy manner, pulling a wooden toothpick out of his left uppers. I hadn't heard the English language mangled like that since my corner-boy days.

"Ms. Markham."

"Not here. Left an envelope. Name?"

My heart did a one-way bungee jump.

"Ocean."

"First name," he growled.

"Johnny," I said as I reached out, but he'd already walked away.

I waited, listening to the East River lapping the wharf while some reprocessed, leathery celebrity faces came and went through the hail of green light showering the doorway which made them look worse than their photos in *Hello!* magazine or the characters I'd represented in night court.

The last thing I wanted was to be recognized sitting in a car outside this joint like I had nothing better to do. Looking at the rusty, peeling Brooklyn Bridge, I pretended I was going somewhere, maybe Brooklyn of all places, and purposefully blew some cigarette smoke down river as I started to consider just how small I was getting in this world. I waited patiently for the letter. The swaggering dope had gone inside and was taking too long. The son of a bitch probably had the letter in his pocket but was waiting for me to go crazy with anticipation.

A half hour later, he strolled over looking slightly more friendly. He came to the window and said, "Sorry pal, but we get lots of creeps around here. I checked out your registration. So you're Johnny Ocean."

"I know that. What time was she here?" I asked, trying to determine if she was dodging me.

"A few minutes before you," he replied.

"How few?" I prodded him.

"She was in a new black stretch," he volunteered. "I didn't talk to her or really see her. Her driver just handed me this here envelope and told me to give it to some guy name of Johnny Ocean. I turned it in to the manager. I was told to make damn sure the letter wasn't given to nobody else, 'specially Bill Rogers."

"So now you can give me the letter?"

"Some ID, like, proof that you can drink legally."

I showed him my license, and he handed the envelope over. I

scanned the FDR for a black limousine while I fingered the thick, engraved, eggshell-smooth packet and decided to read it at home. My mind was racing angrily forward. Bill Rogers?

"When is the last time you saw Bill Rogers?"

He said, "Oh, he's down here plenty, sometimes with Mrs. Markham," like I was stupid for asking.

I drove off at 2:00 A.M., angry at Pandora for the no-show but thinking legal. There were other clients I never met face-to-face and my reasons for wanting to see her in the flesh weren't connected to the case. Concentration was the name of the game—to act like a professional and control my emotions.

When I arrived home, I found what looked like a large bouquet sitting on the table in the foyer. The wrapping paper had colorful scenes from Central Park—bicyclists, couples strolling, rollerbladers, horses pulling Victorian carriages under trees filled with autumn leaves. I laughed quietly, thinking they were from her, and went up to my bedroom. What better place to read two letters from Pandora. They must have been sent right after we spoke on the phone. She had it all planned. I pulled the card out from under the white crêpe wrapping and read:

I love you, motherfucker. Well, let's put it this way: I'm not *in love* with you. In fact, maybe I don't like you that much. I'm laughing at you. And so is she. You'll never get into P's box, because I'm in your way.

Bill Rogers

It wasn't a bunch of flowers inside the wrapping, either. It was a bouquet of long, wrinkled, limp carrots with their leaves that resembled a bunch of decaying fingers. Rogers had to be the one who set up the shooting, or was that too obvious? The telephone rang.

"Johnny, Pandora," she said urgently before I could say hello.

"I went to meet you," I said, with *you stood me up* in my voice.

"Couldn't do it. I saw Bill on the steps to the club when I pulled up, so I wrote you a quick note and dashed off."

"Yeah, I got the envelope."

"Did you open it?" she asked.

"No, I'm saving that for last. It's been one of those nights."

"Yes, it's been a wild night."

"What was so wild about it?"

"Licking the envelope."

"What about the stamp?"

"That's for next time, if you can handle what's inside." I tore off the end of the envelope and slipped out three pieces of paper. One was a neat handwritten message, dashed off in blue ink:

This is the original. Put it in your safe-deposit box, but call me first.

The second was a general power of attorney to John Ocean from her, properly notarized in New York County. That was un- usual, but some clients don't want to bother with the day-to-day stuff. She trusted me to sign all legal documents on her behalf. I could withdraw 170 mil right out of Morgan Guaranty or sell her apartment at the Caprice out from under her. She gave me the power to sign her life away. I was flattered.

The third was the original promissory note for 170 million dollars on starchy bond paper, signed *Marcel S. Markham.* That jerked my head back. The promissory note in Pandora's posses- sion would seem to indicate that Babette never had any intention of collecting the money, so she'd returned the original note to Marcel.

"How in the earth did you get your hands on the original promissory note?" Waiting for each word to come out of her mouth, hopefully in perfect order like, "Babette left it in Marcel's possession," I held my breath.

But no, she answered, "I found it. There it was in among Marcel's papers. The best way would be to go through the case without the note so they couldn't prove it was a loan and they wouldn't have any case? Am I right?"

Pandora sounded like she was teaching the law of evidence. A promissory note is supposed to be in the possession of the lender, not the debtor or his estate. I could see where she was going—no note, no case.

"What does that mean?"

Was this another client asking to have evidence destroyed or magically disappear? I retrieved the file and got out the copy of the note. It was too blurred to match it to the original.

"Well, Babette won't be able to show any written proof of the loan without the original note." Then she added, "You can destroy it, you have my consent."

Marcel didn't tear it up, so Babette could get around the huge gift tax. That piece of paper would show the IRS that there was proof of a real loan agreement. Between brother and sister the 170 million was a gift. Even the IRS would question why the note was in the debtor's hands.

"But what if there is a copy?" She was figuring all the angles with me as her protractor.

A copy of a promissory note would be hard to get into evidence. The law requires the original. Now I understood about the safe-deposit box, the power of attorney. If anything happened to the note, I was in deep shit because it would be under my control. If I wouldn't destroy the note, she was trying to get me to ditch it in my personal safe-deposit box.

"You wouldn't want me to commit a crime on your behalf?"

"Of course not."

"I don't do that as well as some other lawyers, and I could be disbarred, maybe do some jail time. Maybe you should think about getting someone else to do the case."

"Don't get so hot and bothered," she said. "I don't want you to

risk anything other than your precious time to handle my case."
Then she whispered, "We're just getting to know each other, but
I can talk openly with you. It would be a relief if the note just
didn't exist. They'd never be able to collect. Can't you forget I
ever sent it to you?"

"I heard you say you wanted me to behave ethically," I said.
"Didn't Hargrove tell you that the deal with Marcel and Babette
was phony? That it was just a cover-up? The promissory note was
a gimmick to hide the fact that the money was a gift from Babette to Marcel."

Innocently, she replied, "No. I don't understand legal language. What's a defense? Is that important?"

Her naïve reaction ran my emotions from pillar to post.

"Those letters in your file say quite a bit. Now I understand
why you don't know what's been going on through Hargrove, because the note was in your house, not his office, so he didn't know
that Marcel had it, not Babette. Possession: nine-tenths of the
law. The note is in your pocket, not Babette's, so how could she
enforce it?"

"I get it." Finally.

"The written word is what most cases turn on. Haven't you
ever been involved in a lawsuit before?" I asked.

"No. Of course not. I don't count divorces. Do you?"

"So you didn't bother to read the file and the letter between
Marcel and Edgar?"

"Just a few documents. That's why I hired Hargrove. And now
you."

I didn't believe her but decided to pretend I did.

"There's a very revealing letter in the folder from Edgar to
Marcel."

"Edgar? What letter?"

"It's about a loan between them. The letter says in very clear
language that Marcel was going to be forgiven . . . that is, finan-
cially forgiven, all the money Edgar loaned him."

"I never heard of that letter. Rupert Hargrove didn't mention it. Where did it come from?"

Barkis moved in next to me and groaned.

"It was at the bottom of the pile of papers you sent me." I stopped and repeated myself. "The bottom."

"Not possible."

"Possible, hell it's a fact. You want to see it, tonight at the Veranda Club?"

I poured a drink and lit a cigarette on that temporary victory.

"No, I don't doubt it. Just shocked that Edgar had been so generous," she answered, backing off. "But Rupert must have known about it. He's seen this file. Edgar was a control freak who doled out the money in dribs and drabs until he died. He kept people nice and dependent. How much was forgiven?"

"Five hundred thousand, if I recall. Small by the numbers in this case." I didn't say anything about her claim that Hargrove saw the file that *she* sent to me.

"Ten thousand was a lot of cash for Marcel. So now I finally know all of Marcel's loans accumulated to five hundred thousand—if that letter you say you have is real. Marcel could have very easily written it himself. I wouldn't put it past him."

The characterization of her deceased husband was deeply uncharitable for a woman who held $170 million thanks to matrimony.

"Why? Didn't you trust Marcel?"

"What's the difference? He and Edgar—they're both dead," she stammered. "You think it'll be a real fight for us to get that letter into evidence? That letter could help us show there was a history of gifts between us and the Longwoods."

"True, that might create evidence of a pattern," I answered. "But until I've read the whole file and studied the case I don't know exactly what everything means."

Maybe it wasn't Hargrove's fault that he didn't raise the gift defense. Maybe he never saw this file, but if he did, he blew it.

Since Hargrove was still trial counsel I didn't want to get into a controversy with him about the file. That would just sound like me accusing him of malpractice—not pleading the gift defense.

Going easy I said, "I don't think he sees the case the same way I do, but I suspect he didn't raise the defense in the court papers that the hundred seventy million from Babette to Marcel was a gift. That would shock Babette. Hargrove never developed that strategy."

"What are you going to do about it?"

"Not so fast. Don't forget, I'm only in for the deposition. There isn't much I can do about these great needs you have. The first thing that has to be done, without delay, is to make certain there is a proper defense—that all of the money was a gift."

"How do I do that?"

"Get Rupert to plead it."

"I don't want him to. I want you to do it."

"That's possible."

"How?"

"Just call Rupert and tell him I'm taking over the entire case," I said in my most Southern Californian casual.

"I can't. I'm afraid. I hate confrontation. I'm just not good at those things. You must do it. After all, I just gave you power of attorney."

Barkis got up from under my desk. He sat down in front of me and growled once.

"The law doesn't permit me to take over another case unless the client informs the outgoing lawyer. You have to telephone him."

Suddenly she turned cold, even a little angry. "Okay. Consider it done, Mr. Ocean. But no more money than we agreed on. Unless we win. You'll stick with the sum I gave you, then I'll pay you more."

"That would normally cost ten thousand a day if it went to trial, not including all the preparation and expenses. But I can't come up with an exact sum until I read everything and take the deposition."

Barkis looked at me skeptically, as if I were charging way too little. I never would have made this kind of pact in a case involving bucks this big if the client weren't Pandora. He was probably right.

Then suddenly, just as I was about to strike this vague deal, the telephone line went dead. I looked at the phone. Barkis looked at me. Maybe her behavior was even getting to the dog.

The sun was coming up as I returned the receiver to the phone. It seemed normal to be slaving away on Pandora's case in the wee hours. But I was no longer in my world.

CHAPTER SIX

"Ocean, the lawyer?" the voice on the other end of the phone asked.

"Bingo."

"This is Lieutenant Slice, Victor Slice."

"Who?" I remembered this forgettable cop.

"Cut the crap, Counselor."

"That doesn't make us pen pals. What do you want?"

"We found a Bill Rogers. Must be one of your best buddies. He said your name before he went unconscious. He's been shot. Right now there's a bunch of doctors operating on him. Maybe they can save his life. You're going to have to come down to the station house. We're at the 19th."

My hand dragged my watch up to my eyes. "It's seven in the morning. Are you kidding?"

"No." He hung up.

If I didn't cooperate with them it'd create a problem. I grabbed Barkis from the corner of the now fringeless "Tree of Life" Persian rug he'd been chewing up for the past three years, jumped into the car, and was at the 19th Precinct in ten minutes. Barkis hates police stations and cops almost as much as he hates the vet.

When I walked in, a beefy Irish captain who might have been

Dyson's brother took me in to see Chief Detective Windows up on the second floor. Cops were hanging around, parking the squad cars, pouring out of the building, or running up the steps, reminding me of the expression "Police stations are like whorehouses, dicks moving in and out."

I wound up in what might have passed for a waiting room and not someone's office. Slice and Windows were waiting for me.

"What do you know about this guy Rogers?" Windows snarled.

He lit the end of a half-eaten cigar and put his leather shoes up on a well-worn, once walnut-colored rolltop desk that looked a hundred years older than any of us. Slice walked around in a half-circle like a dog in tall grass getting ready to sit down.

I barely moved my lips. "Nothing."

"That's hard to believe. Your name was on his breath. What was left of it. You got any hobbies, Ocean? What do you do with your spare time?"

"What happened to him?" I ignored the accusation.

"Blasted to outer space with an eight-hundred-dollar Remington 12-gauge," Windows retorted. "He was pepperoni but still able to grind out a message with what was left of his face. We'll find out who owns the gun, but that means nothing right now."

"I don't own it, so where's the fit?"

"Your name in his mouth makes you a suspect. You and that Pandora—what's that, Pandora's box? I bet you opened that one." Windows turned to Slice, giving him the opportunity to admire the boss's wit.

"Do *you* have any interests besides busting balls? I get it, I'll bet you're a gun collector."

Slice cut in, "Tell the lawyer about your hobbies, boss."

"Hobbies? Yeah, I have a few, I ain't no college boy like Slice here who writes cop novels. I don't collect guns. But you were close: I collect gums."

"Gums?"

"Sports chewing gum. I get into all the games I want with my police pass, right down on the field. Professional athletes only. Ordinary Bazooka, that can be star gum. When they spit it, I grab it. I got Joe Namath's gum from the Jets-Colt's 1969 Super Bowl in Miami—I went with the Jets as security, a nice Wrigley spearmint. Larry Bird's gum from a Knick's playoff game with the Celtics in 1990. It's pink, probably Topps. And about a hundred more wads. I got a Shea Stadium collection, a U.S. Open at Flushing Meadow collection. McEnroe, U.S. Open 1981, championship gum, beat Borg in the finals, sugarless. I keep 'em in glass boxes, just like butterflies. They don't have anything like it in any sports-trading stores. Yet. One of these days I'll sell them at that fancy auction house, Sotheby's, so my kids can go to college."

"I can't wait to see the sales catalogue."

Then Slice took it upon himself to inform me, as if I didn't already know: "Rogers was married to your client. Pandora Park Avenue Princess. Why's that babe running in low-life circles? Who are their friends?"

As if I'd answer a question like that even if I knew. And wouldn't I like to know just one of her friends so I could figure her. The cops always raked their claws across any client of mine. That got me pissed.

"What's she hired you for? Gonna defend her murder rap if he croaks? And what's Rogers got to do with you?"

"I'll ask him and you can hold his hand."

"Not right now, he's under the knife."

"You know lawyers can't divulge why they've been hired, not even to their mothers. As for what kind of ax Rogers has to grind with me, all I can tell you is I don't know, and if you find out anything from him, be kind enough to call me." I was serious. I wanted to know if Rogers was the one who'd winged me.

Slice, drawing on his college education and general street sense, lunged at the obvious. "You were shot in your office. Who do you think did it? What about Mr. Rogers? Some family, Bud!"

"I told you, I don't know, and I *don't* know. The only Mr. Rogers I know is the television guy with the green cardigan. Gentlemen—Windows—I've got to be going. My dog is waiting in the car. You don't want to be on his bad side."

Windows turned up the anger. "I don't like lawyers, never mind the amateur detective bullshit. You think you're a fucking private dick! You're just a dick. This guy Rogers has some connection to you, I think personally, and I want to know what the hell it is."

"You got a stick of gum?" I pointed to his shirt pocket.

"Don't be a fuckin' wise guy."

The door behind me swung open and a female police officer came in with a note, handed it to Windows.

"Rogers is dead."

For a minute, no one said anything, not from shock but out of some sort of strange occupational embarrassment. I broke the ice. "Where's the body?"

"Lenox Hill," Slice responded.

"Do you mind now if I see what the son of a bitch looked like, since he talked about me so much?"

Windows cut me off. "That's police business. You said you didn't know his face and now he doesn't have much of one left. But I'm gonna want to see *you* again."

As I left Slice told Windows that they'd have to beat it over to the hospital before Rogers was shoveled into a drawer in the morgue.

I drove there myself, restraining Barkis by the collar. Sensing I was getting screwed around, he was dying to take a chunk out of someone, probably Slice or Windows. I called K on my cell phone and told him to meet me over at Lenox Hill Hospital. That was a problem, he said, because he was very busy, occupying the early morning prayer and memorizing Rudyard Kipling's "If," which he now insisted on reciting: " 'If you can meet with Triumph and Disaster / And treat those two imposters just the same . . . ' "

After parking illegally on East Seventy-seventh Street between two yellow and white ambulances marked LENOX HILL HOSPITAL PARAMEDICS, I jumped out of the car. Mercury's winged staff wrapped in snakes—the caduceus—was mounted over the entrance to the hospital.

"'If you can bear to hear the truth you've spoken / Twisted by knaves to make a trap for fools.'"

"K, stop the poetry reading and report over here," I said, getting angry.

"'Watch the things you gave your life to, broken, / And stoop and build 'em up with worn out tools.' Sir, my presence would be of no service. I will call my good Sikh friend Dr. Rangit Singh, a young respectable physician, to aid you in the hospital. You may remember that he was in the street in front of the house asking me about a Green Card some days ago. He will be on the first floor wearing a dark blue turban and looking for you."

I clicked off.

After finding out where they'd taken Rogers, I squeezed into a packed elevator and went to the third floor. The coast was clear— no Windows and Slice yet. Moving toward the nurses' station, I eavesdropped on an intern talking to a orderly. He was vamping about a guy who'd gotten mauled on the FDR Drive, and how he'd just finished stuffing the vital organs back into the victim's body.

I ducked around the corner, hid in an empty office, and waited. I would have fallen asleep, but the antiseptic surroundings and the fluorescent sky of the hospital corridor kept me awake. A Sikh ambled down the corridor toward the nurses' station under an indigo turban, an idle cell phone in his hand. As he crossed in front of me, I reached out and yanked him in.

"Oh my Lord, are you Mr. Ocean?" he said, perusing some X-ray equipment and confirming his identity, "I am K's good friend."

"I need a favor, Dr. Singh. A Mr. Bill Rogers is dead. I have to verify it, but there are too many people around and I can't handle it alone."

"I will lighten your burden by making you a doctor." He laughed.

"How's that?" I whispered.

"Sir, you must wait a moment and you will see."

Peering through the door I saw a young, blond doctor. The name tag read DILBER WAYNE, M.D. The nurse next to him pulled off her operating mask and said, "Rogers looked pretty horrible at the end."

"Appearances don't matter then." Dilber just shook his head.

Just then my favorite cops ran down the hall. I could swear Slice saw me. But I was wrong; he intercepted the doctor, striking up a conversation with him a few feet from where I was standing.

The poor physician was questioned and small-talked continuously in a semiliterate fashion by Mr. Ivy League, who claimed he'd attended Brown in an effort to rise to an M.D. level.

Windows cut in, "Rogers, Doc. That's what we want to know. Did you talk to him, did he say anything?"

That filthy sensation arrived again. I could almost feel his cigar breath coming through the door, backing me up.

The doctor looked at the floor and said, "Didn't say anything other than 'Ocean,' and 'Pandora,' Officer." His words crossed the nurse's comment, "Leave the dead alone," as she brushed up against the knob, pushing the door in against my nose.

"When he came in I knew he was a goner, but we did what we could." As the doctor finished with the cops, his soft hands gestured a "What can you do?"

The doctor invited Slice and Windows down the hall to the operating room to see the body before it was dispatched to the morgue.

Turning, I caught Rangit in the corner with his turban off. His long hair hung down to his ankles. Of course he had never cut either it or his beard. I realized that he was tucking up another turban. This one was white.

"Why are you doing that?"

"Sir, in my country, you can purchase fine material, five yards of pure cotton from Dhaka in West Bengal, for turbans that you can hold in the palm of one hand. I came to assist you with an appropriate disguise. K said you could help with the Green Card, but we can talk later."

"Later," I hesitated to agree.

"We are in a hospital acting as honorable physicians and we must dress according to the rules," he said, handing me a long white coat, complete with a blue plastic M.D. name tag hanging on the back of the door.

"Sir, the operating room is down the hall and that is where they probably took Mr. Rogers. Let me help you into this turban and white coat. Put this silver bracelet, the *kada,* on your right hand."

"Great, thanks for being so helpful." I put on the Sikh bracelet and the turban. Minus the beard I looked like a Sikh doctor.

About ten minutes later Dr. Singh and I strode out to the corridor and split up. He went toward the front door.

I walked into the operating room, but it was too late. Clad in green uniforms, Lenox Hill maintenance workers were mopping a crimson floor. One of the crew, a friendly Hispanic with a gold earring, removed his headphones from a yellow Walkman and said that two *pendejo* cops had examined a male body full of gunshot wounds. I was in the right place but at the wrong time.

He directed me to the morgue. "Doctor, down to the basement take a right and hang a left, all the way to the end, you can't miss it."

In no time I was in the elevator going down and taking the turban off at the same time. Rolling it up and putting it inside the coat, I got out and ran down the hall, zigging and zagging between rows of blue laundry trolleys, not knowing exactly where I was headed. Trying the door at the end of the hall, I found what I was looking for.

Inside, as in all morgues, there was an absence of life. It wasn't a large room. A sign read: DISPOSE OF ALL SOILED LINEN IN PROPER CONTAINER AND DO NOT LITTER THE FLOOR WITH DISPOSABLE ITEMS.

It reminded me of K saying, "We are all disposable and finally cremated in my country."

This was good company—dead bodies stuffed into stainless-steel lockers manufactured by Jewitt. Nice paneling. Each one had its own chrome handle and a temperature gauge reading forty degrees. Like they were slot machines, I yanked each shiny lever. That was the game—pull the arm, win a stiff. Each compartment was very obliging, serving me one corpse after another on a tray. But no jackpot.

Diligently I searched for Rogers's cadaver until I noticed that every door had a white label with the tenant's name, not the landlord's. That was a big help because I didn't have to bother reading the time and date of death marked on a small piece of paper wired around the big toe.

Hearing the sound of the swinging doors opening, I yanked my head out of number 22, turned and faced a body being whisked in by an orderly followed by a young, dark-haired, shapely woman in whites who stared me straight in the eye.

Caught.

"Hi, just wondering which one I'd inhabit when my number was up," I said loudly, greeting her like an old friend. But she wasn't. The orderly walked out, leaving me standing with a severely sexy Asian woman.

The two of us stood squarely in the center of the cold room.

I made a move to break the silence. "Allow me to introduce myself, I'm Doctor Ocean."

"Yes, Doctor, what can I do for you? Are you from Pathology?" she asked giving me the once-over. She reached out to my coat. Lifting my collar, she read the name tag.

"Singh? Are you Indian? Are you a Sikh?" Damn, Rangit had given me his name tag.

Sheepishly I looked down at the blue and white plastic tag on my coat. I'd bungled it.

I didn't answer her question, instead steering the conversation toward the gurney. Looking at a pomegranate that was once a human face, I said, "If he'd stayed in bed today, he'd still be alive."

Stepping back, she asked, "That's not something a physician would say. You couldn't be a doctor." She had me, momentarily.

"Death is something I deal with every day," I snapped back and quickly asked, "And you're on hospital staff? What department?"

That backed her up, taking the heat off me.

"I'm the—" she started to reply.

"Your name?" I wasn't quitting. She had a sizeable diamond on her right hand. What was a nice rock like that doing in a place like this?

"My name is, uh, Y," she stumbled.

Now I felt as if I was onto a small piece of the Rogers puzzle. "And you're just down here slumming?"

"Oh, I was doing someone a favor, checking on this poor guy. I'm leaving." A last look at Rogers's remains and she began to move away.

"Really, and who would that be?" I hit the ball back.

"I'm an obstetrician." Deuce.

"What floor is obstetrics?" I asked. Now our relative power bases had been reversed. She seemed frightened.

"Fifteenth."

"Sorry, Doctor, there are only twelve floors in this hospital. I believe Obstetrics is on the sixth floor," I said, just making it up as I went along. "So what are you doing here? This is not a room you'd get confused with maternity."

"Well, maybe I made a mistake. Are you on staff?"

"No, as a matter of fact. I had an appointment to meet a pathologist. Looks like he's not coming."

Our mutual curiosity had intervened and was overcoming the tension.

We walked out of the morgue, into the hall, and as the doors closed behind us I said, "Didn't get the name."

"It's Chinese. Y."

Y joined the players with one-letter names, like Mr. K, but we were nearing the tail end of the alphabet.

"You want to have a drink?"

"Enough adventure for one night. Take my number and you can call me later."

We elevated up and walked out of the emergency room to the street.

It was the afternoon, the sun shining through the east corridor of Seventy-fifth Street.

"You don't have to call me," she said. "Let's have a drink around the corner from my apartment, about seven. I live in SoHo, on Wooster Street, in a loft. There's a bar on the corner of Wooster and Prince."

I agreed. Whoever she was, I had to find out. Whether or not it was the hottest pickup of my life, it was also my job.

CHAPTER SEVEN

I set the alarm for 6:00 P.M., went down like a ton of bricks, and didn't get up until the clock must have read six plus in phosphorescent digital time. The alarm blared for ten minutes. I used the shower to wake up and ran out the door straight into the end of a late afternoon and the drone of a New York City jackhammer.

I grabbed a taxi and realized as I opened the door that I was on my way to play with a very dangerous toy. But strangely, that didn't bother me. I went downtown via Broadway and walked into the joint, sandwiched between an organic-clothing store and an art gallery on the corner of Wooster and Prince Streets. I asked myself, is this going to be the Bohemian phase of the case?

At 7:15 Y arrived wearing a tight-fitting black skirt with a silvery linked belt, a yellow pullover, bright red lipstick, black pumps, and no jewelry. Her hair was tied back in a long ponytail. She was overqualified for a role in this movie.

Before I went into another world looking at her, I asked the bartender for two coffees, but Y stopped me. "A daiquiri, please."

She sat on a black vinyl bar stool and slowly crossed her legs as I canceled the coffee idea, ordering the drink for her and a vodka for me. An innocent face, but the red fingernails were a dead giveaway. She knew her way around the schoolyard.

The walls of the bar were plastered with sixties posters, and the paint was flaking. Loud house music, the stink of ashes and cigarettes, floors sticky with stale beer made me wonder what the hell we were doing there.

Before I could utter a word, she turned to me and said, "Dr. Ocean, you're a complete stranger to me. I wouldn't know you unless I met you in a morgue, and yet here we are, having drinks. Maybe you're a vampire. Or a freak who picks up girls in offbeat places." She hesitated, mixing the daiquiri with one long finger. "I shouldn't be talking to you, but here I am. Something's wrong with me."

"Works both ways."

We laughed and then she said in a somber tone, "That dead guy, Bill Rogers, worked for someone in my family."

She gazed at her drink.

"What kind of work did he do to wind up like that?"

"It wasn't job related. His brokerage firm did some financing for my family."

"Who in your family?"

"That's a lot to talk about to a stranger. I'm not ready to get into it yet."

I inched away. "I realize I'm prying into your personal life. An occupational hazard, I'm afraid." I didn't mean a word of it, and I didn't like lying even though it's the lifeblood of the profession.

"I don't mind, really," she said, delicately as a lady applying a spray of Shalimar. "Doctors never mean any of it personally, I hear. I only met Bill four or five times."

She had clammed up, but her looks were a great excuse for me to enjoy this hard work. I asked if she wanted another drink. When I suggested something stronger, she said she loved tequila. Telling her I had to go to the bathroom, I walked down to the end of the bar and pretended to buy a pack of cigarettes from the bartender. Y had her back to me. The place was getting crowded, so she couldn't see me if she wanted to. The bartender and I had a short business conversation.

"Tequila. You have any Patron Tequila?" I asked.

"Only one bottle, ten bucks a shot so you gotta be rich." He rinsed out a glass and placed it in a rack.

"Here's a hundred, you're a good man, serve me water, my girlfriend gets the Patron."

"Love it, I don't blame you. She's outrageous." He went to get the bottle.

When I returned her daquiri was empty. I drained my drink just as the bartender brought us two fresh glasses, some salt and limes. Inside of twenty minutes we downed three shots apiece.

"What about Rogers's family?" I couldn't help returning to the subject, and being measurably loosened up by spirits, she complied.

"Old New England. They made farm equipment or oak furniture or hammers and nails, or, you know, they just made some things that should last forever. But they lost everything around the time of the Depression. Bill had a small trust fund that ran out just a few years ago. Then he started his own firm and was beginning to do all right."

"So, you knew him fairly well?"

"Well, like I said, I did and I didn't. He was always very angry about his ex-wife. It went on nonstop but he kept away from the specifics. All I heard was bitching, whining packed in between him muttering the name Pandora. My father called it 'Yankee talk.' Whatever she did to him was apparently brutal."

I was having trouble concentrating on her words now; was Y distracting me, or was I feeling hazy? I couldn't tell. Somehow, my eyes kept drifting up her long, beautiful legs and I couldn't control it. Losing sight of my mission, I thought about one thing—I wanted her. But after Pandora's name came up I knew I was sounding too much like a lawyer. And legalese just doesn't get you laid.

"Sounds like Rogers was a problem and Pandora found a solution."

"I hear she's very sweet but there's a dark side." Y didn't grin. "That leads me to the next question. Why were you at the hospital?"

No answer. Instead she gave me another picture of my supposed assailant. He was a pathetic dilettante who drank his way through life's best years. He could never make a big deal happen. So Rogers, the WASP with no money, winds up with a menial job in a bank, running the trust department in Chinatown, of all places. It wasn't long before he stopped working altogether, siphoning a livelihood off from one of Y's family members, whom she described as "kindhearted."

"Who's the benevolent family member?"

"My father," she continued, sounding progressively sexier, "is the most, well, I should say the *richest* man in Chinatown. I don't use his name because every Chinese person in town would want to borrow money from me. Have you ever heard of China Manpower?"

The tequila was working overtime—Y was talking up a storm. No one shuts up after one drink of Patron.

"Yes, of course. It's traded on the New York Stock Exchange."

"My father started it and is the largest shareholder."

A chill went through my nuts. The stakes zoomed up in the case and my life was suddenly worth less today than yesterday. Just about everyone knew who her father was. But I knew more than most about Emanuel Ling.

"He might be rich but he's made a lot of shareholders' lives very comfortable," she said proudly. "One night Rogers showed up at my father's house. That's how I met him."

"So it was love at first sight?"

"No, nothing ever happened between us. It doesn't work that way in my family. I'm an only child and my father was born in

China at a time when the warlords were fighting each other for control of China."

"When was that?"

"Oh, I'd say around 1910—when you were a freshman in college."

"No, high school." I clarified things, "I'm well preserved."

She smiled but quickly became serious. "My father's parents were killed violently—decapitated—right in their own village. Happened in front of my father who was barely a year old."

That unexpectedly made me feel for her and my arm went around her shoulder.

She picked up my glass from the bar and casually ran her finger around the rim. Just when I thought things might not get personal.

"What were you doing at the hospital?" Hadn't I asked that question before? But it bubbled up in my mind and the lights were swimming around us, making her even more desirable.

"Dr. Ocean, you sound more like a private detective than a shrink. The police called me. I think I convinced them that Bill was a good man and didn't have *that* coming to him."

"Good man, bad habits." I wanted to stay on this subject but my mind was wandering. "So you're very close to your father?"

"I'll tell you about it some time," she added.

"When?"

"As soon as we get out of here."

"Sounds good to me." I offered her my hand. One for the road— she threw a fourth shot downstream. Those shapely legs unhooked and slid to the floor. She raised herself from the bar stool, slipped an arm around my waist, and moved close to me. I bent down and looked into her eyes, which were welling up with honest tears.

Her voice faltered. "Seeing Bill like that, *anyone* like that, is a shock to my system. I don't know about you, but I'm only human, I feel for anyone who is a victim. He was a kind man who just couldn't figure things out."

Clearly she was not a chip off the old Ling block. Hearing about Emanuel Ling in New York is a given. Early in my career I represented a tycoon from Chinatown who told me that almost every business south of Canal Street and north of Wall Street was connected to a Ling company name. But behind this intricate business network there was no end to hair-raising personal stories that went around about the mysterious Mr. Ling, all of them probably true, including his preoccupation with mortal combat back in China. Just for savage amusement, Ling would have beautiful young women shanghaied directly off Shanghai's streets or yanked from its infamous whorehouses. No ransom. It was a variation on what some notable Chinese did—beat, tortured, and finally pulled the intestines from the bodies of young women. While the women lay dying they could still see naked men tying those organs around their bodies.

Y's father despised women. It started in Shanghai, where prostitutes were at the top of the list. They would have to fight without weapons. A winner might be released, but only after her tongue was brutally cut out. Rumor had it that Ling's thirst for female blood sports hadn't abated in New York. More than one source said the price of Ling's amusement ran high and only white female combatants could satisfy him. He'd become westernized.

Her tears ran down my cheeks as she pressed her face to mine and we kissed. Her breathing increased in intensity and I felt her tongue in my mouth. Her warm hand went inside my shirt, massaging my back close to where I'd been hit. Now I was really feeling stoned and couldn't understand why. Maybe she was the one who'd shot me. I pulled my head back slightly and stared at her, trying to assess Y as a new lover or as my attacker. She appeared childlike, pure, naïve. Well, *almost*.

"Let's go someplace," I suggested. "My house uptown?"

"All right," she agreed simply.

I walked away from the bar, thinking that I could fall in love with her. This was happening too easily. She stood next to me, her arm still encircling my back. All systems were go.

We walked down the street and must have looked like one of those raw new love affairs, blitzed, kissing, and hugging openly in the street as the August sun crumbled into the darkness. "Romance is more acceptable when it's dark out," the social code fluttered by while my head spun like a Javanese ceiling fan. Three glasses of flat water couldn't produce this result.

Just as I was about to hail a taxi she said, "Why don't you come home with me? I'd be more comfortable there. It's not far."

A few minutes later, we were at her front door standing on the hallway's beige carpet. It could have been the thirty-ninth floor in a glassy, modern high-rise but it was just the seventh level of an old factory that had been renovated. She had the entire floor and a guidebook view of Manhattan through large windows on all four sides.

She excused herself while I lit a slightly dented cigarette and wandered into the living room, which was full of period Chinese furniture, most of it Ming Dynasty. There was an impressive display of green jade and porcelain in showcases lining the walls. Chinese rugs were unfurled on the slick, parquet floors—blue and gray, with five-clawed dragons wrestling in lush lagoons. An enormous pair of carved limestone lions—Foo dogs—sat immobile on either side of the fireplace. Whatever I knew about antiques wasn't nearly enough to judge this collection.

On the coffee table in front of the couch was an old photograph in a sterling frame of a rugged-looking Chinese man. It had a faded nineteen-forties appearance. The photo was taken outside, with palm trees in the background. I assumed it was Y's father. I couldn't help staring at his commanding, deep-lined face. It was bony and squarish. He had a crew cut, salt-and-pepper hair, and although he was long on looks, there was an unmistakable hollowness in his eyes. This cold-blooded freak wouldn't think twice about wasting me.

Under the table there was a shelf full of thick, beautifully bound, gold-leafed red-leather photo albums. I pulled out the one on top, and it wasn't light. Turning the first page, I was immediately impressed. The photographs were of Shanghai in the 1920s, each captioned with exquisite handwriting. The park along the river called the Bund, Soochow Creek, and all the landmark spots of the city were beautifully captured and placed with meticulous precision in the album. On the following pages were sepia-toned portraits.

Y came up behind me and put her hands on my neck. "Snooping?" she said, but she didn't mind.

"Just killing time."

I turned around. Even though she was blurry, I could make her out. She was wearing a short, pale blue dressing gown. Her black hair fell loosely to the middle of her back. I flashed on Pandora and wondered what she was doing, wearing, and with whom she was talking. Then I realized that I'd only laid eyes on Pandora once—long ago—and didn't have the right to imagine anything.

Pointing to the album, I said, "That's your father. Who's the puffy cheeked guy next to him?"

"That's his adopted father, Charlie Soong."

"Any relationship to the Soong sisters?" It seemed to please her that I was up to speed.

"He's their father. You know the Soong sisters? So you know they were a legend in China, right at the top of the government." Pulling the album closer she said, "You're about to meet the girls." She turned the page over my shoulder. "Those are the Soong sisters. Weren't they beautiful? Each one has a first name that ends in Ling. Ling means life." Pointing to the photo, she showed me, "There's Ching-ling, glorious life, married to Sun Yat-sen. Next to her, married to Chiang Kai-shek, is May-ling, beautiful life. And last is Ai-ling, friendly life, married into the Kung clan, China's richest banking family. My father was named after the girls."

If Ling meant life in Chinese then bullshit must mean truth.

"You don't even know my first name," I said, trying not to sound hopelessly clichéd.

"I don't have to know your first name until *after* we have an affair." She laughed. "But you know mine so you have an advantage. You can't complain that it's too difficult to spell, can you, Dr. Ocean? What a peculiar name. . . . Are you a good swimmer?"

"I have an excellent stroke." Then I kissed her, pulling her down beside me on the couch. For all I knew, this felt like Pandora. I wanted to trust Y but it was against my nature. Those were the rules of the game.

"Don't you want to see the rest?" She asked.

"As soon as possible."

"No, I mean the album. Here's a picture of my father with Chiang Kai-shek and Charlie's son, T.V. Soong. You know Sun Yat-sen was the father of Chinese communism and Charlie Soong raised the money for the revolution—"

The history discourse wasn't as interesting as she was or how high I felt. I kissed her again, long and hard, but she pulled away.

"I want to show you one more picture. You'll think it's very funny." Flipping the page, she showed me a shot of two college guys standing on a soccer field.

"That's my father at his graduation from Harvard in 1935. That's T.V. Soong next to him."

"Your father went to Harvard?"

"Rich Chinese sent their children to the West to be educated. The Soongs sent Dad to Harvard, Harvard Business School as well."

She wore a sweet perfume. That gave me a melancholy feeling that Y was a loner, which was the reason she was so proud and eager to show me her family history. It was disturbing to be romancing Y with Ling's photo staring me down. It didn't help when I felt Y's hands on my thighs.

Seconds later, I was on my back in her bed.

"I hope you're not uncomfortable."

"Head's been spinning ever since we went to that bar."

"Must be the tequila."

"Tequila, I didn't have a drop." I blew it.

"Then what were you drinking?" Her eyes blinked.

"Water."

"You told me you were a lawyer, not a doctor, don't you recall that?" Was she messing with my mind? I didn't remember admitting that.

"I didn't say I was a lawyer."

"You might have, you're a bit wasted on Quaaludes. Dropped one in your glass when you went to the bathroom. Thought it might make you more accessible."

"Very considerate move on our first date. Can't wait for you to meet my family."

"Are you feeling out of control? Scared, Johnny?" She knew my name, maybe more. "Are you mad at me?"

How pissed off could I be? I deserved it. "No, I'm a big boy, just make sure the door is locked. I wouldn't want Dad to walk in on us."

Her hands rubbed my back and legs. She moved her head along my stomach like a boa. At the same time, I felt her nipples hardening, and I started to kiss her neck. Gradually I went down on her, easing her thighs apart. I could hear her moaning, nearly crying as I caressed her with my tongue, bringing her to the tip of a climax. I moved up her, and she ran both hands up and down my shaft and toyed with its head until it was going to burst on her stomach and ripe breasts.

I went inside slowly and she received me gently. Exquisite sounds of pleasure echoed throughout the loft as she came, and this time I went along for the ride.

We were playing with sex, resisting each other. Both of us were expert at that game. I forgot completely about the case.

Afterward, hours must have passed while she slept. I suppressed the urge to rifle through her things. Paneled screens, lacquer objects, and glazed vases defined the room. It was cold, austere. There was a large black chest with ivory inlay that I figured contained china and silverware.

I lay next to her against a stack of pillows, smoking a cigarette and watching her. She was turned on her side toward me, breathing gently, seemingly oblivious to the fierce world on the other side of her front door.

Once again I began to think about the job I was hired to do. No vacation even though I was entitled to a few hours off. Hell, I was working hard except for a moment or two. Any other lawyer would have billed Pandora for the time.

I considered checking out Y's apartment for clues, more information about Ling's relationship to Rogers. An office would be a good starting point. Only there wasn't one. Based on what I'd seen so far, there'd be plenty of great panties and garters to thumb through, but no documents.

I liked Y and even felt sorry for her. It seemed to me she didn't have any idea of who her father was. She stirred, and the wool blanket slipped off her thigh, revealing her small, well-manicured vagina. I tried to touch her. Just as my hand reached for her, she rolled away. I didn't want her to rest; she was too enticing. I ran the flat of my hand along her calves, then up between her thighs.

She moaned and reached for me slowly, whispering, "Johnny, oh Johnny, I'm so afraid. Hold me, oh please, hold me, I'm having nightmares, I . . ."

"What's the matter? Please, tell me. I can help." I pressed her for an answer.

"My family could care less. They just use me like everyone else they can overpower, because I'm good-natured." She closed her eyes, hugging me. She seemed too fragile, which made me suspicious.

All the blankets were around her and I started to feel the cold from the air conditioner. My back and arm hurt like hell right where the bullet had entered. It hadn't bothered me for days.

She came around, drowsy, frighteningly affectionate. "You can trust me. I have to look like I'm working for them but I'm not. You're representing"—she hesitated, shaking her head before continuing—"Pandora. But Bill had nothing to do with any of this."

Although I nodded, I wasn't agreeing. Through the large windows, I glimpsed upper Manhattan—a chaos of lights sprinkled across the honeycomb; one of them was Pandora's apartment. Knowing how powerful Ling was, and that Y was probably lying, I listened to her words like a man who walks outside into a light drizzle and suddenly finds himself in the center of a blinding hailstorm.

She pulled the corner of the sheet up and wiped her eyes.

I had to get back to my office to speak with Pandora, K, and Eyeballs, Inc.

I slipped out of the king-size bed, my feet landing next to a pair of bronze dragon's talons. Pushing my hands against my ribs, I exhaled deeply and headed to the bathroom. Before I turned the faucets on to wash my face, I opened the medicine cabinet and downed some aspirin.

Watching my very sexy new friend lie there, I stood in the doorway. A lamp cast golden light over her body, and I wondered how many times other men must have walked out of the bathroom and looked at her, possibly thinking the same thing. I wasn't ready to leave the loft yet.

In that moment, I had more of a sense of Rogers, knowing the thin line between life and death. Maybe at the end of the case, I'd wind up as fucked as he. They'd find me blown away by a 12 gauge mounted over the mantel at the Explorers Club.

In the morning I dressed, kissed Y on the forehead, and went out the door. She was beat. I'd call her later. Y was going to be valuable to me, I told myself, no matter how dangerous she was.

CHAPTER EIGHT

When I got home the first thing I did was leave a message for K and Eyeballs to fully investigate Ling and Y. I would have spoken to K, but he'd left a note telling me how long he'd walked the dog and what the dog did and didn't do with a lot of "Sir" this and "Sir, you should have seen" that. And there was a long list starting with "Honorable Sir" (always Honorable when money is involved): "Dog needs a new large leather leash, a dog spray to keep Barkis off the furniture, a new squeaking yellow football, and many large bones."

I decided to go out and buy the leash, but on the way I was going to stop by the Black Curtain where I figured André would be doing his morning bookkeeping and receiving food and liquor deliveries. When I arrived, he was out front, uncharacteristically sweeping the sidewalks, something Frenchmen just don't do in America. I walked up to him and started the usual small talk, segueing into anything I might have missed at the Curtain.

He looked at me quizzically. "You did not enjoy the last show?" he asked. I didn't understand and looked at *him* quizzically.

"The star was *your friend* Pandora. She is a great little actress, no?" I was stunned.

"You mean her, the one in your shows, in chains?"

He shot me a weird smile.

"Mon ami, quelquefois elle vient au Rideau Noir, pas pour manger." (Sometimes she comes to the Black Curtain, not necessarily to eat.)

"André, was that really Pandora?"

But before I got an answer, a salesman asked André about a special on 1982 Château Lafite and off they went, leaving me hanging.

I ditched the leash idea and returned home, still shocked that I hadn't recognized the face of the client who was always on my mind. I had only a couple of days before I was to take Babette's deposition. Time to focus.

At my office Mercedes handed me a memo.

"Just got a call from the court and they faxed this over."

It was a court order that Bellicoso obtained that scheduled all depositions to take place in the courthouse, so as to keep law and order between both sides. My job was to crucify Babette, but now it would all be played out at the courthouse, a stage where Bellicoso had the advantage.

During the time left I worked on the facts and researched the law—the only two elements in every case.

Some good information surfaced about Webb Hartford. Eyeballs had grilled a physician colleague of Webb's who knew him as the sensible, stable doctor who tried to be a friend to everyone. Stanford, Phi Beta Kappa. Every scholastic award had come his way and he made it a point to flaunt his superior intelligence at every opportunity. That hadn't exactly been Pandora's view, which made me wonder whether she had lied to me again, except there was one story about Webb that we couldn't corroborate. When he was in medical school he'd been accused of selling Merck, or synthetic cocaine. A large vial of the stuff was found in his room, but he talked his way out of the situation, saying he was using it to treat a horse with a lame foot, a condition called laminitis. He wasn't a vet.

We didn't restrict out investigation to Webb. Mr. K also had his Sikh friends looking into Ling's financial empire and his security.

I kept on with Ling's daughter, seeing Y as much as I could, but it was infrequent because of my preparation schedule. Each occasion was a boost for the case, because she filled me with sex and inspiration. Sunday night before the deposition I saw her. She'd read about a West Side Italian restaurant in midtown. It had an outdoor garden—she'd wanted a romantic night. We arrived about 8:30 and the place wasn't crowded at all. The garden was filled with flowers and marble statues. It was ours.

After we ordered some Chianti, I realized I didn't want to talk much. Not only was I distracted by tomorrow, but I'd become closemouthed about the case.

"Johnny," she leaned forward. "What's wrong? You're so quiet tonight." The waiter brought some bread and the wine I ordered. I paused until he left.

"Got a lot on my mind," I replied.

She reached over for my hand and whispered, "We don't have to talk when you're under pressure."

"How do you know that?"

"Tomorrow you have to be in court. It's on your face."

Hiding my concern about how things would go with Babette was impossible.

"You never really got an answer." She smiled coyly and drank some Chianti.

"An answer to what?" I didn't know what she was talking about.

"About what father thinks about us."

"Or if he knows."

I waited for her answer.

"Probably he knows and hasn't made up his mind how he feels about it. That could be good for us."

More than ever it hit home that the case, Ling, and Rogers were joined. Was I really interested in her or was it my job that brought us together? Thanks for the introduction, I told my license to practice law, because with or without the case, she was one of the best-looking and sexiest women I'd ever met. But I could tell she was frightened. I could sense she was all too aware of things she shouldn't have known, and for her there was no way out; she was sleeping with one tear-filled eye open.

"Johnny, I've made a commitment to you because once I've made love with a man, he's my man, and we should spend every night together," she said and looked at me waiting for an answer.

"Y, I can't do that while I'm up to my ears in this case."

After we finished dinner those words repeated themselves a thousand times that night. While she wanted me with her all the time, I should have been there to protect her. But the case was demanding and I had Babette's deposition in my face.

CHAPTER NINE

Deposition day arrived. There was a message at the answering service from Pandora: "Good luck. Sorry I can't be there. Call me after."

What she was really saying was, I hope I'm not wasting my money and I hope you put Babette through so much hell that she'll drop the case. All heart.

After a gulp of black coffee, I picked up my files and headed for the door. K wanted to go to court with me, but I told him it wasn't necessary. The court wouldn't allow him to sit in on the deposition, anyway.

I ran out the door and grabbed a yellow taxi down to the courthouse. It was hot outside but boiling inside the cab. As I put my knees up against the front seat below the filthy acrylic window that should have been closed, a garlic-drenched souvlaki special downdraft smacked me in the face. The driver was having breakfast and giving the radio dispatcher his lunch order. The traffic was brutal, and I wondered what the rest of the world was doing on its way to work.

"Get me two subs with onions, olives, Genoa salami, oil, blue cheese, provolone, tomatoes, the works, partner," he barked into the gray hand mike, dangerously swerving from lane to lane. "I'll be comin' in around eleven-thirty to gas up."

"You eat that shit by the bucket, you're gonna die in the driver's seat," the dispatcher warned as we lurched to the court-house curb.

As I paid the fare and left the cab in front of the court at 31 Chambers Street I was suddenly overcome by a sick feeling that the deposition wouldn't go well. Maybe it was the conversation about the food that did it, or was I going to choke? Passing through the shadows of the Surrogate's Court's curved bronze mullioned windows and doors, I entered the hallowed ground where estates are settled. The Siena marble foyer exhaled a whiff of the construction corruption scandal that had cost the taxpayers millions, just like the infamous Boss Tweed courthouse across the street. The goddess theme is enshrined in a ceiling mosaic in the foyer of the Surrogate's Court.

Miles to the north, on the roof of Grand Central Terminal, Mercury is clustered between Hercules and Athena. The god of lying, commerce, and false oaths, he points straight at the Surrogate's Court. Grand Central splits Park Avenue and the city and was erected just as the Surrogate's Court was finished in 1911. It's called a terminal, not a station, because it is the end of the line. Speaking of lines, one drawn straight from Mercury's hand south-ward bisects the mural of Themis.

I made my way to the Foley courtroom, named after Surrogate James A. Foley (1888–1946). Nearby Foley Square is named after Thomas F. Foley (1852–1925), a saloon keeper and sheriff. Both Foleys were Tammany Hall loyalists.

More than a century ago, the Foley Square area was submerged under the Collect, a metamorphosed island of garbage and swamp that hastened the departure of the area's respectable citizens. The Collect quickly devolved into a smelly warren of bars, brothels, and shanties, which became known as the Five Points because five streets intersected there. It was said that a murder was committed there every day.

The residents included the world's second highest concentration of Irish after Dublin, hundreds of immigrants, and freed slaves living in a defunct brewery that today is the State Supreme Court. Life in such relentless squalor spawned Irish street gangs—the Forty Thieves, Plug Uglies, the Dead Rabbits, the Kerryonians, the Chichesters, the Shirt Tails, and the Roach Guards—forerunners of the Italian and Jewish gangs that eventually came to dominate crime in the city. Pigs, goats, and cows wandered around, as they do in India today, in the epidemic-infested streets. Even Charles Dickens was shocked by the dilapidation and general destitution that he witnessed on his 1842 trip to New York, recording his observations in his book *American Notes*.

I trudged up the stairs to the fifth floor, through the corridors of marble that change color on each floor, and into the world of *Longwood v. Markham*. I entered room 503, the south courtroom, Judge Macefield presiding, and found myself alone but for the gold-framed oil portrait of Surrogate Foley hanging behind me. He was thought of as the foremost scholar on estate law in the thirties.

I was about a half hour early, which gave me time to set up my files and notes. The Foley courtroom, with its mahogany paneling and two red marble fireplaces on either side of the bench, overlooks City Hall Park. Some people call it the DeFalco courtroom. Surrogate DeFalco was indicted for fixing cases, believe it or not, in other courts. IN GOD WE TRUST was emblazoned in brass letters on the wall behind the bench. God's okay, but what about the judge?

The courtroom was never used for depositions, but an exception had been made for Bellicoso's client. I had documents and correspondence that I'd show to Babette to drive her right out of her head. The strategy was to distract her and foul her already warped recollections, ultimately making her sick, tired, and scared of the case.

Because of a legal technicality, Babette's money was now in her sister-in-law's hands. But it was possible that Pandora had already spent it. As usual, the court orders were imprecise in this regard. The written decision by Macefield seemed to bar Pandora from using the funds without actually *freezing* them.

In these circumstances, a lawyer is taking a chance if he advises a client to use the funds. Macefield was giving me enough rope to hang myself if anything happened to the $170 million. This is a game judges play to keep lawyers they don't like in limbo. There was no legal basis to freeze the assets of anyone living in New York, unless the person is planning to leave the state with the bucks. But Macefield made up the law as he went along, that is, along with Bellicoso.

A half-hour went by. Ten-thirty and a bit. Macefield's rules did not apply to Bellicoso. He and his client would be strategically late. I buried my head in documents until the court reporter arrived.

A minute or two later, I heard a peculiar sound behind me, a weird falsetto, like the voice of a granny talking to herself about strange noises in the attic of her Victorian mansion. The voice was talking to itself, laughing.

I wheeled around and saw Babette Longwood. She looked about forty-five or fifty, although I knew her to be older. She was still winning the stay-young battle—with the help of cosmetics and an occasional facial tuck. She had all the Park Avenue artillery: Kenneth-coiffed blond hair, a pink cashmere dress, a diamond-and-sapphire ring with matching bracelet, and an Hermès scarf casually knotted around her neck. A tan blazer rested on her narrow shoulders. She walked slowly. Was it from the brain damage? Was Pandora telling me another story or was it true?

Not too long ago, Babette had caused a lot of men's heads to turn, from investment bankers to Hell's Angels. She was competition for Pandora then. Those days were behind her, but she had plenty of style left. It was still Babette Longwood, or what remained of her, formerly of Beverly Hills, California, the wife of the late Edgar Longwood.

She walked unhurriedly past me, accompanied by a very thin, elegantly dressed, gray-haired man a little under six feet. He wore a bespoke lightweight gray wool suit, expensive white shirt, silk navy-and-white striped tie, shined wingtips, and a square gold wristwatch. His cufflinks were engraved with a family crest. I thought he smiled at me—he had that dubious charm—but I may have been mistaken. His delicate, smooth white skin was undisturbed by age. The face said he had gone to the right schools, parties, and churches.

Bellicoso was not around, which surprised me, since he usually stuck close by a client like Babette.

Babette's dapper friend walked quietly across the room and introduced himself to me from the other side of the long, thick, mahogany counsel table. He was Webb Hartford.

"Mr. Bellicoso is on his way. He'll be here shortly."

That was disarming. He didn't have Pandora's personality, but he was impressive. He was a very smooth operator, managing Babette in a 170-million-dollar conflict.

I overheard Babette ask him, "You know I don't like to wait. Do something, call him on his cellular phone."

"Darling, he will be here shortly, be patient." He put his hand on her arm and she seemed to accept his explanation for the moment.

It was nearly 11:15 and nothing had happened.

Bellicoso appeared like the orange juice that arrives after breakfast is finished and the check is paid. His nose was fleshy and thick like the rest of his gray-haired head. The body was stocky, over two hundred pounds, and the possibility loomed that he was very fat underneath the dark pinstripe suit. Banging his square black vinyl Samsonite briefcase down on the shiny surface of the counsel table, he immediately arranged boxes of paper clips, a pair of scissors, a stapler, pens, legal pads, and some other office supplies on the table. Eyeballs had a blurb about Bellicoso, told by one of his ex-secretaries. He had an office-supply fetish, demanding that supplies had to be lined up like tin soldiers. All adhesive materials, like custom-printed mailing labels with his firm name on them, had to be stored on the correct side of the closet on the third shelf in rows. There were labels for everything in the office, filing cabinet number 1, desk lamp number 3, telephone station number 4, copy machine number 1. He had the best collection of preinked rubber stamps: FIRST CLASS, VOID, DRAFT, CALL ON RECEIPT, FAX, DON'T FAX, RECEIVED, FILE, OK TO PAY. Adversaries complained that they never received letters from him, just stamped messages on letterhead.

After breaking open pads of different colored Post-its, Bellicoso went into a huddle with Babette and Webb. With their faces turned into the bright sunlight, the three began to whisper to one another. Babette was incapable of talking softly. I managed to hear a few things, mostly about money that she'd transferred but had always expected to be repaid. Bellicoso grunted a few facts to Webb and revved Babette for the moment she would step into the ring. I could see that she had been a very difficult witness to prepare and that Bellicoso had his work cut out for him—as I had with Pandora. Preparing witnesses for trial or depositions is hard enough as it is, because a clever lawyer on the other side will create a question no one could anticipate.

With his pink fingers spread out on the counsel table as if he were going to do a push-up, Bellicoso leaned toward me and did a fine impression of Jimmy Hoffa: "Let's get started, kid. Ms. Longwood's time is valuable."

"You're late," I responded without looking up from my papers, assembled in a nice abstract pattern before me. "Sit down and we can begin."

"We'll begin when I sit down and I'll sit when I choose."

Babette sat beside Bellicoso. Next to her, Webb, armed with a heavy sterling silver pen and a yellow legal pad, looked like a Ken to her over-the-hill Barbie.

The reporter asked Babette for her name and address.

"Baaa—bette" was her answer, as if she were identifying two separate people. Obviously, this proceeding was going to be as painful for me as it was for her.

Suddenly, before I had a chance to pose a question, Baaa bette stood up and, with a wide sweep of her left arm, wiped the counsel table of all the paraphernalia that I had so meticulously arranged. Then, clear-eyed and in her muddled falsetto voice, she hollered, "You son of a bitch!"

I remained composed although inside I recoiled. "Are you addressing me, madam? You don't even know me."

"Don't say another word to her!" Bellicoso said, as if it were my fault.

Webb immediately wrapped his arm around his patient and audibly whispered, "This will be over soon, let Vito take care of him." She sat.

It took a couple of minutes to pick up all the papers. No one helped.

"Let the record reflect that Ms. Longwood has identified me as the descendant of a female dog and cleared the counsel table of all legal materials, including the remaining questions that were to be asked of her during the deposition."

Their eyes bore down on me. I was an insect they wanted to smash against the wall.

"Now, Ms. Longwood," I started, "I strongly urge you to maintain a level of decorum that befits your station in life, or we will have to have the judge supervise this deposition." I didn't believe for a second this judge would ever do it, but I wanted the statement on the record documenting that she had misbehaved. "Would you kindly give the reporter the balance of the information pertaining to your address?"

This time she broke out into a wide, childish grin and, nodding repeatedly, let loose a blur of sounds to the effect that she was ready to go forward.

I felt like I was diving into an empty swimming pool.

"Ms. Longwood, did you ever transfer or loan money to your late brother, Marcel Markham?"

"Objection!" exclaimed Bellicoso.

"What is the basis of your objection?" I asked.

"The question is unclear," he shot back, intending to disrupt me with a baseless protest.

"No. It *is* clear. You're not objecting, you're just being objectionable."

"Keep your questions in reference to the subject matter of this lawsuit. And let's get the time frame of the transaction," Bellicoso instructed me.

"Okay," I agreed for the moment. "From 1975 through the time of your brother Marcel's death in 1995, did you loan him any sums of money?"

There may have been other telling transactions between sis and bro; now was the time to find out.

"Yes."

"How much?"

"One hundred seventy million dollars."

"When?"

"June 1985."

"Do you have an agreement to prove the transaction occurred?"

"Interruption and objection," Bellicoso burped.

"Basis for it? And by the way, you can just call it an objection."

Bellicoso said angrily, "Look, I can call it 'interruption' if I choose. People in out industry call it that."

"When I deal with hoods, it's an *industry,* but when I deal with real lawyers, it's a *profession.*"

"I'm going to come across that table, and you're never going to talk that way to anyone again!"

"Your ass couldn't make it through a turnstile. Relax, Counselor, I like threats."

Bellicoso's large hands were now clenched fists, seemingly pushing through the tabletop. The knuckles were indeed a bright bony white. 'White Knuckle.' At least some things live up to their reputation, I thought and smirked to myself about shaking up Bellicoso. Whether lawyers who claim they are *friends of the court* admit it or not, the objective is to rattle the other side from start to finish. It is easier to do it out of the presence of the judge.

"Wait and see who you're fooling with," Bellicoso threatened.

"A highly spiritual individual. But that's just my opinion."

I thought about my next question while I gauged whether Babette felt intimidated. Webb had a knifelike grin plastered on his face. Even though I smiled back at him, his expression never changed in what is usually a wrestling match of facemaking. At that moment, I imagined that Babette would have preferred it if I were representing her. Maybe Bellicoso should have been Pandora's attorney.

Bellicoso regained his composure. He stood and tightened his large Windsor knot. Smacking his lips, he ran his palm alongside his chin as if he needed a shave and then slid both hands into his suit coat pockets. He could have been a third-base coach in Little League.

"I think we'll go and see the judge, Ocean. There's only one way to get through this deposition with you. You need court supervision."

He turned on his heel and headed for the double mahogany doors. Under those circumstances, I was forced to go with him, leaving behind the court reporter, a dumbfounded and forlorn Babette, and Webb, who appeared neat as a *GQ* mannequin.

A few minutes later, I was seated next to one of the gray metal secretarial desks in the anteroom of Humphrey "Ringside" Macefield, Justice.

His Honor had started out in life as a prizefight referee, later working his way up from presiding over second-rate dope, theft, and forgery trials in the criminal court.

There was a heap of old *New York Law Journals* sloppily stacked on one of the unused secretarial desks alongside a dusty IBM Selectric typewriter. I had read all of them, concluding that there is no other daily in America with the distinction of generating so much potentially useful information that so few people read, understood, or cared about. It was no comic book.

A small male clerk, getting very long in the tooth with a chaotic beard and a beaklike nose, approached me. I thought he was going to peck out the message that Macefield was ready to see us, but instead he officiously ordered me not to read the papers—a "breach of courthouse protocol." He was one of the judge's political sinecure clerks. The White Knuckle was on the other side of the room, playing up to a minor bureaucrat. You never know when a filing cabinet or two has to be surreptitiously opened for an important lawyer. I was certain that Bellicoso wanted some forbidden information and was pressing the weakest button to get it.

As soon as the clerk left, I picked up the *New York Times,* which someone had left around the waiting area. When I finished reading, the Deco wall clock read half past twelve. I scanned the room for Bellicoso and instead saw a solitary clerk, a huge stack of legal papers and an old tan-and-white speckled pigeon pacing proudly on the birdshit-splattered windowsill. I went over to one of the secretaries. She was good-looking, in her forties, with silky highlighted hair, long legs, and a shapely can. Pointedly carnal for a New York courthouse employee.

"Yes, Mr. Ocean. How can I help you?"

"Oh, you know me?" I half-asked. "And what's your name?"

"I've read about you, your notorious cases. The woman with three husbands, that one who married the multimillionaire from

Long Island. Murdered him supposedly . . . Then he showed up at the trial to testify that she'd only attempted to kill him. My name's Rita, Rita Strife."

"Yes, the 'Multi' case. We called her Multiples around the office."

I laughed. She laughed, as if we knew each other. "Where the hell did Bellicoso go? We came in here to see Macefield. What a hard life, Ms. Strife. Gotta listen to guys like me all day."

"No problem finding Mr. Bellicoso."

"What do you mean?"

She reached over and pulled a cigarette from her bag, along with a book of matches.

"The judge and Bellicoso saw each other early this morning. They must have lunch or coffee at least once a week, members of the same party. Find Macefield, you'll find Bellicoso," she answered calmly.

Typical of that courthouse—the judge and the adversary plotting behind closed doors. But in New York State, even your judge friends will tell you to keep your mouth shut about judges' behavior and their rulings. They'll gang up on you, even the State and Federal ones together, in hurtful ways one can't begin to imagine.

She ran highly buffed, tomato-red nails through her hair and smiled at me as if she hadn't just told me things a judge's secretary is supposed to keep secret.

"Do me a favor, will you?" I tried a hand at being needy and ingenuous.

"Sure."

"Can you buzz the judge? I don't want to disturb him. If he's there, ask him if I can see him with Bellicoso. We need his assistance with the deposition in the Longwood-Markham case. He knows about it, I'm certain."

She called the old boy. He got on the intercom first and explained, obviously not aware that I was outside his wood-paneled doors, that he was very busy with Mr. Bellicoso. Then she informed His Honor that Mr. Ocean was waiting and it involved Mr. Bellicoso. The judge and Bellicoso were probably just putting the *x* on the fix.

"What did His Highness say to my request?" I asked when she put down the receiver.

"You know, Mr. Ocean, you're cute. Don't you want to know what's *really* going on behind these closed doors?" She was serious.

"Sure I do. But first get me in to see the judge with Bellicoso. Then you can tell me all about it after we're married."

The next thing I knew, Ms. Strife put her lovely legs together, stood like an obelisk, and marched right to Macefield's chamber doors. With both hands, she slid the eight-foot-high doors into their side pockets and I walked into His Honor's chambers. Behind one of the grandest carved wooden desks seen since the days the Doges ruled Venice, sat Macefield with the White Knuckle at his side.

Pink-skinned, white-haired Macefield was blazing with hostility. It could only go downhill from here. He and Bellicoso appeared to be going over some figures and Bellicoso was on the wrong side of the desk. Vito must have entered through the little-known side door. Judges are not supposed to speak with one lawyer without the other being present. It is a legal taboo called an "ex parte," or one-sided conversation. I didn't know whether to bunt or punt. If I brought it up, he would try to bury me. Did I have an advantage that I could leverage into having Macefield disqualified? Or was I just going to earn his eternal hatred?

"I thought you wanted to see Mr. Ocean, Your Honor," Ms. Strife coyly whispered to Macefield while I hung back.

"No, it's all right. Have Mr. Ocean sit down and Mr. Bellicoso will do the same. He's welcome to the rights and privileges all counsel have in this court."

He spoke with all the sincerity of a flight-arrival announcement at the airport.

It could not have been a grander display, starting with red velvet valanced drapes reaching upward like hungry hands to the gold-leafed ceiling moldings above six-foot-wide windows. The chambers were the size of the plaza at the Plaza Hotel. The floor was covered with a thick vermilion rug. It could have been a Maxfield Parrish mural of a court proceeding.

I sat before Macefield's desk and readied myself for the dropkick across Foley Square.

"Your Honor, the purpose of my waiting for so long outside was to get a ruling on the problem Mr. Bellicoso and I were having with the Longwood deposition. But I see Your Honor has been conferring with Mr. Bellicoso—"

I was interrupted by an unearthly growling. At first, I thought it was Macefield, then realized it was Angel, Macefield's Doberman, who suddenly surfaced from under the desk. Macefield grabbed his spiked collar and smiled at me just as Angel bared his teeth. To this beast I was a Big Mac.

Angel was a courthouse celebrity. Sometimes he sat under the bench at Macefield's feet when Macefield presided. During a famous trial in a packed courtroom, Macefield suddenly blurted "Shit!" leapt from the bench and dashed into his chambers as a large puddle of urine soaked the carpeting around the court reporter. Angel faithfully trotted behind His Honor and quizzically cocked his head at the laughing spectators. Everyone knew the story. Since that time Angel wasn't seen around the courtroom very much.

"Mr. Ocean, I know who you are and I am not the slightest bit amused or intimidated by you and your tired tactics." Macefield folded his hands into a small tent. "Mr. Bellicoso and I have known each other for some time. I have seen him socially on many occasions. We visit each other's weekend homes in the country. Make note that it makes no difference."

This was the same absurd rationale of an adulterous couple

who believe that being seen together in public dispels any notion that they could be having an affair.

Macefield continued, "He has had many matters before me. Furthermore, for your continuing edification, I played squash with the deceased Mr. Markham." Skipping over the political connection, he pushed himself away from his desk and reclined against the back of his chair. "I have had lunch many times with both Babette Longwood and her sister-in-law, Pandora. In short, I am no stranger to the parties or their attorneys, although, I hasten to add, I am meeting you for the first time today. How do you do, Mr. Ocean?"

So not only was Macefield tied to Bellicoso, he was in up to his eyeballs with the client. "I am fine, Your Honor, except for what I see as everyday deposition problems. Mr. Bellicoso says we need judicial supervision because he and I are unable to agree on certain minor issues. A court-appointed referee, in my opinion, is not necessary."

Macefield leaned back in his chair and fingered the bowl of a matte-black pipe that looked like it had never been lit. His watery blue eyes wandered to the face of his political friend, across his law clerks, blinked down to the carpet, then danced over to me.

"Mr. Ocean, if you would like, I will send this matter to the other Surrogate. Because of my knowledge of the case and acquaintance with the parties, you may feel that I should recuse myself. You have such a perfect right."

I was full of anger, but what difference did it make? He knew exactly how to talk the talk without walking the walk. The bastard could just send the case over to Surrogate Mitchell down the hall, make a phone call, and tell his crony to fix it up real good and screw Johnny Ocean to the wall. Then the bias would be entrenched forever. Better to keep Macefield in the case and reveal his prejudice to an appeals court later, if that became necessary.

"No, Judge. Your integrity, honesty, and impartiality are beyond question."

That's the way the game must be played when a judge offers to pull out so quickly, because disqualification is the most harmful thing that can happen to a lawyer if he instigates it.

"Very well. My chief clerk Mr. Cedric will supervise the deposition. I trust that's acceptable to counsel?"

We were all dismissed until that afternoon. As I left chambers I looked back at Cedric who was grinning with false pride starting his new assignment.

The entire process depressed me more than bad weather during a disastrous love affair.

After lunch, I would start up again with Babette. Meanwhile she, Webb, and Bellicoso probably went to eat at one of the countless second-rate restaurants near the state courthouse while I stayed behind to work.

I returned to the empty courtroom and waited until 2:00, when the deposition would continue. It resumed with everyone in his appointed place: Cedric at the head of the table, Babette and Webb flanking Bellicoso on the other side of me. The court reporter reminded Babette that she was still under oath.

The questioning continued.

"Now Ms. Longwood," I began, "is it not a fact that you loaned your late brother the sum of one hundred seventy million dollars sometime in . . ." I used the word loan because it was part of a line of questions I was going to use to trap Babette into admitting it was a gift.

Bellicoso bellowed, "Objection!"

"Sustained," said Cedric. "That question is for the court to decide."

"Why?" I asked. "What's the basis for sustaining the objection?"

"Calls for a legal conclusion, that the money was a loan. Proceed."

"Did you transfer in any manner the sum of a hundred seventy million dollars to your late brother during his lifetime?"

"Yes," Babette said.

"Was it a gift or a loan?"

"Objection, same reasons," my adversary explained.

"Sustained."

I tried again. "It had to be one or the other."

"I'll permit the witness to answer," said the Surrogate's Surrogate, "but I will do that without waiving the claimant's right to move to strike the answer at any time up until trial."

"It was a loan."

I began to understand the only word in Cedric's legal vocabulary was "sustained" when it came to responding to Bellicoso, except to give me a few token "overruleds."

I turned back to Babette. "Who's idea was it to make this loan to your brother?"

"His!" she said, too late for Bellicoso to object.

"And what were the circumstances, Ms. Longwood?"

Bellicoso caught up. "I object to the form of the question."

"I object to the form of you!" I couldn't help it, but lawyers say things like this all the time.

"Mr. Ocean, I warn you!" Cedric whined.

"And was there a loan agreement drafted?" I often start each question off with "and." It makes the witness think that it is a throwaway question or one of the last questions. It's when they relax that I get the answer I want.

"I don't understand," Babette stammered. Her hand crept toward the White Knuckle's knuckles. Then she took a deep breath and inclined her head as if she'd received bad news. This witness didn't know what documents she was litigating over.

Bellicoso didn't say anything and Cedric directed her to answer.

Babette, after a long, intriguing pause, offered, "I seem to recall signed papers . . . documents . . . signing something that I think Marcel signed as well." She looked around the courtroom, seemingly lost.

"Signed what?" I didn't rush the questions. "Exactly what was the piece of paper?" Long pause. "Can you identify it?"

"I don't really know or understand what you mean . . . a piece of paper, yes, that I recall, maybe an IOU. But what was written on it? That I don't remember." She never signed the note and she didn't know what she was talking about. Only the debtor signs a promissory note.

Then she looked at Bellicoso with a wacky but sweet smile and asked aloud, "Vito, help me?"

Bellicoso leaned sideways behind her and talked into her hair. "'I don't know what you mean' is your answer."

"Did anyone ever tell you the document to which you referred was a promissory note?" I asked.

"A promisor what? Don't know what it means."

"Did you read it when it was signed, if it was signed?"

"Said something"—Babette's voice quaked—"about a sum of money. I think it was in the millions . . . dollars . . . and that I would get the money back sometime, or during a five-year time period. . . . I don't know, don't you know? Otherwise how would you know to ask me? You must know!"

"I am sorry, Ms. Longwood, but I remind you that I am the lawyer and I'm here to ask the questions. If *I* sued *me,* I would have to come up with the answers."

A blast from Bellicoso to Cedric. "Tell *him,*" Bellicoso snarled, his chubby fingers pointing at my nose, "to treat Ms. Longwood with respect. Otherwise, we'll apply to have my legal bill for the day paid by Pandora Markham's counsel."

I ignored him. "I am not going to call for production of the promissory note for the sum of a hundred seventy million dollars, or whatever amount, at this time, Mr. Bellicoso." Just to see Vito's reaction I played it very dangerously close to the edge of the promissory note, parked in my file. He didn't look as if he could, or wanted to, produce a note.

Vito's face turned an angry white. "I'll take it under advisement as to whether we'll produce the original promissory note unless there is a court order requiring it. Isn't that correct, Mr. Cedric? Mr. Cedric!"

Cedric had nodded off. His head snapped back, and he mumbled, "Proceed gentlemen, proceed," as his chin once again found his chest.

The issue was now out in the open, but I wanted to keep it low-key. I didn't comment on the way Bellicoso implied he had the note. I knew he was bluffing because *I* had it and would wait for the trial to produce it. Everything in its own time. Bellicoso purposely hadn't made a request for me to produce the promissory note in my files because it would have been devastating for Babette if the note were in the debtor's possession with her knowledge. But if I produced it at this moment, they would have ample time between now and the trial to fabricate an excuse for Pandora having the note. They could argue it was an obvious, intrinsic part of the fraud that the note disappeared or was in Marcel's possession. Angrily, Bellicoso waited a moment for Cedric to revive, but there was no hope.

I continued, "Did your brother ever make any payments to you?"

"Not due until later. But he died."

There was no point in going into the fact that the loan had a low interest rate and wasn't due for ten years. It was more important for me to establish in every way possible that the money was a gift.

"And do you know who the lawyer was who wrote the agreement between you and your brother?"

"No."

"Assuming a lawyer wrote it," Bellicoso mused aloud, but I decided to let him get away with it.

"I don't know," Babette said weakly.

"Kerrigan, James Kerrigan. Does that name refresh your recollection?"

"Remember meeting him once, maybe twice. He's a lawyer."

"Was the lawyer working for you and your brother, Marcel?"

"Don't know."

I was now dealing with a witness different from the hysterical creature who had swept the papers off the desk and cursed. Now she was placid, unexcitable, acting as if whatever drug she'd taken was kicking in. I had to find out what made her tick, get my hand on the lever and exploit it.

"Well, what do you think?"

"Objection." Bellicoso finally tried to save her. "She answered you."

The referee was still asleep, so I didn't raise my voice to her lawyer. "Let her answer, and I'll end this line of questions."

He agreed and let Babette speak.

"I think he was."

"Was what?" I was pulling teeth to get these childish answers.

"The lawyer."

At that point, I stopped and had to take it on faith that a sensible law court would construe her answer to mean that the lawyer was both hers and her brother's. There was an excellent chance that could be a conflict of interest, which would go a long way toward proving that the lawyer just helped Marcel to a nice gift from Sis, which she never intended to collect.

"And did you ever loan or give any funds to other members of your family or close friends? Such as Webb Hartford, your doctor—Ms. Markham's brother?"

"Objection. Irrelevant."

At this time, a fatigued Cedric returned his attention to the proceedings and capriciously snapped, "Overruled! You may answer."

After this laborious ruling, he went out like a light, but I caught a break and wasn't about to wake him.

"No."

"Never?"

"Once."

"When and how much?"

"About two years ago, when Marcel died and Webb helped me through a difficult time."

"The question is how much?"

Webb maintained his cool façade, but a tiny muscle twitching almost imperceptibly in his clenched jaw betrayed him. It inspired me to take another series of swipes at Babette, especially with the White Knuckle at bay with Cedric in a coma. I smiled into the next question, which was the same question.

"How much?"

Babette looked at Bellicoso but didn't get a response from him. Vito couldn't clue her in in front of me because I'd put it on the record.

"Two hundred."

"Two hundred what?"

"Thousand."

"Was the money to Dr. Hartford a loan or a gift?"

I could swear Babette was being subtly elbowed by Webb, but I said nothing.

Finally Babette responded.

"I . . . don't . . . How would *I* know?"

"Who would, uh, know?"

"No."

"Permit me to finish? Who then, if not you?"

"No."

Goddamn those inscrutable, legally acceptable answers like "no" and "I don't know."

"Well, let's try it this way, Ms. Longwood. Do you know who thought to give Webb, your doctor, the—"

"No."

Unperturbed, I forged ahead. "Please, madam, permit me to finish, Dr. Hartford the—"

"No."

"—money?"

"No."

"I see."

But I didn't see and neither did she. No one would ever be able to reconstruct the circumstances. There never has been a legal case in which someone put together what actually happened. Ours is a world where events occur in the form of half-truths. I took a minute to figure out which door I should try next.

"Who currently handles all the financial transactions for you? That is, who writes the checks and does the bank statements, et cetera, et cetera?" This was the easiest question for the White Knuckle to raise an objection to, and in his position he should have. But what happened was nothing. That's a lawyer working hard for his client.

"Webb."

"Does he have the power to sign your name?"

"Never. I would never, oh no, no, no. I sign all the checks with my name."

"But does he put them in front of you?"

"Yes."

"Do you read the checks before you sign them?"

"No."

The next question I already knew the answer to.

"Do you ever look at the checks to see to whom they are made out?"

Then came the long wait and again I expected the word objection to roll out of Bellicoso's mouth, but it didn't.

"No."

That was another key breakthrough. I knew I was in. The strategy of portraying it all as a gift to Marcel was in full gear. Pandora was going to celebrate this one with me. I was saving her millions.

"And how long has this practice been going on, with Dr. Hartford preparing your checks for signature?"

"I don't know."

I looked over at Hartford. He smiled at me as if he were in my camp; I smiled back as if I were his pal.

I wanted to stop, to go call Pandora. I wanted a hit of her excitement.

They were waiting for the next question, Babette on the edge of her seat and sanity. I lit a cigarette, looked at them thoughtfully and then at the ash forming, the curvilinear smoke rising. Snuffing out the cigarette I got up.

"Sorry, I have to go to the men's room. I must take a few minutes."

Bellicoso's mouth moved, but he didn't say anything. Cedric moaned but didn't awaken, and I left the room.

I headed down the corridor past a stiff line of Surrogate's Court denizens. These lawyers represent the dead or dying, spending their entire lives waiting for their clients to expire so they can deal with the heirs, or as one of my lawyer friends used to say, "The hairs of your estate." The courts permit these lawyers to sell everything the deceased left, or somehow to dispose of it side-by-side with the executors and then take their commissions. This is the courthouse of the dead. The veritable funeral parlor of the law.

I got down to the pay telephone. It was the old "Ma Bell" variety, paneled like a coffin. I sat down and closed the door, which switched on the ventilator and light switch. Civilized. I dialed under the hum of the fan. Pandora's telephone number. Timing. At this moment, it seemed right.

No answer. Must have rung forty times. I held the phone in my hand and stared at it as if it were an unflushed john. Pandora had no interest in the case. She didn't even want to stick around for a report on her financial future, to see who was going to pay for the spa where she was probably having her legs waxed and her body massaged, postsauna. That was her afternoon, plus making a few million downtown in the courtroom. I could see an attendant hosing her down with warm water and her thinking about everything except these legal proceedings.

"Dammit. I give up," I said, and pushed my way out of the booth. Maybe I was relieved. Maybe I was going crazy. One rationalization came upon the heels of another. But one thing was certain: I wasn't obsessed with this tough bitch anymore, thanks to Y. During the deposition, whenever I thought about Pandora, the image of Y replaced her.

I went back to the courtroom. Doctor Hartford was at the window speaking softly but deliberately to Bellicoso. Babette was seated like a Sacred Heart schoolgirl waiting for the next question. Cedric was still fast asleep.

It was clear that Hartford was in control. He appeared to be guiding and shaping the case through precise, thoughtful maneuvers. Hartford and Bellicoso reminded me of two senators speaking about how they were going to slide a bill through Congress, or, just as easily, put the finishing touches on someone's downfall.

I tried very hard not to smile at Babette. It wasn't easy. I now found her pathetic. The afternoon was unexpectedly going in my favor. I waited patiently until finally Bellicoso started toward the table, his arm draped over Hartford's shoulder. Hartford stepped to Babette's side and handed her a small container. Babette excused herself and went to the bathroom. At first, I didn't realize what happened. Then my mind computed that it was a drug of some profound influence.

Many times doctors have financial motives and want to be trustees or executors. Who could better influence a sick person than her treating physician?

Everything I'd found out so far about Hartford through Eyeballs led me to the conclusion that he was independently wealthy. Over the years he'd invested wisely in real estate and now owned several miles of Florida beachfront. Further, Eyeballs had discovered that he owned vineyards in Italy and had made a few substantial contributions to various universities, mostly for cancer research. I wondered why he needed a loan.

"Let's resume, shall we?" I said to Bellicoso. "I want to get in as much as I can before four-thirty."

"Counselor, go as long as you like," Bellicoso replied, "but no later than four-thirty."

My adversary was acting very generous.

Babette returned, suddenly raring to go. Whatever she'd ingested seemed to have immediate outward effects. Her face looked clear; her eyes brightened when she sat down.

"Isn't it a fact that as soon as your brother, Marcel, had passed away, Dr. Hartford began preparing checks for your signature?"

"Objection. What do you mean 'as soon as'? It confuses the witness."

"You mean it confuses the lawyer for the witness."

Bellicoso turned to Babette and grandly said, "You may answer."

"Probably, yes."

"Wouldn't it be fair to say that the practice occurred even faster? Within twenty-four hours of Marcel's death?"

"Oh."

"Oh?"

"Probably. I would hope so."

"Hope so?"

"We were both in New York when poor Marcel died. Webb rightly took over what Marcel used to do for me . . . handle . . . all of the business transactions. . . . Why? Is there something wrong with that?"

She turned to Hartford, who by this time was glaring at me. His eyes were grayer in the late afternoon. Then, with no response from Webb, she turned to the White Knuckle who whispered to her, "You're doing just fine, honey."

She liked being called "honey" and smiled broadly at the goddamn White Knuckle. Somehow that touched him, because his face turned salmon. Maybe he was an old beau of hers from the time when she first started prospecting for gold. Another peg slipped into place.

I didn't put any more questions to Babette, deciding instead to quit early while I was ahead.

We all parted company that afternoon and left the courthouse as adversaries always do—in separate directions.

CHAPTER TEN

The telephone rang just as I arrived home. Before I could pick it up, Barkis leaped onto the chair next to me and pushed his wet nose into the phone, almost knocking me over. I managed to pull him away, shouting "Hello!"

It was Gerry Patton calling from Eyeballs. "Ocean, something about Ling that you might want to know."

Gerry had pitched for the Yankees about twenty years ago. Information with a view of how to handle the batters. He'd been with me since he quit the big leagues when his rotator cuff went on his pitching arm, but his baseball vernacular was still intact. I weathered the colorful slang to get information.

"I'll take anything Chinese and hope it fits at this point," I said and planted a cigarette in the side of my mouth.

"Our Mr. Ling is quite an interesting individual, a real heavy hitter with a many-sided mouth. Born in China, speaks English, French, all sorts of Chinese dialects—Mandarin, Cantonese, Hunanese, and others. He was right in there with Chiang Kai-shek, was one of his right-hands.

"My source is Chinese. They're tough to get information from, they all stick together—same farm system. Ling worked his way into top banking circles in China. And then he was out of there in

'49, when Mao took China. Ling went with Chiang to Formosa, you know, Taiwan. While the Cold war was at its peak Ling couldn't leave Formosa. In 1975 Chiang died and Ling split for New York.

"The informer is an ex-employee, disgruntled, a sucker for appliances, computers, CDs, Bush leaguer. Guess the little fuckers are just like us—goddamned materialistic. Hell, you can't blame them, one point two billion and growing."

"What about Ling's family?"

"Ling was married. His first wife was knocked off in brutal way during the civil war by the Communists. No details."

"Was there another woman?"

"Many, they come and go in his life like designated hitters. He doesn't have a high regard for women. He's an opportunist who was *naturally* drawn to politics and finance in Chiang's Kuomintang party. He wound up a cabinet member in the nationalist government."

"What about his business?"

"China Manpower shows up, and there are a lot of related companies, but we don't have that much yet."

"Tell me about China Manpower."

"Right now it's just a name I came across in the state's corporate register on Ling's group of companies. It might be a holding company, but it'll take time to figure out how all of them companies are connected. I don't think we'll luck into a neat organization chart."

"The jigsaw puzzle is yours. Get cracking."

"I'll get on the *Silk Road* and back to you one of these days," he replied.

Population in Chinese known as *ren-kou*—total mouths. The open mouth equals one to feed; therefore you count that way. Ling had a large mouth and was very hungry—his financial empire demonstrated that. He was a Chinese Henry Kravis, chewing up one company after another and spitting them out on Wall Street.

I'd have Eyeballs search for anything about China Manpower, any possible tie-in to the Markham case. So far nothing fell together. Zero. Rogers was the only lead, and that wasn't much.

There was a note from K on the hall console outside my bedroom. It read: "Sir, you have forgotten tonight there is a formal party. You were invited many weeks ago. It would be good for you to have a night off. You must relax and enjoy yourself in the company of a beautiful woman." The note referred to a party a special client of mine was throwing—a charity ball at the Metropolitan Museum.

I called Y and invited her to come with me. We'd never gone out in public, but we'd spent enough time together since we'd first made love that I believed that she wouldn't hurt me. In fact, I felt I thought she'd help if she could.

"Black-tie affairs are agonizing—dressing up like a maître d'. Rescue me."

"Who's going? Anyone you know?" she asked.

"Three hundred close friends."

"Come on. You must have friends, you're a lawyer."

"Lawyer friends, that's an oxymoron."

"What's the party for?"

"Send kids to summer camp in the Poconos."

"Then I'll go for sure. Even though I don't like being uptown. I guarantee a good time, Honorable Citizen." Y said it as if she meant it and hung up.

Park Avenue residents have causes. Family names become synonymous with diseases similar to the way public highways are adopted by celebrities. In New York charitable activity has a double purpose: it's fashionable and a good Samaritan insurance policy that's supposed to keep the rich out of hell. Every day, any person who can afford it gets hit up for a contribution to some event chaired by a businessman or his wife. The donations range from $250 to $10,000 a plate, depending on the table.

The cavernous space of the Metropolitan Museum endows its

reveling benefactors with a very personal nocturnal sensation of ownership when the daytime general public is erased from its grand staircase and huge halls. Many of the museum's wings and rooms are named after such affluent party animals who cherish these black-tie dinners followed by dancing around a relic in a glass box.

About eight o'clock Y arrived at my house. Mr. K's resonant, loud greeting from the front door could be heard all the way up in my bedroom. Excitedly he delivered her to the third floor where I was knotting my bow tie, about to put on my dinner jacket.

Following K, Y appeared in my bedroom and sat in the chair opposite the fireplace. Barkis parked at her side, demanding his petting due. From the dressing-room mirror I silently watched her while Mr. K regaled her with his routine.

"My boss will be right with you. Honorable Miss you are so lucky to know him. He is an attorney of high repute, a man over six feet tall, brown hair, blue eyes, and well educated. You are also a lovely one, such beautiful long, dark hair, a wonderful black dress. The material is very light, from what fabric is it made?"

"Chiffon, I believe." She laughed, pleasantly dazzled by the Mr. K show, gently running her hand over Barkis's head. She wore a very low cut, décolleté short dress, narrow spiked heels, a thin diamond necklace, and a matching diamond ring. Her hair swept around her neck and covered one breast.

Mr. K was far from through with this ritual. "My boss is preparing himself, he wants to look his very best. Miss, permit me to take you on a brief tour of the house while he is dressing." Before I had a chance to warn her about K's standard house junket, he had her in tow and was well into the guided tour.

"This is my boss's bathroom. The bathtub is from France, the taps are made from solid gold, the walls were hand-painted by a famous artist who is seen on the television. And in there"—I knew he was pointing to the dressing room—"that is where he dresses. He has ninety custom-made suits from London, England,

and one hundred made-to-measure shirts. He believes in fine dress and the maxim 'Cleanliness is next to godliness.' This belief is required for the courthouse, where he never wears the same suit twice for a case, nor the same shirt. He has the finest double-sided cufflink collection in the world."

"What if the trial lasts more than ninety days?" Y asked, closing the bathroom door.

"That would never happen. My respectable boss finishes off his opponents in less than thirty days," K retorted.

Although I'd heard K rattle off the same routine countless times, it still amused me. Charming her with more embellishments, K escorted her upstairs, explaining the paintings, furniture, and sculpture. I didn't know that I owned a Rembrandt and a Rodin.

His voice tapering, K elaborated, "This is the gymnasium where my boss works his body after he goes for a daily race in Central Park. And opposite is the music room where he plays his grand piano for two hours each day."

To K, jogging or running is a race even if one person is involved.

And I hadn't played the piano in a month. The last time I worked out in the house gym was years ago. K's monologue continued step by step as they came back down to the third floor.

"Thanks for showing me around, Mr. K. I'm sure the boss appreciates it. How many other women have you said the same thing to this month?" Y asked good-naturedly as she sat down in the armchair.

K shook his head, giggled, and rendered another half-truth. "No, Miss, you are the only one. I must state the real fact. My boss has a special place for you in the core of his heart."

It was time. I came into the bedroom and kissed Y.

"K, that's enough for one night. Please bring Ms. Y and me two glasses and a bottle of Cristal. We are celebrating Y's first visit to my home."

"Very fine, Sir, drink is good, and also to have friends come to the house. They should come more often and you should accede to my wishes about the little ones," he announced.

"Enough, K. I thought you were on your way to get the champagne. Please do not bring up that subject again."

"Sir, it is the best thing. The little ones will know how their father sacrificed his own labor for their benefit."

"No more, K."

"Their lives will be based upon the golden principles of Johnny Ocean and they will multiply."

"K, I said enough."

"Sir, your name must survive."

Feigning obedience, K moved backwards on to the landing, bowed, and said, "Sir, sorry, very sorry, it will not happen again."

Y appeared quizzical as I sat opposite her. The exchange was bewildering, as it had been to so many other guests.

"That was confusing, Johnny. Who are the little ones?"

"Children. K wants me to get married and have a family. He thinks every woman that ever walked in this house is a candidate for pregnancy."

"That's not the feeling I get, Johnny. You seem too independent" She crossed her legs.

"There may come a day when I'll weaken." K arrived with the drinks.

After a few toasts we left.

The Metropolitan Museum is a neoclassical building that would make a perfect courthouse. Aside from the architecture, the museum has an abundance of wasted space. It would be a beautiful sight except for its two rows of incongruous fountains that resemble an unaesthetic irrigation system. At night the building's facade is showered with light as the fountains gush two nondescript curtains of water.

We walked up the grand exterior three-sided stairway, past the welcome desk in the Great Hall. After we picked up our place cards, we stood in a line for twenty minutes, hosing through the Egyptian art rooms toward the party. Socialites would be squirted into the Temple of Dendur.

An old female vocalist sang "I've Got You Under My Skin" in front of a small orchestra. The theme of the night was forties. After I paid my respects—exchanged lawyer-client hugs with the host, who was surrounded by parasites—Y took me aside and insisted, "C'mon, Johnny, let's dance. I love ballroom dancing."

"No, I never dance, just not in my nature," I replied moving away from the dance floor.

"Is that because you can't?"

"How about ballet?"

"Too macho, try something simple first, like ballroom."

"I'm uncoordinated and everyone is watching."

"No one cares. Give it a try, please."

That face could not be turned down. We went on to the dance floor. It was more like a packed E train during rush hour. Fortunately I could easily disguise my weird Elvis Costello moves and not feel as if I was in front of a police lineup.

Finally the orchestra broke and we went to the bar. Ordering two double vodkas, I looked up at the angled windows enclosing the museum's north side and checked out the guests in the reflection. Even though I knew some of them, I didn't make the effort to do the rounds. Besides, I didn't want to give anyone the opportunity to offer their usual New York City compliments to me. Anytime I attend a party or go to a public place, someone inevitably says: "What's that prick doing here? Who the fuck invited him? That bastard sued me."

This was a genuine Pandora affair. At any moment she was going to run up behind me, put her hands over my eyes, and say, "Johnny Ocean, guess who?" I'd bet she'd be at one of these tables with a man, surrounded by people I'd never seen before. Even though I felt guilty, I wanted to take a quick tour of the room to see if I was right. The large crowd was milling and mingling.

Everyone here except us had seen one another at a similar engagement the week before. This phony gregarious process has been repeating itself since ancient Egypt.

After we had two more double vodkas, Y dragged me back to dance while I was busily scanning for Pandora. A slow song was playing as we moved, bumped, elbowed, and banged into one couple after another.

Then it happened. A one in three hundred chance times a million. A blond woman I didn't look at carefully crashed into us with a man I instantly recognized as Webb Hartford. Our eyes locked the way prizefighters' do in the ring during final instructions by the referee just before the opening bell. Webb pulled Babette back in an artful step, and they shuffled themselves toward the orchestra, seamlessly blending in with undulating waves of tuxedos and gowns.

"What happened, Johnny?" Y asked.

"Nothing, someone I saw that maybe I'd like to avoid," I answered, wondering if she knew them.

Then I saw Babette and Webb racing toward me. Babette was waving her arm and I could hear her say, "Mr. Ocean, I'd like a word with you. Wait right there. Wait!"

Immediately I backed up. No way could I talk to her when she was represented by a lawyer. That would be an ethical violation, putting me permanently in the penalty box. Immediately I'd be taken off the case. Babette knew exactly what she was doing, and it was consistent with her contacting Pandora.

"We've got to move out of here. Now! They're coming for me. This is crazy." I sighed and rapidly moved in the direction of the entrance.

"Come, let's hide. I know a great place," Y responded, not wasting a second.

Taking my hand she lead me to the other side of the room, then back through the Egyptian rooms to the Great Hall. "I have a surprise for you."

Two guards stood near the columnar entrance to the south wing of the museum. From that distance I could hear the orchestra playing an upbeat number, "When the Saints Go Marching In." One of the two guards danced around on one foot, entertaining the other who'd turned to give directions to three guests as they emerged from the cloakroom. We sneaked past, slipped into the darkened Greek and Roman wing, and ran through Belfer Court. I looked over my shoulder. No sign of them, but I couldn't be certain.

She pulled me toward the first gallery on the left. The hallway was full of statues; the entrance had a sarcophagus on one side, and there were two statues of wounded Amazons next to the doorway.

I struck a wooden match. It echoed. A sign read: GALLERY CLOSED FOR RENOVATION, but the door was unlocked.

She led me inside and I held her tight as she wrapped her arms around my neck.

"This is something you probably do all the time, Johnny, tell your women you're being followed."

"Wrong. This was your idea."

"That is a meaningless detail. Now that we're here," she whispered.

"I need to research if it's legal in a public building. I've never done it in the Museum of Modern Art, never screwed in the Frick, the Museum of Natural History . . ."

"What's the matter, can't get hard in front of Tyrannosaurus rex?"

"Depends. What does she look like?"

"An older version of me."

We kissed as I backed her against the square base of a white marble statue of a nude woman in the center of other figures. I held her flat against it while Babette and Webb faded from my thoughts. A line of moonlight streaked through the tall windows over the two of us, lighting the sculpture above. Y's face, her red lipstick, and her white skin were a soft cushion I could have fallen into and never returned. For a second I stared at one of the statues.

"Baby, I'm over here. What's up?" Y purred, and a second later her fingers were between my thighs.

"Nothing, I was just thinking, the room, this sculpture." Alongside the wall, just feet from me, there was a sculpture of that rogue Mercury. I slowly pushed the shoulder straps of Y's evening dress off her shoulders, around her elbows, down her arms.

My hands went around her small waist. I could feel the marble under the statue as I kept her close to me. Y's black satin bra dropped to the floor.

He teeth tugged at my bow tie, undoing the knot, pulling it around the shirt collar, unwinding me. We were alone except for a gallery of figures staring at us. She gently pushed herself into me. "Take off my dress."

"I'm trying," I replied, fumbling.

"It's one of those complicated French numbers. Let me help you." She unhooked the back, moving a zipper around the waist and then downward. The soft, sheer material dispersed, leaving Y standing in stockings up to her thighs—except for the jewels. I stroked her nipples. Y and I were beginning to sweat, the temperature rising.

I could hear footsteps approaching. Coming closer.

Y could have cared less, unfastening my belt, running her tongue up my neck as that uneven, horny surface of crocodile strip was drawn through the loops of my tuxedo pants.

"Johnny, I want you in me," she whispered.

"That's where I want to be, in you in the Met," I answered as she began to kneel. More footsteps.

"Get down on your knees, put your mouth on me."

Gladly complying, I sank to the floor, put my hands on the lace elastic tops of her stockings, and spread her legs apart, tasting her. The way she moved made me twitch.

"I want you to lick me just there on the side, just on the side of my— Move your tongue, make me come with your tongue."

She angled her hips away from me and turned around. Her palms were over her head against the statue, her forehead against it. "This is bad behavior, Johnny," she said, arching her back, extending herself to me, losing her breath on the words. "Take me from behind."

I pushed my zipper down and was inside her, swimming in a swift current.

"Take your pants all the way off," she breathed in my ear.

Y gasped, "Fuck me hard, Johnny."

Reaching around, her fingers encircled my shaft. Then she gently moved her hand back and forth.

"Pull me apart. That's what. . . ." She moaned.

For a moment I lost my breath, then I finished her sentence, "I want."

Holding myself back against her muscular ass, resisting the urge, I knew I couldn't make it last. The moonlight splashed off the statues streaming light over us.

With my arms around Y, I came.

The other figures in the room participated. Women danced in a state of ecstatic frenzy in relief alongside Hercules, the demigod who was enslaved to his own passions.

The door opened. How embarrassing and how would I explain this to Pandora? Babette and Webb finding me, naked with Y. Next stop the police—maybe Windows—then a criminal-court judge putting me away for indecent exposure. Macefield would love it. The lights were switched on. I grabbed Y and hid her against the plinth of Pandora. Neither one of us moved.

It was a guard. He entered the room and stood in the same spot for minutes. Then the lights dissolved. We dressed quickly and left.

We walked down Fifth Avenue and couldn't stop laughing about the party.

It was about 2:00 A.M. when K pulled me aside as I came in the house with Y under my arm, telling me he'd uncovered some information I asked him to research. Discreetly excusing herself, Y went up to the bedroom.

"Sir, I know that you are enchanted by this lovely Y. She is very charming, but there are some things you must know."

"At this time of the night, is this some kind of K-Y joke?"

"Sir, you are feeling good, but I don't understand such American humor."

"All right, K, let's be serious."

"Yes, the sooner the information is imparted to you, the stronger you'll become. You may be weak emotionally."

"Not tonight, K, I have been pressing business upstairs."

"This will only take a moment." He walked with me whispering, "The Chinese government—I don't want to offend the young lady—under Chiang Kai-shek was run by opium dealers who controlled Chiang." Laughing, he said, "They had very funny names, Pockmarked Huang, Big-Eared Tu, and Curio Chang. They ran the Green Gang. Before becoming president of China, Chiang was a murderous gangster and a member of the Green Gang. These nicknames are humorous, but the rest of the story is not." His tone became coldly serious.

"How did you find this out?"

"It is written, sir, well documented in history books. Those not written by Chinese. There are many parallels between Chinese and Indian history. The same thing happened in my country with the British through the East India Trading Company: They sold opium to the Indian people just as they did in China. Then the Chinese began selling opium to themselves in the beginning of this century until Chiang's government took control of trade."

"Chiang was very corrupt."

"Mr. Ling worked directly for Chiang. He *had* to have been involved in the opium trade. We are further investigating this underworld figure and his connections. Gerry will be calling you because he knows much more.

"Sir, you know there is no love lost between the Indian and Chinese people. We have been to war with them, and India has had many border disputes in 1965 over Tibet and even parts of Mount Everest. There was a war between India and China, resulting in the Dalai Lama being expelled. Quite right, sir, I don't like the Chinese, not at all."

"What about her?" I motioned upstairs.

"Sir, I never pass judgment on beautiful women. That I leave to the perspicacity of the boss."

"K, for tonight, just bring me another bottle of champagne. We can finish the discussion tomorrow."

Y was sitting on the bed waiting for me.

"Long talk with Mr. K? Hope you weren't speaking about me." She smiled but I knew she sensed that we'd been doing just that.

"All good things. He's concerned about his boss's welfare and checks out everyone who enters this house. He likes you very much."

K delivered the bottle packed in an ice bucket, wished Y a good evening, and left for the night. We drank a few glasses and talked awhile, laughing about the night's escapades. Just before bottle number two emptied Y turned serious.

"Johnny, I lied to you in the hospital." She took a long sip, and I knew I was just a bit ahead of her on the clearheaded meter. I was feeling no pain and she was very intoxicated.

"How's that?" I was surprised but not shocked because I'm skeptical about everyone.

"Rogers."

"What about him?"

"The reason I went there was not because I liked him and we were friends. My father ordered me to go to Lenox Hill." She sighed as though this confession had taken a load off her mind.

"Why?"

"He wanted me to confirm that Rogers had been killed. That's all I know. He never explains things to me. Johnny, my father can't talk. His tongue was cut out by the Communists."

That shook me, but within seconds I was sure it was Mao himself who gave the order to put a stop to the sound of Ling. The Chinese were well known for cutting out tongues, beheadings, burying people alive, poisoning, mutilation, and torture.

"You might be in danger, Johnny. But I'm going to help you. I don't want to see you hurt." She was taking a grand step.

"Tell me what he's doing that might threaten me."

"That's something I don't know. There was something between him and Edgar Longwood, some bad blood that goes way back. That's all I know. You'd have to get into his offices in Chinatown to find out."

I was convinced that she was telling me as much as she knew about a difficult subject. If Ling killed Rogers, then maybe he was on my side. That was a joke.

"How can I do that? Your father's place must be like the Pentagon, crawling with security."

"Yes it is, but I know what to do. The downstairs security switches at certain times of night, and I can get a key to his office. This weekend is Labor Day and there are only a few people around, otherwise it's a military headquarters. There's also a back door where deliveries are received, and I have the security code. Once you're inside, the office is up the steps."

"So what should we do?"

"If you come to my place tomorrow, I'll have the key for you. Then you're on your own. If my father ever found out I'd be finished." She leaned over, picked up a pen, and wrote out the code.

"That's the last thing I want. Are you sure you want to do it?"

She gently put the paper in my hand. Putting her head against me, she sighed and she didn't answer right away.

"I'm sure. The last thing I want is you being shot at again."

"It doesn't make the situation any better, but I'd do it for you."

The last glass of champagne overwhelmed us and finally we fell asleep about five in the morning.

She must have left late that morning while I was still out cold. At best my feelings were deeply confused. In my sleep I tripped through a number of scenarios starting with Y, but I was paradoxically drawn to the wrong woman. The situation couldn't be helped.

I slept on into the afternoon, severely hungover. About 1:30 the phone rang, sounding like a fire alarm. No, I'd leave it alone . . . but I couldn't, because it wouldn't stop.

I picked up the receiver and smothered it in the sheets. That didn't help. The muffled voice of Mercedes downstairs, screaming into the phone, came through the receiver and up the stairs.

"Johnny! I have to talk with you!"

The big compromise—the phone traveled to my ear but I said nothing.

"I know you're very busy in bed with your panda bear and . . ."

All I could hear was a radio blaring Bach's Double Violin Concerto. In my state of mind I chose not to tell her to turn the music down and to behave like a secretary. Who was I to criticize anyone after last night? She'd probably get up and walk out the door.

Today she was being extra efficient but it didn't count. Talking to me was like speaking to a pile of empty beer cans.

"The judge called."

"Judge what?" In what case? In what county?

Mercedes answered, "Macefield, Bellicoso's bagman in residence."

"He called himself?"

"No, it was his court clerk. I *did* get his telephone number. Do you want it?"

"Of course."

"He said it was urgent. Macefield wants a conference right away on the Longwood case. But first, he wants to speak with both sides on the phone."

"Just my luck."

Mercedes gave me the number. Barkis leapt into bed on top of me, nosing me to death. I pushed him away, nearly cracking what was left of my very throbbing head.

Before I could make the call, His Honor's man Friday phoned, informing me that everyone was to be at the courthouse no later than three. There was to be a big unscheduled conference with the court, all about the progress in the case and moving it ahead on the calendar. Even Macefield got on for a minute.

"Listen, Counselor. I looked over part of the deposition transcript the other day, and I conferred with Cedric. I don't want this case to be around the courthouse for five years. I want it moved—fast."

That voice meant business, and I could feel I was about to get the business. There was hardly a case in the Surrogate's Court that was younger than five years old. The dead gallop once again through court files.

Twenty minutes later, I was trying to pull myself together in the shower. I thought about what I was going to say in court, although very often that's a waste of time. Everyone's personal agendas get played out before the formal argument. So what occurs is not the result of planning. It happens on the spot, or on the way to the spot.

I shaved neatly, the razor slicing through my splitting headache. Who knows? If I had some success, I might even get the chance to see Pandora after the conference. I pulled on a dark blue suit with wide lapels, knotted a lavender-and-blue tie. I took another breath, wondered why I ever became a lawyer, put it out of my mind, and went downstairs.

Jimmy brought my car around in less than fifteen minutes. I reached the courthouse, ready for Judge Macefield and his merry band of law secretaries. The sun was white-hot, endowing the courthouse with a stunning pearl-like texture. I was walking into a hot oven.

The day was already moving against Pandora Markham, and I was going to have to pry open the rusted fist of justice and point its index finger away from Pandora's bank account. Themis, goddess of justice, wasn't exactly in her corner now.

I was certain that Pandora had gone through some of the inheritance, but I still hadn't seen a freeze order. She didn't deserve the bread any more than her fancy sister-in-law, Babette, but somehow the guy up there above the cloudline favors certain people with luck . . . and the rest of us with hard work.

I was in Macefield's anteroom once again. For the second time Bellicoso was not to be found. The bastard was in with the judge. I knew that they were, once again, kissing each other's asses.

About a half-hour went by. I examined every square inch of every plaster crack in the walls and ceiling. I finally went up to the judge's clerk to say something, but he was on the phone. It was 4:15.

I waited; a judge in chambers is incommunicado. No one with any legal sense does anything to upset the judge. But in the final analysis, I'm not a good example of lawyerly self-restraint. Standing in front of the clerk, I said, "Tell His Grace that I cannot wait any longer, and if he isn't going to see the lawyers in the Markham case, Mr. Bellicoso and I are leaving."

"What?" The clerk placed one hand over the mouthpiece. "I don't see Mr. Bellicoso."

"You don't?" I replied. "I could swear he was just standing here."

The clerk picked his nose.

"Just, just a minute," he barked into the mouthpiece and hit the hold button with a clean finger. Like a car braking hard, he turned to me. "What did you say about Mr. Bellicoso?" His face was pinched with anger.

"I said, he left and I'm leaving."

In that second, I was calling my own bluff. I couldn't just walk out the door; I had no choice but to face the Muzak they were playing. The clerk called the judge.

"You can go in, Mr. Ocean. His Honor will see you now."

I walked into the den of iniquity only to stumble on a replay of the previous meeting with Macefield. The troops were lined up as if they were listening to the "Star-Spangled Banner," only they were waiting for me.

Before I could take the room's legal temperature, Macefield boomed, in front of his raft of law clerks and the White Knuckle, "Counselor, take a seat right in front here, next to Mr. Bellicoso."

"I thought you left," I whispered to the White Knuckle, who sneered at me.

"And miss you getting reamed?" Bellicoso cackled under his breath. "By the time this case is over you'll be shitting my initials."

"Then that will make both of us famous."

Macefield cut in, "You're late, and I understand you don't appear on time for court conferences. Your reputation precedes you. I don't tolerate tardiness. If there is one thing to know about me, it is the word *punctual.* Lawyers are fined ten dollars for each minute they are late in my courtroom."

Experience shut me up. I wanted to kick the incompetent bastard in the teeth, but, like most seasoned lawyers in that situation, I didn't try to argue. "Yes I'm sorry," I replied. "I won't be late again, Your Honor, but I was hung up in terrible traffic."

"Mr. Ocean."

Macefield's hand whisked through a pile of papers, through another larger batch, and then through his hair. Nothing was said for a moment, until he pulled a clump of his right eyebrow forward.

"I want this case to *move.* Move, move, move, move, *move.*" His hands shot forward, Richard Nixon-style. "I don't want it to linger, and I think you plan to make this matter something that'll span a lifetime, a meal ticket."

His eyes rollerskated around the room and slowed on me.

I didn't say a thing.

"Judge, I know you see what's going on here," Bellicoso said. "This lawyer thinks he's going to prolong the inevitable. He's being dilatory, it's crystal clear. If that's going to be the case, this court must exercise some control over the estate of Ms. Markham's late husband. Otherwise, it may be totally dissipated. For all we know Pandora Markham has spent all the money and gone through the other assets that are in contention in this lawsuit. I insist on an accounting forthwith."

Bellicoso placed his fat, backslapping hands on the armrests of his red leather chair.

"I've read the pleadings," Macefield said. "You have no real defense here, Counselor Ocean. According to this court's rules, I'm capable of awarding Ms. Longwood all the counsel fees here—that could well be into the millions—and all the costs, if you persist and lose." His voice thickened with intensity.

"I'm just doing my job. I am a lawyer taking a party's deposition, and I plan to finish what I started."

"The hell you are!" Macefield yelled.

"Your Honor, now that you have taken the time to advise me on the weaknesses of my client's case, I respectfully request that you do the same for my adversary, so that we both may consider the risks of malpractice and notify our carriers. Otherwise, I would not feel my client was getting fair and impartial treatment at this conference."

Macefield knew that put him on the spot. The scales of justice have to weigh, at least at the outset of a case, equally on both sides. He shifted a little in his chair, adjusting his position as if his confidence was shaken, and he no longer could sit or spit quite the same. He was trying to determine the cleanest method to screw me over and, at the same time, create an unassailable record of the proceedings. The man in the robe has the power, but if he really gets too far out of line, he can wind up standing in front of the bench.

One of Macefield's law assistants passed him a note during this quasi-ecclesiastical ceremony. The judge's heavy eye contact with Bellicoso made me uncomfortable. Obviously, they knew how to communicate in these kinds of circumstances. After a minute or two, Macefield unfolded the paper and read it over to himself, moving his lips slowly.

Then he motioned with his right hand for his clerk to come forward, and he whispered something in her ear. She shook her mouselike head back and forth rapidly, which said, in no uncertain terms, that what Macefield was about to try seemed illegal.

"Mr. Ocean, where is your client now?" he demanded.

And what a good question it was. It clattered in my head like a wrench that skidded down a cast-iron pipe. Bellicoso leaned forward as if he were going to eat me alive.

"I don't know," I replied. "Haven't spoken with her today."

"As you should know by now, most of the assets of the estate are frozen. I'm going to reduce the income Mrs. Markham is receiving and issue an order permitting her to draw an allowance from the estate for the next six months of, say, six hundred dollars a week; however, she may apply to the court if something extraordinary happens and she needs additional funds." That was ridiculous. It was more a threat than a final ruling.

"You don't have the jurisdiction to do that," I protested. Macefield was exceeding his powers, and I was compelled to speak up. But I was going out on a limb. "There has been no demonstration that my client is wasting the assets of the estate; that must be shown on paper. Where's the evidence? I haven't seen any proof of such behavior. This court can't merely accept Mr. Bellicoso's assertion that my client is dissipating her rightful inheritance. Let Ms. Longwood bring on a motion and prove it."

I had nothing to lose.

"Are you going to tell me what my powers are, Mr. Ocean?" Macefield bellowed.

"No, but that is the law."

"Your Honor, I must come to the aid of the court," Bellicoso interjected, rising about three inches off his chair. Macefield waved off the White Knuckle. Vito sunk back into his chair like a fastball whipped into a catcher's mitt.

"I tell you, Counselor," Macefield said, "I have the power to put your rear end in the slammer over the weekend for your remarks. You are in contempt of this court. Should I call in a court officer? I've done it before, and I will do it again."

"You can't hold me in contempt for making an argument, and you've never put anyone in jail as Surrogate. Can we put all of this on record, Judge? Can we get a court reporter in here?"

Macefield backed off. "Tomorrow we are going to have a trial right here in this courthouse," he roared, "and all discovery, including depositions, is hereby closed. That is my order. It will be in writing if you gentlemen want to wait a few minutes. Since Mr. Ocean will not agree to reduce the income of the estate to safeguard the property, I am left with no choice but to proceed posthaste, since we may be dealing with perishable assets."

"Judge, I never said that Mrs. Markham wouldn't abide by your order, but if this court issued such an order, I would want time to go to the Appellate Division where I would request that the order be stayed until the issue was reviewed. And you know how long that could take."

A trial on such short notice is nearly impossible to prepare for. But I was representing the defendant, which meant that Bellicoso would have to present his case first. That would give me some extra time. Babette, or whoever Bellicoso's first witness was, would be on the stand for at least a day.

I wanted clarification. "Your Honor, have you ordered the estate to restrict Mrs. Markham's income from the estate of her deceased husband? Is that still your position?"

Macefield's eyes rolled as if he'd been insulted by my stupidity before subjecting me to another saliva bath. "Obviously not, Counselor! All matters will be resolved by a full and complete trial. Maybe your client can dispose of all the assets of the estate tonight by paying your legal fees."

I could live with the sarcasm. At least I wouldn't have to tell Pandora that even more of her money was now tied up.

Macefield and Bellicoso had set a trap. A good lawyer won't allow his client's assets or the income from an estate to be frozen. Macefield had railroaded me into a quick, fixed trial "in the interests of justice," he said.

Now I was faced with preparing seriously for trial on astonishingly short notice. It would be easier for Bellicoso; he would have an associate work out all the questions for him. He'd read from a script the same way he and Macefield had just acted out their screenplay for me.

I left the courthouse and headed straight over to Pandora's apartment house. I had to have a sit-down with her so we could start preparing her testimony. There was no time for the usual phone Olympics.

The doorman told me he'd met Pandora when he started a couple of months ago. He said she was one of the more elusive figures in a building stuffed with those well-to-do who prefer to live discreetly, whose names rarely make the papers by choice. That was true for Pandora except when she *wanted* to see her name in pulp. He pointed to the service door around the side of the building and said that anyone who wanted to make an unobtrusive exit or entrance used it, implying that was the way Pandora often came and went. He rang the apartment. There was no response.

The image I had constructed so carefully began to show signs of wear and tear: Pandora leaving for society balls every evening, the doorman tipping his cap and opening the limousine door for her and Mr. Perfect. This new Pandora was secretive, suddenly publicity-shy. I hadn't seen her new picture in any of the columns lately. When had that started? Already I knew she was a client who didn't want to see hide nor hair of her lawyer.

No point in hanging around the Caprice. With luck Pandora would show up when I wasn't there. I called Mercedes from my cell phone. She told me that at about 5:30, Macefield's law secretary phoned to say that he'd been taken ill and the trial was to be put off for at least a week, which'd give me time. We'd be notified when a new trial date was set. I doubted Macefield was really sick, but it was a welcome break.

After that call to the office, I went back downtown to meet an old friend, Rolfe Marauder, a New York County Supreme Court judge, for an early dinner in Chinatown not far form the building where China Manpower was located.

Sitting at a worn, chrome-trimmed Formica table in the back of the Hong Fat, I waited for the judge. This rendezvous was no simple reunion. Ten years ago, Marauder had settled a case involving Ling, and I knew he didn't care for the Chinese heavies. The courthouse clerk maintains an index of all lawsuits by plaintiff's name, and I had Gerry Patton look up all the cases in which Ling had ever been a litigant. We cross-referenced the list with the judges who presided in those cases, until we came up with one I knew well.

I met Marauder when I was a P.I. and he was a police officer. Later it went beyond friendship when, as a lawyer, I did his very rough divorce as a pure favor. Then he went to law school at night and was eventually elected a lower-court judge. He worked his way up to the highest trial court in the State of New York, the Supreme Court. The State Court is nothing like the Supreme Court in Washington. It's just a series of rooms for matters involving over fifty thousand dollars.

While I waited, nibbling on a few brown noodles, watching waiters dart back and forth between the tables, the kitchen, and the cash register, I wondered what really went on at the Ling empire. Marauder was always late. He often worked overtime.

I went to the phone to try Y while I was waiting. I pushed a quarter into the world's largest coin collector and dialed the number. No answer.

The judge's rugged six-foot-two figure walked trough the door, searching for me in a sea of wontons and scissoring chopsticks. Even though he was over sixty he was well built, probably weighing not much more than he did when he played quarterback for Fordham. Even his face had a muscular bristle about it. His jaw jutted out like the corner of a square table.

Through all the comings and goings of the frenetic waiters, he couldn't see me tucked into the tiny, sesame-steamed alcove in the back of the establishment. I let the receiver hang and went to meet the judge.

"Johnny, hello, been trying to find you." He reached out and gave my hand a squeeze with the strength of a boxer.

"Hey, Your Honor, be right with you, got to make a call," I answered, just as he was pulling off his vented car coat. I returned to the phone to try Y again, but when I got there one of the waiters was on, gabbing away. Although I couldn't understand a word of it, I could tell the conversation—an avalanche of Chinese—was going to go on for a while.

After I returned to the table, Marauder talked about several flavorless, if not unremarkable, commercial cases involving Ling which he knew about but wasn't the judge. Somehow or other they were settled out of court.

"But have you ever had a case with him or any of his companies?"

He nodded. "I was getting to that. We had a hot matter with the infamous Mr. Ling. He sued one of the big Wall Street firms, Longwood Securities."

I was all ears.

"It was between Edgar Longwood's firm and Ling. It never should have gone as far as the courtroom. It was quite a clash between these two gazillionaires. These lawyers from big firms went at it in the corridors. My clerk told me one of them was hospitalized with a broken jaw. A bloody personal-injury litigation between the lawyers kept those coals burning long after the main fight ended."

"What about the main case?"

"On the outside, the fight involved what looked like a legitimate legal problem. Longwood Securities was a public company, but the majority of the stock was owned by Edgar Longwood. Ling had shares in Longwood Securities and had sued, claiming its owners mismanaged the company. Ling tried to take control of Longwood, insisting on being elected to the board of directors."

"That's typically a greenmail tactic—the attacker gets paid off and goes away rich."

"Typically, but Ling was a pit bull. He wouldn't let go of a very stubborn Edgar who wouldn't quit either."

This wasn't out of the ordinary. More often than not, wealthy businessmen litigate over ego, not principle.

The judge downed some mint tea and told me more. "After Edgar died it was quickly settled by Longwood's executors. They paid a few million dollars to Ling and refused to pay more. The Surrogate's Court strongly recommended the settlement."

That I could clearly envision. Executors try to sanitize estates because they want no blemishes on their fiduciary skin or their right to executors' commissions.

"The amount didn't please Ling. Longwood wasn't afraid of Ling because he had as much clout as anyone in New York, perhaps the United States. Maybe Ling should have used a different collection system to begin with."

"You mean Guido services of Brooklyn and Staten Island?"

He didn't answer that one but smiled and ran his hand back through a thick head of long gray hair.

"Why China Manpower pursued that case with such a vengeance is a mystery," Marauder said, "but I learned a lot in chambers from the lawyers. The court file contains nothing important, but, after six or seven years of heavy litigation, I got to know the adversaries quite well. Both Ling's and Longwood's attorneys became very informal. Since they didn't speak to one another, they let their hair down with me."

"What did they have to say?" I asked, knowing that lawyers have a tendency to get close to a judge in a complex litigation that goes on for years. Confidential information that has nothing to do with the case has a way of finding itself imparted to the judge.

"There was bad blood between Ling and Longwood that goes way back. They had some big business between them that soured. Ling knew Longwood around the time of the Second World War."

The waiter poured us more tea and placed two steamy bowls of wonton soup in front of us.

"That far back would make things difficult to reconstruct," I prodded, taking in a spoon.

"The facts aren't," the judge said disgustedly. "The American people were brainwashed by Roosevelt and Madame Chiang Kai-Shek, who regularly visited the States before, during, and after the war, preaching her ass off to the White House and the American public for aid to China. It worked."

"I always heard Madame Chiang was a great lady."

"Depends on what side of the Pacific you're on. She was a celebrity here and people treated her like she was Grace Kelly or Jackie O, but she was just another full of shit 'Don't Cry for Me Argentina' megalo."

He shook his head as if he'd just sentenced her to life without parole.

"How much did we give China?"

"Over five billion, but most of it went to line Chiang's pockets. Not a penny back. The United States was taken by Chiang, who had a personal interest in everything from pistachios to drug smuggling. The irony—he sent Madame Chiang to live in the United States. He left her for another woman."

"Why the hell did we support him?"

"Because the corrupt little bastards rode into town on the pitch that the Japs and Hitler were about to take over the world, and on top of everything else the commies would control China."

The egg rolls were served. Marauder cut one in half with a fork.

"Sounds like another instance of the U.S. getting sucked in with our wallets wide open." Three more heaping courses arrived: crispy beef, Peking duck, and sweet-and-sour pork. I dished out a plate to Marauder and handed him a set of chopsticks.

"Never eat with wood." He pushed my hand aside, picked up a knife, and continued. His Honor was on a roll. "Even though the Chinese wouldn't fight the Japs, we still tried to get a military force up under Chiang, but he repeatedly made deals with the Japs behind our backs."

"I always thought the Chinese fought the Japs." I raised my voice over the commotion and took a bite of the pork. It wasn't very tasty, could've been dog.

"Chiang wimped out, gave up huge territories. The Japs took Manchuria and dealt opium out of the north, killed about two hundred thousand Chinese in the process. Chiang dealt opium out of the south. So by supporting Chiang we kept the world's biggest dope operation going while China smoked itself numb."

"Probably too stoned to fight."

"Right you are. Finally we had to mop up the Japs ourselves with the A-bombs. All I know is that our taxpayers' bucks went over there and never came back. Mr. Ling was right in the middle of it."

The judge had finished off the crispy beef and was well into the Peking Duck. If he'd used chopsticks the meal would have tasted better, but you can't give a judge advice.

Dinner was over before 8:00 P.M. without fortune cookies and litchi nuts. I had to get moving.

CHAPTER ELEVEN

Y lived only five minutes away in SoHo. I took a cab, hoping to catch her so I could get the key.

But when I arrived, her apartment building was ringed with detectives clothed in department-store suits. As usual a flock of excited journalists hovered around the cops.

In the hallway outside Y's front door Lieutenant Victor Slice met me.

"Ocean, as usual, you turn up in the best of places," he said in his agitated way.

"What's going on?"

"Not too much. We got a call from a neighbor who claims she heard a racket, like someone being slammed into a wall. We rushed over and found the pad all torn up. I don't think it was renovation at this time of night. Some real valuable stuff has been destroyed, but it doesn't look like robbery. A lot of great antiques, artifacts, were in there—vases of whatever you call those pots. Ceramics?"

"Is she all right?"

"No body and no clue as to where the hell the owner is. We're talking Emanuel Ling's daughter, not just the girl next door. The boys found a few things of yours lying around in there. If I was you I'd go right ahead and worry like crazy."

"Worry about what?"

"Maybe yourself."

There was no question he was right. I was being dragged into a possible murder case as a suspect, and I was worried sick about Y's well-being.

Before I could answer, out came the rest of the entourage, like cheap hors d'oeuvres on a metal tray at a badly catered wedding: Windows, his assistants, a few detectives in rumpled trench coats. They ignored me and conversed, attempting to connect bits of criminality as I slipped away.

After leaving Y's place, I couldn't stop thinking about what Y had said about what could happen to her if her father found out about the code. That didn't seem possible, but I was driven to get to the bottom of where she was, what happened to her. The best place to start was Ling's offices. I cabbed uptown, got my gun, a few essential tools and headed back to Chinatown, very distraught. I was going to go for it with or without the key. I left K a message, telling him what had happened at Y's apartment and where I was going.

As Y told me, only one guard stood in the front of the building. I went around back. No one in the alley. A thick steel door led into the building above a delivery bay. Making certain there wasn't another entrance, I took fifteen minutes to check out the rest of the premises. Finally I punched in the code Y'd given me and entered. One flight up and I was at the office door.

Breaking and entering is a specialty of mine. Mr. K has schooled me well on how every window and security device works. When he first arrived in New York, he took a job with the Lexington Lock and Security Company, a dubious entity owned by two partners who had P.I. licenses and had served time for aggravated trespassing. Neither K nor I have time to wait for a process that doesn't work anyway.

Still, the key would've been handy. I faced off against a steel door which was equipped with a full mortise lock: a pin-tumbler, latch, and dead bolt. It could have been drilled in seconds with a 5/32 bit that I didn't have handy. But that would have been too noisy and would have destroyed the lock, leaving aggressively obvious evidence that somebody had been poking around. Unzipping my pocket-size tool kit, I fingered a few implements. I tried out a feeler pick, which didn't work, so I switched to a rake, inserting it into the key way. It was left-handed, so I picked to the left, positioning the tension wrench on the left to hold the tumbler in place. My pick tunneled away, imitating the jagged ridges of the key.

It didn't take long to align all the pins. I moved the tumbler a full turn to the left, retracting the dead bolt, and then clicked the latch open with a half turn.

A narrow hallway unfolded before me. At the end of it was Ling's office. The door was locked with a simple latch. I slid a flexible metal shim up the doorjamb against the latch. The door sprung open.

It was the largest room in the suite, but still humble and nondescript—Communist style. For about three hours, I nervously pored over files and documents. In Manhattan alone, Ling owned over six hundred buildings. There were businesses on Fifth, Park, and Lexington, ranging from dry cleaners to electronic-parts manufacturers to health spas to shipping lines.

It was close to midnight.

Just then, I heard a noise and saw a long shadow along the wall in the corridor. It had a strange, cobra-shaped head. There was no time to find a hiding place, so I dropped to the floor and crawled out of Ling's office. The shadow disappeared. Behind me was a maintenance closet. I slowly eased the door open.

Inside there was a man standing there like a mummy. I wheeled around and cocked my fist to throw a punch.

"Sir, it is I," K said in a plaintive voice. "You would not strike your humble servant, would you?"

"K, what the hell!" I was shaking a bit, and trying not to raise my voice.

"Sir, did you have your dinner?" He held out a bag of Sunkist oranges and a knife. "I have just come to make certain that you are healthy, wealthy, wise, and, above all, safe. I know about Mr. Ling, and I was concerned. You must take now, sir," he added, gesturing with the bag. "*Coolie, goolie joolie*—food, clothing, and shelter—are the elements of life and are necessary, Sahib."

"You know I just came from dinner. You're concerned enough to give me a heart attack. Where did you get that crazy coat you're wearing?" K's coat made him look like the villain in a nineteenth-century melodrama. He also had on black sneakers—a hip nineties cat burglar. A speck of light from the street glinted off the stainless-steel Sikh badge of three swords, the *khanda,* pinned to the center of his black turban. "Sir, that was Chinese food. Ten minutes later, you are still hungry. I received this coat from my son, Sonny."

Even though I left him a note, I never expected him to show up. This was the K method: turn up in the oddest places at the weirdest times, and usually with fruit in a bag. No one knew how he managed to know where everyone was even when they were not supposed to be there.

"Sir, I am your devoted servant. *Ika nika hee, dos re nee maney,* that is my motto. I abide by it. 'In life, one must lead and one must follow.'"

I was about to close up shop, but K spotted a small maroon lacquered cabinet about two feet high, tucked away in a corner with some magazines piled up on top of it.

"Sir, have you taken notice of this? This piece of furniture. It is most unusual and from a foreign country, the land of China." The piece must have dated back to the Ch'ing or Ming Dynasty. We both had an appreciation for Chinese furniture. Over the years, I had spent many days at museums all over the world, studying and collecting the best of Chinese furniture makers.

I went over to get a closer look. It was a beautiful piece, probably worth more than fifty thousand. Inside were about twenty compartments.

"A couple of them might have false backs," K informed me. Chinese cabinetmakers are known for crafting inset or secret locks and secret compartments in their desks and cabinets. "The Chinese do not think like Westerners," K said wistfully and shook his head. "Very cunning and very mysterious." K closed both fists with his thumbs buried under his fingers. "They are of the view to lose their life but not to lose the penny. Among other distinctions," K said quietly, "their thoughts are formulated in tight, calculated dimensions. They are not predictable."

Investigating the interior, I found that each compartment was hand-painted with double and triple borders. On closer inspection with a penlight, I could discern the symbols quite clearly—the waves of an ocean and the swastika which is the ancient Tibetan symbol of good luck. The Chinese use it as the basic element in carpet border patterns, the symbol is continuously linked together, meaning endless good luck. My Chinese tycoon client had given me a rug as a present and explained the design.

There was a sailboat, a sampan, painted on the waves of the top compartment. As I went down the line, opening drawers, I noticed that the sampan moved forward, one wave for each drawer, until the voyage ended on the second to last drawer. A man and a woman suddenly appeared in the boat.

"Sir, they may be in some sort of trouble. Perhaps they are eloping," K ventured.

I released the inset locks slowly. K slid the drawer out. A second drawer shot out from the cabinet's side. Inside sat a piece of paper with a painting of the Imperial Palace in Peking, dated July 18, 1940. A small piece of paper explained that.

K whispered, "Ah, very fine. Ah, very good, sir."

It was embossed with what must have been symbols of the Imperial Palace—of most any Chinese religious celebration for that matter—a Buddha and vases of lotuses and peonies. The symbols were hand-painted and gold-leafed. The aesthetics were good, but what it said might even be better.

The paper was written in Chinese, scrawled out in ideographs along with another sheet of paper attached. I would have to get a translation. I asked K to make a photocopy at the machine located by the door, but he said the Xerox machine was too complicated. So I did it. I'd turn the photocopy over to Mercedes to deal with it. She knew all the good translation services in town. There would be no problem. We'd send one copy to Columbia University and another down to Chinatown. I had to be careful who I dealt with because they might be connected to Ling in one way or another. The old bastard even owned a mozzarella factory in Little Italy.

We closed up the cabinet, carefully replacing the drawers and latching them. My watch read 12:30 A.M. Time to get out of there.

The morning came with still no word about Y. The first thing I did was put Eyeballs on it, telling them to spare nothing to uncover everything about Y's whereabouts. I was damn worried. The police had called a few times, but the questions seemed perfunctory. They sounded like they were checking me out as one of the last people to see her and just waiting for the body to turn up. I was restless and wanted to deal direct. I called Windows.

"Any news about Y Ling?"

He breathed loudly into the receiver and said in a toneless voice, "I don't know why you give a damn. You screwing her?"

"It's a living. Purely professional." I yanked the phone cord as if it were tied around his neck.

"Look, Ocean, why don't you just go your way and let the New York City Police Department go theirs, because there is nothing I'm aware of in the department rules that allows us to work side by side with some rich broad's lawyer who's part-timing it as a private dick. You get it?"

"Yeah, but not from the same class of babes you do." I was getting very pissed.

"I thought you were one of them queers."

"The only person I'm queer for is you, darlin'."

"I'm a happily married man."

"Give my regards to your husband."

"Enough with that kind of talk, you fuckin' pansy."

"What's the word? I've got a personal interest, but then again, that might not mean anything to you since it's a woman."

"Well it does, and all I can tell you is she's still missing and the condition we found her apartment in tells me that she's in a lot of trouble. Up to her neck, if it's still connected to her body . . ."

Enough. I slammed the receiver down.

Horace the new night man handed me a letter, which he said had been hand-delivered before he came on shift. It had that special smell and look. I opened it and read it through once just for the experience and a second time for content.

Johnny,
    Call me. I am dying to know how everything went in court.

Pandora

The original of the Chinese document was in my top drawer. I stored it in the wall safe and called Pandora. The number had been changed with no referral message. Typical.

I lit a cigarette and went to the liquor cabinet. After dropping a few ice cubes in a glass, I poured myself a double vodka and instinctively walked to the phone to call Pandora again, forgetting that I didn't have a working number. Just as I touched the phone, it rang.

Windows's voice came as sharp as an arrow from a crossbow. "Ocean, I told you I'd get back to you."

He never opened a conversation with anything other than your last name. I could hear him calling his wife by her maiden name: "O'Hooligan, call the deli. The Jets are getting killed, and we're out of cheese balls."

I braced myself, knowing from the sound of his voice there was a reason for the call other than courtesy. Windows wasn't the type to call back, ever, without bad news.

"The Y girl—you know, the Chinese babe? The one you're so interested in? Well, she's been located." That was a strange way to put it.

"What do you mean, 'located'?"

"What I mean, Ocean, is that she can't talk to you right now. There's a slight problem. She's a little bit dead."

As much as I'd expected that, I never could have been prepared for it. My stomach wrenched and I couldn't hold back the tears. I didn't want to control it. Windows's horrific voice kept asking me if I was still there, but I buried the phone under the couch cushions and tried to pull myself together. A long time later I hung the phone up and looked in the mirror. My face was swollen and my eyes were two ugly tiny slits. The phone rang again, seconds later.

"Why'd you hang up on me, Mr. Ocean?" Windows demanded.

"How did it happen?" I asked and shuddered.

"We found her in the basement of her building. Don't think she was there the first time around. Been shot once—neat, professional—right through the neck. A beautiful piece of meat left on the floor, bleeding to death. Neighbors say nothing, except your fortune cookie led quite a life. And that's all she wrote."

"Who found her?" I was freaking.

"The super. He was working on the furnace. She was around the back, dressed in one of those Chinese numbers, a shiny green one with the slit up the side. Maybe he thought he was going to get lucky."

My emotions were running all over the table, and I hoped my shaky voice wasn't a giveaway. I kept thinking I got involved in a simple civil case that was more about murder than money. When the pilot tells you the flight will be smooth, somehow there's always turbulence along the way. That's Dyson Airlines.

I desperately wanted to feel sorry, to say something for Y, but I had to stay cold and professional if I was going to find out who killed her.

Without another word, I let the phone hang off the coffee table as Windows yakked away until he realized this time he was talking into space. Silence. That meant he must have hung up and decided not to call back again.

I had warned myself about a lot of things. Better to quit. Better to dump this case before it's too late. Stay alive for another case, when the odds of getting wiped are ten to one instead of two to one. Better to take on a few mild-mannered claims—housewives slipping on grapes at the A & P, speeding tickets. Word process a few contracts. Form a couple of corporations, and stay clear of the machine-gun fire.

But no, it wasn't going to be that way. Pandora had me. And I was bright enough to know how dumb I was.

Wicked. The night was going to be wicked. The thought of Y dead was enough to keep me housebound. I didn't want to sleep, but I wanted peace of mind, a resolution.

K called and I told him about Y. He kept saying over and over, "Oh, my Lord, oh, my Lord, she was a very nice and gracious lady. I am very sad, sir. She was very devoted to you as well. Sir, we will miss her, oh, oh, oh, oh." Then he hung up.

I was a pro, up against other pros. Like me, they had cold vodka and brains. Only they killed, I didn't.

It was time to get out. Certainly Pandora could replace me, and she could vent those considerable charms on more men like me in this big city that is brimming with lawyers who won't admit they love intrigue and pretty women. Bullets are another story.

I was getting drunker. I went for the phone to call the answering service. Was the call from Windows a mistake? It slipped out of my hand and skidded across the coffee table, crashing on the floor. I knelt and picked it up. I had a great respect for telephones, but it wasn't mutual, considering all the trash that had filtered through them to me over the years. I was feeling sorry for myself, wanted something to make up for Y getting whacked in the basement and Pandora's evil, self-involved ways.

Screw it. There was no way I could stay at home. Forget the answering service. I went out to get drunker. There was the night—hot, steamy as a busted radiator valve, and I needed to cool off.

I walked down Third Avenue and rolled into a funk bar emanating Meters riffs from a good sound system with a sub-woofer. The bar was practically empty. Me and the woofer, what a pair.

The Body-by-Jake bartender brought me a draft, then a bottle, another bottle, and my head began to go into a pleasant boozy spin. I didn't want to talk to myself anymore about the case, and I didn't.

This was a joint I used to hit years ago when I first got my P.I. license. I remembered the cases that I took on. Following middle-aged, obese husbands around to fleabag neon-lit hotels at the request of their even more obese wives. Paranoid wives calling me in to sweep their apartments for bugs and cautioning me not to get the place messy. The shit stuff. Suddenly it was like I never left. This case merely involved high-class shit wasting human life. I hadn't come any great distance. I had about five more tepid drafts and felt my stomach painfully bloat into a medicine ball.

When I drink like that, I just put my head down and stare at the bar from one-sixteenth of an inch away until I'm ready to go home.

Time floated by on an ocean of Budweiser.

In my stupor I charted the entire case, drawing every damn diagram, writing a million different stories in my mind to explain what had gone down. It seemed unlikely that Babette would have anything to do with killing anyone, but who else could it be? Pandora was the one who had something to lose and nothing to gain by doing away with Rogers and Y. Rogers and Y—now both dead. That meant something, and it had to mean that the same person wanted both of them out of the way. I had to get out of there. As I placed a fifty on the moist darkwood bar I got a call on my cell phone. Patton.

"John, get a load of this. Weird coincidence. That bouncer from the Veranda Club is hanging around the Black Curtain. We put a tail on him."

"What the—?" I was surprised.

"He may be looking for you, but I think you better be looking for him," Gerry continued through my mumble and he was right.

"Done."

"Good, I'm going home. Can you handle it?"

"Done." I folded my phone closed.

Right up Third, around a corner, two blocks west, under the open awning, through the glass door, and there I was, sliding safely into table number 4. If I had to work it was great that it was familiar territory.

André was there but pretended not to notice me as his black mane swept around the room like a weeping willow in the wind. Very unusual for him to be unfriendly. Katrine, a great-looking Austrian waitress I fooled with about a year ago, was wearing black tights, no bra, and a cotton top. Her lips were painted bright red, and she fidgeted with a Camel. She asked me if I was alive, and before I had a chance to answer, André punched up the music and killed the lights. The black curtain split and rolled out to the sides of the stage. The bouncer wasn't anywhere.

A four-man band dressed in black stood on stage, their backs to the diners. They went into a huddle and slowly began to rap. The patter escalated to harmonies that soon evolved into a song backed by typical, predictable licks. The crowd was surprised to see the curtain lift; apparently there hadn't been a show there in a while.

André was continuing to purposefully ignore me, yakkety-yakking at a customer who was only interested in what was happening onstage. The lead singer began to hum into a mike. He looked familiar, but maybe it was because he was a rocker of the Britain-circa-1970 vintage, complete with spiked hair, rough complexion, and sweat. Returning my stare, he yanked the mike stand closer and began to sing in falsetto: "I'd like to get to you / I want to get you / I need to get you / And when I do, that'll be the end of you. Well, well, well."

He rocked back on his heels, shook his hips, and nearly toppled over several times as he screamed the refrain into the mike. The gyrations—the manic writhing, the coked-out grinding—took him shimmying around the stage and out to the tables. The performance lasted about fifteen minutes. I looked long and hard at the creature in skintight leather and said to myself, I should have ordered in.

Finally the curtain closed, and André turned to me and nodded his head, a cue for me to come to his table. The applause was fairly enthusiastic, which only meant that a lot of the regulars had better things to do that evening than turn up at the Curtain. I downed the rest of my vodka, pushed the table to one side, and rather unsteadily made my way to André on the other side of the room.

"André, who's the singer? I want a word with him, tell him to step into the street."

The sidewalk wasn't far away but it seemed to be, and I knew why. I was blitzed. The chanteur stood by the curb. The convulsing performance had stopped.

"Hey you," I said. "I know you from somewhere and I'm gonna get to know you well."

"Really, wise ass? You want some company?"

"I'm dating myself. And after your music, we'd like to be alone."

"Why don't you go fuck yourself?"

"I don't do virgins."

"I ought to belt the fuckin' shit outta you," he growled. I could see his right hand balling into a fist—just when I was going to ask for his autograph. I could imagine that fist pulverizing my face.

He shoved a wooden toothpick in his mouth, then it came to me. The dim-witted bouncer didn't seem to recognize me. And tonight, he was raring to put my lights out and demolish my sound system. In this vodka-muddled state of mind, I didn't give a damn. I thought I could take him under the weather with me. Easy.

"Aren't you the singing bouncer?"

"I'm off tonight. Haven't seen you lately."

For a second, I thought that I was sobering up. Hoping like hell he might have something useful to tell me, I laid off the sarcasm. "What's your name, anyway? I forgot."

"Brian. My friends call me Crowbar."

"Look Bri, the night I came by the Veranda, what time did you see Pandora?"

"I don't remember seeing her. Well, wait one minute. I know I was surprised 'cause I hadn't heard her name for a long time. But that's not unusual—that group of assholes she runs with hit a different club every other night. But I didn't see her that night. I just remember . . ."

"What?" I asked, now momentarily sober enough to follow a more complicated narrative.

"There was a man in the back of the limo. No, wait a second, there might have been someone else, but some white-haired guy handed me the envelope. There could'a been a woman with him. I guessed Mrs. Markham was there with him in the backseat. Now hold on here, did I say 'Hello, Mrs. Markham'? Anyways, I didn't get an answer. I didn't think about it. That happens to us slaves. A lot."

"Did you get a look at her?"

"Don't remember."

"Think about it, Bri."

"Nothing to think about. A hundred cars come in every night."

"Think!"

"What's in it for me?"

I stood back, looked at the light traffic running up Madison, and thought this might be a hustle. But the answer wasn't in one of those cars.

"Buy you a drink inside? I have a Curtain card." I tried a joke he wouldn't get.

"I get comped in there. So fuck your drink."

"Yeah, I could see you getting off on that."

"Get offa my ass."

Well, maybe I was drunk.

I slapped a hundred dollars into Bri's palm. "Bill Rogers. Let's try that for starters," I said.

"Came down to the club a few times, like I told you that night. And the cops was there askin' about Pandora. You asked about her. They was inside waitin' on Pandora."

"Why?"

"They wanted to know what time she was comin' in and who she was with, and they told me it had somethin' to do with some lawyer named Ocean who got shot workin' on a case or somethin'. And then you show up with your dog in a Bentley. Anything else?"

"That's nothing I didn't know before."

"That's bullshit."

"Before I put another nickel in your meter, baby, I want a sample of the work. *Capisce?*"

"Russian, eh?"

"No. Just an expression I use when I talk to wise guys like you looking for a handout." He shot me a right in the stomach—a thunder sandwich. I didn't keel over, but I felt the punch solidly. I started throwing every fist I could. Trash cans tumbled into the street like dominoes.

His boat-sized shoe came at my face. My hands grabbed it, twisting him to the sidewalk. It sounded like a condemned factory collapsing. The bartender and a couple of waiters were pulling at my neck, and two husky customers were down on Bri. I bet his mom called him Bri when he sat at the kitchen table eating eight eggs, three quarts of milk, and a couple pounds of steak as she looked on and thought about how much she liked to see her son eat—eat up and get real big and healthy, and go out into the world and become a successful bouncer. I ate sparingly. My mother wanted me to be a C.P.A.

My nose and a few ribs felt broken. I think I busted a few teeth out of Bri's mouth, because my knuckles were gashed.

"C'mon, c'mon, you want a piece of me?" Bri howled.

"Yeah, I want a piece of you. That little brain of yours will be coming out of your ear," I yelled.

Bri and I hit the street, and it began again under the lights of Madison Avenue. I managed to free myself and smashed away at his bloody Formica face, fighting the stiffness in my shoulder. He grabbed my throat with one hand, closing his fingers around my Adam's apple. I stood and my foot shot between his meaty thighs, whacking him in the nuts. He rolled into the gutter away from me.

"Cut the shit," one of the customers shouted. I could just make out a siren squealing several blocks away.

Bri wasn't going to put up any more of a fight. There were too many onlookers by then, and any minute the cops were going to show.

"What the hell did you fly off the handle for?" Bri shouted. "I was about to give you some dope, would've saved yourself a lotta walkin' and talkin'."

"How's that?"

With his right hand, he pushed himself off the ground.

"Believe me. I can help you," he said.

For a he-man, he wasn't very tough on the inside. Or the outside, for that matter.

"So talk to me."

"Pandora hasn't been around the Veranda for about a year. And Rogers? He wasn't there the other night either, probably off with those creeps who work for Mr. Ling. And I ain't seen none of that ritzy-titzy mob since Rin Tin Tin ate Kennel Ration on TV. You been had."

"What?" I broke a sweat that had nothing to do with the fury of the fight. "What did you say?"

"Some old geezer, some old fart who looked like a billy goat brought that letter down for you and said to tell you it was from her, maybe he was just a messenger. Yeah, the dude I described in the limousine."

"What else did he say?"

"He gave me twenty bucks."

I ran my hand along the back of my neck, feeling the soreness, making me more inclined to kill this son of a bitch. But he was telling the truth. No reason to make up a story, and he didn't seem to have any idea of what was going on in the case. However, he knew the dramatis personae.

"And you're looking to make new friends? Is that why we just happened to walk into the same bar tonight?" I asked, knowing I'd never get a straight answer.

"That's life."

Now we were talking like two businessmen making a deal. The moon shined down on our punched-out faces full of mañana's aches and pains.

It was time to head home.

Bri walked me up Madison, and our odd alliance was struck. The story was that a certain gray-haired man—slick-looking, well-dressed—met regularly with Rogers at the Veranda. Pandora wasn't present at those meetings. The man and Rogers would have intimate conversations at the bar, in the parking lot. Sounded like thick dealings.

Bri's help was limited. He didn't know the man, never went out of his way to ask. Didn't even know if Mr. X was a member of the club. The whole thing didn't interest him until he found out that Rogers got blown off the planet. When I asked him about Y, he denied knowing her, much less knowing she met her maker in a boiler room. Bri was neither a master of deception nor of description. Most witnesses are just as deficient; lawyers suffer through the process of extracting information from the swamp of mediocrity. So I thanked Bri for the broken tidbits. Just getting them had been a deeply painful experience. The case was a domestic daisy chain—all the players knew one another or had been married to one another. Now there was a new boy in town, a gray-haired phantom. He might have been Rogers's bookie, or a fellow lush or just another waste of time.

When I got inside the front door, I saw a package—it was getting to be a pattern—waiting for me inside the front door, neatly wrapped by someone who had *beaucoup de* time to waste. Upstairs, I opened the gold wrapping and found a soft, black, leather-bound address book. Inside, Pandora had quite artfully written her name, address, and new telephone number in dark blue ink. The rest of the book was blank. It was just another clever handkerchief drop, keeping me interested by way of a little gesture.

I didn't waste any time. It was 4:30 A.M. I dialed it.

I ran my free hand across my jaw, finding small islands of dried blood in my 5:00 A.M. shadow. There were large lumps and there were small ones. I could barely touch most of my face. She picked up, knowing it was me.

"Did you get my present?" Her voice was chilling. I thought of Y's body on a cold slab at the Medical Examiner's office. That made me feel guilty.

"I can always use my client's telephone number." The pain from the fight jabbed at me each time I delivered a word into the telephone.

"The closer we get to the trial, the more you're going to need to be in touch with me." She stopped short. Silence.

Then she said, "The whole thing frightens me, lawyers especially. First, I get sued for millions. Then Bill is dead. Look what's happened since you've been representing me. Now what if I have to go to court and testify? The police have been around here tonight, looking to talk to me about Bill. They told me about that woman you asked me about, Y. She was shot in the neck . . . what a way to die. I don't want to be next. I'm scared. Maybe I should just give the money back."

She burst into a strange staccato weeping. It was the first time she seemed at all normal, and of course my heart went out to her, even though she'd already made it clear that she had no feelings for anyone except herself.

Recovering, she asked, "When is the next court date?"

"Tomorrow, but it may be postponed."

"You let me know."

The sun was coming up. I leaned across the bed and drew the blinds. And then she disconnected me as I asked myself, "If Windows and Slice got into the apartment why hadn't I?"

CHAPTER TWELVE

Around 5:30 the next afternoon I went for a walk up Park Avenue. There was nothing on my calendar. Destination Pandora.

At a pay phone across from her building I called the office to see if there were any messages. The answering machine picked up.

Betty put me on hold for a solid five minutes. Instead of getting pissed off, I put the time to good use, scanning the windows on the Caprice's eighth floor as I paced the street. I thought about Pandora and the nights she had spent on the phone in that apartment, double-talking me to death. What was going on in her scheming little mind?

From Park Avenue I looked up at the apartment as if it were moving.

Betty finally came back on. "You got a call here from a Brian. Don't know him—sounds nice. Is he married?"

"Yes. What did he say?"

She gave me a number, and I dialed it. It was the Veranda. The bartender dredged up my bouncer-source right away.

"Johnny, this is Bri," he reported, in the tone of an employee on the job. "How much is my pay?"

"Five hundred a week. Let's see how the first week goes." I

didn't mind giving him money for information and welcomed his new and improved attitude. "So what's up?"

"Last night there was a scene here when I was busy kicking your ass. Right after that, the cops showed up again . . . a Lieutenant Windows and some other cop name Slice. They left business cards and interviewed some of the staff. I never saw a cop's card except on TV. They were digging 'round for shit on Rogers and Pandora. They want me to come down to the station. Now why the hell would they be askin' for me? Unless . . ."

"Unless what? Don't hold out on me, Bri."

"What if they wanna know about the night I gave you Mrs. Markham's letter?"

"Who gives a damn? Tell 'em. Ever see any of the Chinese heavies around the club?"

"You mean guys deliverin' sweet-and-sour pork, some shit like that?"

"Forget about it. Confucius say: 'Just tell me what happened last night so I solve today's problem'."

"The bartender said they wanted to know when was the last time Rogers came 'round. Didn't say a word about Rogers joinin' the cadaver club. They wanted to know who he hung out with at the Veranda. They talked to everyone. Said they might be back."

"Did they mention a woman named Y Ling?"

"No, but I saw her on TV. Man, she had the angles. She must of been a stripper or something."

"Brian, wipe the drool off your chin and tell me what happened with the cops. Anything else? I gotta be somewhere." As I said "somewhere," I raised my eyes to the eighth floor.

"Nothing. That's all I got." He was acting more and more like a hamster than a skull-cracker.

I hung up, called Pandora, and got no answer. Good. I went over near the service entrance and waited on the street for the locked door to open. A short time passed, then a blue-haired, stern-faced matriarch exited with a large white poodle. They were equally coiffed—she at Kenneth's, he at Château Pom-Pom. Her dog pissed up a storm, probably killing most of the ivy patch around the base of a pear tree opposite the entrance. The poodle's right leg went down, and they turned and marched back into the building.

In life, timing can hinge on a dog's urge to take a leak—just ask Humphrey Macefield. I caught the door and entered the rear stairway, which led directly to the service entrances for each apartment. Racing up the eight flights, I was closer than ever to headquarters. The elevator would have posed too much of a risk. The tenants would be heading out for dinner—the 6:00 to 8:00 P.M. lobster-thermidor-and-rice-pudding crowd.

There were only two apartments to a floor, and I wasn't sure which one was Pandora's until I heard an older woman and an exotic bird having a conversation in 8B. I entered the main hall, but Pandora's front door was locked with a fancy piece of brass hardware.

I returned to the service entrance. It had a simple cylinder and no dead bolt. For a graduate of K's lock-picking school, it should have been a snap. But there was a heavy chain on the inside as well. After about twenty minutes of playing drop-the-screwdriver, I was able to release the doorjamb plate; the chain fell to one side.

After repairing the chain lock, I walked through the kitchen, which looked as if no one had cooked a meal there in ten years. The forties walls could have used a helping of new plaster.

There wasn't a sound in the place. The layout was strange. There was one long central corridor, an avenue of closets. Each door bore a framed white sign describing the contents: SHORT EVENING WEAR, LONG EVENING WEAR, SHORT SUMMER SUITS, SUMMER SLACKS, SUMMER TOPS, FURS, SPORTSWEAR. A whole closet devoted to bikinis. It wasn't much different from a department store.

A door at the end of the hallway opened into a large bedroom that had been meticulously worked over by an East Side decorator. The furniture was flaming Moroccan. The floor was layered with Persian rugs. The room had Bohemian charm.

After all of these weeks of telephone talk, there was the bed where she lay playfully twisting the cord as she coaxed me into one sexy little corner after another, trying to checkmate me.

But the phone that I imagined rang so much was dusty; it looked like it hadn't been used for a few days. She was probably off visiting Tuxedo Park or Locust Valley. Predictable, but it made for an empty apartment for me.

I started to rifle through her desk, a small Victorian secretary against one wall. Nothing. I slid each drawer out with care, looking to see if anything had been taped to any of the panels. I opened a closet door.

I scanned the place for a safe. There didn't appear to be one in here or elsewhere. I was about to leave when I noticed that the trompe l'oeil walls to the bedroom were actually sliding doors. Pushing one of them to the side, I saw the fluorescent light go on automatically, flickering. Instinctively, I wanted to replace the bulb, but I was already doing my share of those in her life.

Right in the front was an old suitcase covered in expensive tan alligator, with the initials P.M. on a gold plate near the handle. The bolts clicked open easily. I fished through silk side pockets and compartments, not really knowing what I was looking for. I was desperate to find out anything—anything at all—about Pandora.

Inside was a disorderly pile of documents: shares in her cooperative apartment mixed in with blue-chip stock certificates, a modest life-insurance policy, and recent brokerage statements that showed she was far richer than she described to me. But the bulk of the $170 million wasn't in the market. There was her divorce judgment against Rogers. When she sought to end the marriage, she charged him with cruelty.

My eyes fell upon a thin sheaf of paper. It was Pandora's will, dating from the time she was married to Rogers. I'd drafted hundreds just like it myself. Moving to her desk, I read it carefully. She had left her entire estate to Rogers. I was surprised she didn't have a prenuptial agreement, because that's common when a rich woman marries for the second time, especially to a nut like Rogers. But Pandora had chosen not to cut him out in a prenup or in her will. In fact, they had made *mutual* wills, leaving everything to one another, depending on who died first.

Clipped to the back of the papers was a 1996 letter from Rupert Hargrove, telling Pandora she'd forgotten to nullify her will when she divorced Rogers, and imploring her to come by the office and sign a new one. If there had been a separation agreement between her and Rogers, they might have waived their rights to inherit from one another. But no, Pandora and Rogers had no separation agreement. She'd sued him for cruel and inhuman treatment, and the divorce was granted on those grounds.

Hargrove had told me about their nasty trial with all the vitriolic trimmings. There was the time Pandora threw a bottle of vintage claret at Rogers in Harry's Bar. Their last Christmas together, Rogers pulled a smoldering log out of the fireplace, merrily wrapped it in the drawing-room drapes, and thrust it into Pandora's arms, screaming, "Look, bitch, if this doesn't make you hot for me, there's more where that came from."

Most couples file for divorce in January after having suffered through Thanksgiving, Christmas, and New Year's together.

It was easy to compute: since the will didn't have CANCELED written across the signature page and was still in her papers, it was in effect. That was wildly careless for someone with serious assets. Like a lot of clients I'd had, she probably thought she'd eventually get around to it. Still, she played such hardball negotiating my fee that it was difficult to comprehend why she didn't immediately follow Hargrove's advice and get the will changed.

I flipped to a third document. It was a note from Marcel:

Darling,

I know this sounds ridiculous, but if it were not for Bill, we never would have met. I feel terribly guilty about taking you from him. If anything happens to me, whatever I leave you, I want some of it to go to Bill when you pass away. I know you understand.

Marcel

Here was another insane gift: Marcel feeling awful about skating off with his best friend's girl, and the guilt trip had a price of $170 million. This wasn't the Catholic Charities—it was a crazy bunch of rich jerks who didn't know what to do with the bucks.

I went to replace the briefcase and noticed that men's clothes were hanging in the closet: the shoes were size nine, not Marcel's eleven; a dark blue pinstripe suit, another one in gray—both of them made by one of New York's best custom tailors. I saw a pair of brown-and-white wingtips that I'd wear to the University Club if I were lunching with Jay Gatsby. I tried on the jacket. It was just about my size, a 40. I held out the pants, which were close to my length. Marcel had weighed two hundred pounds and was about six foot three. No way were these his clothes.

I should have known. She was living with another man. All this time I'd suffered through the case, deluding myself that I had a chance, imagining there was no one else. The only relief was to see that whoever he was, he hadn't fully moved in. Outside of the few suits, there really wasn't a male presence in the bedroom.

But in the bathroom, there was a straight razor, shaving cream, and aftershave. I advanced through the premises on my dual quest—to find out more about my client and to discover all I could about any competitor for her affections who might be in the picture.

I continued to take inventory. Pandora had a great library off the living room. A lot of first editions. Every piece of furniture was a collector's item—beautifully lacquered side tables and Chippendale armchairs.

Any moment she could be back, so I had to beat it—not that I would have altogether minded being caught. Returning to the bedroom, I took one more look in the closet. In the corner of the walk-in, cedar-lined room there was a chest of drawers. I switched on a lamp on top of the dresser. It was stuffed with lingerie. A red bra and a pair of red silk bikini panties stared back at me. Too bad I was going to miss the late show.

As I started to close the drawer, my right hand crossed my face and rubbed my lips. Pandora appeared in my mind, holding her hand out to the man in the blue pinstripe suit.

His fingers unbuttoned her dress carefully as if the contents were fragile. She wore no makeup, no lipstick. The dress slithered down to her waist. He ran his palms over her shoulders, stroking her violet nipples until each stood rigid as an eraserhead.

She cried out, pulled his head up to hers, and violently thrust her tongue in his mouth, pulled it out and said, "Touch my clit, touch my goddamn clit, now. . . . Put, put your fingers inside my cunt, one at a time. Get it, get it good, that's so good," she murmured, and his hand obeyed.

Slowly she unzipped his fly and pulled out his hard-on as he slammed her back on the breakfast table. A maid entered and began to set the table around them for breakfast. A butler poured mimosas into tall crystal glasses. Spode china and silverware rattled around them as he fingerfucked her rhythmically. She slid off him and dropped to her knees, stroking him, then taking his cock in her mouth, relentlessly sucking it as she grasped the small of his back with her hands and pumped him into her.

One thing I knew as I stood flat-footed in Pandora's bedroom was that she'd made love to many men. So why was I being jerked around? I couldn't even screw her in my own fantasy.

An oyster-hued moon floated beyond a formation of skyscrapers outside her window. Closing my eyes, I was being tricked again, dying to get into that glistening orifice, like last night on the phone. It was 8:00 P.M.

My mind hung on Pandora like an old laundry bag on a door hook. I should have handed it off to the maid and told her to watch the starch. There was a knock at the door.

Quietly I raced down the corridor and planted my eye against the peephole of the service entrance. It was a handyman carrying a black toolbox. As I waited for him to pull out a passkey, a bead of my sweat sailed to the linoleum. He stood on the spot for about five minutes, determined bastard, perversely pressing the bell until I thought the chimes were going to summon the hunchback of Notre Dame.

Just as he fumbled for the key, I flung open the door.

"You're here from the magazine, right? But you and I have worked together before. Morocco! The Mamounia. In Marrakesh. Your book, did it ever come out?"

His eyes blinked. "My book?"

He pulled out a grimy, coffee-stained spiral notebook with "Our Lady of the Saints" printed on the cover. "My book says there's been a report of a gas leak. I gotta check out the pilot light on that there stove."

"Francesco, you think I forgot that time you pretended you were with housekeeping and burst into my room to count the bags of smoked almonds and Jack Daniel's empties in the Mamounia minibar? Let me get that for you," I said, grabbing his toolbox and heaving it onto the same kitchen table where minutes before, Pandora was breakfast. "It's a good thing you showed up. The caterer's on the way, and we're going to need that oven. He must be downstairs. Be right back."

I took off, down the back stairs and out the service door. The caterer wouldn't have anything to worry about. But maybe I did. Pandora had an electric stove.

CHAPTER THIRTEEN

The minute I got home I dialed Hargrove. I wanted to double-check the will. Of course he wasn't in. What would Hargrove be doing in his office? He usually worked two days a week and left mid-afternoon. I left a message with his service to call me right away.

I asked K if we'd had any word from our Chinese translation scholars. He said no. K was wearing yellow Bermuda shorts, a Jimi Hendrix at Woodstock T-shirt, a bright red turban, black socks, and unlaced red Nike high-tops. He was in the kitchen, stirring a pot of brown basmati rice with one hand and holding a cup of tea in the other. A veil of steam swirled around his ghost-like face as he put the tea down. Without turning, he said quietly, cutting an onion into the pot, "Sir, we must pray. Now we are nearing the beginning of the trial. We must come to the point, like this grain, which is sharp on the ends, not round like ordinary rice."

The pungent scent—coriander, cumin, red chilies—was suffocating.

"Sir, you must take," K said, pointing to a full bowl.

Ignoring the food, I dialed up Eyeballs and got one of the

night-shift secretaries. I told her to get one of the investigators to call me as soon as possible on the Ling matter.

Nothing happened for several days where the court was concerned. Macefield had pneumonia and would be out for at least a week. It was the standard unforeseen delay that occurs in every case. In the interim, I worked intensively on the case and did what was needed to keep up with the rest of my practice.

In the midst of my research I wasn't taking or making calls except to try to reach Pandora, but it was no use. I wrote her a letter explaining what was happening with the trial and still heard nothing. If the trial went forward and she was unreachable, could I explain that to Judge Macefield? I could just picture him politely granting me an indefinite adjournment.

The Sikh intelligence network fanned out all over Manhattan on the case. Night after night K returned to the house, snapping his fingers in front of my eyes, chanting the fugue refrain: "Sir, the client, she is not available. She has slipped away and, moreover, she never turned up. *Lurki chali gaei tay mur kay kaday na hei.*"

It was a good thing for Pandora that Macefield was laid up. I even called Hargrove again since he hadn't called me. Our conversation led nowhere. I had to reveal that I was searching for Pandora. It was embarrassing. Had he ever seen the original promissory note? No, sorry. Didn't understand what I was talking about when I asked him if he'd researched the gift issue. Just as I was about to say good-bye, I hinted there was a memo, a document in the file indicating that Pandora had never changed her will.

Hargrove told me that he'd been on her case to do it, but she kept making and breaking appointments. Sounded familiar.

Her call finally came in while I was out. I eventually reached her from a pay phone in the street, but her line was on call-forwarding—I could hear the tone change. I half expected a man to answer. But it was her.

"Pandora, it's your lawyer."

"Johnny!" she said. I'd never heard her so excited. "I'm so glad you called. There are some very strange things going on, and I am so worried."

It came as no surprise that pressure was being applied to her, the same way Ling had come on to me.

"What's happened?"

"I think someone is going to kill me." She was getting hysterical. I tried to calm her down; she only went more out of control.

"Who's after you?" I asked her.

"I . . . I . . . don't know."

"Do you have an idea?"

"No . . . no, except that someone's been in my apartment."

"What?" I pulled my feet off the desk and sat up straight.

"I can tell. Certain things are moved around in the dressing room." For a moment she said nothing; the silence roared.

"The armoire. It has to be shut a certain way; otherwise it won't close. The hinges are uneven, and when I came home, one door was wide open and the back door to my apartment was unlocked. Also, I have a silent alarm system—motion detectors—they were triggered. It was reported to the police, but in this city, by the time they arrived, whoever it was had left."

There was no armoire and no silent alarm. Fishing to see if I'd mistakenly contradict her. Did she think it was me? If she had definitive proof, it could ruin me. I didn't flinch.

"Did they take anything? Anything valuable?" I realized I should stick to the notion that it was a theft. It would deflect the attention away from me.

"No, no, dammit to hell, no. That's just it. They didn't take a thing. Nothing. And it scares me, because they were able to get into the building. Johnny, you have to help me."

Since when did I have to uncover the mysteries of her life outside the convoluted legal side of the case? Now she was asking me to catch myself. I changed the subject quickly.

"Right now, I have to concentrate my efforts on the trial. I'm certain Macefield is going to call it for some time in the next week. That's what we've got to prepare for. If we win, everything else means nothing, this other stuff will go away. Someone, probably Babette, is acting desperate, maybe she was there trying to find some evidence against you." I tried to sound reassuring.

"I'm getting so paranoid. And today, some of my mail was opened . . . and there was an empty envelope." Her fright was discharging. She was turning aggressive.

"You won't believe this—it was from Babette. So I called her but last time all her talk came to nothing. Her lawyer never said a word to you about settling. But all I got this time was a machine."

"Well, try again. Time's passed. Maybe now she wants to end it. Maybe she sees the wisdom of not going to court, not airing all the dirty laundry that's floating around the Longwood legacy." Or maybe Babette was sending around a party invitation, a favorite pastime of the East Sixties residents. Time clearly meant something different to her than it did to me. She skated around the hiatus, kicking ice in my face.

"Yes, Johnny. I haven't heard from you. It's been so difficult getting you. I've had to find out from other sources what you're up to." I bit into that lie.

"Which other sources?"

"Rupert."

"You mean Rupert Hargrove?" I couldn't believe that she called him first.

"Right . . . the lawyer with the brains."

"Then we're in deep shit."

"You've got the balls." She said nothing about her own disappearance. "So you needed his advice?"

"I wouldn't exactly call it advice. I called him about your will. I came across it in the file."

I hesitated, knowing I'd screwed up. Now she'd ask me how I

knew about the will. But then I figured I could cover it, saying that Hargrove had sent it over with the rest of the papers and brought the issue up with me. So I pressed her. "About the will you made, where you led with your heart instead of your mind." My words bounced off a silent backboard.

"Oh, that will. That's been attended to. There's another bit of paper, a . . . what do lawyers call it? A codicil?" She was lying. "I did that right after we were divorced, and anyway, what the hell business is it of yours? I don't want you to do anything but what I hired you for. That's why Rupert is my regular lawyer. Damn it, Johnny! Stop right there and don't do anything except what you are supposed to! I have enough problems today."

The yelling ended there, and I just looked at the phone as if it had the plague. I was about to slam it against the coin box, but I got a grip. I decided to bluff.

"There was a copy of a letter to you in the file. Hargrove reminded you to change the will, like any competent lawyer would."

"I can leave anything to anyone I want. So I left everything to my ex-husband. So what? After all, Marcel died!"

There was a long pause. She broke it with a small, intimate laugh that I couldn't help but like.

"Actually, Mr. Ocean, I don't mind. You have to try and understand me, and anyway Bill *is* dead, so what is the difference? He can't possibly inherit. Isn't that how you'd put it? You're the first lawyer I have ever had who takes . . . such a personal interest in a case. And . . . that, *that* is a hard thing for me to become accustomed to."

"Anyway," I switched the subject back to the court, "the case is on the court's quick calendar, as I said in my letter. As soon as Macefield feels like it, the trial will begin. Could even be the same day he returns. He's got pneumonia—supposedly."

"That doesn't affect me," she said.

The cure for her problem was to make it my problem, no matter how infected the case was with her culpability, but she was only half correct. Technically, Pandora was not obligated to testify, but if she didn't in her own case it would look odd. The burden of proof was really on Babette's shoulders to enforce the validity of the loan. Babette was claiming Marcel had no business leaving the 170 mil to my client. But Babette would also have to prove that a fraud was practiced on her by her deceased brother. Or, in laymen's terms, she'd been screwed by a family member. A common occurrence for the last five million years. After all, if you can't hustle a blood relation, who can you con? Some countries have special family-fraud laws. In Switzerland, if a relative steals your money you have to sue your kin within ninety days, otherwise forget it.

"You won't have to testify, so there's nothing to worry about, and—"

She interrupted, plunging a stiletto right into my gut. "I won't take the stand. There is no need. I told you that from the beginning."

"Did you?"

"I had no knowledge of things, dealings, or anything that was negotiated between Marcel and Babette. How could I get in between those two? No one was able to do that. Where I come from—the way I was brought up—if you are a woman, you know nothing about financial matters. That was left entirely up to the man of the family—Marcel—although I know money wasn't his forte."

"You never told me you wouldn't testify. Do I have to tell you that the no-witness case is the toughest one for a lawyer to prove? The judge will want to hear from the person defending, that's you."

"I'm a defendant. I didn't do anything wrong!"

"You're the executrix trying to get the will probated. In the Surrogate's Court, since Babette is making a claim against you, she's called the claimant."

For the moment, I projected how the case would play without Pandora's brilliant contributions. I would take a few choice whacks at Babette and the other witnesses that the White Knuckle would drag into the Surrogate's Court. There would be a raft of maids, butlers, and other employees of Edgar and Babette, who would state, for the record, that they witnessed the deceased, Mr. Marcel Markham, cheat, con, trick, and defraud his poor little billionairess sister into forking over her late husband's bucks. The scheme would snake its way through the drawing room, the library, all the way down to the wine cellar of this plush Fifth Avenue abode. It made for as much chicanery as one would find in the boardroom of any Wall Street brokerage house.

The phone disconnected. At least I was well out of the woods on the break-in. I didn't know whether she hung up or not. As I reached for change to redial, I began to see the case like a sick plant. She'd hired me to spray the slugs but wouldn't allow me to use any pesticides. She'd inherited all the money rightfully, and we had the makings of a great case, especially in view of Babette's deposition. Now she was refusing to tie things up. No testimony. Nada.

"You there, lawyer?" she said after picking up on the fifth ring.

"I'm back," I answered that insulting tone.

"If I had a lot of money, I'd pay you an even larger retainer, just because I love to hear the sound of your voice at least once a day," she said with uncharacteristic sweetness. She was shuffling and reshuffling her moods, looking for a winning hand.

"I've heard that the best way to overcome temptation is to yield to it."

"Have I ever been tempted?" she asked.

"You and I were booted out of that Garden of Eden a long time ago."

"Is that where we met?"

"Yes, I recognize the face."

"And what about the body?" Her voice dropped off.

"Looks as good as the day we ate the fruit."

"Thanks for the compliment."

Before I could answer she switched subjects.

"I gave you a large retainer but I didn't want to interfere with your other cases, and I don't want to impose upon you. I realize you need money for the trial," she hurried on, "but you never did finish with Babette, like you promised—that the case would be done within the deposition stage, that she'd give up. Now we have a trial on our hands. A damn trial."

"And I'm going to have to try it, the hard way. On top of it, there are a thousand legal issues that are going to make a librarian out of me."

"Well, what's it going to cost?"

"Nothing more. I told you I'd throw in the trial for the two hundred thousand."

"Now you're unhappy about the arrangement. What's it going to take?"

If she wanted me to feel comfortable, I was graciously accepting it.

"I'll stick to my word."

"No, you're regretting it and I want your absolute best. So tell me, what else do you want?"

I gave in. "Fifty thousand for the first four days and after that, like I said before, ten thousand a day, including all the preparation, but not any costs like expert witnesses. If the trial lasts less than four days, I'll charge you a flat thirty-five thousand, which has to be paid up front. I take no part in any settlement. You get every penny of the verdict."

"What do you think I am?" she said. "Maybe I should have stuck with Rupert."

"Fine with me. Call him if you think he could successfully take on Bellicoso and the court."

"No, no," she said, switching again. "I want you. You're my lawyer. I appreciate you so much, and there are other things that you can do for me when the case is over."

Her voice rose excitedly on that hustle and I was turned around. Just like that we were back on track.

The next day while it drizzled I dictated some questions for trial to Mercedes, as well as Pandora's new retainer agreement, and reminded Mercedes to get on the translation of the Chinese document. Hands clenched behind his back, head bowed, wearing a bright yellow turban, a black linen suit, and tennis shoes, K worriedly paced back and forth in front of the office. The window was partially open and I could hear him reciting a prayer in Punjabi, barely aloud. He was becoming increasingly concerned about whether all the necessary investigation of the connections between the Longwoods, Y, and Mr. Ling could be completed prior to the trial. Whether or not it related to the case, K was dedicated to my safety and security.

As I was dictating, K entered and said he was praying for his friends, success against my enemies, and for Pandora's payment. He had been listening while I was speaking to her.

Pandora sent a messenger to pick up the agreement. A few hours later, the same messenger dropped off a cashier's check for thirty-five grand along with the signed agreement.

With the cash in the till, I already felt more secure. Then the phone rang. It was André.

"Johnny, you said to call if there was something for the Mrs. Markham case. Maybe I have someone who can help. See for yourself."

"I'll be there."

I didn't hesitate. At the Black Curtain André was bartending, which he seemed to be doing a lot of these days. Threading through a sidewalk full of linen-costumed cocktail drinkers I got to André. A cordless phone was pressed to his ear. He caught my eye and instantly poured me a stiff one. I was in an Absolut Pandora mood.

"Ocean, you want the usual table in the back? I kick them out. No, sit at the bar instead. Got a moment or two, we talk. I will be off the phone. Someone is bothering me . . . one fur coat, they claim it was ripped off from the restroom six months ago. Is this place responsible, *maître?*" André asked, kiddingly.

"Coat-check cases, that's section 201 of the General Business Law. Not my specialty, André." I sipped the drink unwilling to trade advice for vodka.

The Curtain was noisy. The crowd was fanatically smoking, yakking, drinking, and eating. There was hardly an empty table and the Curtain customers, studded with red wine, *salades vertes,* and small talk were having late-night kicks, bistro style.

While I waited for the maestro, I pulled up a stool at the end of the bar and as my shoes hit the brass footrest I believed things just might fall into place. At least Pandora's fee was straight, plus she and I had ended on a good note. A small celebration was in order, and I was at the Curtain anyway.

All of that had me swigging and waiting for André, who pointed to the clock and motioned for me to stay. It was around midnight. The Black Curtain was really cranking, the music turned way up. The diners were getting rowdy and compulsive about their Bordeaux. Having finished his business for the moment André poured himself a scotch, lit a cigarette, and started toward me.

Scribbled in pink script in the big art nouveau framed bar mirror was CHAMPAGNE BY THE GLASS, $10.00, KRUG $20.00. It should have read LIFE BY THE GLASS, FAIR MARKET VALUE. That commodity sure seemed to be cut-rate in the Markham case and getting cheaper by the hour. White votive candles burned in glass boxes methodically placed around the zinc bar as if a religious ceremony was about to take place.

André was understandably detained, speaking to a gorgeous creature sitting next to him at the bar. The face had understated, refined features that gave off a pearl-like radiance. I looked again. Okay, I got it—she was drop-dead dazzling. Her platinum blond hair was combed upward into curls, and triangular silver earrings dropped from her pierced ears. Caressing the side of her neck with her long fingernails, she teasingly took the drink from him. She placed her hand next to his; her slender fingers slowly, deliberately crawled up his arm, like a tarantula on a mission. She turned, her eyes and mine locked in a glance as André waved me over. When I came and sat next to her, she turned away from me, placing her hands on the bar.

Her dress was black, sleeveless, low cut, and short. I checked her out from behind, as I'm sure she expected. What I wouldn't do to get that back against the wall. She toyed with the ridges of a small gold cigarette lighter as if games of distraction were its purpose.

Crossing her black-stockinged legs, she asked André, "Is Johnny Ocean still working for Pandora on that big case you told me about?"

So much for trusting a bar owner. Again she revolved, checking me.

André answered, "On the job. See for yourself. This is Monsieur Ocean."

I didn't get her name; maybe he never said it.

"Do you know Pandora Markham?" I asked.

"That slut? She's one of my best friends." A laugh.

"Really, when's the last time you saw her?"

"I don't speak about people when they're not around to defend themselves. You're her lawyer." Case closed. Her hand brushed my arm. "You like looking at me?"

"I appreciate beauty. But you know what men say about attractive women?"

"No, tell me."

"Show me a beautiful woman and I'll introduce you to the guy who's tired of making love to her."

"You've been around the wrong men."

"Or the wrong women."

"Is it hot in here or is it just you?" she said.

"It's us."

"Every time I touch a lawyer I get burned."

"You must like the way it feels."

"Heard a few interesting things, that might make you think," André interjected. He pointed to her, "Chérie, she was in here the other night with me when two cops came in."

She shot me a shrink-wrapped smile and leaned against André as he continued, "I don't remember their names."

"Slice and Windows?" I was boiling with curiosity.

"Oui, that is it. Inspector Monsieur Lice and Monsieur Fenêtres."

Then his attention turned to a shouting waiter.

"Table 8 wants to pay with paper, no plastic, for two hundred fifty dollars."

André studied the out-of-town check and said to me, "So these guys were discussing the famous Edgar Longwood."

The woman pulled on a cigarette and André spoke through a cloud of her exhaled smoke. "They were joined by Webb Hartford. He's a nice man, a gentleman, comes here often. The three of them spoke about the famous Edgar Longwood."

André put up a finger for me to hold on and I sucked in a deep breath. Evidently he was indecisive about the check, holding it in one hand like a dead fish.

I ordered another. André excused himself to deal with more restaurant business—one of the customers complained about an extra bottle of wine on the tab. I watched the episode while she downed a martini.

André returned and de-Mastercharged the Beaujolais.

She decided to take up the conversation where André left off.

"They talked for a long time about Edgar Longwood with his physician, Webb Hartford."

André listened like a doctor with a stethoscope.

She continued, wanting me to hear every word, "The police seemed to have a lot of respect for the doctor. They had a few drinks, shook hands with him, and left. Webb Hartford was carrying a beautiful bag made out of seal skin. I liked it so much, it made me want to study medicine. Then I heard the cops talking after Webb split."

"What'd they say?" André stepped aside.

"Edgar must have paid Webb plenty, especially to hike to Wall Street during the day. Each time the Doc showed up, Edgar invited him for lunch and the Doc stayed, ate in the executive boardroom, just the two of them."

"This was one M.D. who had time on his hands," I said to myself, feeling confused.

"You should relax, it's a free country. I like to talk, just don't have my own show. The cops even asked me to have a drink. Not for me."

Her lips parted; her tongue flicked her teeth for an instant. Very pretty, very twisted. Who was she? Had I pushed some coy button in a fairy tale and this creature emerged from the Curtain's darker recesses? Damned if she didn't look like someone. Had I slept with her? There was no way I'd forget that. Slipping further from sobriety, I threw down another drink that had somehow found its way into my hand.

The next sound I heard was André over the din asking her to come with him. I turned away for a second and when I looked back, she was gone and so was he.

That was about 1:30 and I stepped out of the Curtain toward my house. The street seemed like a grimy, empty tunnel that I was rambling down holding a wet sack of weird facts that André and the babe left me before disappearing into the void. As I arrived at the corner of East Sixty-seventh and Madison, I began to regain my senses, having a sudden inspiration—an urge to read the files. What could I discover about Webb's visits to Edgar? What exactly did Webb do for him when Edgar got really sick? Were they friends like Marcel and Edgar? Delayed reaction—why didn't I focus more on Edgar to begin with? After all, that's where the money came from, and if it weren't for the Longwood greenbacks, there'd be no case.

I nearly tripped over a pair of large feet sticking out of the darkness. They belonged to a panhandler dressed in loud plaid pants and red high-tops. It was hard to make out his face; he was slumped against the corner storefront, an arm hanging over a polished brass-plated standpipe. Homeless, careless, comfortable, sleeping, doesn't have my legal problems, I thought. He was holding a cane.

Then, out of the first doorway on East Sixty-seventh two husky guys moved like a mass of flesh toward me. Behind me the walking stick scraped the concrete.

I wheeled around just in time to register that the shiny cane was arcing toward me. A silvery handle shaped like a ball at one end flashed off the streetlight. I reached up and grabbed it, like a foul ball at Yankee Stadium. I could see that this batter was Chinese. Then the lights in my head seemed to go out instantly. The night game was over.

When I came around, a tall man was standing over me. His head was shaved and he had bony cheeks, a broad nose, and a cleft chin. The rest of his frame looked bloated from steroid-enhanced bodybuilding. His thick arms rested like wings on his lats as he removed a .38-caliber snub-nosed revolver from his jacket.

A black gun barrel was firmly pressed between my ribs; his other hand slid inside my coat to the shoulder holster, removing my piece. His back-up crunchers stood nearby, their arms folded.

"You gentlemen are going to need a lawyer tonight. You aren't getting away with this. You got the wrong guy," I advised my captors.

"We're swimming in the Ocean. We checked the atlas," my assailant cracked.

"The last thing we want is a case of mistaken identity."

They were Ling's boys and this was no mistake.

As the two-inch barrel of the gun stuck in my side, a black late-model Rolls pulled to the curb, driven by a Chinese chauffeur.

The tub of cement shoved me into the backseat and piled in next to me. But the car just stayed put. The driver turned the radio on. News. Is that what I'd be tomorrow? My keeper cracked his finger joints and knuckles, then folded his hands like a kid in grade school.

This was no way to end it—stuck inside a car with three Chinese with my nose pressed up against the rear window, like a hamster.

Then the car moved. I didn't hear the engine being turned on. The somber quiet of a Rolls went tongue and groove with Chinese silence. Cruising downtown, I put my head back against the soft leather seat, closed my eyes, and hoped to get out of this one alive.

My fat captor opened a cabinet in the back of the passenger seat. It was a minifridge. He pulled out a can of Coca-Cola, popped the top, and guzzled it.

"Company refrigerator. Against the rules to give you one." He pointed to the empty, crushed it to the size of a quarter.

"So what, my Bentley's got a fax machine and a fridge."

But my wit was wasted; he said nothing while the soft drink trickled down his cast-iron pipes.

Five minutes later, we stopped in front of a five-story stucco building on First Avenue in the Sixties. The façade was covered in a graffiti mural of a pair of scales. One side of the scale had a hanging red heart inscribed "Freedom of Soul." A skull hung from the other side. An idea of perfect balance, but it wasn't justice. Supporting the scales was a column made of two words: Life and Death.

As if the graffiti were not enough of a statement, the building appeared to be under permanent construction. The street side of the building was covered with three floors of galvanized pipe scaffolding protected below by coils of razor wire.

We sat in the car, listened to more news. No one made a move to get out of the car. I surveyed three jaundiced-looking storefronts under the scaffolding which didn't appear to be in business. A Famous Ray's pizza parlor, a cigar shop with a long, thick yellow sign overhead reading OPTIMO, and another store selling HEALTH AND BEAUTY AIDS. I could do some shopping there.

A black guy wearing cutoff jeans and no shirt wandered over, carrying a red and white Coca-Cola paper cup. He had one arm. The other had been chopped off at the biceps, about five inches down from the shoulder. His belly button was a disaster area— his umbilical was probably cut with pliers. His bony rib cage billowed like abacus beads.

He bounced toward the Rolls on white basketball shoes, arriving at the driver's window. "You dudes got some breakfast change?"

One of the Chinese in the front took out some coins and dropped them into his dirty paper cup. All the door locks released simultaneously. I was prodded out the back and onto the sidewalk flanked on both sides. At the top of the building, in raised brick, was written, POWER IS KNOWLEDGE, 1949.

The Rolls purred away, blending into the night. With the gun snugly against my back, I was quickly escorted to the entrance. We walked right through the Optimo store to the back, past shelves and racks of cigars, cigarettes, chewing gum, and magazines. Humidors, pipes, cigar cutters appeared to be for sale.

A false wall painted with smoking and candy products opened to a dark hall.

One of the Chinese sparked a match, went to a metal wall box, and flipped a circuit breaker. Bright light showered a large steel door, revealing another beggar sitting on an orange crate, wearing a dirty blue quilted ski parka. A smoldering cigarette hung between his chapped lips, which were streaked with syrupy pencil lines of nicotine.

The panhandler's only hand gripped his soot-covered left ankle. He grimaced, punched some numbers on the door's combination lock, and turned the knob. The tips of his filthy fingers pushed the door open. We went single file down a dirt floor passageway. My escort stayed tight on me during this fifteen-minute, multilevel hike.

We reached a large, well-lit ebony door, with a square knob about chest high, between two thick raised panels.

"Turn it to the right," the voice behind me ordered.

The door opened onto a flight of stairs. The walls were faced with rectangular glazed white tiles. I was pushed down the steps, less respected than an outworn appliance on its way to the junkyard.

At the bottom was a vast platform. A train car sat on the tracks. Unlike underground transit stops, this one had no sign indicating our location. The letters CMC were tiled on the wall. China Manpower Corporation. I was in Lingtown inside New York City. Powerful people love railroads.

The Chinese were associated with the early railroads in this country. Much of the low turnover labor that laid the tracks leading west in the 1800s, especially for the Central Pacific Line, was Chinese. The coolies were hard workers, and Ling probably had his own army of coolies lay this track under Manhattan.

I was shoved into the train car. A windowless, air-conditioned, conductorless, wood-paneled, upholstered parlor car. I sat on a large brown leather armchair. A game of chess, in progress on the bar, waited for someone to make the next move. On a dining table an elaborate buffet had been arranged, consisting of eggs benedict, espresso, smoked salmon, kippers, caviar, and toast, presented on a large silver tray. An open magnum of 1985 Dom Perignon was lodged in an ice bucket. One champagne glass was provided. A fire crackled in the hearth of an eighteenth-century Georgian fireplace, straddled by two more brown leather club chairs, over which there was a large, gold-framed ancestor portrait of an elderly Chinese man. The *New York Times,* The *Wall Street Journal,* and the *Herald Tribune* were on the table. An elaborate setting for a lawyer's kidnapping. The car slid out of the CMC station while I ate breakfast.

About half an hour passed. The car pulled into another ghostly station. I tried the door. It was locked. Through a tiny glass panel I could make out wall tiles reading CMC. The latch clicked open.

A large ornate door on the platform opened onto a wide corridor, which lead to a room in the distance. The ceiling was lined with recessed gallery lights reflecting on Old Master oil paintings hanging from fabric-upholstered walls. There was a text alongside each work of art: *Marcelle,* by Henri de Toulouse-Lautrec, stolen in December 1968 from the Museum of Modern Art, Kyoto, Japan; *Nativity,* by Michelangelo de Caravaggio, stolen in October 1969 from the Church of San Lorenzo, Palermo, Sicily; *Portrait of a Man* by Antonello, stolen at night in May 1970 from the Malaspina Museum, Pavia, Italy; *Holy Family,* by Antonio Allegri da Correggio, stolen at night in May 1970 from the Malaspina Museum, Pavia, Italy; *Bearing of the Cross,* by Antonio Allegri de Correggio, stolen in December 1970 from a residence in Milan, Italy. And last but not least was a triptych from Siena, Italy. Chased by the police, the thieves threw the triptych out of the getaway car's window. It was supposedly recovered. Wrong, the text said. That was the copy; the original was hanging here. The detailed history of each painting contained a chronology of Interpol's—and other law-enforcement agencies'—attempts to recover the works.

At the end of the gallery's glossy wood floor, a figure was

bracketed by four freestanding columns. Otherwise the room was empty—and freezing. An overhead vent clicked on, whirred, pushing out more cold air.

As I walked toward the figure, a soft light began to glow overhead, illuminating a large bronze statue of a thin, reclining Chinese man dressed in a military uniform. He had an undistinguished face with a puckered mustache under his small nose, reminiscent of a certain German dictator with whom he identified. His hand rested on his crossed legs. The eyes were weary and watery. There was a plaque fastened to the base of the statue. It read, GENERALISSIMO CHIANG KAI-SHEK, TO MY FRIEND EMANUEL LING, 1945.

Peering around the room, I noticed an alcove. Inside, under a dim yellow lamp, an old Chinese man cloaked in a long, dark blue, gold-trimmed robe sat on a platform. Whirlpools of deep wrinkles covered his face and a Fu Manchu mustache touched the shoulders of his white cotton soutane. His arms hung over the sides of a rosewood Ming dynasty armchair. He wore beaded slippers. This had to be Emanuel Ling. The lips moved but he said nothing.

Leaning toward me as if that would help, he made a sound that approximated a muted wind instrument. In that instant I imagined Ling in the 1930s at Harvard with his hair slicked back, wearing a maroon boatneck sweater and beige linen pants, studying on a beautiful autumn afternoon in the Widener Library. Later that day he meets his girlfriend and, bluejays chirping away, they lazily stroll arm in arm along the sun-soaked Charles River. She's a pretty twenty-year-old sophomore from Boston, studying Chinese at Radcliffe, and planning to visit China in the summer. On the weekend, I could see Ling carrying a green plaid blanket and a flask to the Harvard-Yale football game, saying to his roommate, "Let's go to the rathskeller for a beer after the game."

Ling's robe opened as he leaned toward me, exposing gnarled and crippled legs. Varicose veins bulged from corrugated calves and knees. Even a kidnap victim could feel compassion. He'd seen better days.

Temperature-controlled showcases, filled with orchids that were equally frightening and beautiful, surrounded him. They were meticulously labeled—*Paphiopedilum,* some of which are known as Winston Churchill, a leopard-spotted variety shaped like a sac hanging from a bow tie placed on an oyster shell. There was *Thrixspermum Formosanum,* which originated in Taiwan; a plain white orchid; *Esmeralda Clarkei,* colored like a brown and fawn tiger; and countless others.

Ling relished extremes. I didn't have to meet him to confirm that conclusion, but I now saw that he'd experienced as much torture as he'd shelled out. This encounter was probably like a thousand others—the cards were in his hand, his deck, his game, his casino.

The walls were covered in Chinese scenes—junks gliding through the mist up the Yangtze, chrysanthemum flowers scattered along the border. The room was paneled with hand-painted coramandel screens that were inlaid with mother-of-pearl designs, encrusted with jade and ivory figures and semiprecious stones.

To the left there was a small rosewood side table on which lay an open gold box containing a stack of papers. As if he were feebly brushing away a pesty housefly, he extended a slender finger, dragged his uncut nail back and forth on the pile, indicating that I should take the top sheet.

I did just that.

The paper contained Chinese figures. I handed it to him. He scribbled the words *nu* and *woman* next to it. I didn't know what the hell he was doing.

Beneath the Chinese characters, the note read, "Women. They are no good."

The old man waited. It was my turn to talk. If I backed off he'd kill me in a flash.

"Let's not play any word games, Mr. Ling. You've had me around all night. Why am I here?" The attitude was working; the old man was taking all the grief I could dish out. "I'm not your underling." That didn't seem to amuse him.

His passive manner changed. Those eyes didn't cut me any slack. I'd never forget that penetrating, black-hearted stare. Out for blood and nothing less. The momentary pity I felt for this bastard quickly dissolved.

One of his hands swooped toward me like a rake, then the other. I stepped back. He handed me another sheet of paper:

You have meddled. Now you are the prey of countless hunters and you will be destroyed. You must not defend Mrs. Pandora Markham in the controversy. This is not a matter for the courts, it is for the tongs. That's my property, my money. Because of your actions, Y is dead.

Stunned by the reference to Y, I was unable to hide my reaction. It was hard for me to swallow Ling's thinly veiled claim that he killed his own daughter, but it was possible. Was it my fault?

Ling was deadly still, expressionless, experienced in steering silence to action. He rang a small gold bell. Two bodyguards, size XL, entered from a door behind us and stood on either side of me.

A video projector lowered from the ceiling. Show time. A large white screen unrolled on the wall behind me. The projector clicked on.

Two Chinese heavies were gripping Y by her arms. She was wearing black and red silk pajamas. She was frantic. Duct tape was tightly wound around her mouth. Ling indicated that she should be allowed to talk, pointing to his own mouth and then to her.

One of the men took out a black jackknife and cut the tape around Y's mouth. She didn't raise her voice as she spoke respectfully to her father. Ling regarded her. To him she was wasn't family, she was garbage.

"Father, you should not do this me. Mr. Ocean does not love me. He will not be blackmailed by you. He is not afraid of the consequences if I am involved. You cannot stop him from doing his job." Her eyes reflected the unspeakable agony she'd suffered. "Father, let me go." She broke down and was instantly subdued as the camera panned to Ling, whose ancient hand motioned to silence her, to take her away. The screen darkened and it sounded as if she was being dragged across the wooden floor by her hair.

One of Ling's men returned and stood in front of us. "Mr. Ling regrets, sir, that he might have inconvenienced you." He spoke to me in a loud, clear voice. "You are free to leave."

"I can't say that the pleasure has been all mine, gentlemen," I answered, turning to leave. My foot stepped right into a padded box behind me. Instinctively I yanked my foot out as if a shark were about to take off my leg. It was a wood coffin, a perfect fit for my unscheduled funeral. Fear burned through me. What the hell was this?

One of Ling's men got me in a bear hug, picked me up, and forced me inside.

"Wait, wait, wait." My shoulders jammed against the sides. There was no way to wrestle out of it. The last thing I saw was the quilted white crêpe lining. The lid closed. These bastards were going to suffocate me, kill me in the dark.

A lock at my foot and one at my head was snapped into place. Everything I knew about Ling rushed through me. I remembered that Chiang Kai-shek would deliver an empty coffin to someone who had not complied with the Generalissimo's wishes. If Chiang was not obeyed, the coffin soon held the dead body of the unruly individual. Ling was going to execute his objective tonight without any preliminaries.

No space, no oxygen, just the smell of me at close range. My face pressed against the inside of the lid, sucking in wood grain, desperately searching for a patch of air to breath. The coffin was lifted, listing, juggling me off to nowhere.

I screamed out, but the words only flew a centimeter from my mouth and died, wilting into dried saliva. I didn't hear anything while my body jostled around inside a package of hot claustrophobia, sweating like a living being on a conveyer belt headed into a crematorium. They had to be kidding. This was New York City, not Shanghai in 1930.

Life was over, was all I could think about. Death with a $200,000 price tag. That fucking Dyson, he didn't get me into a case, he got me into a casket. How long would it take for K and the police to know I was dead?

My imagination went berserk, back through cases where people were walled up in brick fireplaces, thrown into the sea trapped in steamer trunks, locked in refrigerators, buried in the back of hydraulic garbage trucks. After my life's work, I wind up in a box, directly below eight million New Yorkers.

I blacked out. To this day I'll never know how much time passed or where I was. Then a cool breeze. The lid over my head lifted and I was pulled out by my arms, by the same guy that stuffed me in. I didn't believe I was alive.

Ling's bodyguard stared down at me. He shoved a gun into my stomach. We were alone in a room that looked like a basement.

"Mr. Ling would like to leave you with a story of ambition."

Not a problem. I'd do anything to keep breathing.

"Li Lien-Ying, the Grand Eunuch of the court of the Empress Dowager, was once a shoemaker. One day he didn't go to work. Instead he watched the Empress Dowager's eunuchs parading though the streets of Peking. Afterward, Li was unable to rid his mind of the splendor of the Grand Eunuch. In the back of his shop, he gathered his testicles with one hand for the last time and he snipped them off. When the pain stopped and the incision healed, he reported to the palace and applied for a job as a eunuch. Ultimately, Li became the Grand Eunuch, second only in power to the Empress Dowager. Success, Mr. Ocean, comes with a price tag. You may win this case, but you will lose something very precious in the process."

I was blindfolded and shoved up some metal steps.

We entered a train car that didn't feel anything like the fancy parlor compartment in which I arrived. The luxurious treatment was not available round-trip. This was a ride and nothing more. The car rattled down the tracks as if it were carrying cargo. It stopped and I was bumped out.

A steel grate creaked open and I was thrust up into the daylight. Ripping off the blindfold, I tried to open my eyes but the sun was too intense. For a moment I squinted, standing, taking in the fact I was finally outside. It was an Indian summer day—a sizzler. Sweat drained into my shirt. My body was liberating me from last night's ugly agenda.

I was in the middle of some shrubs and bunches of impatiens in the middle of a garden. The gold-leafed Helmsley Building was in front of me. Traffic whizzed past on either side of me. I was standing in the center of the garden at Park Avenue and East Forty-sixth Street.

A cop crossed toward me. This was a godsend—a miracle that would even me up with Ling. We'd go right back down the hole and get him and his henchmen. Just as I was about to speak, he whipped out his citation pad and flipped it open.

"Can't you read?" he shouted.

A cement mixer loudly idled at the light.

My eyes were still adjusting to the intense sunlight. "I'm a lawyer, what's the problem?"

Wrong response. I should have known better from all the times I couldn't talk my way out of speeding tickets after identifying myself as an attorney.

A small white plaque was next to my foot sticking out of the ground: WALKING ON THE MALL IS PROHIBITED.

While he wrote out a one-hundred-dollar violation, I watched the Metro-North trains moving underground through the grate. Ling shipped me uptown on his railroad. But I knew he and his train had vanished, leaving me facing a few pedestrians, the denizens of lower Park Avenue set free for lunch hour, and a ticket.

I pulled off my jacket, opened my collar, and walked home.

Right on cue, as I stuck my key into the front door, the phone rang. I staggered into the lobby. The ringing stopped when I put my hand on the receiver, *hello* crystallizing on my tongue. Mercedes must have answered it. My mind and body seemed to be going at the same lethargic pace.

Barkis stood in the foyer. He turned and led me upstairs. When and if I got to the third floor, I wasn't leaving the bedroom for anything or anyone.

Once there, my body unfolded on the couch in the bedroom. My brain was wired to Emanuel Ling, the name repeating like a busy signal that I couldn't hang up on.

The phone went off again. This time, I fumbled it up to my ear on the first ring. It was Mercedes calling me from her office on the second floor.

"Out late?" There was a nub of ridicule in her voice, but also the undeniable tone of worry.

"I'll pass you on to my shadow," I groaned into the mouthpiece. "It was one of those nights I proved my dedication to the cause, and no one will ever understand."

"You sound like you had shock treatment. Better take some vitamins, B-12, get that circulation going."

"B-12, where does that subway stop?"

"You're all right?"

"Met Mr. Ling and his henchmen in the middle of the night and went for a free ride on their roller coaster. How did they get off death row? Gotta get some sleep. I'll call you back. Can you work late tonight? And where's that bloody translation?"

"Yeah, I guess so. That stuff from Columbia. They lost the document and just found it again. The guy who was doing the translation went back to China for ten days. So we have to wait. Eyeballs left that message on the service. Your Park Avenue girlfriend must have rung you up a hundred times. She's in a panic over where to find Don Juan. Says she must speak with her lawyer—pronto."

"What?"

Hundred times. That crashed in my head. She was never that desperate. Maybe she was getting to appreciate my long, self-destructive nights spent on her behalf.

"Are you there? Earth to Johnny."

I nodded off, ignoring Mercedes' voice, hearing Emanuel Ling crooning as if he had a tongue "New York, New York."

CHAPTER FOURTEEN

Late in the afternoon I awoke, rubbing my eyes, barely believing I was still alive. One unstable image remained in my mind—Pandora's face metamorphosing into that of Ling's. Then everything was merging into a messy collage of evidence and characters, which meant I wasn't getting anything right. Last night was a frightening wake-up call. Big Brother wasn't going away and neither was I because there was no place to go. From now on it was going to be like this every day.

As I sat up in bed, running on empty, Mr. K, in a lavender turban and white Nehru suit, quietly strolled into the room.

"Sir, you have had a very difficult night, I can see that vision on your forehead. Will you allow me to assist you?"

He stood to the side of the couch holding a silver tray on which there was a pitcher of ice water and two glasses. I drank some water.

"Nice turban. Please no mysterious eastern healing techniques today."

"But your methods are not working. Relax, sir, you must slow down. The work of a trial attorney is very, very punishing because you must reach the precise issue. Such work has led you on extraordinary adventures." He rubbed his hands together and placed them gently on my head like a surgeon preparing a patient for a lobotomy.

"And some near-death experiences," I replied without feeling soothed. "What are you doing with your hands on my head?"

"Sir, don't be worried, something very healthy. Stretch your arms out vigorously and sit up. Do not sprawl on the floor."

I sat in the center of the red and blue Kurdish carpet with my legs crossed.

K spoke in a firm voice awash in tranquility.

"You must regulate your breathing. You are feeling great pressure that must be diminished and dispersed. Those who breathe longest, live longest. So you must inhale deeply, release slowly, slowly, very slowly. Your lungs must contract slowly, slowly, slowly. Yoga gives control and concentration, peace and calm. In my religion we are to remember the name of our Lord constantly and to coordinate it with every breath we take. It is the same as *mala,* which is rosary. Every time I touch a bead, I say the name of God."

I tried to resist the process, like millions of other classic nonbelievers who have not experienced spiritual awakening and colon hydrotherapy sessions, but I found myself gradually closing my eyes. The sound of his singsong voice almost made me laugh, but it was a little too late. I became immersed in the process and gave way to the words. When I had tried to meditate with K years ago, it was an unsuccessful spiritual voyage that ended up with the two of us laughing like circus clowns. Now it was different.

"There are four sources of energy—food, breath, meditation, and relaxation." K's hands were folded in front of his face and his head was bowed slightly.

"Yes, I have been living off the first two for some time," I mumbled.

"These things I have learned from my guru, Punditji. Your

breath will bring new life inside and you will expel the toxins now living in your body. You will then experience a rise in your *prana,* your life-energy force."

"I hope you can expedite this process, K, because I am falling asleep."

"I am sorry, it must be done slowly, slowly. That's it, sir, that's very fine. I see that you are taking long, deep breaths. You are inhaling towers of air, valleys of nature's cleansers. Your senses are being refreshed. A new vision will be coming to you."

"I am doing that, K. I have had much practice and little choice when it comes to breathing," I said as I slipped into a calm, collected state of mind.

"Free yourself from the temporal, carnal world and you will have universal rhythm. Floating, you are floating."

Maybe another hour went by. I came around energized and ready to go at things, even though I had virtually no sleep.

"K, I'm feeling fantastic." I couldn't believe it.

He glanced at the clock on the mantle and said, "*Bohatah chai* (very good). But I wouldn't compare your transformation with that of Prince Siddhartha, who changed into Buddha after six years under the bodhi tree. You have had a transcendental sleep. I am glad for you, sir. Now I am going downstairs to do some office work. But, sir, one more word of advice. Today you are looking drained, a bit anemic. You must take vitamins and especially minerals." He poked an admonishing finger at me.

Ice-cold water from the showerhead poured over my face while I dealt with a serious problem: Ling was expecting something from me that I couldn't possibly do—take a dive. That wasn't going to happen, not in a million coffins.

I dried off, got dressed, and called down to Mercedes.

"Mercy, what's up?"

"The guys from Chinatown called. They couldn't make a thing out of the document you got from Ling's offices and still nothing from Columbia. They kept saying to me, 'Different interpretations, different dialects—some Hunan, some Cantonese, some Mandarin.'"

Just about then, Barkis sauntered in from the kitchen. Pushing his thick paws straight out on the carpet, he placed his black head in between them and slid to the floor. His eyes never left me.

K came on the line. "I am sorry to bother you, sir, I saw your extension lit. Honorable sir, please forgive me, I have been downstairs awaiting your order."

Mercedes hung up since K was upstaging her.

"Sir, your friend—he says he's your friend—called a few seconds ago. Said you were his sparring partner and that you like the way he sings. That was the way he put it. What is this guy speaking about? Does he know my last name is Singh? He's a crazy one."

I called immediately. Someone answered but his voice was obliterated by a shrill racket. It sounded like a demolition site. Screaming into the phone, I asked for Brian. Minutes later, my eardrum nearly destroyed, he got on.

"Johnny, you won't fuckin' believe this, you gotta come down here to TriBeCa." He huffed as if he'd been sprinting. The crashing, slamming, and banging were earsplitting.

"Have the cops been around again?" I asked, but I wasn't sure he heard me. There were thunderous sounds around my words.

"We can't talk on the phone, it's too crazy here. If you don't want to come, I'll have to run uptown so we can . . . but I'd like you to see this place."

"What the hell is going on there?" I hollered.

"I'm at my aggression gym, DAMAGE."

The sounds grew deafening for a moment.

"What?" I asked.

"You like the sounds? It's the real thing. We're breaking up stone walls, refrigerators, plate-glass windows, Pepsi machines. It's a new kind of workout."

I imagined steroid-pumped bodybuilders hurling stoves off

concrete towers, busting up pianos with sledges, jackhammering the floor in denim cutoffs and black tank tops.

Then a *wham* mid-sentence and the line went dead.

Information—the shit I put up with to get it. A few minutes later I threw on a polo shirt and went down to the office to wait for Brian.

I sat behind the desk, put my feet up.

At that moment, Mercedes buzzed me from the outer office. "Eyeballs is on line one."

"Johnny," Gerry said, "all I can tell you is that there was something big brewing between Ling and Longwood. For a lot of years. We've been able to trace some old records. But I need more time."

"Take it."

"And we know Webb Hartford treated Edgar right up until the time of his death. He was at the hospital with him when he died."

As I signed off, Mr. K walked into my office, gingerly approaching the side of my desk.

"Sir, I thought you were going out. Have you had your dinner? You must take something, sir. I have brewed a pot of herb tea with peppermint, spearmint, red clover, goldenseal, and hawthorne berry—my own blend which is good after meditation."

"K, we've already met the spiritual quota for today; tomorrow we'll spend a hour in a flotation tank."

"Sir, I understand. I will leave the tea here. Take it as you like." He placed a large misty cup in front of me and stepped back two paces. "Your friend who telephoned has now appeared on the doorstep. He identified himself as your sparring partner, then he stepped in. He's in the lobby, and I have observed him carefully. Is he a professional football player? Do you mind if I detain him there for a while longer?"

"No, send him in."

He entered lathered up, wearing a perspiration-soaked, skintight red sweatshirt, dark blue lycra jogging pants, a red headband, and running shoes.

Bri looked at me. "Johnny, you coming downtown?"

"Relax, you're sweating. Have a drink with me and Mr. K," I replied. I was in no hurry to go anywhere.

"Mr. Brian, you are with a great man. My boss will solve all of your problems. He is an attorney of great repute. You will find him to be a generous man, a man of learning and perspicacity. Feel as if you are in your own home."

Bri's clammy eyes returned to me and he inquired, "Who's the swami?"

"Where have I heard that before? He's my spiritual advisor. Relax, you're not standing on a magic carpet. How come you're not at the Veranda?"

After another double take at K, Brian started talking fast and furiously. "I'm off tonight, so first I go to my gym and do five sets of tick tocks, one hundred shrugs and two hundred good mornin's. Then I destroyed a piano or two with a sledgehammer, went over to the place I called you from, and then for a long run over here."

"What are you talking about?" I wasn't into the fitness patois.

"Man, you never did tick tocks? You pull yourself up on a bar, tuck your knees in toward your stomach, and turn side-to-side. When you go 'round in a circle, dat's a 'round the clock. Man, that burns like a motherfucka, and good mornin's is standin' up, just bendin' forward with a couple hundred pounds of weights 'cross your back. How you do shrugs is keep your arms straight, lift like five hundred pounds, like they were in wheelbarrow, you lift it and roll your shoulders up to your ears."

"I see. Mr. K might like to do three quick sets of those shrugs or some tick tocks."

K quickly shook his head.

"What's the deal Brian? Why'd you call me?"

"Do somethin' for me and I'll pay you back. Scratch me and I do you. I got some information you'd be interested in concerning your biz," he answered like a kid that won't throw the ball back and then starts to run home with it.

"Some scratch is available. What do know about Pandora Markham and the case?"

Disjunctively he pulsed into a fit of temper. "Yeah, those fuckers. Police—cocksuckers Slice and Windows have been down at the club this entire week. Seems like they're onto somethin'."

"Wait a second, cool down," I said, trying to get a clear story. I wondered whether Bri had ever played Connect the Dots.

"Been looking high and low for anyone who's seen Pandora. They say they can't get a hold of her. I got some info, though, that's . . . real interesting. I got it out of Windows."

"That's a tough nut to crack. What did he say?"

"Managed to get a hold of this," he said proudly. "The stupid shit left his papers and went to take a leak."

I snatched it out of his hand and read:

Longwood left a small trust in his will for Webb Hartford. Asked him to make sure to look after Ms. Longwood if anything ever happened to him. Hartford checks out positive.

I flipped Brian a fifty and he left for the aggression gym, a trip I was happy to avoid.

That inspired me to get right to work—on the more professional side. I asked Eyeballs to get me everything they could relating to Markham's death. There were hospital records, but only a few were available in the file they sent over. Still, these may have explained it all. Markham had lymphoma, which might indicate suicide, especially if the diagnosis was terminal. Was he thinking, I don't have long to live, I'm in debt up to my ears to my sister, I'm too sick to make a go of it? Potent reasons to jump down an air shaft. And reasons that would blow my gift theory to pieces. Or did someone push him? That was another confusing possibility. I called Dyson and asked him if D&S had any ties to an expert who specialized in medical malpractice.

"Jack, I have to ask you something."

He was out of breath.

"Playing one-on-one with my nephew. Call you back in a few."

About an hour went by. K served iced mint tea and cooked me a multi-dish Indian meal.

During the sixth course, Jack telephoned. Modifying my request, I asked him if he had any connections at New York Hospital, where Marcel Markham was treated.

"You're dealing with one of the world's legendary families—and now you think there might be foul play. Whoa, whoa, whoa, tell me about it."

"Whoa, Jack, when it's over I may let you read the file so you can tell your grandchildren about it. But right now, suffer. It's all attorney-client. Can you help?"

Answer, yes. In no time he was able to get some administrative records read to him over the telephone. "Markham had cancer; that's all I know for now, Johnny. Dr. John Aranda is a compadre of a compadre. He can help. He knows the case. It'll be an education for you to trip over there. You're in my area now. All of this is tight hospital security, but I told him you and I are in the case, and anyway Markham's dead, so why not talk to you off the record?"

"I'd like to speak to your friend ASAP. Tonight?"

"Be back at you in a minute."

It was minutes.

Dyson rang back. Dr. Aranda could see me around midnight.

Downstairs Mercedes and K were still pulling Markham files together for the trial—all the evidence, the research, the notes concerning the direct and cross-examination questions for trial. It would take at least a week to form the blueprint for the courtroom.

Mercedes took a break around 11:45 and came into the office

with a pot of coffee. We drained a few cups and I got myself geared up for another long night. I left for the hospital alone.

The doc, as to be expected, had an emergency which lasted until about 2:30. Serenaded by ambulance sirens, I thumbed through beat-up wildlife magazines, witnessing the raw tragedies of a standard Manhattan night whisked through swinging stainless-steel doors.

I was half-dozing when the balding, mid-fifties, round-shouldered Dr. John Aranda walked toward me, his hands tucked into the patch pockets of a long white coat.

"Hi, John Aranda, but my friends called me Jack." He was about six foot three with a small nose, blue eyes, and an angular but soft jaw. After I explained the case, it was clear that he was interested, even intrigued, saying he conferred with lawyers more than with doctors and, although it wasn't his choice, forensic medicine was becoming one of his specialties. He invited me up to the pathology lab.

At first glance the lab looked like a cluster of administrative offices, but once inside it was far different. We passed a seven-foot electron microscope.

He pointed to it. "That's for more sophisticated work, but in Markham's case we would have first diagnosed the lymphoma under a regular microscope, which would have shown the malignant lymphoid cells—or what laymen call lymph node cancer."

He squeezed my neck. "Feel them right here?" I did and didn't enjoy it.

"When lymphoma biopsy specimens are sent up from the operating room, they're frozen so we can make an immediate diagnosis. The rest of the biopsy is fixed in Formalin to perform additional studies."

"Things around here work on a real-time basis." He pointed downward. "Three floors below is the operating room. The patient is on the table, sliced opened. A biopsy is taken from the patient, placed on a tray, put on an elevator—a dumbwaiter—and arrives here. Some other hospitals use pneumatic tubes to transport specimens. We have to make a quick determination whether to cut the tumor or not. That's my job. We might debate the type of cancer and how to treat it while the patient lies on the operating table below and waits. We use a two-way radio system with the operating room." He picked up a batch of charts, moved across the room and then as an aside he remarked, "Marcel Markham's biopsy. I was in the lab that day."

"How well do you remember it?"

He rubbed his temple. "Like everyone else, I'd often seen Pandora in the papers. One of her admiring millions."

He laughed roundly, bellowing until I said, "Join the club, Doc."

The chortling stopped abruptly. "When her husband was admitted for the biopsy, the entire staff was buzzing." He smiled wryly. "The joke was, if we didn't save him, then she'd be available. Every M.D. in the place was scrambling to see her when she visited. And she didn't disappoint anyone." He broke into a long, thunderous laugh.

"I'm certain of that." Was I his straight man?

"If it were daytime, this place would be hopping. Technicians and doctors would be pouring over slides, writing reports. Some of the biopsies come from tumors the size of footballs, like ovarian tumors."

Behind him there was an electric saw. The brand name was Butcher Boy. I'd seen it before in meat markets.

"What's that doing here?"

"Standard butcher-shop machine." He wrinkled his face and gave me a horselaugh. "Cuts human bone so we can analyze it." That was some unfunny sound bite.

The cook's tour of the laboratory was finished and we went to his office—a small room filled with a desk, one black Formica filing cabinet, and two chairs.

"What can you tell me?"

"First off, I love showing people what we do. It makes cancer simpler for others to understand. I study and analyze cell structure appearance—whether it shows up in tissue or blood cells. Markham's lymphoma was unusual in a way. It was an abdominal non-Hodgkin's lymphoma."

He reached into his shirt pocket, pulled out a pack of cigarettes, and tapped it against the cabinet. A cigarette slid into his palm. He reached behind him into a file folder and handed me two pieces of paper. "Take a look at this."

It was a copy of a clinical pathology report.

"It's Markham's original pathology report. I did it. You won't get most of it, so I'll explain it."

While I half-skimmed the report, he talked.

"Markham was a memorable case. Special class, special treatment, special memories." Then he laughed long and hard again. I didn't think that was funny either.

He lit the cigarette and dragged like he was going to smoke it in one go. From the top drawer of his desk, he pulled out a thick, clear ashtray and set it down near the edge of his desk. A small digital clock clicked 3:53 A.M. It made me think he owned three things: the clock, the ashtray, and the report.

"When he was diagnosed in 1994 he was treated for the lymphoma with the MOPP regimen—a very standardized combination of certain drugs. I recall that he didn't react well and his condition worsened over a short period of time."

"You're saying the chemo didn't help?"

"That was it, but his kidneys were also affected by the pressure caused by the enlarged lymph nodes. The tumor spread behind, in the abdomen, the back of the belly. The two ureters on either sides of the body, which carry urine to the bladder, become blocked and distorted under those conditions, and the urine flow is stopped or backs up into the kidneys. The kidneys can't function properly and eventually fail. I saw his CAT scan and made the diagnosis. Markham knew he had kidney problems as well as the cancer. He was in a lot of pain. Dr. Hartford took care of him again, not one of the staff doctors." His hands went up in the air on the name Hartford.

"So is it normal that both kidneys would be affected by abdominal non-Hodgkin's lymphoma?"

"Well, it's rare, but it happens. The kidney problem can abate if the cancer goes into remission, but in his case I don't know if it ever did."

I didn't know what he meant. From my point of view, either it went into remission or it didn't. But I didn't press the issue.

"If the cancer goes into remission, then the tumor mass recedes, the pressure is released on the kidneys, and the flow of urine through the ureters to the bladder returns to normal and is discharged from the body. He was on dialysis, which meant he was coming in every three days because the chemo didn't help. If I remember correctly, Webb Hartford checked on him periodically."

"His brother-in-law."

"I knew that. I conferred with Hartford a couple of times in person and on the phone from Chicago. I had seen him around and certainly had heard enough about him. Like they all say, he's a *brilliant* medical scientist and a surgeon." That science part I'd heard before, but Aranda's touch of sarcasm was confirmed when he added, "Hartford is only comfortable with a scalpel in his hand."

Evidently Webb was the clearance center for family diseases. As a concerned family member, he was expected to provide his professional services. But I took it another way: Control radiated from his bag.

"You seem to know more than you want to tell me," I ventured, putting on my best smile.

This time he unhinged a far more nervous laugh. "No, not at all. I was really only the pathologist, not a surgeon, and I was only consulting on the case. Finally I heard things cleared up from someone."

"Who was that? You mean remission?"

"Well, I don't want to get into that," he backed up.

I pressed him. "I really have to know. It might affect my case." I pleaded like an eager biology student, knowing that Webb had treated both Edgar and Marcel for cancer.

"Markham was living with the kidney problem, but strange as it may sound, his lymphoma was considerably improved, I thought. I didn't really hear about the remission from anyone."

"How then?"

"By accident. But that's not really unusual when you work in a hospital. A small world, you get to see other doctors' charts, scans, X rays. It happens all the time. I was in the viewing room and saw a CAT of Markham's by accident. It showed a total remission of the tumor without evidence of kidney obstruction. The CAT was normal; I checked the date, but Markham was still receiving massive doses of chemo and he was still on dialysis. When I read about it in the newspaper I was shocked—he left the hospital, then winds up dead in an air shaft."

"Did you ever bring this up to Hartford?"

"I kind of did but one of them told me that the remission was short-lived."

"Did you believe it?"

"I don't want to get into that." He stared straight at me.

"Well, how do you explain it?"

"The fact is, if he didn't die of any natural cause, he was a suicide. I stayed away from it because it got so damned political. Hartford swore up and down that he'd cure Marcel, that he could take care of him, and because he was so high-profile we basically left it up to him. Maybe he got frustrated that he couldn't save his brother-in-law and Marcel sensed it, committed suicide." Aranda's chin was perched on his knuckles, the elbows digging into the desk.

"Suicide. I don't think so," I added sotto voce.

The doctor rolled back in his chair.

"It looks to me like Markham did himself in. At that moment I didn't know his condition. I can't put my finger on anything precise. Maybe that's a problem I have, but you've made me think there's a rub there someplace. Stay in touch. If I can help in any way, please don't hesitate to call me."

"I'll keep that in mind, thanks."

I saw "Pandora" written in little script letters in the physician's eyes. Was he determined to connect himself with the case to live out a fantasy? Jack probably wasn't any different from me—he wanted to prove something to her; he wanted to get her attention. What he didn't know and I wasn't about to tell him was, she'd drive him nuts.

As I got up to leave he said, "Just before he died, I saw Markham at the hospital. He was here for some tests—a battery of tests."

"Tests, what kind?"

"Blood tests," he replied, and I felt rather stupid for almost missing some critical facts.

"And the results were . . . ?"

"I never saw them. Next thing I know, he's in the obituaries." Frowning, he said, "I read his very carefully." He wasn't laughing anymore.

"I'll bet you did, Doc."

CHAPTER FIFTEEN

During the time when the trial was put off, I researched federal and state case law on gifts between family members, and I didn't go out unless I was accompanied by K and at least one of his gun-toting Sikhs. Reading this stuff was a large sleeping tablet, but necessary. Federal tax law held the answers to the question of whether Babette was trying to circumvent the gift-tax consequences. If I could prove it was not an "arm's-length" transaction between Babette and Marcel, then I would be more than halfway home. Arm's-length refers to the position of parties to a transaction. They must be independent of each other—no bending of the rules, no side deals or motivations like making a money gift appear to be a loan. That frequently occurs between family members and that's what we had here.

There were various indications of gift that I had to raise at trial. If no interest is charged, especially to a relative, the deal clearly looks like a gift. The note carried interest but I could argue it was never collected and it was too low. Forgiveness of a loan could be strong evidence of a gift. Getting Edgar's forgiven loans to Marcel into evidence was crucial because it showed a pattern. But I could be stopped by Macefield on the grounds of relevancy.

I could just imagine him: "Where are we going with that theory, Mr. Ocean? We aren't trying the Edgar Longwood tax case in this courtroom."

Pandora only clocked in twice and didn't discuss the case; rather she was full of fear since the break-in. She repeatedly said to me, "Sleep is out of the question, even though I have hired a bodyguard. But if they get by him there's nothing but a door and me."

What could I add to that accurate appraisal? Although I had the Sikhs and my gun protecting me from Ling, I knew anyone could be had. The trial was breathing and I could feel its breath around the next corner, so I didn't have much time to soothe her nervousness. I had to win.

Eyeballs kept up the search for the missing parts of the saga. China's history from the late 1800s to the Mao takeover in 1949 helped to put things into perspective on Emanuel Ling. Eyeballs accumulated data on the inner workings of the Chiang government, the banks, and Ling's actions as Chiang's proxy. They were getting there, but I needed time away from the trial prep to see if it tied into the case.

Less than a week after Macefield took sick, a phone call came from the court.

"Counsel, this is Cedric. The trial date is a time certain," he announced like a proud father telling a crowded room of his daughter's engagement.

"When?" I asked.

"Tomorrow, nine-thirty sharp. Call your adversary and let him know." He hung up.

When I called Bellicoso's office he was gone. The message was left with no guarantee he'd get it in time for tomorrow.

In the morning, Mr. K and I drove down Park Avenue, snaking through the perpetually darkened base of the Helmsley structures around the Metropolitan Life tower. Both buildings straddle Park Avenue, hiding Grand Central Terminal from the north.

As we came around the south side onto the aqueduct behind Grand Central I turned, looked back at the statue of Mercury, and asked K if he knew who Pandora was in Greek mythology.

"Sir, she is like Eve in the Old Testament, the first woman. Pandora brought with her all the evils and sicknesses of the world in the jar, which she unleashed."

"Very good. And what do you know of Mercury?"

"Sir, Mercury, I know it as a planet and an element, nothing more. It is also called quicksilver. It is used in thermometers to measure temperature because of its sensitivities. Every metal has its merits and demerits. Mercury is the only liquid metal and it takes the shape of the vessel in which it is placed. That is its merit, but it is a deadly poison."

"That's why you didn't recommend it as one of the minerals I should take to improve my metabolism."

"That is a good joke, sir." He chuckled.

After braking at a red light on East Thirty-fourth Street, we continued on down Park Avenue South, then across East Fourteenth Street to a jammed Broadway.

Mr. K raised his eyebrows and placed a single finger over his mouth. "Sir, I did not know the stories behind much of Greek mythology, but are you saying that corruption is to be expected in estate matters?"

"It is unavoidable."

I cut through Twelfth Street and took Bowery down to Pearl, driving through the underbelly of Chinatown, which leads right into Foley Square, northeast of the Surrogate's Court. Every morning on Pearl Street, in the esplanade between the federal and state courthouses, Chinese men and women zealously practice T'ai Chi.

Mr. K studied their movements and said in an excited voice, "Sir, I approve of such exercise. It is a type of yoga. I have also noticed that your health has improved, your spirits are high because we will be victorious in the courts."

"Right, so long as Mr. Ling and Judge Macefield are on our side."

After a left turn through Foley Square, I parked a few blocks from 31 Chambers Street. As we reached the front of the courthouse, the day had changed. It was no longer warm. No one could predict this kind of weather in the beginning of September. It was metallically sunny, icy cold.

The Surrogate's Court and other stately limestone buildings hunched over Foley Square like a convocation of vultures watching lawyers clad only in summer suits cross the windswept concrete prairie that separated the courthouses. Countless corrupt politicians in white shirtsleeves had given rabble-rousing speeches in this sacred square using the backdrop of neoclassical architecture to buff their images. I was only seeking to get a fair shake out of Foley Square, and to leave it undisturbed.

Until I understood the practice of law, I loved the profession. When I was in school I'd walk around courthouses touching the columns, studying the statues of legendary justices, reading the words engraved under the pediments: "The true administration of justice is the firmest pillar of good government." I believed that the institution was the wellspring and essence of truth. When my fingertips tripped along those concrete columns, I made contact with God; the law was my life. William Butler Yeats said, "Every argument carries us backwards to some religious conception." He could have said the law is a religion because in these sacred buildings God is inscribed on the walls of each courtroom. Witnesses have to swear on a Bible that they are telling the whole truth, nothing but the truth. Didn't I have reason to believe justice would be done in the presence of the Lord? Unless I was going to join the clergy, what other profession would bring me so close to the Almighty? Each time lawyers enter these wood-paneled rooms, our lives change. We open our mouths, become agents of God invested with the duty to argue who is right or wrong, who goes to jail, who goes free, who is condemned to die. These are religious acts.

But the Corinthian columns of the Surrogate's Court's are thirty feet above street level, far too high for anyone to touch.

Mr. K and I walked through the lobby, and just as I wanted to point out and explain the murals to him, he asked sardonically, "Why isn't there a painting of one great hand washing the other in every courthouse foyer?"

"I'm pleased that your interest in law and mythology grows."

I pressed my shoulder holster and checked my gun as we approached the courthouse metal detector. I wasn't traveling anywhere in the city without a firearm while the Chinese godfather was breathing down my neck. Showing the two court officers who manned the detector my attorney's picture ID, I was permitted to walk around it. Surrogate's is not a high-security courthouse.

We entered courtroom 503. K carried the hefty litigation cases. Nine-thirty. Just as I had expected, it was as empty as Alcatraz. I'd arrived before the court reporter, the judge's secretary, and the court officer. K gave me a Sikh blessing, wished me luck, and returned to the office. I was alone.

In the Surrogate's Court there is only one counsel table for the lawyers and parties. I would sit on the right with Pandora, if she ever showed up; Bellicoso and Babette would be on the left. The center of the nine-foot-long counsel table was laid with the usual lawyerly spread—a stack of Dixie cups and a black plastic decanter filled with water of an indeterminate age. Staring at the mahogany bench trimmed with miniaturized fluted columns, I pictured the man who'd be sitting there, banging his gavel every time I argued a point in favor of my client and sustaining Bellicoso's ill-founded objections.

I unloaded the two black leather litigation briefcases.

There were about a thousand precise questions I'd written out for Ms. Longwood and Co. There were other witnesses I anticipated, including Webb, an expert witness, a sympathetic accountant, maybe Kerrigan, some compliant employees or servants. They would verify Babette's testimony and bolster her credibility. There are two tiers of falsehoods in estate cases—those who lie supported by those who swear the lies are true.

But what of my invisible client? She'll never show, I said over and over to myself. I wasn't a stranger to these situations, sitting in the courtroom alone with the cold elements of the case, without the benefit of any assistance from the client.

Sometimes it's better that way. In my first trial ever, the client, a Mr. Garrett Cassell, destroyed his case. A single document was our most important piece of evidence. I waved it in front of Cassell's face on about fifty billable occasions in my office in the presence of his square-bottomed wife, advising him on each pass: "When I ask you in court, 'When did you receive this piece of paper?' You will answer, 'Late March or early April 1982,' and you will say that you received it in the mail." That was his story when I was hired.

When Cassell took the witness stand, the question was put to him: "When did you receive this piece of paper?" A long, painful pause followed while the document hung in his face like a bullfighter's cape. The question was repeated many times. After that unrehearsed pause he answered: "I don't know."

On the heels of that response the trial associate who worked for me, a forty-five-year-old graduate of Harvard Law School, ducked his head under the counsel's table. That less than professional piece of body language immeasurably assisted the judge in assessing my client's credibility. To compound the problem, I then asked the question twice more, and my star witness again replied: "I don't know."

Babette's crazy recollection was going to be Bellicoso's main trick. She would have to have spent weeks with him sewing that patchwork quilt together. No one ever knew what was going to happen once any witness took the stand, never mind the Babettes of the legal world. I would extensively use the deposition transcript to cross-examine her. That testimony was a mess and Bellicoso knew it. She'd have to contradict her own statements to present any kind of a case, and that would put us way ahead.

Around 10:00 a gangly, pink-skinned man arrived. His cheeks and nose were blistered. Pointing to his face he mumbled, "Sunlamp, fell asleep." His spongy-soled, brown Thom McAn's squeaked on by as I surveyed his tapered, tight-fitting suit. Another hard night with Peggy Sue. His skinny red rayon tie was slightly wrinkled and soiled. The suit jacket was inches too short. He had shaved or scraped his face, leaving a wilderness of nicks, cuts, cactus stubble, and black sprouts. His face said, *You're lucky I'm here, don't piss me off.*

Ceremoniously he placed his gray metal stenography machine on its tripod, then inserted a block of paper into the feeder deck. "Mr. Reporter," as every stenographer is known, and that packet of blank paper labeled LONGWOOD V. MARKHAM would soon spell out the future of this affair.

Handing me his business card, he said, "Just call me Barry." Like all court reporters, he made his living from selling copies of trial transcripts. The price, six dollars a page. It always pays to befriend the court stenographers because testimony is only as accurate as their recollection. In every trial there's heated argument and more than one person speaks at a time. The reporter takes down the voice he hears, which is not necessarily what was said.

We waited for my adversaries: the attorney, his client, and the judge.

All cases in the Surrogate's Courthouse are tried before judges. There is no rationale for that rule except that under New York law it is a court of equity, and questions of equity are decided by a judge. Equity means fairness, which is just a turn of phrase used to screw the clients out of a jury trial. Another ridiculous rule of the Surrogate's Court is that the lawyers can elect to have an advisory jury of six persons. This "jury" can only render advice to the judge, who is not ultimately bound by the jurors' factual conclusions and doesn't give a damn what an advisory jury thinks. Fact-finding is made by juries in most other courts, unless the parties opt for a judge trial.

Enter one of Macefield's law clerks with a squeaky-clean profile: asleep by eleven, fleshy but not fat, ex-choir boy, attended Fordham or St. John's, father was a crony of Macefield's. He never smoked a joint, drank a drink, beat his meat, or understood the difference between Cindy Crawford and Barbara Bush. He fastened the middle button of his brown tweed coat, yanked the bottom down, and toddled over to me.

"Mr. Ocean, has Mr. Bellicoso arrived?" His forehead was sweaty. He stood on his toes and peered over me, as if I were hiding my adversary.

"I haven't seen him," I replied. His face became sullen when he heard I wasn't keeping tabs on Bellicoso.

"The judge would like to see the two of you in his robing room for a conference before the trial starts," he insisted.

Without giving me the opportunity to react, he turned on his heels, and, switching my POV to his sports jacket vent, he disappeared into the robing room. Inside Macefield was waiting for the games to begin.

While I paced like an expectant father, I checked the time. Ten-thirty and still no sign of Bellicoso. His late habits were getting on my nerves. But the judge would tolerate it. I went out the door, down the corridor to take a piss, smoke a cigarette, and work up some more anger. Just then I spotted Bellicoso in his blue-pinstripe-and-overstarched-white shirt, coming toward the courtroom holding a thick manila folder. Two male assistants trailed behind carrying square black litigation briefcases.

When I returned to the courtroom Babette was sitting between me and Bellicoso. She looked impressive, wrapped in boutique jewelry, encased in a silver-gray jacket, a tight-fitting black skirt, stockings and heels. Too bad Pandora didn't want to come down and strut her stuff for Macefield and the truth. This was also a private duel of beauty and bucks. Or was it just going to be a talkathon between me, the White Knuckle, and the judge, that would put the court reporter, the court officer, and the fly on the wall to sleep?

Bellicoso had smugly spread out all of his legal folders on the table like he was arranging a place setting for the wedding of the year.

Directly behind me, in the first row of seats in the gallery, sat Webb Hartford, trying as hard as he could to get me to stare at him. I had handled a thousand sidecars like him. Nothing fazed me in the courtroom, not even the judge. I was going for the win. The worse the pressure got, the better I'd perform.

While Bellicoso and I mentally danced around each other, I suddenly realized that I hadn't told Bellicoso of Macefield's request to see the lawyers in his robing room.

"Morning, Vito. . . . Judge wants to see us," I said, appraising his associates who could have been the two assistants in Franz Kafka's novel *The Castle.* As I spoke, Babette got up and sauntered to the far side of her counsel, leaving a trail of Chanel No. 5 in her wake. Webb protectively craned his head closer to the railing separating us.

Absorbing the courtroom choreography, Bellicoso smacked his lips. "Let's go, Counselor, I'm ready."

I rapped three times on the robing-room door. One never enters a judge's chambers or robing room without knocking. No answer. The two of us waited. There is always a silent delay entering hallowed ground.

The door opened and three lawyers walked out single file. One of them was a middle-aged veteran, slickly dressed, alligator litigator I'd seen around the halls. He'd logged thousands of courtroom miles. With his hand covering his mouth he said to Bellicoso and me, "You're next, but we have a conference with the judge that we're finishing, should be done in about twenty minutes."

His voice dropped about a decibel as Bellicoso turned to go back to his seat. "By the way . . ."

"By what way?"

"You're Ocean. Look, friend, you haven't got a goddamn chance. . . . Settle. I heard it directly from Macefield. He said he was going to bury this Pandora Markham. She's got no case and he's going to throw it out of court. She's your client." He pulled a straight index finger across the base of his throat and flashed some jaggered, graying canines.

"Will you go on record with that? What's your name, telephone number? I'll call you later," I replied reflexively although I had my doubts that Macefield made such a statement.

"No, man, I'm just tipping you. It's your ass, not mine. Take it for what it's worth." He put his arm around one of his colleagues and walked out to the hall.

At about noon, Macefield's law secretary emerged and informed us that the judge was going to recess for a long lunch. We were to return around 2:30 so we could resume our wait.

During the break, I rang up the office. I got Betty at the service, who told me to call Gerry Patton. I did.

"Johnny, got a message for you. K went over to see that doc you spoke to a few days ago, Jack Aranda. Didn't say why he was going but he seems very interested in the cancer stuff. You know how he loves to play with his chemistry set. And the police department is starting to take a look at where the money came from in our case. They're very interested in Edgar Longwood."

"How'd we get that information?"

"One of K's Sikh buddies works at One Police Plaza. He overheard two detectives talking about the case."

"That wouldn't be my new best friends Windows and Slice by any chance?" I asked rhetorically.

"Home run, Counselor. Got something else I think you may find useful, part of the scoop on Ling. I followed up on the information you told me about his life in China."

The usual hallway lawyer-and-client chatter funneled into my ear. I strained to hear what Gerry was saying.

"Can you speak up?"

"I've been pinning down Ling's banking connections. Like I said, he was in the best company. All the things your ex-girlfriend told you checked out."

Hearing the reference to Y was like an electric cattle prod.

"When Ling was a boy in the late twenties he was Chiang's procurer—knew young babes, the underground nightlife scene in Shanghai. Ling was Chiang's mirror image, similar deprived backgrounds as kids. Chiang trusted him more than anyone else with money matters. Couldn't have given a shit about the Chinese people or politics. They milked the country any which way they could, from opium, prostitutes, gambling, and then they hit the mother lode—banking and the United States. Ling went from batboy to cleanup hitter for the generalissimo and the Green Gang. All of them were pure criminals."

"What kind of responsibility did Chiang give him in the government?"

"Chiang controlled China, but he had his hands full and couldn't always watch the store. Ling was put in charge of buying arms throughout the world for the Nationalist army. Starting in the thirties they spend close to one hundred fifty million bucks a year on arms, and our Mr. Ling runs the show. Not hard to understand the rest. Ling is hooked in with the U.S. arms tycoons and Washington right through the war."

"Nothing ever changes. More Asians sleep in the White House than the Mandarin Hotel in Hong Kong." I scanned the pay phone area. Paranoia is a healthy disease.

"Chiang became a billionaire using a shitload of our money that was supposed to be foreign aid. Not one member of the inner circle ever filed personal income tax returns. They were the Marcoses, taking whatever they wanted, whenever they wanted, while the Chinese peasant had his pants rolled up, ankle deep in water grasping a handful of seeds."

"No wonder they lost the revolution."

"The Green Gang massacred the Communists in '27, so the Commies head for the hills and organize under Mao. Chiang ran the Reds out, not because he cared about political doctrine but because he was a capitalist mobster, only after money. You know what side we were on—Commies out, capitalism in—business as usual with China. Pleased the hell out of the West, namely the U.S. and Europe."

"A real pretty picture."

"Not that simple. Chiang and Madame Chiang manipulated Roosevelt and the Democrats all during the war to pour money into a losing cause—China. All together, the Chinese ripped us off four to five billion in aid. What a joke on us. We never got a dime back. Most of it disappeared in the hands of the Chinese mafia."

"That dough sounds like the capital base of the empire he's built here in Chinatown. Does that piece fit into China Manpower?"

"Grand slam. Ling's running the same scams in New York, except it's heroin instead of opium. He does have some legal businesses. He controls plenty of real estate—a strip right up Fifth Avenue to the Bronx, twenty-five thousand apartments in Queens and Brooklyn. In the Caribbean he has an empire, not to mention Atlantic City."

"How did Ling get the money into the United States?"

"That's when my game got rained out."

"It's all a great case against Ling for raping China, but it doesn't connect to the Longwoods."

"It's early in the season, Johnny. Did you know Shanghai means 'by the sea'?"

"Call me when you know what Emanuel Ling means."

Two hours had passed. I had to be back to conference the case with Macefield, as ordered. Before I returned to the courtroom, I dialed Mercedes.

"Glad you called, boss. The guys from Columbia U. just telephoned. They want to meet with you, but they're busy until later today."

"Tell them to send over what they have."

"Emanuel Ling telephoned."

I felt a spike of pain. Then I recalled that Ling doesn't speak. "Ling?"

"Someone asked for you. I said you were in court. He said, 'Tell him that Mr. Emanuel Ling has telephoned.'"

The shivers zipped up my spine. I didn't need this the first day of the trial. "Any number?"

"No." Just a short, naked *no.*

I told her to try to reach Ling through China Manpower and to make sure she left word that I was busy in court but to make the message extremely polite.

Life goes on. The next order of business for Mercedes was to arrange a meeting as soon as possible for me with the Columbia linguists. They had to get on the ball. I headed back to the courtroom, feeling as if I were the manager of a small, confused conglomerate.

When I got upstairs, Bellicoso and his client, her doctor, and the judge's law clerk were all seated together in the courtroom in the front row, scoring brownie points with one another. I could hear the *ding, ding, ding*s. The clerk was looking for a job out of the state system, and Bellicoso was winning his respect. They were speaking about the case, but I couldn't catch anything significant. Their eyes swiveled toward me like lawn sprinkler heads on a timer. I was an intruder.

The clerk informed me that His Honor had returned from lunch and would see us immediately.

Macefield was seated behind a small, green metal table in his robing room, wearing a blue suit, white shirt, and flowery blue necktie. He hadn't yet slipped into his blacks.

"Sit down, Mr. Ocean. Sit down, Mr. Bellicoso," Macefield said, his finger beckoning.

"Tell me, Mr. Ocean, just what are the facts in this case?"

He wasn't asking me for my version of the facts, he wanted to know what the case was about. I wasn't angered because it was predictable. Macefield pretended not to recall the matter. Judges never seem to remember what happens from one day to the next, using the excuse that they have many cases. Lawyers have just as many cases—that is, busy lawyers—hundreds and thousands of insignificant facts weaving and circling around their craniums like a swarm of insects on a hot summer night.

I placed myself squarely in my chair and was about to start when Macefield took out a smooth, worn tobacco pouch.

"Wait a moment, until I fill my pipe, so I can relax while I listen to you."

"That's all right with me, Judge. Can the lawyers smoke?"

I looked over at Bellicoso, who had cracked a smile. For one crazy second, I assumed I had a fighting chance to be friends with Macefield, but he didn't answer my question. "Your Honor," I began, "let me tell you what the facts are in this—"

"Facts, damn it!" Macefield hollered. "You're going to tell me what the facts are? Who the hell are you to tell me anything? Who the hell are you to presume you can tell a judge *anything?* I am the finder of fact, and don't you try to tell me anything. You understand?"

The eyes went quiet, then he stared me down. I was in the first grade. I felt like killing him.

"Yes, Your Honor. I have nothing further to add. I apologize to the court." I bit down hard.

"No, you don't get it. Do you understand?" Macefield looked like his head was going to implode.

"Yes."

"Then say, 'Yes, Your Honor, I understand!'"

"Yes, Your Honor, I understand."

I didn't surprise myself with that obsequious concession, because if I didn't, I was dead. The mea culpas were for the client's sake.

"Gentlemen, let's proceed. It is now three o'clock."

We left the room and took our places. The courtroom gallery was filling like batter in a waffle iron—honeycombed rows of nosy humans. The balcony had yet to be occupied, but the courtroom floor on three sides was nearly full.

Macefield entered, pulling his robe over his blue suit. Everyone was required to stand while he was announced by the court officer.

"Hear ye. Those who have business before the Honorable Humphrey Macefield, Justice of the Surrogate's Court of New York County, come forward and ye shall be heard."

"Gentlemen, do you wish to make opening statements, or should we waive them? If so, be brief, I know the law, rest assured," Macefield stated for the record.

Bellicoso rose from his chair and replied, "Your Honor, I do not see the necessity. We have no jury." He put his arms out as if he were feeling for rain. His eyes mockingly searched the four corners of the room for a reason, finally coming to rest on me. Sheer poetry.

"Exactly my sentiments, Counselor," Macefield called out from behind the bench as if he'd received a Christmas gift. "And you, Mr. Ocean?" he asked, expecting me to roll over.

"Your Honor, I would like to make some opening remarks. I'll be brief."

"Do you really think it's necessary?" He childishly pulled at the shoulder of the robe and sulked.

Bellicoso gathered his notes, while Babette, calm as a lily pad, glanced at Webb.

"Mr. Bellicoso, since Mr. Ocean is giving an opening statement, you shall have the opportunity to go first, when you are ready."

Vito didn't hesitate—he was fully prepped—stepping sermonically to the podium which was placed just in front of the gallery. Telling the court he would waive the opening was a Bellicoso move from the old school of sandbagging. He stooped like a deferential pilgrim, adjusted his reading glasses, and read carefully from his notes. This is the textbook approach of senior litigating partners in large firms. Just a reading of paper according to Hoyle. No fire, no brimstone. Most judges like that style and abhor flamboyance.

On the other hand, I fully exploited what some lawyers call the "well" of the courtroom—center stage. That's the space for ranting and raving between the counsel table, the bench, and the jury box. That's the spot my trial-practice professor, Martin Louis, called the cockpit. "That'll be your workshop and electric field."

Webster's New Collegiate Dictionary, Ninth Edition, defines "cockpit" aptly: "A pit or enclosure for cockfights, a place noted for especially bloody, violent, or long-continued conflict."

On the last day of class Professor Louis admonished us well before the bar examination, "This is the arena where the gallery gets to see and hear lying cocksuckers tell their cockeyed, cockamamy, cock-and-bull stories to cocksure lawyers and judges, under oath. But that's where you'll craft and deliver your best arguments and actions to the judge and jury, hopefully wrapped in packages of persuasion. This is where the cockfight rages, testimony is ice-picked, witnesses raked over red-hot coals; where judges scream like banshees and hold attorneys in contempt. It's the rink, the ring, the diamond, center court where hell froze and where we, the officers of the court, listen to echoes of an eternity of injustice. It's where you as lawyers will stand flat-footed with your asses hanging out for the client, arguing right and wrong, life and death even though you haven't a clue as to what really happened. It's where you've summed and been summed up, walked the box imploring each juror to believe your client, cross-examined witnesses and crossed the judge. All in the name of that void called the Truth.

"But you're in the cockpit on your own, flying by the seat of your pants—a frustrated actor dodging bursts of flak fired by a frustrated lawyer—the judge in a frustrated theater."

But the cockpit had its limits; in this case there was no jury. Bellicoso gestured with the eraser end of his pencil. "Your Honor, this is quite a simple case—a straightforward one, if you will. My client is a widow. She inherited a large estate, took part of those assets and made a loan to her brother. That loan is now due and payable with interest. The fact she is wealthy doesn't mean the money was given away to her brother or anyone else. A false picture has been created in pretrial proceedings that it was an artificial transaction, that it was not a true loan." Bellicoso's eyes panned the room snapshotting the bench, Babette, me, the court reporter, and the gallery.

He spoke for another twenty minutes, covering some odd cases that he tried to compare with ours, drawing on his trial experiences in family-fraud matters (which were next to none).

"My client is an honest, lovely, refined woman who legitimately loaned her brother a hundred seventy million dollars, and if she didn't make such a loan she was defrauded, cheated in the name of family. Ms. Longwood loved her brother and trusted him to repay the loan. But he is not alive today; his wife is. We are faced with a shoddy defense—that there was no loan but rather a gift made to Marcel Markham. If Marcel Markham were in this courtroom, he'd either admit that this was a loan or he'd admit he defrauded his sister out of a hundred seventy million dollars. Loan or trick, either way that sum is due my client. It is my reasoned belief that she's the victim of a terrible and despicable fraud, suffered as a result of her generous nature."

So Bellicoso revealed, acting for the claimant, that he had two routes to go down. The first was to keep Babette on the narrow path and have her testify that it was a loan; the other involved the more complicated plan of having me confirm on cross-examination that she was not capable of comprehending her affairs, and as a consequence, she was defrauded by Marcel. Either way, Pandora lost. Bellicoso plans were not unshrewd.

Pausing as if there were a jury hanging on each word, Bellicoso waited for the picture he'd painted to dry. Macefield grinned like a clown and nodded approvingly to Bellicoso.

Then more olive oil leaked from the bottle as Bellicoso applied to the court for more time.

"Your Honor, I apologize, I have a comment or two to add. Please indulge me. . . . Some people are never satisfied, even with the fairness and advantage of a family business transaction. A confidential relationship existed and Ms. Longwood's confidence was exploited. A loan of this magnitude would not be possible unless the parties were related. But that doesn't account for anything other than a legally enforceable transaction. The note called for interest and a debt is owed. I will prove these facts to this court beyond a shadow of a doubt. By a stroke of good fortune, Pandora Markham is charged with the administration of her husband's assets. Suffice it to say that, without the generosity of Babette Longwood, the estate matter of Marcel Markham would be merely a matter of counting hundreds of dollars, not the millions of my client's that we are discussing here today.

"However, we are faced with a much different situation. The sum of money sought is a hundred seventy million dollars, but with appropriate legal interest—eleven and one half years interest at seven percent—the total is $301,100,000 as of today. This money does not belong to the estate of Marcel Markham and it certainly does not belong to Pandora Markham. It is rightfully the deceased's sister's property and must be repaid forthwith."

Bellicoso closed with his hands extended toward the bench as if Macefield were going to toss him a bag of gold coins. I could have predicted Bellicoso would go too far and begin to argue my case, nearly saying that the transaction was less than arm's length, and that if Babette and Marcel weren't sister and brother, a loan of that size would never happen.

But the court thoroughly enjoyed the opening. It was pure theater, as usual.

There was a surge of conversation behind me. The journalists protuberated. The *New York Times* and the *Daily News* milled about in gossipy coils, made notes, and chatted with the court clerk.

The *Times*'s "At the Bar" column was ethically scoured and dry. It would report this case in a very flat manner. These articles emphasized the law and only quoted what lawyers said in court. But there would be more and more reporters climbing all over this case and the courthouse as the days progressed. The remaining seats in the gallery were occupied by lawyers killing courthouse time, clerical personnel, retirees, and bag ladies. The last two categories surfed from courtroom to courtroom, depending on the testimony and celebrity of the case. Longwood against Markham deserved a better crowd.

Macefield gaveled twice. "Mr. Ocean, be brief. Read my lips: I have heard it all before."

I didn't want to go forward unless I could get additional media support. Hal Samson was missing. He was one of the regular courthouse reporters I knew from the press room at the State Supreme Court. I was surprised he hadn't shown, but he was probably doing the morning routine: checking today's new court files for items, phoning in updates of old stories, and grilling the clerks for scoops, rumors, or tip-offs.

I had been so damn distracted by Pandora, I'd overlooked reading the newspaper coverage. When it came to the press, I assumed Macefield, like most judges, knew how to cover his ass. That was the trade-off for having the press monitor Macefield. My hopes to artfully bury him by fashioning a transcript that would condemn his bias and rulings would be dampened if Macefield played to the journalists and was careful on the record.

"Your Honor, may I have a moment to gather my thoughts? Mr. Bellicoso has raised an interesting legal point and I want to respond to it."

Macefield accommodated, "Motion granted, we'll take a five-minute recess."

No sooner had I turned around then potbellied, North Carolina born Hal Samson, the little king of torts and legal news, strode into the courtroom. As usual, he arrived fly unzipped; filthy, cracked granny glasses; tousled, dandruffy hair; a circle of ketchup stamped around his mouth, talking a mile a minute about the latest courthouse scandal. He sat down in the press row, looked my way, and winked.

Hal knew me from the beginning of my career and had covered every major case I'd ever tried. The closest thing to an ally in that courtroom was Hal, a true eccentric who adored the law more than any lawyer did. The only thing he loved as much was college basketball. He'd gone to UNC and was a Tar Heel fanatic. Every trial lawyer in New York knew about Hal because we'd call him for information, for research, and for his opinion on which way a judge would go on an issue. He knew it all and filed every state court opinion that'd been written for the past twenty years in a beat-up metal cabinet. If it wasn't there, then it was in one of Hal's countless hog-tied paper bundles, scattered, podlike, around the press room, together with every college basketball stat imaginable. If you didn't know the law, Hal was only too happy to tell you. No charge. He answered his phone, "Sleaze, Slime, and Grime, we charge by the minute, phrase your questions ahead of time." Hal could locate a case archaeologically buried in one his mystery bundles faster than a computer wiz on Lexis, simultaneously stuffing a greasy hero into his mouth, phoning a hot scoop into the city desk, and writing notes with his pudgy free hand.

Hal looked at me with an ear-to-ear grin. "Johnny, this was on my hot, hot calendar. A typical Ocean show. I've been reading the court papers right along. Your writing style, I have to say, must make their skin crawl; you really know how to piss a judge off. When are you going to learn that you have to grease the wheels of justice to get anywhere in this courthouse? Like my Daddy used to say, 'Boy, when those wheels grind, they grind real fine and they're gonna pulverize your ass unless you watch it.'"

Hal laughed, said his father was a poetic postal clerk, but I agreed with the principle.

"You've got a tough one here *and* you're Carolina playing on Duke's court."

I didn't say anything, trying to keep my spirits up, wanting to feel otherwise. Macefield returned and ordered me to continue.

The war began.

I spoke in my courthouse voice.

"Although Your Honor has requested that I be brief"—I caught Macefield getting enraged and enjoyed it—"I will concisely frame the key issues. One hundred seventy million dollars changed hands, a fantastic amount in any day and age even though we're accustomed to hundreds of millions, billions changing hands in national and global markets. No stranger will give you that amount of capital, and no bank will loan it to you without collateral."

For a quarter of an hour I recited the classic cases involving transactions that weren't businesslike which had failed to meet the standards of arm's length, a legitimate business transaction. Then I launched back into the facts of the case.

"The deceased cannot testify, and anyone who has a financial interest in the outcome of these proceedings cannot testify as to what Marcel Markham said. Such testimony is barred by the Dead Man's Statute. Can this court rule that exchanges between brother and sister were arm's length and no different than a standard business transaction between unrelated individuals? With all due respect, I have grave doubts. Dealings between siblings are characterized by nuances and subtleties of blood relationships, comparable to marriage. The normal competitive, negotiative *hardball* atmosphere was absent when this transaction occurred. Shrewd minds were not trying to outmaneuver each other. No one was trying to be cute or clever or make a *deal*. Instead, an arrangement was made whereby a sister was trying to help her brother, not do business with him. There is substantial evidence and direct admissions by the Claimant, Ms. Babette Longwood, that she gave a hundred seventy million dollars to her brother and that, Your Honor, was no borrowing and lending of funds. If it were a gift, it was not a loan and vice versa. It can't be both because they are mutually exclusive."

Then I paused—it seemed that time had stopped—recalling that the promissory note was at my office asleep in the file. I had no duty to produce it. It was never requested. Babette made no demand to take Pandora's deposition. Now it was up to Babette to prove her case. Without a note it is nearly impossible to prove a loan. It perplexed me that Bellicoso never demanded the note.

"Who was Marcel Markham? Let's examine the man's life and career. Called himself . . . businessman-investor. He had no business, no investments. No legitimate third party would loan this old sport money with the expectation of repayment. But he was surrounded by women with resources. He was good-looking, athletic, well-educated. He played piano, sang standards, was a scratch golfer, wine expert, a good husband, a great storyteller, brother-in-law to one of the world's wealthiest men, Edgar Longwood, from whom Mr. Playboy borrowed two hundred eighty-five thousand dollars and never paid back a cent. That was a gift, too. In fact, Marcel Markham's debt to Edgar Longwood was forgiven in writing."

"Objection, Your Honor." Bellicoso was on his feet protesting the reference to other alleged loans, on the grounds of relevancy.

"Overruled, these are merely opening remarks. I will rule on the pertinence of the deceased's other transactions at the appropriate time, but I see no harm in permitting Mr. Ocean to show the court his blueprint and what he intends to prove at trial."

Macefield gave me the left-handed shake, fluffing up the record, making himself look fair. It was just a matter of time before he screwed me silly.

I went on, crisscrossing the cockpit, playing as much to the court as I was to the gallery, using the three-sided audience as my jury.

"Just how was Marcel Markham going to repay his sister a

hundred seventy million dollars? That's a question best answered by Babette Longwood, since the creditor must have had a complete financial profile of the debtor, otherwise how could such a loan be business-like? Marcel never worked a day in his life and didn't have a job up until the moment he died. Do we, the people, just suffer through another tax scam? The tax laws have far different consequences for gift givers, and that is something that Ms. Longwood knew at the time such sum was transferred to her dear deceased brother. If it were to be a gift, a tax in the sum of more than eighty million dollars would have to be paid. If it were characterized as a loan, payable ten years or parenthetically nowhere down the line, then it would be a disguised gift, hidden behind a paper curtain called the promissory note. Seven percent interest is interest that Babette Longwood could have made from any bank. She didn't have to take a risk and lend it to her brother without collateral. The Longwoods come from a securities background. No one in their position would stand for an annual return of less than twenty percent."

If nothing else was gained up to now, Babette and Webb no longer appeared calm and collected. The realities of a trial were bracing, and they were going through the painful acclamation process.

Macefield listened but nervously fidgeted with his robe, pulling the sleeves tight, as if there were a draft in the courtroom.

To my satisfaction Webb now appeared unraveled and flushed.

A nervous smile tripped along Babette's lips. Maybe she was starting to enjoy the circus and the game of pick-a-judge-and-win-bucks.

"I will prove beyond a doubt"—I shifted my gaze from Babette to Macefield—"to this court that the claimant knowingly, intentionally, and wrongfully gifted these funds and jewelry to her brother, Marcel Markham. The cash and other items rightfully belong to Pandora Markham.

"This respectable court is well aware of the principle. As stated so well in *General Stencils, Inc. v. Chiappa,* 18 N.Y. 2d 125, a 1966 case and still good law today, you cannot commence a lawsuit to recover an asset when your wrongdoing resulted in the loss of such an asset. A wrongdoer cannot take refuge behind the shield of her own wrong. The United States Supreme Court has espoused the doctrine, and the principles remain the same. Babette Longwood may not take advantage of her wrongdoing."

"Objection! I move that such remarks be stricken from the record." Bellicoso was on his feet, swiftly moving to the bench, waving his hands at the reporter. "The executrix's counsel is accusing the claimant of committing a crime—tax evasion. I can see what is coming. I object, I object, I object!"

"Gentlemen, approach the bench sidebar," Macefield gruffly ordered.

We stood before Macefield like two hungry hounds waiting to be fed.

"Gentlemen, you understand the duality of such allegations even though an opening statement is not evidence. Mr. Ocean, you may have much to lose if that's what you're setting out to prove. You claim the IRS didn't get its gift tax because Ms. Longwood defrauded the government, and if that is your point I will allow it in opening remarks but the government is not a party to the proceeding."

I didn't want to talk him out of that ruling. By playing the tax gambit, I knew they would argue that Marcel defrauded Babette. They would say that Marcel fooled her into making a gift and all along she thought the transaction had all the characteristics of a loan.

"So I will reserve on Mr. Bellicoso's objection. However, this is a problem I see for you, Mr. Ocean. The old five badges of fraud, in case you've forgotten them, are: One—a knowing misrepresentation of, Two—a material fact upon which one, Three—relies to one's, Four—detriment, and Five—suffers damage. That is New York State fraud. The precise fraud which you are defending. Did your client's husband defraud his sister as well as fail to pay the note? Those are questions I hope you are prepared to countenance." He sank into his leather chair.

"Well, Your Honor, it may come down to her fraud pitted against Marcel Markham's alleged fraud. That's the way I see the proof developing. She could be barred from bringing this suit because she has *unclean hands.*"

Macefield and Bellicoso didn't like those points of law driving them into the backcourt as the man from Mars explained the law and alluded to unclean hands. It meant that if Babette had done something wrong, she couldn't get relief in an equity court. Equity courts like the Surrogate's frown on litigants with unclean hands.

Finally Macefield said, "Let's resume, Mr. Ocean."

I wasn't overconfident or bluffing Bellicoso and the court. The legal points were correct. I was sure of myself but at the same time well aware of the rule of life that you never know the evidence that's roaring down the pike against you.

Then there was the matter of my client.

While I was rolling a pen back and forth in my right hand, addressing His Honor with my very well thought-out opening remarks that frame the legal issues in this trial and save this beautiful creature's fortune, she was probably pouring herself a cup of Earl Grey tea and reading *Vogue.*

But I was disciplined enough by now. I wouldn't get stuck in my Pandora fantasies. I wound down the opening.

"This frivolous action attempts to recover what was once given away."

Bellicoso said, "Note my objection."

I ignored him. "Furthermore, we will call witnesses who will demonstrate every element of such proof." I stopped cold.

The court reporter removed his thin fingers from the keys of the machine like a concert pianist finishing a long composition. I moved out of the cockpit, sat down, and turned to Bellicoso as the court said, "Counselor, you may proceed. Your first witness. Please have the witness take the stand to be sworn."

Babette briskly rounded the counsel table and went to the stand like a trained seal. Bellicoso massaged his face with his right hand as if he were trying to wake himself out of a bored stupor, then perused his notes while Babette was sworn in by the court officer.

With a stack of legal papers between his hands, he strode to the small wooden podium, the invisible box from which lawyers are permitted to question witnesses. He set his papers down and asked her a series of preliminary questions ranging from where she went to school, to the facts of the marriage to Edgar. She seemed steady. Her speech had improved. Of course, most witnesses talk straight on direct examination when they've had the living hell rehearsed out of them in lawyers' offices for two or three full days before the trial.

"Did there come an occasion when your late brother and you had a discussion concerning your inheritance from the estate of your late husband Edgar Longwood?"

Bellicoso's pencil rapidly moved across his legal pad, running a line through the question, eliminating it from the list before she had a chance to respond. He wanted her off the stand ASAP.

"Marcel was very interested in money, you know?" Her voice was faint coming through the microphone, sounding like she was trying to be heard on a bad overseas call.

"No, I don't know," Bellicoso answered her, like they were having tea in Babette's kitchen. "Could you tell this court about that? Please elaborate."

I didn't object. Macefield wanted me to, so he could get the court to sustain an objection of mine for the record. But Bellicoso was nervous and would make his own witness talk . . . too much.

"Well, Marcel, my brother, took care of me, took care of my books and, and, he and I never really spoke of money, except when Edgar was sick."

I watched her take a drink of water.

"Did Marcel write checks for you?"

"Yes, he did do that."

"Did Marcel review your bank statements?"

"Yes, he did do that." She examined the room and seemed to focus on Webb. He was stoic.

"Did he speak to your banker on your behalf?"

"Yes, all the time."

"Did he discuss financial matters with you at any time?"

"No, not really." Again her eyes crossed over to Webb.

"Did Marcel ever show you any documents to review regarding your funds?"

"No."

"Bank statements?"

"No, not really." She seemed suddenly cool.

"Did you not have access to these documents?"

"No, sir."

The answers were too clean. The direct went on like that for close to two hours with the usual colloquy between Vito, me, and the court. I began to catch Webb consistently touching his head or his body to signal the "no" answers. I'd seen it a thousand times. When he did nothing it would be a "yes" answer. I moved my chair and stood as if I were studying a file, placing myself directly in the line between them, forcing her to see me every time she searched for an answer. I stared at him. Refusing to meet my eyes, he knew I was on to the game.

Babette eagerly said, "Let me go back to the other question, about Marcel taking care of me. The subject of money came up . . . more frequently. I didn't mind. He was my brother, I loved him. You know we were close." She looked curiously at her counsel.

"Yes, please go on." Bellicoso prompted and I heard Hal Samson release a prescient sigh tucked into the whispering gallery.

"What is there to say? You're my lawyer. You know what happened," she snapped. He recoiled.

The court officer, the gallery, and even the stenographer laughed loudly. Macefield went pale pink.

"Ma'am, please answer the questions, regardless of whether you believe your lawyer knows the answer," Macefield guided her.

"Yes, sir. I didn't mean any offense to your court. . . . What was the question?"

Babette sounded as if she wasn't through insulting the White Knuckle.

Macefield took his glasses off, placed them on the bench; his eyes lifted to the wall clock like gulls leaving a beach. He checked his watch. It was nearly 4:30. Surrogates don't work past that stripe even if they're entranced by the testimony.

I requested that some of the testimony be read back just to break Bellicoso's pace. The stenographer read back the section.

"After Marcel, I mean . . . damn, what's his name? Edgar passed away, then Marcel came to me and . . . I wanted to help him."

She stopped and gazed at the room, flipping through the faces like the way she would a stack of vacation photos. Clearly Webb was her objective. Her eyes went to him. I was no longer blocking her view. That was it. I had to stop them now.

"Objection, Your Honor, I believe the witness is being signaled by Dr. Webb Hartford, seated in the front row of the courtroom." I pointed directly at him. "I request that Dr. Hartford be removed from the proceeding."

Jumping to his feet Bellicoso hollered, "That's preposterous! He's not even a witness. There's no basis whatsoever to exclude him. This is just another of Mr. Ocean's infamous courtroom tricks. He's trying to provoke a mistrial."

Macefield didn't say anything, ignoring a very serious complaint. He waved me and Bellicoso to the bench for an off-the-record sidebar. Issuing an icy ruling, he hissed, "Application denied, Mr. Ocean, only children play these games. Gentlemen, I'll see you in the morning at ten sharp. Good day."

The judge stood, made a statement on the record about the matter being resumed tomorrow, and scurried into his robing room.

The crowd seemed nonplussed by Macefield calling it quits right at that point, but I didn't care because I made my record. Tomorrow my adversary was faced with the old problem of communication between lawyer and client. Babette couldn't depend on Webb's signals. But all in all, the day had been a good one. So far it had been close to a replay of the previous encounter with Babette when I took her deposition. Although I didn't think much of the opposition to begin with, they looked even worse than I anticipated. I just didn't want to get overconfident.

I rushed to tell my client, as usual. The great success of Babette's deposition had fallen on Pandora's unappreciative ears. Would she react the same way today to the trial's events?

The revolving door rotated me out of the courthouse like a Coke bottle spinning off the assembly line. Then I stopped dead in my tracks and carefully scanned the area for Ling's guys. It looked safe, so I walked on, thinking about the trial.

Would Bellicoso really argue this insane, defenseless woman in her debilitated state was defrauded and exploited? The short answer was yes and that's why she was hostile to her own counsel. Bellicoso was intent on staging a freak show, demonstrating that she was incompetent. All of it at the paying client's expense. Babette probably wanted me to prove that she was sane, but that she was not immune to fraud; that she knew what she was doing— sanely and legally she made a bonafide loan to her brother but the deceased made it seem like a gift; and that Marcel took advantage of his sister who happened to have an extremely generous nature.

I arrived home, went into the office, scanned a thick stack of phone messages, faxes, and mail.

Shit, forgot to call Ling. That wasn't smart. The negligent approach wouldn't work, and this wasn't a great time to forget about Emanuel Ling. I reached for the phone, hoping Mercedes had written down the right number for him.

I got an answering service. It efficiently informed me that Mr. Ling would try to return my call within the next ten minutes. It'd have to be someone else's voice—a flunky. The phone rang right back.

Dammit, it was Bri.

"Bri, what's going on?"

"Ocean, I've been around, working for the cause. That's how I'm in the park."

"What park?"

"Central," he said as if it were his home address.

"I confess that I don't know why you'd be there, especially at this odd time."

"I'm in trouble. Cops picked me up. I'm at the station house, Central Park precinct near Eighty-sixth Street."

"That's a weird place. Nice architecture. Sounds like you've been arrested."

"I've been booked. You're my phone call. They came down to the Veranda again, picked me up for questioning, arrested me, now they're gettin' ready to charge me with somethin' downtown."

His voice growled big trouble.

"Don't get into anything with them. I'll be right over. You want me to be your lawyer?"

"Of course, of course. That's why I called you."

I went into the kitchen, poured myself a drink, and checked on the hound. Barkis was sitting by the door to the library. He wasn't in the mood to care about my comings and goings, and he hadn't touched his bowl of dry-meal-and-rice dinner. Then he surprised me, raised himself off the floor and lumbered downstairs. I decided to take him along just in case Ling was lurking in the park or outside the door. Could I get Barkis on a diet of Chinese arms and legs? Time was racing. I had to review Babette's direct-examination transcript for tomorrow. I ordered daily copy, an invaluable tool for cross-examination. It was being typed and would be delivered at ten this evening by Barry.

Before I left I peered out the window on the first floor. No Lingites visible. I drove into the park from the east side, up to the medieval police station. After squeezing the Bentley in between two ratty squad cars, I walked across the cobblestone courtyard, through a pile of leaves, and into the gothic precinct. It sits roadside, a concrete-and-stone, single-story structure on the capillary linking the East and West Sides. Once more into the big blue breach. Barkis sat in the front seat, pressed his nose against the windshield, and waited.

Inside a voice shouted to me from the back of the room. Windows.

"Hey, Ocean! Over here, you want to see your client? He's in the back room." Windows was biting into a cigar.

"Same cigar?"

"Yah, gotta smoke the same one 'til I solve the Y thing, then the city issues me a new one for the next case."

"That's if you solve it. Better quit smoking, you'll be on this one for a while." He grabbed my arm and pulled me toward him. "I wanna talk to you, mouthpiece man. When you get finished with the client back there . . . you may be his roommate."

"Okay. Apartments are hard to find in New York." I removed his hand. "You're very touchy for a cop. Next time I'll bring my CDs. We can slow dance in the stationhouse." He made a sick frown.

After entering through a thick metal door, I met with an un-handcuffed Bri in the back room—a bright, unevenly plastered, funky white seven-by-seven interrogation room, complete with an unenclosed toilet. CRAPPER was crudely painted on the wall above it.

Brian had been heavily questioned for the past eight hours, and as human nature would have it, I looked at him as if it were my turn. Windows's jacket was hanging on a wall hook.

Bri sat opposite me on a small metal chair at a square, white wooden table. He didn't look like the jock in my office the other day. His face had a pasty appearance, his forehead was sweaty, and his shirt was soaked in perspiration around the chest and armpits. One eye had a shiner and the other was badly bruised. The bouncer looked like he'd been bounced. The cops had obviously worked him over good. Bri tried to wink, but the purple lid only half closed. My gaze moved down to his lower lip where I read the word *guilty* sitting there, big as the Hollywood sign in Los Angeles. I shook that out of my head.

"Fell down, Johnny. You're gonna have yourself a good time with this one . . . murder one."

"Who?"

Bri's elbows moved forward like wobbly ice skates. "The Chinese babe. She was a woman who got herself 'round. You know, the chick with the body that never quit."

Out of nowhere the mention of Y's name roasted me from the inside out, and I knew it'd sting more and more as each lurid fact reached me. It couldn't be helped. I lost it, had to know right there and then if Brian killed her. I lunged across the table and pulled him against my face. "Tell me if you murdered her, you piece of shit, or I'll break you in two, right the fuck now."

Brian blinked and cried out, "What, what the fuck are you doing?"

"Fucking tell me."

"No way man, never killed no one. I don't even know that bitch, what the fuck are you doin', you suppose to be my lawyer?"

When he said the word *lawyer* my hands released his collar and he fell back into his chair. Realizing that I blew my cool, I made up a story that was at least half-true to cover my personal reasons for losing it.

"The cops think I'm in on this murder. You better be giving it to me straight. I'm putting my ass on the line for you."

"Swear to Christ, John, swear."

As I cooled I pretended to myself that Y was still alive, but that didn't help. I couldn't believe that Bri had done it. Ling was the last one to see her alive. Things were muddy because they always are in these situations; criminals are professional liars. As much as I disliked Windows, I knew he wouldn't make this bust unless there was evidence.

"Are you sure they are going to charge you?"

"Yeah, they are for sure." He thumbed his chin stubble. "There's no telling 'em anything, except what they want to believe. I told them they had the wrong guy, and that I didn't know the broad, except that I saw her coming into the club a lot, like I told you." Those big droopy basset-hound eyes didn't draw any sympathy from me, and he told me before he didn't know Y. That surprised me.

"If you want me to represent you, better tell me all of it." Meanwhile I read the sign on the wall: CENTRAL PARK IS NOT A WALK IN THE PARK. ITS RESIDENTS ARE PICKPOCKETS, MURDERERS, CHILD MOLESTERS, MUGGERS, THIEVES, AND GOOD CITIZENS. HAVE A NICE DAY AND WATCH YOUR ASS.

I gave him a cigarette and he talked around the smoke, politely tapping the ashes into his palm. My mind was on Y and wandering like a ball on an uneven surface, leading me to where I knew I wasn't capable of doing two things properly at the same time. While he talked I didn't try to stop him as I stepped into the great abyss of personal conflict of interest. Furthermore, I didn't know whether Ling killed Y; I only was invited to the video in which she was last seen alive.

In these types of rooms I had interviewed many clients/psychos. Like all the others, he made calm, well-reasoned sense for a man who might spend the rest of his life in jail. Not waiting for him to say anything, I jumped in on all fours, asking him, "Do you know Emanuel Ling?"

"Don't know him personally." His eyes bored through my chest, and huge hands massaged a small flower vase that sat on the table. PROPERTY OF THE CITY OF NEW YORK was stamped on the side. Everyone in this city bears the mark.

"Before, I didn't tell you 'cause I didn't think of it, but I thought she was sexy, really got me going whenever I saw her going into the club, but I never approached her. Never went no further than thoughts."

I pictured him choking Y with those NBA mitts.

"I knew she didn't have anything for me. Never looked at me once. I didn't have enough class for her. But now they say I went over to her place with a gun, blew her away, dragged her down to the basement, left her hanging 'round the back of the boiler. That's not my way. I don't need to do no one, I don't do contracts on good-lookin' babes. Hope you know that, Johnny. Hope you know that about me. They didn't even prove to me she's dead." The back of his wrist swiped across his wet brow like a bar-code reader. I could hear his mother saying, "Brian, you're a mess."

"No, I didn't know that." But I said to myself, "No Bri, I thought Y was all right. She was just fine, just had a small buttonhole in her neck and she'd be back with us in no time." This was all a nightmare. Brian was screwing up my head, but listening to his unstreamlined, stressless tone, I believed, probably because it was early on, that he didn't do it. Bri was stupid, not evil.

"Do you have an alibi?"

"Yes, but I don't think I can get anyone to back it up. I was alone for a while that night, then I went to the club and worked the lot."

"Did you punch in?"

"Nope, was working for cash."

"Didn't anyone see you there?"

"Yeah, think one of the Filipino busboys saw me, but I don't speak that and he don't speak English." As if Brian did.

"And with Filipinos it's one day yes and the other no. Can't trust 'em. The cops don't know about that, and no, we don't get paid by the hour or on the books at the club, most of the time. We get a small salary, the rest in cash tips, so we use the time clock but not all the time and not that time. They gives us the lot as a valet concession. They don't give a shit about the cash in the lot."

It had been a long day plus tax. Trying to stay alert, I ran my hand through my hair, slowly reconstructing what Windows had said about Y. I was too tired, had to call it a night with Bri. Flashes of the Markham trial were intervening.

It seemed ridiculous, but the bail question has to be asked of any defendant. "Bri, you got any cash, assets, some big bucks like two hundred fifty thousand or some collateral for a bond? I can possibly get you out on bail when they arraign you. I'll have to take a break from a trial I'm doing, but it can be arranged for me to be down the street at the Criminal Courthouse tomorrow or the day after. In the meantime you'll be in the tank."

"How's that? Forget the two hundred fifty. I got nothing, but my mom's got a house in Queens she owns clean."

"You're going have to ask her to put up it as collateral for the bond, if it's worth two hundred fifty—otherwise you won't be out of here. And the judge might ask for a lot more." He didn't reply. "They'll be taking you downtown sometime tonight or tomorrow. Let's hope we get a decent judge."

On the way out I ran straight into Windows, firing up a match with his thumbnail. The flame hissed and flared inches from my face. A smelly cloud of smoke introduced him, along with the coarse voice of police authority. "Got yourself another client . . . this time a winner, a real payday."

"That's right, Constable. I take what comes through the door. Wasn't born with a silver spoon in the mouth or a metal badge in my—"

"Maybe a steel plate in your head. You have what it takes—a line of bullshit from here to Maine," he said sarcastically. "I had it rough growing up, just like you, but I knew the difference between being a lawyer and being a lawman."

"One works the client, the other works the general public" jumped out of my mouth.

"Ocean, that's the kind of cops you deal with."

"The ones on this case?"

"You wouldn't be offering me a bribe, would you? Your stuff's too high class for the likes of a poor fella like me from the other side of town. I don't have bodyguards hanging around, like some patrons of yours," he said caustically, his anger barely tolerable.

"I don't get the reference."

"You don't come in here representing one of the bouncers from the Veranda without being connected. You know that your client's on someone's payroll, not some nightclub. I don't mean W-4's—tax forms, and all that good shit . . . for the past ten years. The bastard got a record as long as a Rockefeller's bank statement."

"How's that?"

"That's for you to get straight with your client, and the boss who's going to pay you to get his employee off a murder rap that's airtight. Yeah, this'll be a good one, get him off for killing a very rich Chinese babe. What's in it for Brian? He didn't even get to bang her. Got to be some strong motive. Connections, I can figure them out."

That threw me back to my own goal line. So far there hadn't been any clue that Bri worked for Ling, and maybe it wasn't true. I had seen the video. Although I didn't want to react, my instincts took over and I responded, "I don't know who his boss is."

"Yeah, sure, sure," Windows snapped and went to the door without waiting for me to react. Then he added, "The kid killed her real good and professional. That's not the kind of job he could pull on his own."

And I didn't want a job done on me. As I left the precinct I slipped my gun into my pocket. If Ling surprised me on the way home, at least I had quick access.

CHAPTER SIXTEEN

Closing the door slowly as I entered my house, I turned to see if Windows or Ling's henchmen were behind me. Now I was suffering from double paranoia. Was I losing it? Would a world-class marathoner turn around in the last hundred feet of the twenty-sixth mile to see if second place was gaining? Breaking all the cardinal rules, I was getting too personally involved in the case, in a contest with Windows and my own client, not to mention Ling and Babette.

After I poured some hot coffee, I read through the transcript, the files, and my notes for tomorrow's theatrics. I sat in the library scribbling some questions, when out of the hallway darkness K silently entered wearing a white Nehru jacket, black pants, and a black turban.

"Sir"—he beckoned with one hand—"have you taken something? A drink is not enough. Allow me to bring something. I have prepared a wonderful Indian dinner. It is becoming late but I can go out and get you something."

I rocked back in my chair. "I'm not hungry. Where have you been? I haven't seen or heard about you for days. You know the trial has begun."

"Yes, I am aware, there is no problem. I have been busy, busy,

busy. You must prevail, even if the client does not." He snapped his fingers; he turned on the chandelier and then adjusted the dimmer.

"I'm working on behalf of the client, I'm her representative. Why do you say that?"

"Sir, you must hope that such purposes are one and the same. You must protect yourself against this client. Your enemies will be vanquished. The court will scrutinize everything and the client must tell the truth. Sir, may I tell you something, not in my Punjabi language but in your own tongue of English jurisprudence?"

"Why not?"

"No doubt the wisdom that is born after the event will engender suspicion and distrust when old acquaintance and good repute may have silenced doubt at the beginning."

"Who said that?"

"Your own legendary Judge Cardozo did in 1938."

"I hope that's not this case."

Pushing some law books aside, he said softly, "You must travel to the root of the problem. You are almost alone in this case."

I put those thoughts on my mental shelf, knowing he had a point. But between tomorrow's possible cross of Babette and Bri's arraignment I had my hands full.

K's bent brown fingers pointed down like a divining rod over a well. "Mr. Kerrigan, the attorney for both parties and draftsman of the note, can be helpful, sir, even if it is not to his interest."

"I agree, K. He can be of great service."

"And possibly this young man, too," K announced, turning away. "Enter Mr. Yung."

A small Chinese man, no older than twenty-two, stepped into the room. His long hair was combed into a pompadour above puffy red cheeks.

K gestured toward him. "Sir, this is Mr. Mickey Yung. He is a fine person, a student at Columbia University, and he has something to tell you. He has been waiting in the kitchen upstairs, trying one of my paneers, dal, rice, and some chapatis. I made them for you—not to worry there is plenty left."

"I can smell it."

"He has brought you some valuable information."

"Mr. Ocean, I'm pleased to make your acquaintance. I've been working on your project. I have waited over two hours for you. The rice was very tasty, but the dal and paneer is not agreeing with me. I'll speak quickly."

"I apologize that the cooking got to you first. Have you translated the papers?"

"Yes. It was difficult because it was written in old Chinese." Hurriedly he took out a folder, put it on my desk.

His finger traced the words he'd translated as he read them aloud. "One million Webley & Scott's, .45s. One million .45 Colts. One hundred thousand 38/200 Smith & Wessons. Eight hundred thousand Al Thompson machine guns. Ten million hand or stick grenades (made in Germany). July 18, 1940."

Mickey went on, "There is also a list here of armored cars, and other military vehicles. There are five thousand of each vehicle. This document is signed on behalf of the Chinese Nationalist Government, Emanuel Ling—or in Chinese—Ling Emanuel."

It was apparent that Mickey wanted to exit quickly.

"Is that all?"

"No, Mr. Ocean. The second item is an invoice to the Chinese government from Longwood Securities for the listed arms. That's it. I must be going. To whom should I submit the bill for my services?"

"You can give it to Mr. K, and he'll see to it that it is taken care of immediately."

"That would be good. I need it for tuition. Columbia is very expensive," he said, retreating to the door.

"There's a men's room on the first floor."

He picked up his book bag and ran downstairs.

As I heard his feet rushing over the steps, K said, "Sir, sorry, I must have undercooked the curry. I was very busy, busy, busy. And before I forget, Eyeballs has found these banking transfers from the Chinese government to Longwood Securities." He placed some papers in my hand.

Now I could see a tangible connection between Ling and Longwood. I took a deep breath and reviewed the documents. My life inside and outside the courthouse finally merged. There was a purpose in Ling's quest to get me out of the case and it was wired right into Longwood Securities. Is that the reason why I was shot? Was Pandora being aloof with me because she didn't want to be in the middle of these two titans? I just didn't have a clue but I had something to go on.

I reached for the phone, punched at the keypad like a caveman trying to figure out how to use a new implement, and called the uncooperative client.

The phone rang on past the point where I thought she was home. It was after midnight and I was about to get tape instead of the spicy live act.

She picked up.

"Hello I'm home," she answered. "I was out, just got home a little while ago, relaxing."

"Reading, watching TV?"

"Having a drink, listening to Cole Porter. That was a great era. You should have lived then, representing the young and beautiful movie actresses. Glamorous women in trouble. That's more your type, Johnny. They would understand you better than I do."

What the hell was she talking about? She was in trouble up to her ears.

"Pandora, I hate to raise the subject, but today was the beginning of the trial."

"How did it go? Just don't tell me that I'm going to have to testify."

This time, I didn't take a step toward relaxing her. Nothing was said for minutes. I didn't allow myself to break the silence, letting her just breathe into the phone. The cool voice would have to tell me sooner or later that she was going to testify.

"Tell me, Johnny . . . I don't have to come to court. . . . I told you I would never do that. . . . I know nothing about what happened, and if they subpoena me, forget it, I'll refuse."

"Refuse what?"

"I won't testify."

"Is that a limited-time offer?"

"Don't be funny."

"Do you know Brian, the bouncer at the Veranda Club?" I just threw that in to see where it went.

"Don't change the subject."

"The big, blond-haired guy that parks cars and works at the club, the guy who gave me the envelope with the promissory note. The one I never put in the safety-deposit box."

"No, I don't know him," she said, ignoring my crack about the safe-deposit box.

She was lying, stupidly, but I also knew she wanted me to continue this line.

"He's been picked up by the police, questioned for quite awhile by them."

"For what? And how does it concern me?"

"The cops claim that he murdered Y."

"Y? What?" She stumbled, then recovered. "What the hell would—what would a person like him be doing with her?"

That's all she said. She seemed to become frightened, and then came more of the deadening silence.

"Look, I wanted to get ready for tomorrow. It's a key part of the case. It could be made or lost, depending on what Babette has to say. I might need to call you during the daytime."

"I'll be out, that's something I cannot help. You're supposed to take care of the case."

"Are you certain you don't know Brian?" Still testing her, I wanted to see if she'd lie again.

"Positive."

Another line rang. I told Pandora I'd try to call her back, knowing she wouldn't tolerate the hold button.

A female voice said, "Johnny?"

She sounded exactly like Y.

"Mr. Ling wants me to communicate a message to you." Fear replaced my excitement.

The pretty-sounding Chinese telephone voice melodically chimed, "It is Mr. Ling's wish that you follow his instructions, that you do nothing further involving Ms. Longwood and the lawsuit concerning her sister-in-law until you read his letter. It'll be delivered in a few minutes."

"Is this Funeral Express or Federal Express?" I asked as Barkis put his paw on my leg.

She hung up.

It wasn't more than the prescribed few minutes before the doorbell rang. Continuously. The jerk had his thumb glued to it. I went to the chest of drawers in the office, pushed a full clip into my Glock. The sound of it slipping and snapping into place calmed me down as I slid it into my pants pocket. If it came to violence in my house, this time I was going to do the shooting.

As I stepped into the darkened foyer armed to the gills, two of Ling's tough guys busted through the front door, breaking it off the hinges. Reeling, I saw that one of them was carrying a small package that wasn't tied with a pink ribbon. My first thought was "bomb" when suddenly the lights flipped on. Mr. K appeared at their side in the foyer, greeting them with a sweep of his hand. "Welcome to my boss's home. Is Mr. Ocean expecting you?"

The unexpected emergence of Mr. K took them aback. With a confused expression, the larger of the two large men monotoned, showing teeth the size of mature acorns, "I am Mr. Yang." He pushed his finger out at me. "You are to read the contents of this package and to come with us to see Mr. Ling."

"I can't watch that movie twice in one month. What else is playin'?" I replied.

"Please, my friends, Mr. Fang—" K started.

Mr. Yang grumbled, "The name's Yang."

"I don't care if it's Yin or Yang, Tang or Fang," I replied.

The bowling-ball face didn't think that was very funny.

K's hand again swept back majestically. "Honorable gentlemen, have a seat, feel as if you are in your own home, make yourself comfortable. My respectable boss will take care of everything."

"Who's the swami?" Yang said.

K bowed, hands clasped in front of his face, and began speaking absolute nonsense in Punjabi (The car is crazy, the czar ate all of the salad and now you won't be able to drive to Canada). They looked at K like animals confused by the sound of humans.

"Let's go, Mr. Ocean," Yang ordered.

"Sorry, Mr. Yang, I'm going to bed. I've got to be in court in the morning."

"You don't understand. Mr. Ling has summoned you." His voice was firm, "You'll be coming with us." His hand slid inside his suit coat for something that wasn't a Hostess Twinkie. I backed up into the sound of a low growl. Barkis. I can't recall an occasion when Barkis didn't bound downstairs when the doorbell ran. Every visitor received an introductory nose bump from Barkis, or if he didn't like the person, entry to the house was blocked by a wall of steel ribs.

Mr. K choreographed himself between me and the Chinese characters, and he uttered the usual K crisis mantra, "Now, be cool, Mr. Fang. Please, this can be discussed, gentlemen."

That Barkis growl quickly morphed into a vicious snarl, then an ungodly, grizzly cry.

Yang shoved K across the room, propelling him into the wall. It sounded like a door slamming. I was afraid K was dead as he slid to the floor like a collapsed marionette. But advising them calmly from the floor, K said, "This matter can be amicably resolved by talking it out, please."

Barkis leaped in the air. His muzzle knifed past my face, speeding for Mr. Yang's throat. In an instant, Barkis's teeth were locked on to Yang's shoulder—130 pounds of killer Rottweiler toppling 250 pounds of Chinese hitman to the ground. Yang's gun skidded noisily across the floor toward Mr. K, who scooped it up like a cricketer shortstop.

Blood gushed geyserlike out of Yang's suit coat. Protectively holding his throat, he howled for help as he lay in a red puddle that was growing rapidly into a pond beneath his twisted face. Barkis hadn't found his jugular, yet, but he was chopping and channeling his way there, biting into Yang's hands. In less time than it takes to grind a pound of flesh into hamburger, Barkis must have punctured his hands, neck, and shoulder twenty times. The Rottweiler only released him when the other thug made for the door.

Barkis snagged him, clamped his ankle, and pulled him down to the floor. A loud bang that sounded like gunshot was followed by gnashing of bone. His ankle had been crushed, the Achilles tendon snapped like a guitar string. I'd heard the same noise once before playing football.

A second later K had the gun in Yang's bloodied face. Barkis was yanking the other punk out the door by the leg, his teeth in the porterhouse of the man's thigh. Before I moved they were gone, leaving streaks of blood on the sidewalk.

The blood-soaked package lay by the door. I picked it up and felt the soggy bottom. It had been floating in Yang's blood. I carefully opened it and pulled out a piece of paper. It was the same stationery of the Imperial Palace that was in Ling's office. Only this time it wasn't written in Chinese. No translator need apply.

It read: "You have broken into my sanctuary and have stolen

documents that were to be seen by no eyes except mine. You will return them or die."

Even though I was safe for the moment, Ling's guys weren't through. If anything, they'd multiply and come back like pods planted at night, opening in the morning and chasing me in the afternoon. Again and again they'd be at my door, on my tail, and in my hair.

"You think that we should report this to the police?"

"From your tone, I think you will not," K replied and pressed his lips together.

"It means calling Windows because sooner or later it would get to him and we'd be up all night at the stationhouse answering thousands of questions." I walked in a half circle, bothered by the lack of options. "Not to mention how much he hates me so he's going to do nothing for me."

"And Mr. Ling is not about to file a complaint," K added.

"Thanks for being in the right place at the right time," I said to K, although it was far from the first time we'd been in a scrape.

K bowed and became very somber. "Sir, it is my Sikh duty to help victims. You may not be in such a classification, because you are very brave, but my Sikh brothers and I are bound to help you or anyone who is in trouble, whether or not you ask for help. Our swords may be used, but I am optimistic that others will see the wisdom of a better solution."

As I started back to the office, I heard K praying and reading form the Sikh Bible known as the Holy Granth. Mr. K was asking God that there be no more violence in my house (he did not mention the rest of the world), that there were to be no more lawless acts committed upon me by Mr. Ling. And he requested of the Sikh gurus, specifically Guru Nanak—a great prophet and intellectual, warrior, sage, and poet who died in the sixteenth century—to provide protection for his boss.

Stopping in the office, I faxed the translations to Eyeballs with an explanatory note.

Upstairs, Barkis was lying on his side, fast asleep in my bedroom, showing no ill effects from the encounter. But I didn't feel comfortable. Wasn't it just a matter of time before Ling had me back in the coffin?

K's prayers notwithstanding, I took an alternate route to the courthouse, parking near East Fifty-ninth Street, then took the subway downtown to the courthouse. On the other end of the city I'd had one of the roughest nights of the decade. The better part of it I'd spent figuring out what time I'd return to court, what streets I'd drive down, who would answer the telephone, where K could safely go.

Just before saying good night, K had observed me, worried and puzzling over how to protect my domain and him. He said, "Don't concern yourself with me. I can float above these dangers and my God is always watching out. Go, sir, live your life in the ordinary cautious manner and everything will be fine."

In the courtroom it didn't look like everything was fine. The opposition looked okay. The White Knuckle was ready to start another day in the courtroom looking fresh and well rested. Webb, decked out in a navy wool suit, crossed his legs primly in the same first-row seat. Babette, clad in a creamy white silk blouse, a pearl necklace, and a gray knee-length skirt, nodded to Webb. A short sable jacket rested on her shoulders. I gave Bellicoso credit for pulling *her* off. But I still maintained, like a mad scientist with a secret formula, that Babette would never put on a convincing case. It was my ace in the hole.

Waiting for the judge to appear, I lapsed into my least favorite subject—Emanuel Ling. He was after my life, but if I thought long and hard enough about the reason—I arrived at the same unclear place time after time. There were a limited number of possibilities with whom Ling could be allied in the case. Babette was the first choice that I rejected because Edgar and Ling had a bitter lawsuit. That also eliminated Webb. That left Pandora, but I was fighting to get her the pot, so she had to be dropped from the list, not to mention Ling's warning to drop her case or die. Windows and Slice. Were the cops on the take to get me indicted for murder? That would get me off the case in a hurry.

The evidence was the lawsuit between China Manpower and Longwood Securities. What Marauder said at dinner now framed all of my thinking: sometimes a lawsuit is a pretext for some other hostility between the same folks. The Imperial Palace document was a solid expressway into the secret lives of Ling and Longwood.

When I looked up from the table, Macefield was on his way to the bench. After the usual "Hear Ye's" Babette was recalled to the stand. Her words from the previous day replayed in my litigator's head: "I didn't mind. He was my brother. I loved him. You know we were close."

The White Knuckle opened his file. "Returning to where we left off yesterday, describe for the court exactly what happened between you and your brother Marcel when he approached you for a transaction concerned with money."

"Objection! Leading the witness, Your Honor, and that's not where we left off. Her last statement was 'Then Marcel came to me and . . . I wanted to help him.' Page thirty-six, line four."

Macefield reacted and ruled, "It's all right, Mr. Ocean. We don't mind a little leading around here and please don't tell me the nature of the objection. I attended law school. I will figure out why you are objecting and make an appropriate ruling. It is not necessary to establish an exact base from yesterday's testimony."

She answered even though there was no question.

"My brother told me that he would need the money . . . some plan about making antique, art reproductions, or maybe it was ice-cream stores. I just can't remember." She gave Vito a strange look and raised her voice. "He opened big offices on Madison Avenue. He wanted to do that. I can't recall all the details." I liked the hostile tone. She was starting to go against her own lawyer again. Bellicoso looked disgusted and Macefield turned away.

"Let me ask you, Ms. Longwood," Bellicoso stumbled. "How were the arrangements made for . . . question withdrawn . . . what did he say and what did you say at that time? Can you give us the substance of the conversation between the two of you?"

"Marcel said he needed this money. It was well over . . . well into many millions of dollars, and I said—" She stopped short, appearing like a dumbfounded, thumb-sucking child. After a chilling silence, she whispered into the record, "And I handed it over to him."

"Just like that?"

"No, I think he wrote the check and I signed it. No, I think I just instructed the bank to wire the funds into his account or he instructed the bank. That's how we did it. He was my brother. . . . I always trusted Marcel, and we went to his lawyer, and made some type of agreement."

"Who was that, that lawyer?" Bellicoso pressed her.

"I don't . . . I can't . . . oh damn. Look it up. How am I supposed to know things, Vito? You know how terrible I am when it comes to names . . . faces I can remember, but I told you not to ask me anyone's name. Isn't it in your file?"

So far, she was consistent with her deposition that she didn't recall the name of the lawyer, but she was more precise at that time, about the transaction being loanlike. My strategy showing she was rattled at her deposition was workable. Bellicoso was using her nuttiness to his advantage to show that she was taken advantage of by Marcel. It was obvious that the court and Bellicoso wanted to show she was exploited. Bellicoso turned my tactic inside-out. I'd almost set too good a trap for myself.

"You were saying your brother had an attorney, Ms. Longwood. Please try to recall anything about the lawyer." Bellicoso stayed on a track.

"I cannot recall, but I do remember his office. . . . He had a lot of odd scales. . . . He told me he was very interested in weights and measures. I remember he laughed and said they somehow related to the scales of justice. There were . . . scales of all types all over the place—ounces, pounds, grams, kilograms. English, Greek, German, American. Hanging from the windows, used as planters, fruit scales on the table, even scales from one hundred years ago that you could weigh yourself on . . . yes, I remember weighing myself in that lawyer's office. And there were antiques all over the place, like a shop. He had a collection of old pens and bottles of different types of ink."

She stopped and her eyes reviewed the gallery, making certain that no one missed her narrative.

Absorbed by the testimony, another antique, Johnson Howarth from the *Times,* craned his neck toward Babette. Meanwhile, Hal moved closer to the railing, madly scribbling like a courtroom sketch artist, shaking his head.

"He was a very nervous, unattractive man. He had dirty hair, dirty clothes and he was telling me everything about his very boring little . . ."

"Life," Bellicoso urged in a soft, firm voice. He resented the comment on the profession and his own career. I didn't object as she rambled.

"He was shaking when he spoke to me. The nerve of this man to ask me if I were dating anyone since my husband's death. His name was Kerrigan . . . now I recall . . . Marcel took me there several times. He wanted to talk about his scales. That was different. It made me feel uncomfortable. Told me I was skinny, beautiful. This man was strange, not like a lawyer should be. He could never have been my own lawyer." She stopped cold.

"Why not?" asked Bellicoso.

"I didn't trust him. Would you?"

"But he did some legal work for you, including the transfer of funds to your brother?"

"Yes, but that was different. He was my brother's lawyer and in that sense, I, I . . . I trusted m-m-my brother, I trusted his lawyer, the b-b-b-bore-bore, boring, s-s-s-son of a bi . . . bi . . . bitch. Lawyers, and him with those sc-sca-sca-scales, jus-stth . . . stice, justice. It all m-m-m-made sense to Marcel if that's what counts." Babette's eyes flashed intense anger, as if Kerrigan were in front of her in the courtroom, toying with her and the scales of justice. It was effective. For the first time something productive was happening for Bellicoso's case. The precise circumstances of Marcel pulling the wool over his sister's eyes were being related to the audience.

They'd spent rehearsal time with her last night and it stuck. Against what I figured were very severe odds, they'd straightened out many of her problems on the stand.

She went on, "So, after we met . . . as I said several times, he convinced me to give him the money."

That was critical: she let the word *gift* slip out in the form of "give." When the time came, I would jump all over that.

"He?" Bellicoso asked.

"Let's say first Marcel, then the two of them, Marcel and the lawyer," she answered thoughtfully. "The two of them, over a period of those meetings, did a good job on me . . . and . . ."

She wasn't stuttering a bit.

"Please just relate to the court what occurred, and do not include in your testimony what you believe to be the effect it had upon you and others," Macefield admonished her as any judge would.

"Well, the lawyer spoke to me about how to do the loan, and Marcel did the same. I see now that they worked like a gang against me."

I didn't object because Macefield gave her another warning. But now it was out there—double-teamed and defrauded.

"Mr. Kerrigan said we needed a mechanism for me to get the money to my brother, Marcel. Mechanism, I didn't know what that meant. Something to do with mechanics who fix cars?"

Very funny, Babette. That was a joke I didn't thoroughly enjoy, but the reporters certainly liked it, along with some of the spectators. One laughed and pointed to me as if I were too serious, that I should relax and enjoy the legal humor. Easier said than done. This witness was not only clearheaded but she also could deliver a decent punch line.

Hal indicated that I should read something he held in his hand. His assistant delivered a note to me, but I wouldn't be able to read it until lunch.

The direct examination continued. The voice was Macefield's, not Bellicoso's. "And do you know what Mr. Kerrigan did toward that end, Ms. Longwood, to get the money transferred to your late brother?"

It is not unusual for a judge to take over the examination of a witness when he's looking for something specific or wants to move the trial along. Sometimes lawyers object, but that's not a wise strategy.

Babette raised her head to the bench and answered quietly, meandering through a litany of memorable childhood experiences with Marcel. With Macefield's prompting, she nostalgically traced the Markham childrens' lives, recounting anything and everything she and Marcel did together since childhood. Although she wasn't responding to the question and was digressing, I didn't object. Under these circumstances a good opposing lawyer will permit the witness to babble on, hoping she'll talk herself into troubling admissions.

Her upper lip quivering uncontrollably, she made a pathetic sight. Could this exercise possibly be construed as relevant? Macefield thought so. That testimony lasted an hour and a half and included Marcel's puppet shows, Babette's curbside lemonade stand, Snow White, and hula hoops.

Much to my chagrin, she related to the court a very moving story of her drug overdose, going into great detail about her relationship with Edgar. Because of her husband's demanding travel schedule—he was hardly ever home—she'd become alcoholic and dependent on drugs. The cycle became more punishing when she was told that Edgar had terminal cancer and that she was not going to spend the rest of her life with him.

One night she swallowed enough pills to put a barn of horses to sleep, locked her bedroom door, and read a book that was similar in tone and direction to *Final Exit*. Luckily the maid had a key and found her around one in the morning, slumped over the side of her bed. She was rushed to the hospital, her life hanging by a thread, but she was miraculously saved. About a week later Marcel got her admitted to Hazelden, a treatment center for drugs and alcohol in Minnesota. Webb's name wasn't mentioned and, by the way things sounded, he had nothing to do with her treatment.

For the court's exclusive benefit, she talked about how horrible she felt every day of her life and how the counselor at Hazelden became her first friend, introducing her to a whole spiritual level of life. Rich people have a hard time adjusting to a very rigid rehab program, but she stuck with it and made some of the best friends of her life with others who were in the same boat. Hardly any of them were from her walk of life, but she loved being in a natural environment, living away from New York City, and getting to see inside herself and understand the kind of family and background that caused her addiction.

The rest of the story under oath was all about her long road to recovery. Marcel was there every inch of the way, attending the family program at the clinic, spending every afternoon with her, sitting on the lawn reading her short stories and holding her hand, fully cooperating with the doctors to cure Babette of her chemical dependency. There were no other family members except Marcel on campus. During the two-month treatment period Edgar didn't visit her once, although he was still capable of traveling in his condition. Pandora didn't see Marcel for that entire time. The rehabbing of Babette permanently damaged what could be best described as a fragile friendship between the sisters-in-law.

When she finished speaking it was clear that Babette didn't touch the stuff anymore. She was clean. It was also clear that Marcel either sucked up to his sister for the money or he really loved her. For the time being, Macefield was finished helping the White Knuckle present Babette as a very human, sympathetic character in her own soap opera.

After overpolitely asking the court if he could proceed, Bellicoso returned to his examination. "There was a loan agreement and I recall an IOU. Mr. Kerrigan called it a promissory note. Did you ever see that note?"

"Yes, I did."

"Did you read it at the time you saw it?"

"Probably checked it, but I don't recall now reading it over and over. I trusted them to do the correct thing. He was the lawyer getting a legal fee, and my brother was getting the money."

But it was too late for her to make it clear that it was a loan. She'd already uttered the magic word *give* and said that she was convinced to give; she wasn't under any pressure to do it. She wasn't fooled by anyone so far. Vito was at the front door but he was having trouble making the key fit the lock.

I'd have to subpoena Kerrigan unless he'd come to court willingly. This testimony made him sound like a real shyster. If Bellicoso called Kerrigan as a witness, it would be to corroborate that Kerrigan exploited Babette. Certainly Kerrigan would deny it. Bellicoso would have to attack Kerrigan, destroying the credibility of his own witness. That's legally frowned upon in New York. Only under limited, special circumstances in a civil case can you attack the credibility of a witness you call to the stand. That makes it difficult for a lawyer when presenting a case, or a defense to call the other side's witnesses to the stand as a surprise strategic move. To begin with, the other side is hostile and uncooperative, and if a lawyer is prevented from attacking the credibility of an adverse witness, the examination will be fruitless and embarrassing to the lawyer.

It would be hard to prove that there was nothing unethical about Kerrigan representing Babette as well as Marcel in the transaction. It would be a difficult position to maintain, and it was a perfect setup for Bellicoso to eat Kerrigan alive on cross-examination. I could anticipate the questions and answers:

"Mr. Kerrigan, who decided on the rate of interest, Mr. Markham or Ms. Longwood? Or did you decide it, Mr. Kerrigan?"

Answer—Mr. Markham.

"Mr. Kerrigan, who requested that you draft a promissory note?"

Answer—Mr. Markham.

"Who did you know first, Ms. Longwood or Mr. Markham?"

Answer—Mr. Markham.

"Which of the two clients did you ever meet with alone, that is, without the presence of the other?"

Answer—Mr. Markham.

"Who introduced you to Ms. Longwood?"

Answer—Mr. Markham.

Those exchanges would kill our case. And what if Kerrigan testified that Marcel did defraud Babette? That was hardly likely since he'd be as culpable as Marcel, unless Bellicoso got him to sell out.

Crossing through the cockpit, approaching the witness stand with a piece of paper in his right hand, Bellicoso asked, "Is this the document to which you referred, Ms. Longwood, when you said you were shown a promissory note? Do you recognize this document?" He'd abandoned the podium for this occasion. Macefield told him to have the document marked for identification and for it to be given an exhibit number before it was shown to the witness.

Another promissory note? My mind raced but I couldn't possibly show any shock or surprise. The note in the possession of the creditor was to be expected, as far as any court was concerned. Had Bellicoso broken into my office and stolen it? That was too far out, even for this case. Did someone else give him the note? No to that as well. Had someone forged a second note? Or had Pandora pulled a fast one on me? Did she know there were two notes floating around? That would be tonight's discussion with my star nonwitness.

I stayed cool, waiting for the court officer to present the documents to me so I could object. Which one was the original? The one in their possession or the one I had safeguarded in my file? Now I'd have to call a handwriting and document expert witness to testify if the signatures were the same. If different, I'd have to prove our note had the real signature.

Marked for identification by the reporter, Exhibit 31 was about to be admitted into evidence. The other side is given the opportunity to examine the proposed exhibit and to object to it as admissible evidence. I was nervous. The court officer delivered the note into my moist hands. I read it over slowly, hoping that the sentences would be screwy and at the bottom it would say "copy." No such luck. It looked pristine in every way, having the standard note language and most importantly the signature of Marcel S. Markham. On the spot I had to find a way to counteract this note. I was supposed to have in my possession the genuine thing.

Just as I rose to make an objection, not fully knowing why, except it was a knee jerk, Macefield was called off the bench, saying there was an urgent matter involving a patient. Judges usually say there is an emergency at a certain hospital and that they have to make a ruling over the phone. I never understood that, but I pictured a judge on telephone conference with a group of lawyers and doctors who gathered around a speaker telephone with a straitjacketed patient sitting on a wooden chair in the middle of a white-tiled room. The judge would hear arguments about the patient's mental health and then rule on whether he was competent or incompetent, whether he should be committed or released into the atmosphere outside the hospital.

We sat and waited for Macefield, but he didn't finish the call until 1:00. Lunch. The clerk informed the lawyers and gallery to return at 2:30. The courtroom would be closed until then.

I read Hal's note. It said that he wanted to interview my client in a very friendly and discreet way and had left several messages with her doorman at the Caprice. There was no response. He telephoned but there was no answer. Could I help and would Pandora just meet with him—off the record if she didn't want to be in the newspaper? Also Hal said he hadn't seen Pandora around for nearly a year. I wasn't surprised, but I couldn't do anything for him: it was completely inadvisable for Pandora to speak to the press.

My mind was flying. The first thing I had to do was to call Pandora about the promissory note. I went to my courthouse office, the hallway pay phone. There was no answer. Big surprise. Shouldn't I have figured she'd be out the rest of the day instead of sweating with the rest of us?

Mercedes reminded me that I had to be in court at 3:30 for Brian's arraignment. I'd forgotten to tell Macefield that I needed an early break, so I had to get over and see Bri ahead of time.

I got back to 503 just before the end of the recess. Handling two cases in the same afternoon was going to be trouble. Macefield would give me grief about the time off. Brian's arraignment would be difficult and time-consuming.

Anyway, it was done for me. Without explanation, Macefield never returned from lunch. The Longwood matter was adjourned until the following day.

From the Surrogate's Court down the street to the Criminal Courthouse it was a short walk through cutting gusts scaling off the East River and whipping around Centre Street. Ling wasn't far off, around the corner in Chinatown or right below street level, sitting in a dining car on the Ling RR. He could have me done right here very quickly. Some of the court officers I knew from Surrogate's were walking over to the Criminal Court for lunch. I joined them for the stroll up Centre Street. If Ling was going to do a drive-by he'd have guns blazing back.

For once in my life, I couldn't wait to get into yet another court—one that was not the Surrogate's—and I was eager to find out what Windows and the district attorney had cooked up. The calendar listed Bri's name and the case. But Bri was not going to be arraigned until after six from the length of the calendar.

This gurgling toilet was the criminal justice system. The halls were filled with sports-capped defendants floppily clad in multi-colored, oversized, numbered football jerseys, knee-length, cuffed baggy cotton pants, and airborne sneakers, talking intensely with discount lawyers in pinstripes, calling them counsel, who were being paid a thousand or fifteen hundred to get the defendant off for a mugging, a petty theft, or something much worse. This is where the attorney preps the alibi-ready brother, sister, mother, or father of the defendant. These relatives, as justice takes it course, testify as character witnesses for pimps, murderers, prostitutes, dope dealers, rapists, burglars, armed robbers, or small-time crooks.

This was not exactly the environment of the Longwood Securities boardroom or the swinging night scene at the Veranda. None-theless, it was in the case. There was no question that Y's death was linked to the money, and now there were two courts involved.

The first thing a lawyer does in these cases is confer with the assistant district attorney handling the case. I went around the corner to Leonard Street, where the guard gave me a pass to elevate myself to the tenth floor.

After ten minutes, Fox Carson came out to meet me. We fox-trotted back to his office, a windowless cubicle faced with about forty or fifty crime-related notices and an unused, overpunctured cork bulletin board.

"You're probably the tallest DA and the youngest in the office, Mr. Carson," I greeted him with two assessments that weren't de-finitive compliments.

"Twenty-five and six-five," he quipped.

"Basketball?"

"I didn't think you'd ask." He passed the ball back sarcastically.

"Just trying to break the ice," I replied.

"That's hockey, but I played basketball at Long Island University."

I rested my eyes on Carson's calendar. Next to a telephone number and the initials H, M.D. were the words *poss. witness.* Webb Hartford, M.D.?

"Mr. Ocean, there's some physical evidence that's very convincing and he has no alibi, not to mention all the circumstantial material we have on your client."

"What are the charges?" I asked. I knew they hadn't changed, but I wanted to see if any other counts had been added.

"Murder one, for starters, but we might have more. I think it might be conspiracy, obstruction of justice, maybe rape. We're looking into everything."

"Rape?" The bastard just might have done that and more to Y from the way he talked about her.

"There were witnesses who saw Bri going into Y's apartment, and in all likelihood, your client will be held without bail for the grand jury."

I asked him who the witnesses were, and Carson paused. The former athlete lit a filter cigarette and sucked in a balloon of smoke. "All I can tell you is that you have a tough case and there are a lot of very prominent people involved who want to see that your client doesn't get the chance to pull the trigger again. I think the bail will be very high."

For an inexperienced kid he was strong-willed, but it wasn't up to him to set bail. Word had come down to him that this was a special case and the office was to prosecute it all the way. I could easily see Windows winding up some East Side politician about solving two notorious murders that could be used as a platform for re-election. There was nothing else to discuss with Carson since there was no possibility of springing Brian in a deal with this office.

At 6:00 I went to the courtroom where Bri would be arraigned. After checking in with the clerk and signing in with the desk sergeant behind the courtroom on the same floor, I was taken to one of the holding cells in the back to speak with Brian.

He had about twenty roommates who didn't look like the tuition-paying types. He leaned in, his hands gripping the bars in the usual desperate way.

"Johnny, I hired another attorney, because you're representing the broad who was married to Rogers. I can't trust that."

"You knew that."

"I don't know nothing."

"They say you raped her." I tried to get a reaction from him before I was out of his life.

"Good luck to the DA. I never touched her."

Something told me he was unhappy about me not representing him. He turned and walked away, leaving me standing in the corridor looking at a batch of bad boys in a steel box and thinking that he was either a murderer or a rapist or both. There was no way I could have stayed in a case where I wanted to kill my client.

On the way out I was told a well-known, downtown criminal lawyer was being brought in to handle Brian's case. I knew the name, a former United States attorney. This lawyer wouldn't touch the case unless he received a hundred thousand up front. Criminal lawyers get their money right away, in cash, otherwise they never see a penny from the client. Once a lawyer's name goes down on the attorney's appearance form in a criminal case, the attorney is in the case until it ends. The law protects criminals, even against their own lawyers.

CHAPTER SEVENTEEN

Macefield didn't resume the case for two days. Judges run their calendars any way they choose, and the lawyers roll with the punches from one day to the next, even in the middle of a trial. In the interim, I was busier than an understaffed Greek coffee shop at lunchtime and lying low with Barkis and my Glock. I reread the translation of the arms list. It was impressive proof that money to buy arms for Chiang's army flowed through Ling and to parties in the United States. Longwood was in the middle of it.

I had to call Patton.

"Johnny, I was about to call you. I read the translation. We found some very old banking transactions between China Manpower and Longwood Securities. You can thank Mr. K. Some of his Sikh friends have Federal Reserve access. The Freedom of Information Act comes in handy, too, especially when the right wheels are greased, but some of the records are missing."

"K never mentioned anything to me."

"He made the introductions, maybe he doesn't know the results."

"There must have been a hundred million dollars or more transferred to Taiwan, then Ling in New York, right out of Longwood. Edgar Longwood, Harvard Class of '35, sounds familiar?"

"Same year Ling graduated?"

"There's an even stronger bond. They were roommates."

"What about the bank business between Edgar and Ling?"

"Apparently, money was transferred out of China to Longwood Securities, then Longwood paid the U.S. government for arms."

"So Chiang is using American money to do business with Americans. He wouldn't have had those big bucks unless the Roosevelt government loaned the mafioso Chinese billions. Like I give *you* money to buy *my* house."

"Exactly, great for the Chinese. We were idiots. So, get this. Funds from the Central Bank in China—that was the official government bank set up by T.V. Soong under Sun Yat-sen in 1924— were sent to Longwood, who bought everything from the United States government so the kickback channel could be established. The Chinese people didn't know anything. If the arms deals were government to government, then there was no intermediary to pay off.

"In those days industrial companies like General Motors, General Electric, and Chrysler supplied the war machinery to the U.S. government, who then sold arms and anything needed to China."

"Nothing has changed, the same giants of Wall Street are still selling arms to Washington."

"Right but this is the pennant winner—ten percent of the payments made by China would go into an account controlled by Longwood Securities. That money, together with bucks Chiang and Ling made from opium, was supposed to be deposited in China Manpower's account, which belonged to them. Guess what? There's about two hundred million missing, never paid by Longwood."

"Pin the tail on the donkey."

"Longwood Securities wired funds out of the China Manpower account to Switzerland where Ling, the Green Gang, and Chiang maintained their own accounts. It's similar to the setup used by other heads of State to funnel money out of their own economy.

The Marcoses, Saddam, Mexico, certain African countries, they all have their bucks in Switzerland, which thrives on officials stealing money from their countries and funneling it there. It's the armpit of the world, harbors more fugitives than any other country, only extradites criminals for money laundering and drug dealing."

"It hardly ever extradites them. Anything is jake with the Swiss. They take a cut of everything, just like Ling and Chiang."

"That's right. Switzerland is as filthy on the inside as it is clean on the outside—a wolf in sheep's clothing. It's not a country, it's a clearinghouse for crime."

"So there's the round robin. United States government lends billions to Chiang, who designates Ling to buy arms. Ten percent comes off the top and goes to Longwood, who wires it to Swiss bank accounts. Ling acted as arms comprador for the Chinese government and set up a kickback scheme with his Harvard buddy Edgar Longwood. Very neat. Ling was preparing to come to New York, and his money that was not already in Switzerland was supposed to be held for him by Longwood. In those days there were a lot of commerce between New York and China. New York was full of Chinese who maintained business interests in China and vice versa. There was plenty of room for shady transactions. T.V. Soong lived in New York during the war, until he died in the seventies. He choked on a piece of filet mignon. He had more connections than the Rockefellers, including the Rockefellers, and was hooked right into the Longwood clan. You name anyone with clout and T.V. knew them. But Ling trusted only one man who wasn't Chinese and that was his mistake."

"Edgar."

End of conversation.

No wonder Ling wanted me to lay off. He was after the money Longwood screwed him out of. He wasn't going to get it from Pandora. So he had to get it from Babette. Webb controlled Babette.

One way or another I was going to win this case and I had

more reasons than all of them. My life had been put on the line and it was still hanging there like a wet shirt. All of it was unbelievable, but I had to press on and see where it led. Not one of these powerful individuals could stop the process. Still, I had to question how the case was started in the first place. Did Pandora know what the hell she was up against? Did she care? Was this why she didn't want to testify?

Ling, with Longwood's Washington connections, made the purchase of weapons simple as ordering cable TV. Weapons from the world powers delivered to China's front door. Every detail efficiently accomplished through the good offices of Longwood's Wall Street brokerage firm. The houses of Ling and Longwood and their awesome power were the real claimants in the case. Could I beat them single-handedly?

Was there a chance I'd come out on top? Mao did. Chiang and his entourage economically raped and pillaged an opium-stoned China while the Red Army struggled to capture Chiang's American-made weapons and ammo. They eventually took China away from Chiang.

Despite this breakthrough, I had yet to prove anything. I hadn't given up on Pandora. The sound of her name was enough to give me hope that when the case was finished she'd be mine. Eyeballs had not confirmed to me who was living with her. I felt like a fat squirrel on its hind legs, begging the world for a solid clue.

While I waited for Macefield, I also decided to check further into his background and all of his recent decisions to see who won and why. I obtained a list of all of his biggest campaign contributors. It came from the Office of Court Administration. Twenty years ago, Edgar Longwood and Longwood Securities had generously supported Humphrey Macefield, giving him well over one hundred thousand dollars toward a Surrogate's judgeship campaign that didn't cost anything near that in the seventies. Judges, like politicians, are elected.

In addition, Macefield's father was a Tammany Hall–appointed judge and a power in the Democratic party. He was a cabinet advisor to President Roosevelt, and although I doubted I could prove anything to close the circle, the association between the Chiang government, Edgar Longwood, Emanuel Ling, and the United States government was getting clearer. Macefield was tight with his father, who would politically protect everything Macefield did in the courtroom. This legal political payoff wasn't anything new, and I'd never be able to prove that this case was fixed arguing before the brethren. This invisible way of fixing cases had been going on since the first politician scratched out something he called a speech on a black rock.

At 11:30 I walked over to Third Avenue and Fifty-ninth with Barkis, bought the *Times* at the newsstand owned by one of Mr. K's friends. The story was in the Metro Section, not in "At the Bar." The angle was obvious. The battle over millions between the sisters-in-law. It was a circus but what business isn't? It was well written by Howarth. He made it sound like a pay-per-view cat fight. Every character, including the prime subjects. Babette and Pandora got detailed, libel-proof, portraits painted. The more I read, the more I understood the *Times* was interested in the contrasting characters of Babette and Pandora, loving the odd brother-and-sister twist, posing the question, Did Marcel Markham trick sis into the 170-mil transfer?

The article was slanted in Babette's favor. The inescapable impression was that Ms. Longwood would not bring the lawsuit unless she was owed the money and that it was foolish to think that anyone, however rich or related, would place a hundred seventy million in someone else's hands with no strings attached. The article had a definite politically correct and feminist pen, strongly implying that two men—Markham and Kerrigan—had taken advantage of a woman. In a lamentable effort to show balanced reporting, there was a line at the end about women controlling large amounts of money that was made by men.

On the night before the trial resumed I was still a long way from solving the problems. I had handfuls of evidence that independently didn't mean anything. I was a mad artist throwing paint at a canvas, unable to make a painting.

Then, on a cloudless, bright, cold day I was in a gray suit back in court. No one mentioned the article in the *Times,* but I could sense that it had been roundly read in this room. Babette sat next to Vito, enthusiastically chatting him up. It seemed that she had quite a bit to say to her lawyer before retaking the stand.

A half hour passed with a smorgasbord of sidelong looks, sighs, yawns, table drumming, and edgy whispers. Macefield did not appear and we were about to find out why. The attorneys were summoned into his chambers. He was alone, head inclined, dressed in a charcoal gray suit with a new pink tie, and was writing something behind his desk. One hand turned and pointed like a traffic arrow, inviting us to take seats while he finished working. There was no court reporter present and, without looking up to greet us, Macefield let us know there would not be one. Any objections I had would go unrecorded. If I asked for a reporter, Macefield would deny it. This shit happens.

Suddenly, he stopped writing and stared at me. "Mr. Ocean, what is your factual defense in the action, besides the theory that the transaction was a legal gift?"

"That's what we are resting on, Your Honor, and the theory the obligation was satisfied by way of gift. The parties had a concealed oral agreement that contradicted the terms of the promissory note, evidenced by my client being in possession of the promissory note."

I was forced to tell him what our best evidence was.

"Don't *Perry Mason* me. There is a note about to come into evidence presented by Babette Longwood. Explain that, Mr. Ocean, in today's English."

"Your Honor, I am not trying to be clever. I will prove the parties had an arrangement and the debtor is in possession of the note. The presumption, under such circumstances, is that the debt has been satisfied, or there was never a debtor-creditor relationship in the first place."

"Very interesting, Mr. Ocean," Mr. Bellicoso purred, betraying no sign of surprise, as if he knew there was a second note all along. "You have a note and so does Ms. Longwood. You'll personally have a lot to explain, or your client will, about how it came into her possession."

Macefield looked at me with his lips tightened and inhaled through his nose.

Was my best piece of evidence about to be interpreted against my client and blow up in my face?

"I am inclined to agree with Mr. Bellicoso, Mr. Ocean. Are you telling us that, until now, no one had asked for the note? . . . Mr. Bellicoso had not requested it during discovery?" Macefield was looking at me as if Bellicoso's failures were my responsibility.

"It may come as a shock, Your Honor, but Ms. Longwood's counsel never demanded production of the note, and I have no obligation to produce it under these circumstances."

"I don't agree," said Macefield. "Moreover, there is something of an ethical issue as to how such a note came into your possession."

I could have said that Pandora wanted me to destroy the note altogether, but I refused. That would have blown his mind.

Vito piped in, "There will be a case made out, that is, a case more than sufficient that you won't be able to rebut by false evidence. We have the original note and it will undoubtedly be the only note received by the court in evidence." He added, "The authenticity question will be resolved. Then we can see where that puts Mr. Ocean, Judge."

He was accusing me of forging the note. "Mr. Bellicoso, just because you have what appears to be a promissory note doesn't mean that Babette Longwood didn't gift the money to Marcel Markham. You'll have to rebut the defense."

My mind started doing somersaults, rolling through counterarguments I hadn't given any thought to, which could beat us into pulp: The note had a lengthy term and was payable without much interest—that could be fraud. Macefield would rule: Mr. Ocean, your client's dead husband and that Kerrigan fellow tricked Ms. Longwood into a lousy deal, and you're trying to fool this court with a flimsy gift argument.

Marcel and Kerrigan had the note in their possession—that was illegal because the note should have been delivered to Babette. Macefield would rule: That's like buying a house and never getting the deed or possession of the property.

When trial lawyers think they're ahead of the game, they discover that things are not as they seemed. Their own guns get pointed back at them. My only consolation was that Vito probably hadn't thought about these arguments. Yet.

It was a question of which note was real at this point. I had to know how the note got into her possession.

Macefield, with a face like a gray sky about to go black, instructed me in a low voice, "Mr. Ocean, bring your client to the courtroom. My compass is pointed in your client's direction. I want to hear her testimony immediately following Ms. Longwood's. Furthermore, in the interest of justice and moving this case along, I want you to deliver the promissory note in your file to me this afternoon. Fax or deliver a copy to Mr. Bellicoso's office. If the issue is authenticity, let's study it and get it out of the way. Both of you may have your respective handwriting and document experts analyze the two notes. We will hear their testimony later in the week. All arrangements to obtain the notes can be made through my chambers. My clerk will supervise the procedure."

My beach towel had been yanked away by the not-so-blind lady of justice, exposing my private parts—my elusive client and her secret document. Had I promised Pandora she'd never have to set her beautiful foot in this or any other courtroom? No, but she said I did. I had the macabre image of the sheriff banging on her door, subpoena in hand, dragging her out screaming and kicking all the way downtown, calling me every name in the book.

From the second Macefield finished blasting his order, I began to retreat, not knowing what to do about Pandora. The note problem was something I could easily manage; I had a very competent expert I'd used many times before.

Macefield couldn't legally order me to bring Pandora to testify. Bellicoso hadn't served Pandora with a trial subpoena. How I presented my case was something the court couldn't control, but Macefield hit the nail on the head and was driving it right straight through me.

"Your Honor, I am not sure I can reach my client now," I replied, while my veins pumped the fear of getting caught around my system.

"Go to the telephone and try. Do you want me to give you a quarter? Is that what you're waiting for? Have your office hand-deliver the note. I'm certain you can do that."

"Your Honor, I don't see how my client can add anything in the midst of the witness testimony, and until Ms. Longwood is finished testifying, and I complete my cross-examination, it will be impossible to determine whether or not any other testimony is necessary. I may not have to introduce the note in our possession. Furthermore, I object to the court calling my client as a witness."

Macefield's face twisted like an asp. "I have made my orders! Are you telling me how to run my courtroom? Are you telling me something I don't know about the law?"

On cue, Bellicoso operatically bellowed, "I must come to the aid of the court. There is full and complete support for the court's action. Rule 4011 permits His Honor to order the presentation of proof and thereby he can call witnesses to the stand, and in addition, try the issues in whatever fashion he chooses."

Bellicoso was wrong. That rule only allowed a judge to hear

the evidence in a particular order or sequence, not to call witnesses on his own—that's constitutionally prohibited. But things were moving against me like a typhoon.

Macefield continued, "I have made my rulings, and a group of eminent legal authorities, commentarians, and myself understand it. I also thank you, Mr. Bellicoso, for reminding your adversary that I have the power to call whomsoever I wish as the next witness and to order him to produce any documents in his possession. That is my ruling, and that is the law." He looked like a mad scientist hunched over a smoky vial.

"Can I be heard on one more point, Your Honor?"

"What is it?"

"Can we finish Ms. Longwood's testimony before my client comes to the courthouse and before I produce the note? It appears to me, I respectfully submit, that once Ms. Longwood's testimony is complete, the issues may very well be adequately resolved."

It didn't come close. "Mr. Ocean! Retrieve your client. I expect you back in this courtroom by two o'clock tomorrow or I will dismiss your defense and be done with this matter! Judgment for the claimant will be entered. The note is to be delivered today, no later than today. Gentlemen, call your experts so they can read, diagnose, analyze, test, and whatever else the proposed exhibits." Then he looked at me. "Now, if you don't move, I will have you removed from the building."

His hand floated toward me as if a bolt of lightning was about to emerge and strike me. I backed off with my tail dragging and left his chambers knowing I was close to blowing up. That would only give him an excuse to hold me in contempt of court. It's one of the court's weapons to keep the fix on course.

Before I returned uptown, I went to the telephone in the hall to alert my client and the office.

Ironically, the immediate problem was not Macefield. It was Pandora. No answer at her apartment. I called Mercedes.

Webb walked to the elevator with his arm around Babette,

whispering in her ear. A few spectators were trailing behind when I noticed two very tall, broadly built black-turbaned Sikhs standing to the side. They looked at Webb and no one else. I didn't want Hal or any other reporter to see, so I turned around just as Mercedes picked up.

"Macefield's ordered me to get Pandora in to testify. And we have to deliver the promissory note. It's in my safe. Send the original to Macefield and a copy to Bellicoso. Keep trying Pandora's apartment while I'm on my way uptown. And get a hold of Carmine Lassiter. Tell her to call Macefield's chambers so she can testify about the authenticity of our note versus Bellicoso's. I want everything looked at, including the paper. She'll know what to do and she should start this afternoon."

"Okay."

"Just wait for me and keep trying Pandora's number until you get her, then hook her into my cell number in case I don't get back. Macefield's really pushing me. He's going to dismiss our defenses, and that'll be the opening of the file of Pandora's malpractice case against me."

When I got to the house, I walked into my office and passed a red-lipsticked, animated Mercedes sitting forward behind her desk. With her hands turned out, she explained to me, "Something's not right, Johnny. . . . There's no answer, as if she's disappeared in the middle of the trial. Now that would be incredible. I've called and called, plus sent a note over to her building. The least she could do is stick around, have some respect for all the work this office is doing. Besides you're a wreck. You have really put out for her, but she hasn't for you."

Just as I sat at my desk and opened the file, the phone rang. I picked up.

"Counselor," Windows drawled, his sound muffled by the cigar, "I have some news that might be of interest to you."

"What's that? You haven't exactly been the picture of helpfulness up to this point."

"Nor you to me. I have to do it all myself for the great State of New York, you know what I mean? You're one of those bigshot citizens."

"Careful with the envy, don't spread it too thin or it'll crack. What's up, Detective?"

"I can't get anything more out of Brian. Maybe a smart attorney like you can, especially now that you're out of the case and want to do something for the city."

"That's not practical, possible, or probable. I work for private clients, not for the public. I have my own problems. Right now, I'm in the middle of a money case. The client and I are busy preparing for the trial. All of this other stuff I'm not getting paid to deal with—unless the State of New York retains me."

"That's got nothing to do with the department. That's a civil matter."

Cops always say "that's a civil matter" whenever they don't want to get involved in something complex that's brimming with danger. No crime has been committed, but it's imminent. Domestic violence is the best example. Husband threatens to kill his wife, but the cops don't want to intervene in a civil matter. Two hours later the wife is dead, and now it's a homicide. That's criminal, not civil, and a distinction that costs lives.

But Windows was paying careful civil attention.

"When will it be over?"

I could see him chomping through the question, blowing a gust of cigar smoke into the phone.

"If you spoke to this character for me, I'd get somewhere. You're not his lawyer. Maybe you're buddies, and I can't force you to do anything."

"What's his lawyer say about you intimidating me?"

"Nothing. Giving us a hand, c'mon now, get Brian to talk to you. You're an officer of the court."

"Can't do it, Windows. You wouldn't want me to lose my license. The suspect has his own lawyer. I'm a lawyer. Got to speak to his attorney."

"Well then, I'll tell you about your bouncing little boy. He's talking. Download this into your fancy townhouse."

"Both ears are open."

"He's confessed, in writing, and it's signed. Claims he finished off your old girlfriend Y Ling. One shot in the neck. Lucky it wasn't a shotgun. Like Rogers, we'd have to find the head."

"Nasty joke for a cop," I snapped. He got me emotionally. Yeah, just one little hole in the neck through which a lifetime escaped.

Was Windows trying to get me worked up, to get me to blow my cool and talk?

"The suspect might've even told us where we could find the gun, ammo, everything except his holster. He says there are other people involved but won't talk. But I don't buy into that from a bouncer who never got through a front door. He just trying to take a stab at freedom, sell us something that DA's buy—information for immunity—then the prick goes for a long walk."

The "long walk" meant the little-known New York State witness protection program. Sometimes the state uses the federal system; sometimes the parakeet gets a bus ticket to the Midwest and he gets lost.

"You know the guy. Who could he be working for?" I asked.

It was about time I warmed up to Windows, because if Brian killed Y, I wanted to fry the bastard.

"Brian says Ling owns the Veranda Club." Windows had been fact-checking. Bri's innocence disintegrated.

"And what about the suspect meeting you at the Veranda Club? Said you left a note in a file, saying Webb Hartford checks out."

"Bullshit, never happened."

"Said you were waiting for Pandora one night at the club?"

"Maybe."

"Said you came around the club to ask questions about Rogers?"

"Fairy tales. He lied to me. Told me an old geezer delivered a letter to the Veranda for me. And I think he fired me because Ling hired a heavyweight attorney."

"There are two murders on the stove—Rogers and Y—both connected, in my opinion. I wanted to make sure that Brian wasn't your pal. Just a former client."

"You got that right. Did you ask him who shot me?"

"Yeah, swears up and down it wasn't him but he's got the goods. Just wants to make a deal first. But I don't plea-bargain. That's up to the D.A."

Mercedes slipped me a note. Pandora was on the other line. I signed off on Windows, telling him we'd talk later. The customer comes first.

"Pandora, I have some news for you. I—"

"Why aren't you in court?" she demanded, as if I were playing hooky.

"That's a question I was going to ask you. It's your case. Now it's the other way around. Macefield has ordered you to testify. There's no basis for it. Legally, he's way out in left field. But he's ordered it."

"I told you, under no circumstances, absolutely under no circumstances would I testify."

I didn't answer.

"Whatever else you were to do, you were to keep me out of court. I read the newspapers. It's a spectacle. The press is watching every move. I don't want any of that! Can't you control it? Isn't that why I hired the great Johnny Ocean, the world's greatest trial lawyer? Jack Dyson, damn. I could kill Dyson, just murder him."

It would have been an ideal time to send her back to Jack and go on an indefinite sea cruise. At this point, everyone was against me except Mr. K.

"Don't worry. You'll be fine. The press is no problem." I lied through my teeth. "Most of the reporters are friends. One of them from the *Daily News* even asked if he could interview you. We could practically write it ourselves."

She groaned. "I'm not going to say a word to anyone—not even you, if this keeps up."

"I didn't suggest you talk to the *News*. I'm just telling you it's not as bad as you think," I said, sparing her the gory details of what Macefield was doing to me. "I'll ask the judge to bar the press from the courtroom." I offered her this enticement to get her to sit in the witness chair. Macefield would blow me out the door on that application, but I continued to cajole her, "You can enter the courtroom through the back. No one will see you. No cameras are allowed in the courtroom. You won't be photographed. I can control that without any problem."

The calmer my voice went, the more I felt her weakening, succumbing to reason.

"How will you be able to keep the photographers out?" she asked, easing into the big top. For five minutes I reassured her until she became resigned to the realities of the process.

"I will be ready the day after tomorrow. Twenty-four hours notice is too much of a surprise. You'll have to tell the judge. Otherwise I am not coming."

"Let's see if Macefield will accept the delay. That, I can't promise. He's tough. If he orders you to come to court tomorrow and you don't show, he could dismiss our case. Babette would win."

Only a magician could win that request in front of Macefield, but I acted like I could pull it off, grateful that she was coming to court. Let the chips fall where they may tomorrow.

I rang off, feeling for the first time in the case that we had a rapport and a chance to win. I called my handwriting expert, Carmine Lassiter. Fortunately, she was between cases. I explained the situation. She'd already heard from Mercedes, had copies of the notes, and was on her way to court to see the originals.

Just then Rupert Hargrove called, wanting to know how the case was going.

"Rupert, did you ever get a chance to look over Pandora's will file after we spoke?"

Hargrove hesitated, coughed, cleared his throat, and said he had to requisition the file, that he had just called to check in. I asked him about the file, which meant his poor wife would have to dig it out of the archives. After ten minutes she brought it to Hargrove while we talked about the trial.

"As, I said, I drafted a will for her, changing the previous one, really revoking the earlier will. Not a codicil. But she never signed it, never got around to it."

"Who was the beneficiary?"

"That was it, there were none. She couldn't make up her mind between certain people and certain charities. In the old will she had named her ex-husband, Bill Rogers, the principal beneficiary. He threatened me. If Pandora executed a new will he'd kill me. Thought that happened only in those divorce cases. I said to him, 'Kill me? I don't know if you can kill a dead man.' That man was sick."

"Is there anything else in the file?"

"Well, I was just reading what I said from a note I made in case he did murder me, and it also says a bit further down that I heard from Pandora several months later. Then she didn't want to change the will, which was very odd since she was divorced from Rogers."

So the will had not been changed and it was not going to be. Rogers was tracking the money every step of the way to make certain Marcel paid his debt of guilt.

When Rupert hung up, I called Pandora back. I didn't mention Hargrove.

"Tell me what I have to testify about," she said. "We might as well get to it."

"We'll have to meet tomorrow after court." My posture was getting more professional. We were going to meet and review evidence as I would with any normal client, and I would treat her like a witness and not a potential lover.

"You still have the note, don't you, Johnny?"

"I had to deliver it to the court, otherwise we would never get our note into evidence."

"Why did you give it to them? If you had gotten rid of it, there would be nothing to support the loan in the first place," she insisted, pouting, barely listening to me.

"The cat is out of the bag. . . . I had to tell Macefield that we had the note. They have a competing note, just like twins. One is real and one isn't. It's no longer just what we thought, that we have the only promissory note. You had nothing to do with the note as far as I can tell. It was just amongst Marcel's papers, wasn't it?"

"You think I manufactured it?"

"I just want to be sure about where the note came from. Bellicoso and the court will probably ask you that question. They might try to show you forged it."

"That's crazy. Marcel died and I found it in his desk. That's all there is to it."

"That's what I want to hear. If you testify that you found the note in your husband's possessions, it would go a long way toward establishing that the money was a gift. We just need to prove its authenticity."

She calmed down. She was impatient. In these tense final moments, she didn't want to take any chances of not being prepared.

"The best time to meet is tomorrow night," I said, not telling her, as I probably should have, about the conversation with Windows.

"Look, we don't have to meet. I know what to say. The note is the note and it was in my late husband's papers. I've read so many lawyer thrillers, seen them on television, cross-examination . . . say 'yes,' or 'no,' or 'I don't know.' I shouldn't elaborate on any point. If I am confused, I should say, 'I don't know,' or 'Would you repeat the question?' And I can say, 'I don't recall,' or 'Hmm, I don't presently recall but I might at some future date.' But if I'm forced to answer a question, my response will be to the point. I won't go into any other subjects." She made a breathy promise and added, "What do I know about the dealing between Marcel and Babette other than what Marcel told me?"

"I'm writing up the things you'll have to know on the stand."

"Okay. You will pick me up the day we go to court and we'll review them then. You are still a gentleman, aren't you, Johnny?"

"Of course, I haven't changed."

I heard the door slam downstairs. Mercedes was gone.

"I have another question for you."

"Yes, Johnny, what is it?"

"At any time were you with Marcel and Babette when this sum of money was discussed?"

"Not really. Marcel kept me out of it. She was his sister; I was just his wife, and I didn't have her kind of money. I remember that Marcel borrowed regularly from Edgar, and Edgar never wanted, as he said in a letter to Marcel, to be repaid. They just created the notes for tax purposes, like this case, to hide the gift. You've explained all of that to me." She said all of it in one breath followed by a long, sensuous sigh. It changed the mood, gave me a rush, reminding me of how hot she was, how hot she could get me. In an instant my emotions went back to square one.

I moved the laughing Buddha paperweight on my desk, rubbed it with my thumb, and stayed quiet.

"I have a limousine and a driver; you don't have to pick me up. You're a gentleman."

"Okay."

"Such a gentle . . ." Her voice softened.

"What's that?"

"Uh, uh-huh . . . Ooh, yes, very gentle . . ."

"What?"

"Yes, that's it, Johnny, be gentle. Tell me how much you want . . . you want to . . . you make me tremble, gently now, Johnny."

"What are you talking about?" I asked but I was going wild with the quick, capricious way she had shaped the conversation. Was she playing with herself? Were her long, thin fingers holding her lips open, rubbing her clitoris in a slow but determined fashion? Absolutely. All the lights were off, except for a small lamp nearby that cast a faint orange streak of light along her thighs. One of her heels fell to the floor, then the other, and I went dry in the throat.

"Yes, Johnny, spread my thighs, then tell me, tell me what it looks like there and what you want to do with it. Yes, please touch it there. . . . Tell me. . . . Kiss me there and tell me, describe all of it to me," she murmured.

"I can do whatever you want. I can be whatever you want," I answered. Isn't that what I was supposed to do as her advisor?

"That's what I like to hear. That's what I want to hear. I want you . . . to give in to me completely, to tell me, Johnny. I can see you so well. I can feel you all over, Johnny. You feel so good. . . . Johnny, I want to wait, I want to see you first. You can't hold back. I love it so much when you teach me, that's it, show me the way it must be done. I am whatever you want me to be. I want you. Tie my hands and legs, Johnny. You are the one, the person who must tie them tighter, tighter, that's it, bind me to you and then take me again and again, make me, milk it from me until . . . ooh Johnny, ooh Johnny, you are the one . . . push it in, Johnny."

I was undressed, the phone pressed to my ear, waiting for the moment when she'd tell me to come over. My head was buzzing from the heights she was taking me to. Anything was possible at that moment; the little voice on the other end coated with thick depravity. If I didn't go to bed with her tonight, this call was going to lead me to it within days.

"You want it?"

"Don't make me beg. You know the answer."

"Pandora, you must be filled with my prick, and flooded with pleasure . . ."

"And . . ."

I went white-silent.

"And . . . please?"

"You're caught on the end of it. I'll shove it into you and when I pull out you'll be covered in cum and sweat. You're a sick sex junkie."

"No, Johnny, no, yes, yes, yes, you fucker, you give that to me now. Do everything to me. First down, down there. Kiss it, kiss deeply, let me feel your tongue way inside of me and . . . that's so beautiful, Johnny. It's so beautiful and big for me. Fuck me hard, fuck my cunt, my pussy hair is so wet, dripping for you, all over your dick and balls."

"Can you take all of it?"

"Yes, yes . . . fuck me, fuck the living hell out of me."

She sounded as if she were going out. The voice faded, and I thought for a second she'd fallen asleep.

"Johnny, are you there?" she finally asked.

"Yes." I cleared my throat.

"Are you still hard?"

"What do you think?"

"Well, don't be. I take my orgasms where I find them. Sorry if you feel used, but we have a trial to think about. Big kiss, I have to go."

Of course I could have killed her, but I just answered, without a trace of disappointment, "I'll give you a copy of the cassette when we're in court, and a big kiss to you, too."

"You taped it?"

I hung up on her and threw the phone across the room, mad as a rabid dog. The bitch had done it again. She made a fool out of me. But I mind-fucked her. That made me feel much better.

After a vodka shot, I pulled over an ashtray, lit a cigarette, and felt some excitement about the next two days. Even if the other side had the guns, I wanted a war. Pandora was coming with me. Finally we'd fight them together. I could hear it in her voice, in her soul—she wanted to win, needed to win.

Hours later, about midnight, I climbed into bed. Again, in my sick way, I wanted to talk with her, but that would have to wait until we went to court.

I finally began to fall asleep, dreaming that Pandora and Webb were strung together like two steel cables on the George Washington Bridge. The tension created by one snapped the other. The bridge collapsed.

CHAPTER EIGHTEEN

We were scheduled to be in front of Macefield at 9:30 A.M. Outside of 503, his secretary, Ms. Strife, dressed in skintight knits, snaked up to me—a very sensual welcome sign in enemy territory.

"Mr. Ocean, love that suit, pinstriped, pale blue shirt, very enticing. Nice sapphire cufflinks, you *are* ready to cross-examine Babette Longwood. Every day something different, never the same anything, including shoes," she gushed and smiled as a thin stream of spectators filed in behind us. Since the courtroom seats were taken, they went up to the balcony.

"I love a man who pays attention to detail—and doesn't wear bow ties."

"I do it out of respect for the court. Anyway, you've got it all wrong. You're the big attraction around here. Way hot for the legal system. Over the top. But I shouldn't tell you, Macefield will accuse me of sexually harassing you. Have you been in the courtroom watching the action?"

"Wouldn't you be if you worked here? This is the most exciting thing to happen in this courthouse since the Johnson and Johnson trial. You're in it and my boss has it out for you. Are you holding up? Everyone is dying to see your client."

"Thanks for the compliment. How'd you know about my client testifying?" Spectators were standing in the rear and on the sides of the courtroom. Every seat taken. The widespread news coverage had reined in a crowd. There were four black-turbaned, heavily bearded Sikhs seated around the room, appearing not to pay attention to me. But I recognized one of them I'd seen with K several times.

"There are no secrets in that office. Good luck," she replied and walked inside.

Right away, Macefield requested that sharkskin-suited Bellicoso and I approach the bench for another reporterless sidebar.

"Mr. Ocean, is your client in the courtroom?" Bellicoso adjusted his silver necktie.

"On the way, Judge," I responded firmly.

Asking for time would make him crazy. Foolishly I let Pandora believe her testimony could be put off for a day, but I had no choice. The only thing I could do was bluff and run out the time today.

"For her sake, she'd better show. Proceed with Ms. Longwood." That was some temporary relief. He turned to Bellicoso.

"I've seen your proposed exhibit—the promissory note that you had premarked yesterday—Exhibit 31. Would you kindly call Ms. Longwood to the stand so we may continue? Mr. Ocean has had the opportunity to review it as well. It has all the earmarks of authenticity, Mr. Ocean. I don't know what you have in store, but it will be intriguing."

"Your Honor, I will await the outcome," I answered, not giving an inch to the court's sudden protean attitude.

Babette glanced back at Webb, who stared straight back at her as she took the stand and was handed the exhibit by the court officer. Bellicoso stepped forward, scooping the note from the witness table.

"Ms. Longwood, do you recognize this document, Exhibit 31?"

I glanced up at the balcony. A large group of spectators had gathered and one pointed down at Babette, explaining things: "Now she's the rich one, done nothing wrong. The judge will say that she's innocent."

Babette lifted the single-page document as if it were dirty and wet, studying it for a solid five silent minutes. Macefield was uncomfortable, turning in his chair, gazing at a noticeably tense Bellicoso pacing back and forth in the heart of the cockpit.

At last Babette responded, "I do . . . not, don't re-re-cog-nize the . . . the doc-document but that, th-that does look like the sig-signature of Mar-Marcel."

Macefield was shocked as she started to stumble, stutter, and lose her clarity. He repeated Bellicoso's question. "Ms. Longwood, do you recognize the document? That is, have you seen it before?"

"Ju-judge, I jus-jus-just do not *know*. It may have been in my off-ice at home. The sig-sig-signature looks like my bro-brother's and, and he did si-sign . . . a . . . note to me."

The crowd gasped and went into a beehive buzz over her stuttering. Macefield asked her if she could say with certainty that it was Marcel's signature. She could not. If the witness, especially your own witness and client, does not recognize the document in question with certainty, there is no legal basis for it to be received in evidence. But it was offered in evidence and received by Macefield over my objection, subject to my voir dire. The voir dire is a process by which an opposing lawyer can ask the witness questions about the validity of the representations and the authenticity of documents.

"Do you recognize the signature?" Macefield asked again, underlining the uncertainty of his ruling.

"Yeh-y-yes. I bel-ieve it's Marcel's."

If this kept up, I would have hardly any cross of her since she might prove a better witness for us than for them. I would leave it undisturbed.

"Your Honor, may I conduct my voir dire?"

"You may proceed, Counselor."

I approached Babette. Webb's face was ashen, but he couldn't do anything unless Bellicoso stopped the process. The gallery loved the action, especially Hal, who was sitting on the west side of the courtroom. He was close to the witness chair and to where he knew I'd be in the cockpit—surrounding Babette. I have no use for a podium: The best part of any trial is the cross-examination. The reporters were all experienced enough to know that Macefield was treading on questionable ground and Babette was about as unstable as a witness can get.

Picking up proposed Exhibit 31, I handed it back to Babette and stood to the side of the witness chair, in front of the American flag. I looked around the courtroom to the gallery, forcing Babette to face the spectators. This is a tactic I normally use in jury trials. It would work here. Looking jurors or the court in the eye and lying is harder than lying to a hostile lawyer like me.

"Ms. Longwood, have you ever seen this document before today? And if so, where and when?"

"I th-th-think so. Bu-but I ca-cannot re-re-re-remember where or wha-wha-what or when."

"Where did it come from? You did say it *may* have come from your office at home?" She'd never come through on this one.

"Tha-that's right."

"Well, did it or didn't it?"

"Don't know."

The judge and Bellicoso could have crawled into a hole over that answer, but there was no going back. There were no objections from the White Knuckle. He knew that Macefield would have to overrule him. I could feel the courtroom closing in on Babette. Everyone's eyes were training on her. She felt the pressure.

"Did your lawyer show it to you? Was that when you saw it for the first time?" I was finessing her into the situation Pandora had placed me in, which is where I got the idea for the question.

"That's a poss-poss-possib-possibility. I *don't* know." This was a perfect time for Bellicoso to object on the basis of attorney-client privilege, but it went by him. That was a break. "I do-don't know."

"Well, you say you don't know, so let's see if we can be helpful. I'm going to read you some excerpts from your deposition, which was taken in this courtroom six weeks ago. Do you recall the time I asked you some questions before this trial?"

"Yes."

"Before I get into that let me ask you, do you know what a promissory note is?"

"Yes, I, I do."

"At page thirty-four, line twelve, I asked you the following questions, to which you gave the following answers, under oath. Question: 'Did anyone ever tell you the document to which you refer was a promissory note?' Your answer: 'A promisor what? Don't know what it means.' Question: 'Did you read it when it was signed?' Your answer: 'Said something about a sum of money. I think it was in the millions . . . dollars . . . and that I would get the money back sometime, or during a five-year time period. . . . I don't know, don't you know?' Now did you give those answers to those questions under oath, and were they true at the time?"

"I, I gu-guess I did. Un-under o-o-oath."

"Ms. Longwood, you didn't know what a promissory note was then. And that's what you said, correct?"

I was standing almost behind her, about six feet from Hal, whose head was buried in what he was writing. Next to him was an artist sketching Macefield, Babette, and me in pastels.

"Right." Her face was gray. So was the White Knuckle's.

"So you can't recognize this document today, based on your knowledge when I took your deposition, could you?"

"No, sir, I c-c-c-could not."

Hal madly jotted everything down. So far the *Times* hadn't written up the case extensively, but the *Post* and *Daily News* would splash this testimony onto the second or third page of

tonight's late edition. COURTHOUSE FIASCO—WOMAN SUES FOR
$170-MILLION DEBT, CAN'T I.D. THE I.O.U.

I addressed Macefield, "Your Honor, I object to the admissibil-
ity of this document. This witness can't recognize her own promissory note."

He overruled my objection and admitted Exhibit 31 into
evidence. Bellicoso then asked for a bench conference.

"Judge, I have my handwriting expert in the courtroom. He's
had the opportunity to study both notes. I was going to call him
after Ms. Longwood, but in light of her inability to recognize the
document, I submit it is appropriate to call Mr. Pericles Eliopolus, one of the world's most renowned handwriting experts. I request that Ms. Longwood's testimony be briefly interrupted, that
Mr. Eliopolus be taken out of turn."

I could have objected. This was way out of line. There was no
reason to stop the rest of Babette's testimony. But it was buying
me time with Pandora, so I just shut my mouth.

"Application granted. The witness may be taken out of turn,
but first we'll take a brief recess. Have you're client ready, Mr.
Ocean. This shouldn't take long."

"Famous last words," I said under my breath and walked away.

I sent for my expert, Carmine Lassiter. Taking a break from examining the documents in Macefield's chambers, she came into
the courtroom. Olive-complexioned Carmine, half American Indian and half Italian, cut a striking figure, as noticeable in the
gallery as any one of the turbaned Sikhs. She was able to prep me
for cross-examination, but she hadn't had time to complete her
analysis.

The session resumed.

A man in white shirtsleeves and black silk-striped tuxedo
pants, who I'd previously thought was a spectator, pigeon-toed
his way to the stand. The back of his small head had patches of

wiry gray hair; long sideburns were tied in tiny dreadlocks. Gold jewelry covered his wrists and fingers. As he passed me, his thin lips smiled. He flashed a confident look to Babette, his employer, who didn't seem to understand it. His knees nearly knocked together as he moved through the cockpit to the witness box, where he was sworn in.

Macefield directed him to be seated, even though he was sitting, and asked for his full name and address for the record.

"My name is Pericles Aristotle Eliopolos, but my friends call me Perry. My address is 25-57 101 Avenue, Queens, New York."

Bellicoso asked his first question. "Mr. Eliopolus, what do you do for a living?"

"I'm a questioned document examiner, what the public calls a handwriting expert." In the second he completed his sentence, Eliopolus self-consciously raised his right hand. The wrist was bent, deformed, and the fingers were curled backward.

"For what time frame?"

"Twenty years, and I'm a man forty-five years old, half my life."

"And what is your educational background in your field?"

"I was trained, well educated I might add, because I like to plug the school, at the Brambles College of Normal Review in Heidelberg, Germany. Southwest Germany." His eyes widened and twinkled, as he must have thought that we all knew the institution. I'd never heard of it or Eliopolus.

"What was your area of concentration?"

"Handwriting, handwriting, handwriting, everything to do with handwriting all over the world." His eyes rolled up to the ceiling as if we were stupid.

"What degree did you receive, if any?"

"No degree. There is none."

"Your studies were completed when?"

"About 1968. I speak German and Greek."

Macefield smiled as if the German language was connected to the case.

"Thereafter have you worked in the field of document analysis and examination?"

"Yes, sir. I have examined documents in court. My testimony has been accepted by two hundred fifty judges around the United States alone, maybe more." That couldn't be true. He was starting to show his insecurity very early on.

I interrupted, because I was getting ready to voir-dire the witness, "Does Mr. Eliopolus mean he has testified two hundred fifty times?"

Eliopolus answered, "That's correct."

"Since 1975?"

"Thereabouts."

Macefield was taking notes. He never did when I spoke, but if Vito said something or when his witnesses testified, the judge was writing. That was a bad sign for Pandora, the executrix. Macefield would hang his decision on the findings he recorded.

"Have you been qualified in those trials as an expert witness two hundred fifty times?" Bellicoso asked.

I knew that was a gross exaggeration, but I let it slide. It would have taken forever to voir-dire him over all the times he testified. The judge would stop me.

"No, probably more like two hundred times." His voice grew louder. "I have been, and I might add, I am consulted by the United Nations, Philip Morris, AT&T, and many others. I also was consulted by the district attorney of Queens five times."

"And have you published any articles in the handwriting field?"

"Yes, I have. Actually, I have written articles and a handbook called 'Juries and Forgeries' and that has been published in thirty languages in twenty-five countries." I did not own that text, and I was sure it sold fewer than twenty-five copies worldwide.

"I am the founder and president of the International Forgery Detection Society, based in Vienna, Austria." His right hand floated up again looking like a broken tree limb.

It was then I asked to have a short voir dire. I wanted to test Eliopolus and his credentials right away, and it was a good time to disrupt his composure.

Macefield sighed but granted it.

Stepping directly in front of the witness, I asked, "When is the last time you testified prior to today?"

"Eight months ago." He pulled the mike closer with his left hand and gazed outward, trying to speak over me to the courtroom.

"Was it a New York City court?"

"No."

"Which court was it?"

"In Chicago."

"What type of case?"

"Criminal."

"Do you know the name of the case?"

Flustered, he replied, "I don't recall."

"When is the last time you testified in New York?" He was getting agitated; I knew I'd get to him. That's all I wanted to know. Somewhere in that little head he believed that he was entitled to respect, but he wasn't going to get any.

"I think last year I was in court in New York."

Bellicoso cut in, "Your Honor, this is improper voir dire. Counselor, would you stipulate Mr. Eliopolus is a handwriting expert?"

Bellicoso was right, voir dire is only used in these circumstances to test the expert's qualifications.

"I defer to the court to rule on Mr. Eliopolus's expert status. I won't stipulate."

Macefield ruled that Eliopolus was qualified and asked me to take a seat.

Vito resumed, "Mr. Eliopolus, you were retained by my firm to examine certain documents?"

"Yes, I was, sir."

"When?"

"About three months back."

No denying that took me by surprise. Bellicoso must have known there were two notes, or else that there would be a controversy over the authenticity of his note.

"Did you examine such documents?"

"Yes. I have them with me."

Doing his job, Macefield said, "Let the record reflect that the witness has a file from which he is removing documents. We will have this marked for identification as claimant's number 32, a group of documents." The reporter marked the documents and returned them to Bellicoso.

"I am showing you Exhibit 32. I will list what they are: the last page of the last will and testament of Marcel S. Markham, original of Marcel S. Markham's driver's license, original of Marcel S. Markham's voter registration card. Each document bears the signature that purports to be that of the late Marcel S. Markham, do they not?"

"Correct."

"Now, Mr. Eliopolus, can you describe your method of examination?"

"Yes. I studied these documents under a microscope, at fifteen and at forty-five times magnification. Furthermore, I also examined them with a magnifying glass, which is five to six times magnification, at least. And I have identified Mr. Markham's signature as being on those documents."

"Now, Mr. Eliopolus, you examined this series of documents and compared them to certain other documents, is that correct?" Bellicoso was at the podium speaking to Eliopolus as if he were someone he just met for the first time.

"Correct. I made enlargements of the signatures."

"Can you tell the court if the documents comprising Exhibit

32 were written by the same hand as the person who signed Marcel S. Markham on Exhibit 31, the promissory note produced by claimant?"

"Yes."

"Were there any characteristics that were common to all of those signatures?"

"Yes."

"What were those common characteristics?"

"The common characteristics were that the person who wrote them had an extension in his signature as well as the letter formation. So it was done by the same person."

"What does that mean, extension?"

"Extension means that a certain space was used horizontally, which is common in these exhibits."

"Were there any other common characteristics that you observed?"

"Yes. Particularly at the end of the signature, the line usually ended in a loop followed by an underlying line that goes back toward the first name."

Approaching the judge, Bellicoso asked the court, "Your Honor, I will have Exhibit 33 marked, the note produced yesterday by Mr. Ocean on the executrix's behalf."

I didn't object.

It was a quick way of getting my note into evidence.

Then Vito posed the question to Eliopolus, "Please tell us if you examined Exhibit 33, the executrix's note and compared it to Exhibit 31, the claimant's note?"

"Yes. I found that the person who signed 33 put the *a* in Markham well into the *r* and the cap on the *h* was bent. Such characteristics were not found in Exhibit 31 and 32's signatures." He was cocksure of his answers, smirking his way through expert expressions of certainty.

"Any other differences between Exhibit 33 and 31 and 32?"

"Yes. The last name was extremely bundled and indistinct in 33. Under strong magnification, I determined that there were hesitation marks in the middle zone letters."

"What do you mean by hesitation?" asked Bellicoso.

Macefield was feeling like he had a winner. Things were going down well and he let me know it with one of his trademark glances askance.

"Here you can see in Exhibit 33 there is crowding. The letters are more together." He pointed with his left hand.

The court officer picked up the exhibit and showed it to Macefield.

"Is it your expert opinion that the same person signed both documents, Exhibits 33 and 31?" asked Vito.

"No. My expert opinion is that Exhibit 31 and Exhibit 33 were not signed by the same person and that Exhibit 31 is the authentic signature of Marcel S. Markham."

Thinking he was far ahead, Bellicoso closed the testimony and said, "I have no other questions for this witness."

Macefield peered down at me sitting at the counsel's table and softly said, "Cross, Mr. Ocean?" But I could swear he said, "Cross the ocean."

I greeted the witness, standing directly in front of him so as to block him from Bellicoso's view.

"Good morning, Mr. Eliopolus. Sir, altogether how much time did you spend analyzing this matter?"

"I would say approximately between ten to twenty hours, closer to twenty."

"In one straight go without a break?"

"No."

"Was it all done in more than one day?"

"Yes, I spent the last couple of days here in court working, in the judge's office."

"Where else was it done?"

"My office, several months ago."

"You did some of this work in your office? Did you do it by yourself?"

"Yes."

"Mr. Eliopolus, I notice you were wearing glasses when you started your testimony, and now you've taken them off."

Someone in the gallery removed his glasses, peered down at them as if he were about to be called to testify.

"When you did this analysis, did you have your glasses on or off?"

"I usually don't need them, because I have magnifying glasses, but I used a microscope." He changed his approach and I went with it.

"Why?"

"The microscope only has value for seeing the details."

"You observed the signature at fifteen and forty-five times magnification?"

"Yes, I did."

"What does it mean, 'hesitation marks in the middle zone'?"

"It means a person not signing a real name has a tendency to observe what he has copied. Such a person hesitates for a second here and there, and it shows up under high magnification. When you write it's a fluid process. There is no hesitation in your hand-writing at all. But if you have to be certain that you are writing exactly the same thing you are copying, then you will hesitate."

"And in which strokes of the signature did you notice hesitation?"

"All of them in the central region of each name in 33."

"What parts of the name did you magnify that indicated that?"

"Every stroke of it." He said in a very bitchy way, but I continued to push him on every part of his testimony.

"Every single stroke of it in the middle sections?"

"Every stroke *there,* yes."

"Mr. Eliopolus, what does the middle zone consist of in this case?"

"In the middle zone, all central letters."

"What letters? That is what I am asking you, what letters?"

Eliopolus asked Macefield if he could illustrate this on an easel. Stepping down from the stand, Eliopolus picked up a wooden pointer with his left hand. He went to the easel where he had the court officer mount blowups of the signatures in Exhibits 31, 32, and 33.

"Observing the name Marcel, the middle zone is *R-C-E* and then Markham, the letters in the middle zone *K-H-A.*" He ran the pointer alongside the letters and waited for the next question.

"So in other words, you are saying that the first and last letters are not in the middle zone of names in a signature?"

"Partially they are, but not completely."

"Are you saying when the subject wrote his name, there was no hesitation on the *M-A* and on the *L* in Marcel, no hesitation marks on the *M-A-R* and the final *M* in Markham?"

"Very little, because when a word is started or finished, the writer is less conscious of copying. The writer is more relaxed."

"The hesitation then begins over again in the signing of the second name, because it is discontinued at the end of the first name. The person signs the beginning of the second name with no hesitation and then the hesitation commences again in the middle of the second name. Is what I said correct?"

"The hesitation is in the writing, not in the person, but you are correct."

"What was the reason that you looked at it under magnification?"

"For corroboration."

"You didn't want to leave any doubt?"

"That's correct. That is why one observes it under microscope."

"Did you show your findings to any other colleague?"

"No, I didn't get corroboration from anyone else if that's what you are asking."

"And, Mr. Eliopolus, have you ever had an occasion to examine your own handwriting?" I looked at him squarely. The question made him jumpy.

The process took several minutes, but I was finally just getting a handle on where I wanted to take him and his testimony.

"No, I have not."

"Why is that?"

"There has never been an occasion to do so."

The way his voice fell off I knew he was lying.

"Mr. Eliopolus, are you right-handed or left-handed?"

"Do I have to answer that question, Judge? I'm not on trial." He looked at Macefield for guidance. Macefield directed him to answer the question.

And he was on trial. Neither Macefield nor Bellicoso could protect him any more than if he were a celibate sex therapist.

"I am not right-handed or left-handed." The answer was delivered like, I am not living and I am not dead. Any trial lawyer would love to go deeper on this one.

"That's odd. Which hand do you write with?"

The gallery was eagerly awaiting this answer. The question had developed out of the blue, but that's the kind of cross-examination that breaks a witness. Peripheral questions often lead into the substance.

"Neither. I was born with a crippled right hand and my left hand is all thumbs. It just scribbles. I only use it for signing things, just to scratch out something that looks like a signature."

I felt sorry for Perry but I had to destroy him. Every player in a contact sport tries to aggravate the opposing team's injuries.

"And what you scratch out, is it always the same or is it different sometimes?"

"Different, yes, most of the time."

He stuffed his crippled hand into his other hand as if it were a paper bag and humbly moved back to the stand. That was all he said, but it was more than enough. I didn't have to ask him why he became a handwriting expert since it was right out there for everyone to see. He was envious of anyone who could write his name or express himself on paper. He must have hated Marcel because he was able to get $170 million transferred to him by writing out his name.

"In addition to your activities as a questioned-document expert, you also analyze the age of paper?"

"Yes."

"And isn't it also a fact that sometimes you judge the age of ink?"

"That is extremely difficult, you know, but I have done it."

"So you do it or do you leave it to the FBI lab in Washington?"

"Both. It depends."

"Are you aware that both signatures are signed in either ink or ballpoint, Exhibits 31 and 33?"

"Yes."

"Mr. Eliopolus, you are absolutely certain, are you not, that whoever put the signature on Exhibit 31 was not the same person who wrote the signature on Exhibit 33?"

"Yes."

"Are you aware of an ink, a Parker ink, called Nile Blue?"

"Yes, but I don't know if that ink is on Exhibit 31."

"Sir, did you know that Nile Blue was not available for sale until November 1987, eleven years after the note, Exhibit 31, was executed?" I didn't say that was the ink used (which it was) but it was enough to make him too uncertain to answer any questions about ink.

"No. I did not."

"And did you make an attempt to determine the age of the paper in either Exhibit 31 or 33?"

"No, sir."

"So you did not check the paper of Exhibits 31 and 33 for the presence of *size?*"

"I wasn't asked to do it." He was a goner who just wanted to get off the witness stand.

"You know what size is, don't you?"

"Yes, it is a paper substance that contains a surface so the ink will not run. My client did not engage me to do that work."

"Could you do it?"

"Possibly. I am knowledgeable but not qualified."

That meant they were dead on this issue because Carmine was one of the best at paper analysis.

"You couldn't do it?"

"I might have attempted it."

"What attempt would you make to find out how old this piece of paper is?"

"I would look under the microscope for the composition, texture, and fiber. You can tell when it was made, sometimes who the manufacturer is. The age of paper is difficult to determine, but it can be done."

"Now, Mr. Eliopolus, I'm a little confused. Maybe you can help me. Wouldn't the age of the paper and the ink be useful in your analysis?"

"How do you mean?"

"It would be fairly conclusive if either the ink or the paper, or both, were manufactured after Marcel S. Markham died."

"I suppose it would."

"If Mr. Markham signed the note in 1986 and the ink and paper didn't exist at that time, would it be reasonable to conclude that the note was not signed by Markham and had to be signed by someone else?"

"Yes, I can say that much."

This witness was all mine. I moved back to the counsel table, turned, and asked, "Isn't that the case here?"

Bellicoso screamed out, "Objection," and it was sustained.

"Let's return to a subject. You've testified about forgery many times?"

"Yes, many times."

"Is it your contention that the signature on Exhibit 33 is a forgery?"

Bellicoso stood. "He can't testify whether they are forged. He can just testify whether they are the same or different, Your Honor."

But before Macefield ruled, Eliopolus answered, "That's correct."

"Have you ever been involved in determining whether a signature was a forgery?"

"You call it a forgery, that there are two signatures. I can say yes, one is a forgery."

"What other things did you look at in determining Mr. Markham's signature?"

"Space. The space on the two documents, 31 and 33."

"Isn't it a fact the space available to sign one's name is different on Exhibits 31 and 33, that the handwriting was narrower on 33, because the signature line is closer to the edge of the paper? Isn't that possibly even the reason for the cramped middle zones on 33?"

"Yes."

"So the size and placement of the signature line could cause cramping of letters in the middle zone? Would you concede that?"

"Yes, that's true."

It really wasn't true, it was just an illusion because the space was closer to the edge of the paper, but Eliopolus was agreeing with me. He was really broken and scared after having to talk about his hand under oath and screwing up on the paper and ink.

"I see. How much were you paid to testify here today?"

"Five thousand dollars."

"How much did you get paid for the preparation?"

"I believe ten thousand dollars total."

"And isn't it a fact, Mr. Eliopolus, that when you first looked at these exhibits before, you looked at them without your glasses and then with your glasses?"

"I looked with my glasses later, but it was not really necessary."

"It wasn't necessary?"

"No."

"It wasn't necessary?"

"I can see them without the glasses."

"You could see them without the glasses?"

"Yes."

"Sir, are your findings based on what you saw with your glasses, the microscope, or the magnifying glass? Which of the three is it?"

"I cannot recall at this time."

The man was so shaken he contradicted his testimony that he used different tools to corroborate his findings.

Bellicoso objected again but the answer was on the record. Eliopolus had already testified to that, and although Macefield ordered that the answer be stricken from the record, it is never physically taken out of the transcript.

"Just a few more questions, sir. In your expert opinion, is the signature on Exhibit 33 an attempt to forge Mr. Markham's signature?"

"Possibly."

"So it is possible that an individual can have more than one signature in your opinion?"

"Yes."

"Two distinctly different kinds of signatures?"

"Yes, in some respects." He was prejudiced by his own left-handed signature, stuck with his own testimony.

"Well, but it is possible that he can."

Trying to get the issue out of the way, Macefield said, "It is possible. He has testified to that. The court will in fact take judicial notice that people can sign their names different ways."

I said, "Nothing further."

"I see Mr. Bellicoso is shaking his head, indication that he has no redirect. I would like counsel to approach," Macefield ordered. He sat back for a moment, looked at his trial notebook, thumbed back and forth through it.

"Mr. Ocean, I can see that the executrix will need time to prepare to rebut the testimony." Macefield wasn't giving me anything that any other judge would have under these circumstances. "Gentlemen, I am going to have to change the scheduling of this trial in light of today's testimony. We will stand adjourned for one day, and you may apply to the court for additional time, Mr. Ocean, in order to properly prepare for your expert witness on the matters that the court has heard from the claimant this morning. The court will stand in recess. Copies of all exhibits will be provided to you, together with the originals, so that a full examination may be made by your people."

I felt I had progressed considerably with my cross-examination of Eliopolus. A good trial judge would reject his testimony.

As I exited to Chambers Street with my hand on my gun, Hal hustled up alongside me and piped, "Counselor, you did well. Who's your expert going to be? I want it in tomorrow's edition." I told him about Carmine Lassiter and headed for the garage, watching all the way for trouble. My mind was not on the note.

No matter what happened in the battle of experts, I still had my star witness in the wings. She was the problem and the solution.

CHAPTER NINETEEN

I had spent much time intensively preparing with Carmine Lassiter, the grande dame of the profession. No one would challenge her. She was eighty-four years old, a true intellect who exuded an aristocratic air when she testified. If a lawyer aggressively cross-examined her, it was the end of his case because she knew more about paper, ink, and handwriting than anyone, including wise-ass trial lawyers. It was better to leave her alone.

We returned to court as Macefield ordered. I called my witness to the stand. Carmine's tall frame quickly swept across the courtroom, dressed in a black and red shawl draped over a long, tailored dark blue dress. Her hair was white, went to the middle of her back. She was wearing no jewelry except small silver earrings. The clerk swore her in.

"Carmine Lassiter, 541 East Seventy-fifth Street, New York, New York 10021."

"Ms. Lassiter, what is your occupation?"

Her black eyes arrowed in on me, she sat forward. "I am a forensic document examiner, specializing in the determination of authenticity of documents, handwriting, ink, and paper."

"How long have you been engaged in this profession?"

"Since 1945 I have testified in courts in many states, in federal as well as state courts. I have also testified in foreign countries—Mexico, Great Britain, among others. I received my training in Europe at the Police Academy of Microscopy, studying under Professor Klingerberg at the Institute of Forensic Identification in Vienna, Austria."

Bellicoso, knowing that it was better not to challenge her, stood and addressed the court.

"I will accept a résumé if you have one. I will stipulate she is an expert in examining handwriting." With her qualifications out of the way, I resumed my direct of Carmine.

"Ms. Lassiter, you are being paid to appear today?"

"Yes, five thousand dollars, plus an hourly rate for preparation."

At this time I was standing behind the counsel table.

"You have been asked to examine certain documents that are present in the courtroom."

"Yes."

"You were asked, were you not, to compare the signatures of a Mr. Marcel S. Markham, who is deceased?" I stepped closer to her.

"Yes, I was."

"Are you familiar with Exhibit 31?" I handed her the document and stayed next to her.

"I previously examined it and made notations."

"Were you aware that what you examined, Exhibit 31, has been called a promissory note in this action?"

"Yes, I am aware of that. I have examined many promissory notes in my day, Mr. Ocean." Her answer came close to sarcasm.

"In addition to Exhibit 31, there has also been received in evidence Exhibit 33, a second promissory note offered in evidence by my client, Mrs. Pandora Markham."

"Yes."

"Did you at any time compare the signatures on these two documents?"

"Yes."

"What were your findings?"

Carmine sat back, removed her glasses, and placed them on the stand. "As an expert, I never give an opinion examining one comparison signature. I used the additional examples, several signatures from Exhibit 32. I compared them and made certain notations, comparing not merely the general appearance of a signature, but what experts call the primary characteristics. If the primary characteristics, each letter and its connections broken down, are equally unusual in comparisons, they can be considered identical."

Macefield drew closer and took down some of her testimony.

"And what were your findings?"

"This signature in Exhibit 33 appears the same as the signatures in Exhibit 32. I don't mean exactly. There are characteristics indicating the signatures were written by the same hand. I have made comparison charts, which are enlarged and which I will hold for the court, yourself, Mr. Bellicoso." She looked around the room at the huge audience and added, "And everyone else in the courtroom." That brought a laugh from the gallery.

With Macefield's consent, she got up from the witness stand and moved to the easel where she placed several enlargements of letters.

"The capital *M* in Marcel is the same or similar. That doesn't mean too much, because if it was a forgery, everybody would try to forge the capital letter as closely as possible. But the hidden characteristics way is to check 32. There is large difference as to whether the loop at the end goes up or down. In 33 and 32 the loop at the end goes up, and in 31 it is indistinct. A characteristic I find equally outstanding is the top of the *R* in Markham. The approximate quarter circle at the top is not so pronounced in 31."

"Is there anything else?"

"The *S* in the middle initial is significant. The *S* is very close in Exhibits 31 and 33. Sometimes in the samples of Exhibit 32 it goes apart—it loops—not like in 31 which is more firm, the capital *S,* the loop of capital *S,* how wide it is on the bottom part, the way it is written. See it in 33. But for examination purposes, I turned it upside down and that shows the direct connection between the writing hand and the writing characteristic of making the loop." She took the enlargement and held it upside down and showed it to Macefield, then went on with her analysis.

"A forger would not understand the wide looping in the *S.* He or she will copy every character opportunity in the line; that is, the items that are prominent to the eye; but where the copying breaks down is the failure to reproduce hidden characteristics, like looping details. The forger will not do it correctly because he just doesn't know how."

"Did you have an opportunity to examine the last name on these documents?"

"Yes. Let's go to that subject. I want to discuss the last name. The capital is not the same in 31 as the *M* is in Exhibits 32 and 33. And the rest of the letters are tight, closely bunched in 32 and 33, not in 31." Leaving the easel she returned to the stand and I followed.

"Is it your testimony that it is not possible that the signature in 33 and 31 was written by the same person?"

Bellicoso objected to the form of the question and I was asked to rephrase it.

"In the realm of your experience, Ms. Lassiter, was the person who placed the signature on Exhibit 33 the same person who placed the signature on 31?"

"No."

Bellicoso objected and asked that her reply be stricken, arguing that she could not come to a conclusion concerning an ultimate issue to be resolved in a case—which note was authentic. That issue was to be left for the trier of fact, the court in this case. But the objection was overruled, as I pointed out to Macefield that was the rule in the federal court but not in the state court.

A recess was ordered.

Exiting the courtroom, I walked around the maze of reporters, lawyers who make a second home out of courthouse hallways, gallery members, out to the white marble corridor and down one floor to the men's room.

I turned on the porcelain tap to one of the two 1920s sinks and was washing my hands, killing a few minutes, when Bellicoso walked in. We were alone.

I went to take a piss and he pulled into the next urinal. We emptied our bladders like two horses in a trailer.

Bellicoso spoke first. "Ocean, you'll never get away with this paper shit. You're going to get creamed by Macefield. You'll find out no one buys that kind of crap in this courthouse. You'll fight city hall the rest of your life." He grunted, quickly stepped back, fixed his instrument into his pants, and started to leave.

"Vito, don't wash your hands. It won't do any good," I replied.

That's a Manhattan Supreme Court tradition: follow your adversary into the john and threaten him while he's pissing. Bellicoso was from outside the county but enjoyed the custom. Must be a statewide ritual now, I thought to myself.

When I returned to the courtroom, Bellicoso was talking to the court reporter. He placed a black plastic business card with gold engraving in front of Barry and said, "If I can do something for you, let me know."

I went up to Barry, asked him what the conversation was about, and looked at Vito's card. He'd been in a car accident and was going to hire Bellicoso as his lawyer. In the first place, the White Knuckle didn't take auto-injury cases. Barry must have been flattered out of his mind that he could hire a big-time lawyer. That relationship could affect the transcript. Just as I was about to ask Bellicoso why he was doing business with the court reporter, Macefield entered. I immediately brought the incident up to the court for no other reason than I have an obligation to do it. The client was entitled to a full, unbiased record of the proceedings.

I moved to have the stenographer discharged from the case. In these situations the lawyer has to take such action. No client would want that reporter in the case, and I'd be negligent if I didn't make the motion. Macefield perfunctorily denied my application with the same dismissive attitude he applied to my complaint that Babette was being signaled by Webb.

So now I had the judge and the court stenographer against me. I was running out of enemies. The search for the truth was taking a bad beating.

While Macefield appeared to be studiously reading the court transcript, we sat at the counsel desk waiting. Hal walked up behind me. "Screwed up on the court reporter, Johnny. Watch yourself, Macefield's really got it in for you. You should've taken a Pasadena on that one. Journalists can only help so much in this court, so you better get help."

He faded back to his seat near Webb. The gallery was full. Hal's message was that I should bring in another lawyer who was tight with Macefield to level the playing field. I wouldn't ask for that kind of help if my life depended on it.

I resumed questioning Carmine.

"Have you examined the ink?"

"I did examine the ink. It has substantial meaning. Exhibit 33 was signed with an unusual ink, iron gall ink, which is made from an old recipe from the nineteenth century. Inks come from plants sometimes, pigments, growths on trees. This is a special ink that is derived a specific way. I will give you some of the technical background. I'm not a chemist or a scientist, but I believe it is interesting if you have the patience, Your Honor."

Macefield nodded deferentially.

"Gall is produced on oak trees by insects. The gall is used in making inks—as well as for dyes and cures in pharmacology. Gall insects, of which there are many, including beetles, gnats, moths, and wasps, produce gall on the tree or its leaves. Lord Tennyson wrote in *Talking Oak:* 'I swear and else may insects prick each leaf into a gall.'"

She smiled charmingly at Macefield. "Thank you, Judge. I like to air these wonderful tidbits in stuffy courtrooms."

Macefield loved that and he nodded approvingly. Judges always like to hear the historical background of expert testimony. They enjoy the professorial fantasy and their association with higher learning.

I turned around in time to see the sick expression on Eliopolus, who was seated behind Babette.

"And when Exhibit 33 was signed, what type of ink was used?"

"It tests as iron gall, which of course existed prior to 1985. It's an antique substance and has a great historic look—as does the signature in Exhibit 33. In contrast, Exhibit 31 was executed in a ballpoint for the first name, but the ink appears to have run out and a new Parker ink, a 1997 Parker ink, was used for the middle initial and the last name. The ballpoint pen and its writing element, if you will, wasn't manufactured until after the document was signed, sometime in late 1997. It was used in conjunction with a Paper Mate model 130 which came on the market around the same time. The first name and middle letter were both signed with the Parker ink that postdated the document. Therefore Exhibit 31 was signed in the late 1990s."

I believe that Kerrigan must have given Marcel the pen and ink and ceremoniously had him sign. It clicked because I recalled Babette testifying that beside the scale collection, there were many other weird antique items that Kerrigan kept around his office, like those bottles of ink. One of them must have contained iron gall.

It was remarkable. Carmine didn't look the least bit tired.

"Is it your expert opinion that the same person signed Exhibits 32 and 33?"

She closed her testimony with a yes, and I said, "I have nothing further, Your Honor." We were home free.

Bellicoso cross-examined Carmine for about an hour, but it was inconsequential. In fact, he wound up making her look even better than his own expert. Finally Bellicoso asked for more time because Eliopolus hadn't had time to contradict or confirm Carmine's findings. The court gave Eliopolus another date to be recalled.

"This is an ideal time to break, gentlemen," Macefield announced. "Counselors, I see where this testimony is going, and I have my doubts that it can be proven scientifically."

Was the bastard rejecting Carmine's testimony? It meant he'd have to do the same to Eliopolus, but he came off as totally unbelievable anyway.

Macefield continued, "Right now I want to hear from Ms. Pandora Markham. It will give this trial clarity, like the trumpets from 'Pictures at an Exhibition.' Moussorgsky, trumpets, yes, clarity. I love it when all you hear are the horns. I believe that is far more relevant. And I don't want ten pictures, like the Exhibition, I want one clear one. We will resume tomorrow. Mr. Ocean, please have the executrix in court by 9:30 A.M."

I picked up my briefcase, wended my way through the courthouse crowd, answered a few questions from reporters, and passed an angry Webb and glazed Babette. She didn't seem to know what had happened, but he stared at me as if I had committed some horrific travesty by putting Carmine on the stand.

I went out the back exit from the courthouse and surveyed the street, east and west. The street was Ling free. Then I darted to the garage, jumped into the Bentley, and drove home. One day at a time. I was still in once piece. How long would that last?

CHAPTER TWENTY

The first thing I did when I returned to the office was call Pandora. She picked up and sounded out of breath.

"We're on for tomorrow."

"You don't have to remind me, Johnny." There wasn't a trace of last night's phone fuck in her voice.

"You're out of breath." I stayed just as cool.

"Exercising, getting in shape for cross-examination. Taking the edge off." She laughed.

"Edgy, that's the way I felt leaving the courthouse."

"Why's that?"

"Emanuel Ling, he worries me. I think he might have something to do with why I was shot. That guy is after me."

Silence. Then she said, "I don't know him and if it has some connection to the case, it might have been through Bill. He worked for Ling, but that was way back, before the money was given to Marcel."

Then she switched subjects. "So how did things go today?"

"Expert witness for Babette was on the stand. I think my cross went very well. Tomorrow it's your show."

The mention of tomorrow didn't make her the least bit nervous, and she was impervious to my standard reminder that she was about to take the hot seat. There was no talk of preparation. When I hung up, I asked K to cook one of my favorite Indian dinners. Clad in a purple turban, camel coat, and white pants, K served me while I brought him up to date on the trial. In particular he enjoyed listening to the ink-and-paper analysis by Carmine.

"Sir, and did the honorable justice understand the testimony about the age of the paper or the differences in the inks?"

"I don't know."

As I shoveled in some of his brown rice he spoke about Indian painting. "Single-hair brushes are used to paint details like eyebrows, or even hair itself. Like the ink you mentioned, our colors come from many sources: a lapis lazuli stone, ground to a fine powder, produces blue. Yellow comes from cow urine, *peori*. Red color comes from insects."

He went on and on while I ate a dinner of chilies and paneer. It was delicious, but a big mistake. When I tried to sleep, the spices seeped through my brain, rewinding the trial, wheeling me over and around the mattress all night like a tire aimlessly ambling over miles of desert dunes.

Egg-yellow sunlight poured through my curtains. Eight A.M. I hadn't caught more than two hours of sleep. Hauling myself out of bed, I was still thinking about the expert testimony and mad as I could be about Macefield's comments. And, typically, those remarks weren't on the record.

First the indispensable preliminaries: the shower, where my best trial strategies occur, and getting dressed.

My mind was 100 percent concentrated on Pandora at the trial—not in the bed—doing a good job as her attorney, getting her butt off the hook. Even though I had a thousand bits of evidence and testimony on my mind, I felt an inner calmness charged with composed aggression.

This was the old me, before I met these characters. I shaved, knowing the perspective was changing. The tide had turned.

It was nearly 8:45. While I waited for Pandora, I fed Barkis a slab of sirloin and downed a black coffee.

Still no client. I made a few phone calls and thumbed some unpaid bills.

Then the doorbell rang.

Pandora was downstairs.

On my way Barkis stretched in front of the door, blocking my exit. He knew there was trouble outside.

K picked up my two black litigation briefcases. As we left the building, the lobby telephone rang.

K answered, then said, "I will try to find my boss."

I asked him who it was. Windows. This was a time jam I couldn't afford. Pandora was probably tearing out the upholstery in the car, swearing my name because I was making her wait. Any second she'd take off and Macefield would have my head.

Nervously, I opted to speak to Windows.

"Ocean, we're coming down to the courthouse. We're looking for Webb Hartford, got some questions to ask him. Is he going to be there?"

"Same spot every day—front row center. Love to yak but this is a bad time, I have to be in court. I've only got a minute. Why are you asking about Hartford?"

"We're looking deep into how Edgar Longwood and Marcel Markham croaked. We think Dr. Hartford might have plenty to tell us."

"How's that?"

"We interviewed your buddy, Dr. Aranda. He has evidence that Markham's lymphoma was in remission but Markham was never told about it. I'll bet you know about that."

"Don't assume anything. I tell you when I get lost. I'm listening."

"Look, talk to the swami. He's got a grip on things."

Windows hung up in midair.

I didn't know what he was talking about. But it was 9:00. Pandora was outside fidgeting. Macefield was breathing fire in the courthouse.

I turned to K, "Do you know something about Webb Hartford? The cops are on their way to the courthouse to question him."

"Sir, you must be absolutely of one mind now. You are to think only of this morning and putting your case before the judge. I will tend to all other matters." His hand gently pushed me out the door.

"K, just give me a clue, what—?"

K handed me my briefcase, slipped an envelope in my coat pocket, and shut the door behind me.

A black stretch limo was parked at the curb, not the usual Lincoln town car used by the denizens of Park Avenue. Inside sat the fabled star of my case. My heart began beating like a conga drum in a salsa festival.

Putting my head down, I swallowed and went for her.

I was intercepted at her door by a white-haired driver humming "Here Comes the Bride." He opened the front door instead and showed me to my seat.

That wasn't where I was supposed to be. My suspension of belief went to the next incredible level. I wasn't going to meet her, even in the same car, never mind the same case. An hour before she was to take the stand and we might as well have been talking to one another for the first time. How could I drive to court with a client and not take time to go over last minute details? This bitch was a real prick.

I stole a glance back. Pandora sat in the rear looking totally unconcerned.

She was the classic newspaper photograph of a scandalized heiress. From under a brimmed black hat, her long brunette tresses trickled down below her collar. I wasn't sure that she smiled. Her lower lip was lush, sensuous, and ready for something defined in every man's brain. Her mouth opened—a gorgeous crack in a beautiful, flower-covered stone wall. Her lips pulled back but she didn't say anything. The angular, pale face was more provocative than I recalled in the video, but it was softer, accessible. A string of gray pearls and small diamonds looped around her neck. She wore an expensive black suit that masked the shape of her figure. She could have been on her way to court or to a funeral. But the package inside the clothes was an erotic, slow-burning fire of lust. I checked out every square inch.

"Hello, Johnny. It's been a long time since we saw one another. As you can see, I'm in mourning. Sorry you can't sit back here, but I hurt my foot yesterday. I stumbled over the phone cord getting out of bed and I must put it across the seat."

Her leg was stretched out, covered to the ankle by a beige blanket. Then without any explanation, she hit the electric button and closed the smoked glass partition between us. I just shook my head and didn't say anything.

Which one of us was crazy? Up to now she'd been a phone voice. Suddenly we were live, but separated as if we were talking from my house to her apartment over a line. And we weren't even speaking.

I was stung but I shouldn't have been; I know these kind of relationships never change. Evidently she had no desire to talk about the case, much less to win it. I thought this morning she might say to me: "Johnny, let's drive right the hell out of this shoddy, squalid world and never look back." That was a comic, childish dream. Never happen in this life, this case, with this client harpy.

While I simmered, I opened the letter from K.

Sir, labor as wide as earth has its summit in heaven. Your efforts have brought great laurels to you and to your office.

Forgive me for speaking to the police and Dr. Aranda without your permission.

Your good and faithful servant,

K

I dialed Aranda at the hospital on my cell phone, now glad for the partition separating me from my client.

"Jack, I just got a strange call from Detective Windows. Do you know what he was calling me about?"

"More or less."

"Can you tell me?"

"The medical examiner's office exhumed Edgar Longwood's body. Traces of inorganic mercury were found in his hair."

"But he died over fifteen years ago."

"Metals stay in the bones and tissues forever. But it's most easily picked up by a pathologist in the hair. Fifteen years is not a long time to be dead for that type of thing, but I wouldn't compare it to the dented skull of Tutankhamen."

While I listened to Jack, I could see Pandora in the visor mirror through the hazy partition. I could swear she was staring at me, pursing her lips, running her tongue across her teeth.

"Mercury's the stuff that caused the Mad Hatter syndrome in England in the eighteenth century. When British hatters blocked hats, they didn't know the vapors made them sick."

"*Alice in Wonderland* is not exactly on my legal research list, but I guess it should have been. Where did you come up with all of this?"

I watched Pandora adjust her garter belt and tighten her stockings.

"A visit from that Indian chap who works for you. He was wearing a wonderful yellow turban, very knowledgeable about chemistry." He gave me one of those trademark Aranda laughs.

"What did Mr. K have to say to you?"

"Told me about mercury poisoning and I told him about lymphoma. They both produce the same symptoms—puts pressure on the ureters, cuts off the flow of urine, destroys the kidneys, and bang, you're dead."

"So a doctor would never know if someone with lymphoma really died of mercury poisoning."

"Right, and no one would ever test for poisoning under those circumstances, unless the doctor were an Indian working for a lawyer in New York City."

"I got it."

"Mercuric chloride is a soluble salt. Best known as a disinfectant. It can easily be mixed in food. Eat and die. In the 1930s and '40s, swallowing mercuric chloride tablets was a common form of suicide. The cops are looking into whether Markham was poisoned with mercury, too."

"I never bought his suicide."

"Well, renal disease and mercury poisoning both produce extreme depression. Markham was cured of his lymphoma, but he was probably so deeply depressed from the mercury poisoning he might have actually committed suicide."

I watched Pandora run a brush through her hair ends as the limo headed down Park Avenue. She gazed out the window, looking meditative. Sympathy trickled through me as I thought, Marcel could've been alive today. Her bitterness probably resulted from his death.

Then she tapped on the window and wanted to ask me something, as I told Aranda I had to sign off.

"Johnny," she said, "can I stay in court after I'm through and hear Babette testify?"

"Of course, you're a party and it's your case."

"It's my party."

As the limo sped to the final destination, I thought about the distinct possibility that Babette was suffering from some drug that Webb had slipped into her breakfast. All that talk of brain damage might have come as a result of Webb's concerned "treatment."

I couldn't wait to get to the courtroom and watch Windows and Slice haul that smug bastard Webb out.

We passed the Veranda Club. I imagined it looking naked, ugly, senselessly out of place in the daytime except for that statue of Zeus propped up in front. Zeus, the guardian of law and social order, invested the powers of the law in his consort Themis. Ms. Markham didn't acknowledge the highest Greek God, her creator.

As we neared Foley Square, I had the driver circle to the back of the courthouse and the garage. We pulled inside and stopped. An attendant strode to the driver's window and handed him a ticket.

"We park all the stretches, sir. I'll take it from here," he said politely. The driver stepped out. The attendant got in. At the instant I opened my door to help Pandora out, the attendant's foot went down hard on the accelerator. Nearly thrown from the car, I hung on to the door while he tore across to the other side of the garage.

The brakes screeched and I was thrown forward. Someone reached in, grabbed me by the shoulders, and hauled me out of the front seat and onto the concrete floor.

I thought we were about to be robbed. Not unusual in New York City, morning, noon, or night. I began to yell to Pandora, but that idea died a quick death. The face in my face was Chinese—Mr. Nameless from the Ling railway. His fists tightened around my starched collar as he picked me up and slammed me against the hood of the car. With both of my feet I pushed into his stomach, sending him across the floor and into a support column.

His indestructible frame bounced right back, holding a pistol aimed at my head. One of his companions fastened his arms around me.

Moving in close enough to be me, he said, "Ocean, you were warned."

I couldn't budge, my gun holster uselessly rubbing against my arm. About twenty more tough guys materialized and surrounded me. Did Ling own this place, too?

The rear door to the limo swung open and Pandora got out looking very indignant. "Johnny, what's going on here? Who are these people?" she demanded, straightening her skirt.

"Shut up, lady, and get back in the car where you'll be safe," Nameless barked.

Stepping backward, she opened her mouth to scream. One of Ling's guys planted his hand over her mouth, muffling the sound, and shoved her back inside.

Nameless jammed the muzzle into my mouth. I watched his finger move on the trigger. No way out. This was careless. How could I forget about Ling?

Out of the blue, a deafening blaring of car horns started, seemingly coming from every car on the floor. Then a mass of high beams switched on. The room was washed in a freakish sound-and-light show. The Chinese put their hands up to block the beams. The horns didn't abate.

Nameless loosened the grip on my collar. His face was molded into a contorted expression, configured to sort out bizarre situations.

Rangit, Mr. K's blue-turbaned friend, appeared in front of us.

"Good morning, gentlemen. Allow me to park this limousine. Mr. Ocean has to be in court for a most important trial."

Out of the darkness Mr. K also appeared and added, "He is an attorney of high repute."

Nameless swung his gun toward Rangit. Mr. K calmly warned, "I would ask you to be cool in these circumstances. My boss does not like violence. Things can be settled in a very peaceful manner."

"Get out of our way," Nameless shouted.

K clasped his hands together and bowed respectfully. "I don't think you gentlemen understand."

Rangit yelled, *"Balwant! Baldev! Chernjit! Gobind! Gian! Balbir! Raghbi! Surjit! Pritam! Mohan! Sunder! Gurmukh! Kultarran! Gurmeet!"*

There must have been at least fifty of them with their *kirpans* drawn. As each name rang out, a Sikh emerged from one of the honking cars. Spokes of high-beam light bounced off the long, sharp knifes.

One by one the Chinese dropped their guns to the floor and made the traditional gestures of surrender.

The Indians escorted them from the garage to a destination I could be certain was far from the courthouse.

Pandora left the car. "Johnny, what was that about? I can't go and testify after that."

"Those were Emanuel Ling's thugs."

She looked startled. "Is it something personal between you and him?" she asked, sounding innocent.

"They've been after me to drop this case and you as a client."

"Who is this Ling?"

"It's a long story. I'll tell you after court."

We had to get inside, otherwise Macefield would fine me.

We came in through the rear of the courthouse to avoid the press out front. Like everyone else who enters for the first time, Pandora stared up at the mural of her Greek counterparts on the ceiling. From the look on her face, she felt very much at home.

The only place safe from the press was the waiting area in Ms. Strife's office. I left her there and went into 503 to assess the situation.

The gallery was brimming with the regulars. Bellicoso was seated at the counsel table alongside Babette, with his head buried in yellow legal pads. It was apparent that he had a long list of questions for Pandora. I approached him.

"I haven't finished my cross-examination of your client, Counselor. Will she be retaking the stand after my client testifies?" I asked, just to piss him off.

"I don't have to answer you," he replied and looked away.

My veins were icy as I took my place at the counsel table. I wanted to get it going, get it over. No lawyer looks forward to his client being grilled on the witness stand. But why should I be worried about someone who could teach Darwin a thing or two. Speaking of which, on her own, Pandora found her way through the crowd and entered the courtroom. She sat next to me as if she had done just that every day of the trial.

Macefield walked to the bench with the deliberateness of an executioner. We the People of New York State, on both sides of the railing, respectfully stood just as the "Hear ye, hear ye" rolled off the lips of the clerk. Macefield lowered himself into the soft black leather chair.

The court reporter hovered nervously above the keys, waiting to print the first word to leave Macefield's lips.

"Good morning, ladies and gentlemen. Mr. Ocean, I assume you have complied with my order." If I were Pearl Harbor, Macefield was about to bomb.

This was finally real—fear and passion over testimony. I answered, "Yes, Your Honor, we have."

"Well, then, call your witness. The court is ready to hear the testimony."

I did what I was ordered to do, and for the first time in my career I had the sensation I was throwing my client to the wolves. In a moment, she'd be seated in the oak witness chair, telling these wooden walls the story of Marcel, what happened to the promissory note, how the whole thing was transacted. She would be trying very hard to get the money. She would be the witness, the player-participant. The beautiful face framed in a Surrogate's Courthouse. A perfect female creature, squared off against a system of two vestiges: Bellicoso and Macefield.

Or did they all come from Hades on a coach driven by Mercury?

Babette leaned forward, studying every inch of Pandora. Her jealousy was sickeningly apparent. It was out in the open that envy was major force behind the lawsuit. The witness had everything that Babette wanted—beauty, youth, charisma, and Pandora's enchantingly bent personality.

Pandora moved gracefully to the witness chair. Every eye was glued to the back of that woman. There wasn't a trace of a limp from her injured foot in her swaying walk to the stand. Macefield had done nothing about the press coverage. They were there. Gerry Patton would have said, "Live as a bus full of freeloading fans going to Yankee Stadium on Ladies' Day." I wanted the record of this trial to be public, despite Pandora's request to bar them, so I had ditched the application to bar the press.

But on Pandora's behalf I now had to make the application. "Your Honor, I was advised by your clerk this morning you might exclude journalists from the proceeding. I apply to you to do so."

I kept my eyes fixed on Pandora, who was sitting in the witness chair, staring out at the crowd.

"Mr. Ocean, you and Mr. Bellicoso approach."

At the bench Macefield's sphinxlike face plagued me with another riddling comment. "Mr. Ocean, just when you thought you knew all the answers, I'm changing the questions. I have decided to permit press coverage for the remainder of this hearing. You're fortunate I have refused to allow the press pool to have a television camera in the courtroom. Please proceed forthwith."

I caught Windows, followed by a trench-coated Slice, enter the room and move to the side closest to me. For a moment I thought they were going to whip out their badges and start arresting everyone in sight on behalf of the Furies. Slice took off his Burberry and folded it.

Where was Hartford? He must have found out that the cops were looking for him.

Macefield ordered me to examine Pandora. It shouldn't be up to me to ask her questions. It was as if I'd picked up Bellicoso's briefcase, pulled out damaging evidence, and cross-examined my own client with it.

"I want my objection noted for the record, my vigorous objection to this testimony. There is no reason whatsoever to take the executrix's testimony unless she has been subpoenaed or she is testifying on her side of the case. I ask Your Honor to reconsider his ruling."

Bellicoso joined the act. "If I may again come to the aid of this respected court, Your Honor is within the rights and power which inhere in this court's broad jurisdiction, section 6 of the state's constitution, section 1501 of the Surrogate's orders to preserve and perpetuate its jurisdiction and authority."

"Ms. Markham, were you acquainted with any of the business transactions of your late husband, Marcel Markham?"

I skipped the introduction and the background formalities because I wanted her in and out as quickly as possible.

"Yes, but to a limited extent."

Her head was cocked away from Macefield. She was making no attempt to play up to him. She was avoiding the question. I went further.

"To what extent?"

"My sister-in-law and my late husband had many dealings and, I suppose, many feelings together. I was usually not present at such events."

The Park Avenue head remained positioned. The voice from the telephone was making its long-awaited live appearance—smooth, plainly feminine, and nearly musical. It was impressive.

"My sister-in-law and Marcel, that is, my late husband, constantly discussed his . . . how shall we say, his . . . uh . . . reluctance to work. Marcel said he had an aversion to work that stemmed from his childhood, so he needed to be taken care of. He might have had psychological problems. In the beginning of our marriage, I did the work, including the housework. My acting career suffered, but fortunately I had some money of my own."

The press busily attempted to jot down the nothingness she was saying. Hal's head was dead-cat stiff, transfixed on Pandora. Her testimony felt uneven and dangerous, a tightrope act on a windy day. She was talking way too much. She herself had outlined the drill for the examination, which could have easily applied to this direct—yes, no, I don't know. I could only hope that she wouldn't broaden her testimony too far, leaving juicy bits and pieces for the White Knuckle to chew on during cross-examination.

"Were you ever present when your sister-in-law, Babette Longwood, discussed a transaction in the sum of a hundred seventy million dollars?"

In the swaying sea of onlookers, Webb was not to be found among the many Surrogate's Court practitioners standing in the rear. They hadn't come to watch the examination—they were fans of Pandora.

"Yes." Her voice sounded solid, believable.

"Could you explain? That is, could you tell His Honor when this occurred and what transpired?"

"I will be glad to. I recall that it was in early 1985. Marcel, as usual, returned home around six-thirty. He was wearing a white shirt, beautiful Egyptian cotton, with a green and black plaid tie and a light gray suit. He sat in the family room, drank a Pimm's Cup, and spoke to me about his sister. The conversation was clear. He wanted to borrow money. She was willing to loan, or to make a loan, of some money to him. That simple."

Why the hell was she using the word *loan,* the precise phrase? Didn't Pandora know she could kill us? She seemed to be playing directly into the hands of Babette and Macefield. In this legal horse race a loan would come in a dead third behind a fraud and a gift.

"What occurred thereafter?"

"The sum was a hundred seventy million. He mentioned it and I will never forget that. It is not something you hear every day."

"Were you ever given to understand in words or substance that the transfer of these funds occurred?"

"Yes."

"When was that?"

"The summer of 1985, somewhere around that time, can't recall exactly at this moment. Marcel left a copy of the Morgan Guaranty wire transfer on his desk. Bankers were calling every ten minutes. . . . Maybe it will come to me."

The pressure of the courtroom was quickly wearing her down, I could see it. I was watching the case slowly deteriorate, sink, thanks to her testimony.

"Counselor, would you step down and allow me to probe a few areas with the witness?" Macefield asked, but it was an order.

I had expected he was going to jump in before the cross-examination, giving Bellicoso an edge, but did it have to be this soon?

"Yes, Your Honor, but would you permit me to finish this line?" I still hoped I could save her.

"Yes, proceed."

I had already started to return to the counsel table and was shocked when Macefield permitted me to continue.

Pandora had her head angled at Macefield, making it very difficult for me to speak directly to her.

"What did your husband say to you about the money coming from Ms. Longwood?"

"Your Honor, with all due respect, I object," Bellicoso cried out. "This entire line of questioning goes to the essence of the Dead Man's Statute."

"Please answer the last question, Ms. Markham," I advised her, getting more heated.

The courtroom was anxious and noisy about the impending

answer. Windows moved over to Slice, his policeman's head glued
to Pandora.

"Marcel told me that the money was forthcoming and we
could use it."

"Use it for what?"

"For whatever, for lifestyle."

Macefield turned toward her. She looked away.

I couldn't stop addressing her aggressively. "Did you ask Marcel how he was able to obtain these funds?"

"Yes." She was breaking by bits.

"What did he say? What did he say?"

"I don't recall. She was his sister."

That wasn't better.

"Think about it, Ms. Markham. Think about it. I'd like an answer."

There was extreme quiet in the courtroom. She was burying
us. Bellicoso was grinning wider than Foley Square. There was no
need for her to think about it, but she was thinking deeply about
it. If she said, "I don't know," it could save the day.

Finally she responded, "He said it was like taking it from her,
but it was alright, because she didn't know or maybe didn't care
about the difference." She said this as if the words had been lin-
gering inside her like a virus.

That was the real tablecloth soiler. We were sunk. After all the
work and the strife, it comes down to a deadly single sentence.
Wonderful meal except for the tiny pinch of arsenic.

Macefield cupped his fingers and motioned for Exhibits 31 and
33. They were placed before him in a manila folder printed with
the name of the case in black, block letters. Under the scrutiny of
the gallery, Macefield leaned forward, studying the documents.
He seemed to be reading every word over and over, as if he were a
monocled British police inspector staring at clues. Then he took
both exhibits, stacked them together like pancakes, and handed

them to the court officer, instructing him to place the two documents before Pandora.

"Ms. Markham, would you kindly examine these documents?" Macefield's tone reeked of judicial kindness and humility.

Her long fingernails reached out and gracefully picked up the exhibits. She scanned them several times and then put them down.

"Madam, I ask you again, have you seen these documents, either or both, prior to today?"

She cocked her head and looked at me for direction, just the way that Babette had searched for it from Webb and Bellicoso. Now it was my turn to be the maestro, but there was nothing I could do.

"They look the same to me, except I know that this one, Exhibit 31, the way it is signed in ballpoint for the first name and then in ink. I have seen it before. I know because when Marcel showed it to me, he told me he'd signed it with his gold pen and he'd run out of ink. The beautiful Paper Mate pen I gave him for Christmas."

Then, like a flashy sports car braking on a dime, she said, "But he returned it to her."

Now I was on that spot.

Macefield turned to me slowly. "Counselor Ocean, I am given pause by the origin of Exhibit 33." He slowed the timing of the next sentence. "It really concerns me." He retarded the pace further. "How did its creation come about? Was it in your client's possession or was it in the possession of a third party?"

"I am not at liberty to say, Your Honor. It is a matter of attorney-client privilege, section 4503 of the Civil Procedure law." My eyes were on the judge, not on the client.

"I don't understand, Counsel. What is the privilege? I can quote from the textbook commentaries following section 4503, which I have in front of me, as well as any attorney. The statutes' commentaries were written by my good friend Mr. Vincent C. Alexander, a member of former President Richard Nixon's law firm, Mudge Rose. As Mr. Alexander states, 'Because the attorney-client privilege (like all privileges) is an obstacle to the ascertainment of the truth, New York Courts frequently concur with Professor Wigmore's view that it should be *strictly* confined within the narrowest possible limits consistent with the logic of its principle.' Need I say more?"

"Your Honor, I received the promissory note in a manner that is protected by the privilege. That is the only argument I can make. I will say no more, as only Ms. Pandora Markham can waive the privilege."

"I can see that I must elaborate to be understood. Mr. Alexander states, and, I caution you, in the following sentence at page five hundred seventy-two of the same volume, which may be of aid to you. 'The party asserting privilege'—and I can't emphasize enough, Mr. Ocean, the value of the next words—'usually bears the burden of establishing all of the essential elements.'"

"I am prepared to shoulder that burden, but first I would have to ask my client."

An appeals court confirming Macefield's opinion would take a long time. I was prepared to defy the court and wait. Ironically, Pandora had given me the note to get it out of her possession. If she consented to waiving the privilege, she would have to reveal our conversation about the note. That would include her testifying that she wanted me to destroy it or lose it in some other way. If she didn't consent, she'd look bad because it would appear the note came into her hands in an illegal manner. It was her decision now.

"No, Mr. Ocean, I will approach the issue in a different way. I'll do the asking. I represent the people of this state and they are entitled to an answer because every minute that passes is paid for in tax dollars."

The gallery eyes shifted to Pandora. Another eerie quiet fell over the room.

"Ms. Markham, what is your disposition? Are you willing to

waive the attorney-client privilege, so that you may tell this court how you or your counsel came into possession of Exhibit 33, a signed promissory note in the sum of one hundred seventy million dollars? This document is now in evidence and you contend, through your expert witness, that it is authentic. You may confer with your attorney."

Bellicoso was still standing with his hand on Babette. They were enjoying this part of the trial.

So was Macefield. "Do you know the consequences of a fraud on this court, Mr. Ocean?"

"Yes, I fully do, although this is a first for me. No one has ever charged me with such an allegation," I answered without raising my voice.

The issue was based on nothing more than confidentiality, but the threads of my career were hanging on it. Macefield was accusing me of manufacturing the note. Pandora had to tell the truth.

"There is no need to confer with my counsel. I never saw Exhibit 33 before in my life, Your Honor, and I have to tell the truth." The coquettish movement of her mouth and the sweet tone of her voice offered a free lesson in seduction and deception. "I don't care about the attorney-client privilege. I care about me. I don't know where the promissory note came from. You'd have to ask my attorney."

The onlookers sucked in one universal breath and stared at me.

Macefield asked that the attorneys approach the bench.

"Your Honor, I will have to take my client's statement under advisement. Obviously I cannot say anything until I speak to her."

Bellicoso said nothing, leaned against the bench, watching me as if he just discovered that there is a God.

"I am inclined to reserve my remarks, in light of this evidence," Macefield said. "Mr. Ocean, do you have any other witnesses or any other thoughts? Perhaps I can rule from the bench today and we can dispose of this matter. I am prepared to render an opinion on very short notice."

"Again, Your Honor, I would have to confer with my client," I said, unconsciously pointing toward the witness chair. "I need a day."

The courtroom clock read 1:00 P.M. Time and justice were not on my side.

"Application granted," Macefield said, knowing that he was on sold ground and wanting to do nothing to prejudice the reversal of fortune I was suffering.

Pandora stepped from the witness stand. Everyone stayed put, watching her grand exit after an unforgettable performance.

Shaking her head, she came over to my side of the counsel table and coldly asked, $170 million later, "Are you ready to leave?"

I didn't answer her but hurriedly swept all of my files and legal pads into my briefcase as if it were a trash can. We went through the railing's swinging gate toward the paneled doors at the rear of the courtroom, with me pushing our way through the crowd. I had pissed away every moment of my life since Dyson called me.

"What was that about?" I asked her, barely opening my mouth. "You gave me the promissory note, the one you asked me to destroy."

We exited onto a noisy Chambers Street, hotly pursued by a thicket of reporters, including a swarm of news crews throwing questions at us. "Johnny, what are you going to have Pandora do now, write a check for one hundred seventy big ones? Are you going to recall Babette to the stand? Hey Johnny, did you forge the note? Where did the second note come from? Hey, hey, hey, hey, hey, Johnny, Johnny!"

She didn't answer me, and she wasn't going to.

In a sea of screaming press and flashing cameras, Windows and Slice raced out of the courthouse toward us, but I kept Pandora moving for other reasons. One of Ling's men could squeeze out of the mob and Jack Ruby me into another time and place. There was a thick buffer zone of press between us.

With my hand on the butt of my Glock, the last thing I heard as I slid into the limo was Hal screaming, "Call me tonight at the *News,* Johnny. We'll give you a feature!" What else would they give it?

We sped off. At a red light, Pandora sat back, kicked her black patent-leather spiked heels at the front seat, zipped up the glass partition between the driver and us, and said, "I guess you deserve an answer about what happened today."

"Go ahead. You're the client, you know the facts."

As we eased up Lafayette Street past the Criminal Court, I wanted to rush her inside and have her prosecuted for perjury. I would have given anything to have been the district attorney.

"Sometimes in life one can be fortunate enough to be on both sides of the game. I understand that's called a no-lose proposition."

"I never play chess against myself," I said, angry as hell for taking the case.

She lit a cigarette and crossed her legs.

"That's clever, John, very smart comeback. You're a collection of comebacks."

"We had the real note," I said. "And you lied to the judge. What the hell was that?"

"You should quit while you're ahead. Shame on you, trying to pull off a hundred-seventy-million-dollar scam with that note. Marcel could have just walked over to Babette's apartment anytime and taken that original promissory note and brought it to our house, but he was too honest so I did it."

"You took the note?"

"Whatever."

"You had access to one hundred seventy million and you blew it."

"Wrong again. Doesn't work that way. Emanuel Ling can be a very demanding and demeaning individual. Now Mr. Ling will get his money back from Edgar Longwood. Longwood Securities held back on Chiang Kai-shek and Emanuel Ling. Edgar didn't pay his debts, so Mr. Ling is collecting now."

"What have you got to do with Ling?"

"Over two hundred million is owed to Ling from Longwood, and I am Mr. Ling's collection agent. For a long time he was very patient with Edgar, even used the court system, but that never worked until you came along. You're a great lawyer and we never would have gotten this far with any other attorney."

"I didn't help anyone except you."

"No, you litigated that money right into Babette's hands. It is there now for the taking. She's not about to refuse Mr. Ling or Webb Hartford."

"Try to remember I studied law, not the Chinese mafia. What have you got to do with them?"

"Nothing other than being dead."

"So I must be an undertaker and this must be a hearse."

"I'm not as attractive as Pandora. She was great on that tape, wasn't she? You love women. You should meet some older ones, like Chiang Kai-shek's widow. Lives in New York City. Just turned 101 years old and is still best friends with Emanuel Ling. This is some birthday present, one hundred seventy million plus interest. Here we are, together at last. You and Doctor Webb Hartford."

"And I'm Mother Teresa."

But her voice became Webb's. "You know what a Roman senator said about Caesar? 'Caesar was every woman's man and every man's woman.'"

"You do a good imitation of your brother."

"C'mon, Johnny, don't act surprised. You were fortunate enough to represent the two of us. You even created a promissory note, kept it in your file, claiming it was in my possession as the debtor. You recall that wonderful argument you made in court about the attorney-client privilege, Civil Procedure something or other number 4503, some gibberish. You could try to convince

Macefield that you never knew it was me. But you're bound by the privilege."

I smashed my fist into the window but it bounced off. Shocked beyond belief, I turned to the driver.

"Pull over, pull over! The privilege to represent you? A transsexual or just a cross-dresser?" The car kept going.

"Johnny, please don't be so middle-class. Don't you remember the story of Achilles in the Trojan War? Achilles didn't want to fight, so he hid from the Spartan army dressed like a woman. Then he became the greatest warrior fighting against Troy. When we were growing up, I always pretended to be my twin sister. I dressed up in Pandora's clothes more than she did."

"Babette must be grateful for her physician's theatrics."

"Right, but she'll never see a penny of her money. She couldn't come to court unless I prescribed an excellent tranquilizer."

"You should have just written out a script for me while you were at it."

"The witness stand is a wonderful place to perform, much better than the Black Curtain. Twins, twin notes, which one was real? That was such a great joke. Do you have any more like that one?"

Pandora removed her hat, pulled up the veil, and took small prosthetic bits off her face. She flung the pieces out the electric window like pistachio shells along with the clothes, changing into a suit and tie. Then she pulled off her wig. That too went out the window with her shoes.

It was Webb Hartford. In the flesh. The resemblance to Pandora was exact. Identical twins can't be different sexes, but Webb and Pandora were close enough, and nearly perfect when Webb added the touch of latex makeup. He was a psychopath who could cross-dress far better than I could cross-examine.

"Remember when I told you that a little stealth is necessary in almost every situation? Your response was, 'It's hard for me to do anything except in a straightforward way. You know, lawyers are like that, even in their personal lives.' I told you then that it was a good thing for me to know, and since I would rely on it, I wanted you to have the power of attorney."

"Yeah." I remembered it all too painfully.

"And, Johnny, do you remember, 'I'm just wearing Levi's and a black T-shirt. . . . I like the way you repeat what I say. I would really like to see you tonight. We can meet later. It's important that I see you personally, to show you something that I'd like you to keep in a safe place . . . a safety-deposit box or a Swiss bank account?' "

"I recall the conversation."

"And the sex on the phone?"

"How could I forget that, now that it was with a man."

"I had a fake orgasm."

"I didn't."

"Very masculine. Well at least you got something out of the case, but you'll be the one on trial next."

The limousine slithered up Park Avenue, along the mall, and to a gentle stop at the side entrance to the Caprice.

The black door to the limousine jerked opened. Chief Detective Oliver Windows stuck his head inside and said, "Doctor Webb Hartford, you're under arrest for the murders of Edgar Longwood and Marcel Markham."

"Do you have a good lawyer?" I asked Webb and stepped out, lit up a Lucky, and walked down Park Avenue toward Grand Central Terminal, wondering if Mercury was listening.

A few weeks later Barkis and I wandered the smoke-filled streets of Chinatown, calmly testing my fears as we passed the second-floor offices of China Manpower. Some colorful turbans were trailing behind on the lookout, which helped my confidence. Funny, Y seemed to be walking right alongside, squeezing my hand, telling me that everything was all right, that we could go back to her place and make love forever. That gnarled my guts.

So did Webb Hartford. That psycho had gotten himself a gun-slinging defense lawyer from Davis & Shirling—and claimed that I'd represented the real Pandora, even tried to have sex with her, and that she'd testified in court. Dyson said he couldn't get in between the firm and a paying client. Catch this: He said there was no conflict of interest. Webb got out on bail, not much of which was put up.

But my head was working overtime as I neared the entrance to China Manpower and looked up to see if the lights were on upstairs. This time I wasn't going inside. Maybe Ling was behind his desk, thinking up another scheme like Pandora's will which Rogers read, then forced her to leave everything to him. That had to be Ling's idea. Never leave your last will and testament around the house. Then Ling had Rogers kill Pandora, but Rogers demanded a bigger cut because he controlled all the money. No one blackmails the Chinaman. A shotgun closed Rogers's mouth, and Webb neatly stepped into Pandora's shoes.

I kept repeating to Macefield that Webb Hartford had impersonated Pandora and surely killed her. But he swept that aside like a crumb off the breakfast table, ruling that I had fulfilled my obligation to produce my client while Bellicoso's laughter echoed around the marble corridors of the Surrogate's Court. Babette won.

No sign of Ling or Yang, but I put my hand inches from my waistband holster when I spotted a hearse marked SING SI WANG FUNERAL HOME parked in front of Ling's office. This time it wasn't waiting for Pandora at the side door of the Caprice.

I glanced at the hearse's tinted window, and my reflection bounced back at me like a punch in the stomach. No question I was a patsy, chosen because my legal mind could dream up the fancy gift defense, because a sexy client would have me fighting like a pit bull. Hargrove hadn't measured up on either count. Webb sucked me into a rescue mission, into a hurricane of Ling's threats designed to keep me working up a bloody sweat to save the lady in distress.

That pair nearly yin and yanged me to death while Mercury stood by, his finger showing the way to the Surrogate's Court, tracing the invisible axis of graft, corruption, Boss Tweed, and the stinking Collect that still permeates the court system, Park Avenue, and the city.

Except for the sacred Mall.

I don't know why the gods point at justice but won't deliver. Still, you can bet my tombstone won't read, "Johnny Ocean died a pawn in a high-stakes game." No one can tell me that Webb isn't going to hit Ling up for a chunk when the $170 million comes in. Or vice versa. Put a big *if* before the words *Webb pays Ling*. There's enough double-crossing in this bunch to go around and come around. And the consolation prize is these bad boys are in the sights of Slice and Windows, who are waiting on the forensics. When that mercury evidence comes in, the fight will really begin, but at least Slice, Windows, and I will be on the same page when we try to prove Webb poisoned Edgar and poor, pathetic Marcel.

I turned away from Mott Street, then a series of blasts came right behind me. Before I could move out of the way a crowd of Chinese disguised as dragons stampeded past. It was the eve of Chinese New Year and time I got the hell out of Chinatown for good.

Bellicoso can laugh himself sick, but until the monkey eats the banana, I still have a fighting chance.

I just have to play it out. That's what Mr. K says.